# MIDNIGHT'S LOVER

## DONNA GRANT

D0037341

St. Martin's Paperbacks

This is a work of fiction. All of the characters, organizations, and events portrayed in this novel are either products of the author's imagination or are used fictitiously.

MIDNIGHT'S LOVER

Copyright © 2012 by Donna Grant.
Excerpt from *Midnight's Seduction* copyright © 2012 by Donna Grant.

For information address St. Martin's Press, 175 Fifth Avenue, New York, NY 10010.

ISBN: 978-0-312-55249-7

Printed in the United States of America

St. Martin's Paperbacks edition / July 2012

St. Martin's Paperbacks are published by St. Martin's Press, 175 Fifth Avenue, New York, NY 10010.

10  9  8  7  6  5  4  3  2  1

NNA GRANT

**5! Top Pick!** "An absolutely must read! From beginning to end, it's an incredible ride."            —*Night Owl Romance*

**5 Hearts!** "I definitely recommend *Dangerous Highlander*, even to skeptics of paranormal romance – you just may fall in love with the MacLeods."            —*The Romance Reader*

**5 Angels! Recommended Read!** "*Forbidden Highlander* blew me away."            —*Fallen Angel Reviews*

**5 Tombstones!** "Another fantastic series that melds the paranormal with the historical life of the Scottish high-lander in this arousing and exciting adventure. The men of MacLeod Castle are a delicious combination of devoted brother, loyal highlander, Lord and demonic god that ooze sex appeal and inspire some very erotic daydreams as they face their faults and accept their fate."            —*Bitten by Books*

**4 Stars!** "Grant creates a vivid picture of Britain centuries after the Celts and Druids tried to expel the Romans, deftly merging magic and history. The result is a won-derfully dark, delightful, well-written tale. Readers will eagerly await the next Dark Sword book."
            —*Romantic Times BOOKreviews*

**4 Hoots!** "These are some of the hottest brothers around in paranormal fiction."            —*Nocturne Romance Reads*

ST. MARTIN'S PAPERBACKS TITLES BY
# DONNA GRANT

## THE DARK SWORD SERIES

*Dangerous Highlander*

*Forbidden Highlander*

*Wicked Highlander*

*Untamed Highlander*

*Shadow Highlander*

*Darkest Highlander*

## THE DARK WARRIOR SERIES

*Midnight's Master*

*Midnight's Lover*

*Midnight's Seduction*
(coming in November)

To Kim Rocha
Thank you for your support, for your smiles, your texts and Facebook posts, and for just being your truly wonderful self and great friend.
Love ya, girl!

# ACKNOWLEDGMENTS

Thank you to my brilliant, marvelous, beautiful editor, Monique Patterson. I know I say it all the time, but you are the bomb! Thanks for pushing me when I needed it, encouraging when I hesitate, and for allowing my imagination to truly take flight with these stories.

To Holly Blanck—what can I say besides the truth?—you rock! To everyone at St. Martin's who helped get this book ready, thank you.

To my amazing, fabulous agent, Amy Moore-Benson. Thank you. For everything!

A special note to Melissa Bradley, Leagh Christensen, and April Renn. Thanks for all the help, especially when I needed it the most.

To my kiddos, parents, and brother—thank you! A writer makes sacrifices when writing, but so does the writer's family. Thanks for picking up the slack, knowing when I'm in deadline that I won't remember any conversations we might have. And for not minding to have to repeat anything. lol

And to my awesome husband, Steve, my real-life hero. You never mind spending dinners talking about upcoming battle scenes or helping me work through a spot I'm stuck in. Thank you for the love you've given me, for the laughter you brought into my life, our beautiful children, and the happily-ever-after life I always dreamed of. I love you, Sexy!

# MIDNIGHT'S LOVER

# PROLOGUE

Fourteen years ago . . .

Danielle Buchanan watched a fat raindrop roll down the outside of the passenger car window until it disappeared from view.

"We're almost there, Dani," Aunt Sophie said from the front seat.

Danielle didn't care. She hadn't cared about anything in three months, two weeks, and four days.

That's when her parents had died in a car crash.

She still remembered being woken by the red and blue lights from the police car flashing through her window. Danielle had sat up, listening as they told her babysitter that there had been an accident.

Danielle had thought that was the worst day of her life, but then, days later there had been the funeral. Two coffins set side by side in the church.

Two coffins lowered into the ground.

A coldness had swept through Danielle then. At twelve, a girl wasn't supposed to feel so old, so uncaring, so . . . hard-hearted.

Danielle had gone to stay with her best friend, but Cindy hadn't understood anything Danielle was going through. They had grown from being inseparable to barely speaking to each other. Still, it was something Danielle knew, a place she was familiar with.

Then her world had been turned upside down again when Aunt Sophie arrived. Danielle had learned her parents had given Sophie guardianship over her if something ever happened to them.

Danielle didn't have anything left in her to fight the move from Florida across an ocean to Scotland. What could a twelve-year-old do anyway?

"Dani, honey, I really think you'll enjoy it here," Aunt Sophie said, her accent thick, but her smile bright and kind.

Danielle blinked as they continued up the mountain. The car slowed, and a moment later they were turning right.

Danielle looked around the seat in front of her through the windshield. Row upon row of houses lined the street. They all looked alike.

Aunt Sophie turned her head and grinned broadly. "We're here!"

Danielle tried to smile, she really did. But as they pulled into the tiny driveway all she could muster was a sigh.

She climbed out of the car and looked at the two-story house, then at the ones on either side. There was no doubt she was going to forget which house was her aunt's.

"Come on, Dani. Everyone is waiting for us."

Danielle licked her lips and knew her parents would want her to be happy at her new home. Aunt Sophie waited patiently by the door, a sad smile on her face as if she knew exactly what Danielle had been thinking.

Danielle walked to her aunt and through the front

door. Uncle Henry, Aunt Sophie's husband whom Danielle had met only once when she was seven, gave her a wave, but didn't rise from his chair in front of the TV.

"In the kitchen," Aunt Sophie said as she laid a hand on Danielle's shoulder.

She turned the small corner and stepped into the tiny kitchen where there were two other women. One was washing dishes and hurried to dry her hands as she faced Danielle.

"We were gettin' worried," she said.

Aunt Sophie sighed, exhaustion evident in the lines of her face. "It was a long trip. Dani, this is my best friend, Mary."

Danielle hoped her lips turned up in a smile, but she wasn't sure.

"It might take a while, my dear," Mary said, "but I think you'll love it in Scotland."

Danielle's attention turned to the woman at the table. The woman watched Danielle with eyes as steady as a hawk. Her silver-blond hair, the same color as Danielle's, was pulled back in a loose bun.

"Come here, child," the woman beckoned softly.

Danielle found herself walking to the woman. She stopped in front of her, amazed that the woman could look so young and frail at the same time.

"You look just like your mother."

For the first time since the funeral Danielle felt the prick of tears.

"I'm your aunt Josephine, but everyone calls me Josie. I knew the moment my brother brought your mother to meet us that she was the one for him. They were very happy together. So in love. That's rare, you know."

Aunt Josie took Danielle's hand and smiled. "We shall grieve together, you and I."

Danielle didn't pull away when Aunt Josie tugged her

onto her lap. She thought she was too old to sit on adults'
laps anymore, but Danielle liked Aunt Josie.

"This land is verra old," Josie said in a whisper while
she smoothed her hand over Danielle's hair repeatedly,
soothing and calming Danielle at the same time. "Many
kings wanted this land, and though they might think they
ruled us they never did. There is magic in my Scotland,
Dani. You'll feel it soon enough."

Aunt Josie lifted Danielle's hand until their palms
were held flat together.

"You have magic in you, child," Josie said, her green
eyes holding Danielle's. "Just as I do. I will teach you
about magic and your heritage. You've come home, Dani.
A Druid always comes home."

# CHAPTER ONE

Inverness—Fourteen years later
New Year's Eve

Danielle zipped up her boots that reached to her knees and rose from the bed to stare into the full-length mirror on the back of her door. She turned to one side then the other looking at the slinky black dress that hugged her curves.

"Definitely need to work out more," she mumbled as she frowned at her reflection and sucked in her stomach.

Her door pushed open and Whitney, one of her flat-mates, poked her dark head through the door. "Wow, Dani. You look amazing."

"Sure you won't come with me?" Danielle asked for the tenth time. They had all planned to spend New Year's together with another group of friends two months ago, but now Dani would end up alone with Mitchell. It wasn't that Mitchell was a bad sort, just someone who didn't get the hint that she didn't want to date him.

Whitney laughed and shook her head. "Not on your life. Joe says he has something he wants to talk to me about. I'm hoping he's finally going to ask me to marry him. I've been waiting for months!"

Danielle smiled and hugged Whitney. She was happy for her friend, but it was just another reminder she was alone. Again.

"I want you to call me as soon as he proposes. Well, after you say yes, of course," Danielle said with a laugh.

"I will. I promise. Listen, I came to ask if I could borrow your black heels. The new ones you bought this week?"

Danielle hurried to her closet and opened the Kate Spade box. "Yes, you need to look your best. You know Clair's pearls would look great with your dress."

"I've already asked to borrow them," Whitney said as she took the shoes. "I have the most wonderful friends in the world."

Danielle grinned as she leaned her hand on the door-knob. "I'm just thankful we all wear about the same size. It's saved me a lot of money over the years."

As Whitney walked to her room, Danielle closed the door and her smile faded. So much for a rowdy group of friends to party with. Not that Danielle was a party girl. She was the opposite actually. It had been all of them who had talked her into going out on New Year's. And wouldn't you know everyone else would have something planned with their boyfriends?

Danielle sighed and looked at the clock on her night-stand. It was just after five o'clock. She had enough time to run some errands before she met up with Mitchell and they headed to Blink's. Blink was the newest, hippest nightclub in Inverness, and they were putting on one hell of a party tonight.

After one more look in the mirror, Danielle reached for the bangle bracelets on her bureau and left her room.

She liked the clink of the silver bracelets as she slid her arms into her coat.

"I'm leaving," Danielle called out.

"Be careful!" Whitney shouted through her door. "A snowstorm has been forecast for tonight!"

Danielle inwardly groaned while wrapping her scarf around her neck before she tugged on her gloves. "Just what I need."

She grabbed her purse and keys and left the flat. A blast of cold wind hit her as she pulled the door closed and hurried down the stairs to her car waiting at the curb.

The car, a mid-1970s Mini, had been her aunt Josie's. When Josie had gotten too sick to drive it, she'd given it to Danielle. Danielle loved the car, even if it had gotten more unreliable than not.

She unlocked her door and slid into the driver's seat. As usual, the car didn't start on the first try.

"Come on," Danielle whispered as she turned the key once more.

There was a flare of life, and then nothing.

Danielle rubbed the car's dashboard slowly. "I know you can do this," she told the car. "Don't let me down tonight."

On the third try, the Mini roared to life.

Danielle sat back with a smile on her face and fastened her seat belt. She pushed in the clutch and put the car in first before pulling out into the road.

She drove slowly through the icy, snow-covered streets as the sun sank below the horizon. Danielle would have preferred to get her errands done earlier, but she'd had to stay later at her job than usual.

Wouldn't you know the boss-from-Hell had wanted to clear her desk so *she* could take the next week off?

Danielle was supposed to have left the office at noon, but Isabella had other ideas.

Danielle mentally checked off the places in her mind as she ran errand after errand. Finally, she pulled up to the cemetery and turned off the car. She reached for the single pink rose on the passenger seat and got out of the car.

The snow that had fallen overnight was deep as Danielle meandered her way to the back of the cemetery and the Buchanan plot.

Though her parents were buried in America, there was a plaque with their names and the date they had been taken from her. Danielle wiped the snow from the plaque. She stared at their names and wondered how different her life would have been had they not gone out that fateful night.

It was a thought that haunted Danielle every year. Though the images of her parents had begun to fade in her mind, the memories she had of them would never leave her.

After a moment, she moved to her left and wiped the ice and snow from the large stone cross.

Josie had died on New Year's Eve five years earlier and Danielle came to her gravesite every year. No one was sure what had caused Josie's death. Each year she had grown weaker and weaker until her soul had left her body.

It had been painful to watch, but Danielle never left her side. They had spent countless hours together in the little time they had left. Josie had been the one Danielle had gone to with a problem, the one Danielle had gone to for answers.

And Josie had never let her down.

Josie had been the one who hadn't pushed her to talk, hadn't begged her to get on with her life. Josie simply let Danielle cope with the death of her parents as she needed.

She had warned Danielle that her time was about to end, but Danielle hadn't wanted to believe her. Until Josie's hand had gone slack in Danielle's grip.

"I miss you, Aunt Josie," Danielle said, and placed the pink rose at the base of the cross.

Josie had been true to her word when Danielle had first met her. She had shown Danielle the wondrous world of magic.

It had been glorious. The first time she felt her magic move within her, it had changed her life.

Until they learned just what her magic did.

Danielle bit her lip as she recalled the pain that would bend her in two when she would find an object and not want to return it to its owner.

Of all the magical ability Danielle could have received, she hated hers. She had no choice when it came to using her magic. It forced her to bring the object—whatever it might be—to its rightful owner or suffer unimaginable pain.

Danielle realized that she had been squatting next to the cross for some time and her legs had grown numb from the cold. A large, fat snowflake landed on the back of her gloved hand.

"You always did love the snow, Aunt Josie," Danielle mumbled. She kissed her fingers, then placed them on the cross. "Until next year."

Danielle rose and walked back to her car. The streetlights had already blinked on as the darkness grew. She shoved her hands in her pockets and did her best not to slip on the ice.

The icy wind managed to find a way up her skirt and take whatever warmth she might have had from her. Danielle shuddered and hurriedly got into her car.

To her surprise, the Mini started on the first try. Danielle waited for other cars to pass, then pulled in behind them. She was supposed to meet Mitchell at his flat so they could go to dinner.

If she didn't know her flatmates so well, she'd think they had set this up so she'd be left alone with Mitchell. It wasn't that Mitch wasn't a nice guy. He was.

He just wasn't a guy she was interested in.

Which didn't make sense. He was good-looking, had a great job, and she had gotten to know him well over the last year.

But there was no connection between them. No spark, no chemistry.

It would be so much easier if there were, because Danielle knew Mitch liked her a lot. She could have the husband she'd always wanted. She could have the family and kids—everything.

However, her parents had told her to never compromise, and Danielle never had. She certainly wasn't going to start now.

Just as Danielle expected, there were no places to park close to Mitchell's flat. She ended up parking down the street and walking to his place.

She now wished she had suggested meeting him at the restaurant instead of letting him drive her. That sounded too much like a date, and this was anything but a date.

Danielle walked up the steps to his door and knocked. Almost instantly it opened. Mitchell, his dark hair combed back away from his face, smiled, the corners of his blue eyes crinkling.

"I was getting worried," he said as he motioned for her to enter.

Danielle gratefully stepped in out of the cold. "I had to run some errands."

"I made reservations for dinner."

She didn't move farther inside when he put his hand on the small of her back. "Reservations? I thought we were eating at the pub as we agreed earlier."

"Well," Mitchell said as he ran a hand over his hair in a nervous gesture. "With it just being us two, I thought we could have a more . . . intimate dinner."

It was just what Danielle *didn't* want. She glanced at the floor, hating that she had to begin the evening like this. "Mitchell . . . I like you. A lot."

"And I like you, Danielle."

"But as a friend."

The smile slowly died on his face. "Why can you no' let this progress and see where it goes?"

"Because that would only cause you pain. I don't want that."

Mitchell put his hands on his hips and turned partially away from Danielle. "I had hoped when you agreed to still go out without the others that it was a sign you wanted more."

"I told you I didn't."

"I thought you were being coy," Mitchell said with a shake of his head. "I've waited over a year for you, Dani."

"A year when you could have found someone else. I wish I felt the same for you as you do for me, but I won't lie to myself or you."

Silence filled the small entry as Mitchell refused to look at her. Danielle shifted from foot to foot, unsure of what to do next. She had hurt him, the very thing she hadn't wanted to do.

"I cannot do this," Mitchell said softly. "I cannot go with you tonight and pretend we're just friends and that everything is all right when it's no'."

Danielle nodded. "I understand. I wish you the best, Mitchell."

He still didn't look at her when she opened the door to leave. With one last glance at him, Danielle stepped back into the cold.

The door closed with a loud click behind her as she looked over the snow-covered city. How had her life gotten so messed up? At twenty-six she had thought she'd be married by now.

Instead, she was alone.

She'd always been alone. Since the night her parents died in that awful car crash and she had been brought to Scotland she had been alone.

Danielle raised her chin and squared her shoulders. Alone or not, she was going to Blink to ring in the New Year. It would be so crowded no one would know she hadn't come with friends.

She carefully walked down the icy steps and onto the sidewalk. About halfway to her car she heard a door open and turned to watch Mitchell leave his flat, get into his car, and drive away.

It was good that he wasn't staying inside. He needed to get out and find someone.

Danielle was nearly to her car when a group of young boys came running down the sidewalk. She tried to get out of the way, but one of them slammed into her shoulder, sending her spinning around.

The heel of her stiletto boots slid on a patch of ice and her feet flew out from underneath her. Danielle landed hard on her side, her arm trapped beneath her.

"Bloody Hell," she murmured.

She took a moment to get her bearings and make sure nothing was broken. Her skirt had rucked up, leaving a section of her bare thigh exposed and touching the snow and ice.

Danielle would be lucky if she got out of this without catching a cold. She knew she shouldn't have worn the black dress in this weather, but it wasn't as if she had expected to spend a lot of time in the snow.

She pushed up on her elbow and blinked her eyes. She must have hit her head because everything was spinning. When she was able to open her eyes without feeling dizzy, Danielle found herself at the edge of the sidewalk next to a tire.

It was the flash of something shiny that grabbed her attention.

A shiver of trepidation raced down her spine, and though every fiber of her body told her to pretend she didn't see it, she knew she couldn't.

Hesitantly, Danielle reached into the snow, brushing it aside. In the dirt, grime, and ice, next to the curb was a key. A very old key by the look of it.

Danielle took a deep breath before she picked it up. Instantly, a vision of a castle at the edge of a cliff slammed into her.

*"MacLeod Castle,"* a voice inside her head said.

With her hand fisted around the key, Danielle climbed to her feet and leaned with her other hand against the car next to her.

"Tomorrow. I will bring you to this MacLeod Castle tomorrow."

The pain curled up from the base of her spine, slowly at first, and then grew until Danielle bent over with her arm wrapped around her stomach.

"Now. I will go now," she bit out urgently.

When an object was in a rush to get to its destination, it meant it was of great importance. It had been over a year and a half since Danielle's magic had found something.

She wished she hadn't discovered the key. Because

deep down inside, she knew nothing good could come of this. Because somehow she knew her life would be changed forever.

With Danielle's capitulation the pain ebbed until it dissipated completely. And just as before, Danielle's magic told her where to take the key.

"East I go," she mumbled with sarcasm. "I'm so glad I didn't have plans."

She carefully picked her way to her car, and once behind the wheel, she put the key in her coat pocket.

*"East. Go east. To MacLeod Castle,"* the voice repeated over and over in her mind.

"So much for my night of celebrating."

And wouldn't you know the car started on the second try.

# CHAPTER TWO

Somewhere in the Highlands

Ian's eyes flew open as he lay perfectly still inside the dark, dank cave he had called home for . . . months. He wasn't sure how much time had passed.

Nor did he care.

He didn't move, didn't even blink as he listened. The only sound that met his ears was the shrill noise of the howling wind. But for an instant, he could have sworn he'd heard his brother's voice.

More and more he heard Duncan calling to him, beckoning him to leave the mountain.

Ian scrubbed a hand down his face and sat up. His breath billowed white before his face. A glimpse through the cave's entrance showed Ian the sun had risen on another day.

How many days had he lost this time? It could have been hours or weeks that his god, Farmire, had had control. As awful as that was, Ian feared what Farmire had done while he'd been in control.

It was one of the reasons Ian made his home in such a remote place. The farther his god had to go to appease his need for blood and death, the less likely Ian was to harm someone.

At least that was his hope.

Ian dropped his head back against the jagged rock of the cave and squeezed his eyes shut. By all that was holy he'd never felt so isolated, never been so desolate in all his two-hundred-plus years.

And it was only going to get worse. So much worse.

Ian thought of MacLeod Castle and the people who had become a family to him. He missed the sound of the waves crashing against the cliffs, the aroma of freshly baked bread, and the laughter as they all sat in the great hall and ate.

He missed the other Warriors.

But most of all he missed his brother.

Ian rose to his feet and walked to the cave's opening and looked out. Everything as far as he could see was covered in a thick blanket of white so blinding he had to squint to look at it.

There were no footprints leading to or from the cave, and since it wasn't snowing now, maybe Ian hadn't ventured from his hideout.

If only he could remember . . . But there were huge holes in his memory whenever his god took over. Though he tried to get control over his god, Farmire was too powerful. Also, Ian's grief over losing his twin had only allowed Farmire to gain the upper hand in the first place.

Duncan.

No one had understood the bond between Ian and Duncan. As twins, they had shared everything. If Duncan was hurt, Ian felt his pain. If Ian had needed Duncan, he'd been there without Ian having called for him.

The fact they had also shared a god only strengthened their bond.

Ian remembered when they'd had their god unbound. It had been Deirdre, an evil Druid, or *drough*, who had caught them and unbound their god.

The pain had been excruciating, unimaginably agonizing, with their bones popping and muscles shredding as the god stretched inside them. But it had been nothing compared to the strength of the god now bellowing inside Ian's mind.

No longer was Ian able to share Farmire's greedy and insatiable hunger for battle with Duncan. Now, Ian had to contend with it all on his own.

And he was losing badly.

Ian recalled how he and Duncan had found a way to gain control over their god together. It hadn't been easy, but they'd had each other.

Even locked deep in the depths of Deirdre's mountain prison, they'd learned to face whatever came their way. Together.

It had been Deirdre who had taken Duncan's life. It had been Deirdre who had taken the only brother Ian had ever known.

And it had been Deirdre who had put Ian in the predicament he was in now. The *drough* had known exactly what she was doing when she killed Duncan. She'd known Ian would then get the full powers of his god—and the full rage.

Many Warriors never learned to control their god, and the god soon took over. Which is what Deirdre wanted in her quest to rule the world.

Ian had been a proud man growing up in his clan. He'd even been a proud Warrior, despite the primeval god inside him.

Now, he hid away from the world because he couldn't rule his god. He wondered what Duncan would think of him. Would his twin scorn him? Would Duncan pity him?

Ian scratched his head and felt the long, dirty strands of his hair. The hair felt foreign to him. Ever since they'd been young lads, Ian had kept his hair shorn close to his head to help others tell him and Duncan apart.

The last time he'd cut his hair was before Duncan had left with Logan on their mission to find an artifact that would help them destroy Deirdre once and for all.

They had killed Deirdre once already when they'd rescued the youngest MacLeod brother, Quinn, from her clutches. Though they had killed her body, they hadn't destroyed her soul.

"Unfortunately," Ian mumbled.

Ian thought of the Druids and the pivotal role they'd played in the lives of every Briton beginning thousands of years before. The Druids had been the ones to rule the land, not kings or clan leaders.

There were two sects of Druids. The *mies,* or good Druids, whose magic came from the earth and elements. And the *droughs,* who, upon reaching their eighteenth year, gave their souls to Satan in order to command black magic.

It had been the *droughs* who had called up the primeval gods from Hell to help the Celts send Rome from their shores. Those gods had inhabited the strongest warriors from each family, creating immortal Warriors with the strength and power of the god that had taken them.

When the *droughs* couldn't send the gods back to Hell with their magic alone, it had taken both the *droughs* and the *mies* to bind the gods to the Warriors.

Since Deirdre hunted and killed both *droughs* and

*mies* in order to steal their magic and increase hers, there were few Druids left in Britain. Those that remained stayed hidden.

Ian had never felt animosity, never allowed himself to hate as he did Deirdre. His loathing grew each day his god took control of him. Because Ian knew that once Farmire was in complete control, Ian would be Deirdre's.

"I'll kill myself first," Ian stated, his hands fisting at his sides.

*"Nay, brother. You need to live."*

Ian didn't acknowledge Duncan's voice, though it sounded as if his brother stood right next to him. It was just proof that Ian was going daft.

At least he was alone and his friends at MacLeod Castle wouldn't have to watch as Farmire slowly pulled him under.

But Ian missed the other Warriors.

He missed Fallon MacLeod's calm leadership. He missed Ramsey's infinite knowledge, Logan's teasing, Hayden's eagerness for battle, and Arran's steadfast friendship.

He missed Quinn MacLeod's recklessness, Lucan MacLeod's easy laughter, Galen's constant eating, Broc's silent gaze, and Camdyn's quiet presence.

There was also Larena, the only female Warrior and Fallon's bride.

Then there were the Druids. The MacLeods had welcomed all Warriors fighting against Deirdre into their castle, but they had also made it a sanctuary for Druids.

The MacLeods had turned their ruin of a castle into a home once more. It was a place where no matter what you were, you were welcome to sit at their table and share a meal.

It helped that Ian, Duncan, and Arran had stood by Quinn while they'd been trapped in Deirdre's mountain. Ian had known as soon as he saw Quinn that the Warrior was someone important.

Ian thought back to when he first met Quinn. Quinn had been battling his own god at the time. There had been instances, Quinn admitted, when he had nearly given in to his god.

It was too bad Quinn wasn't with him now to help Ian win this constant battle of wills with Farmire.

Even if Ian hadn't been snatched from MacLeod Castle, he knew he would have left. Only a fool would stay and endanger all that they had worked to protect.

And Ian wasn't a fool.

*"Brother, you must eat. You will need your strength to battle Farmire. The weaker you are, the more control he has."*

Ian knew Duncan was right, but to get food meant he would have to leave the cave. But the voice in Ian's head, whether it was his brother or not, was correct.

He did need to keep up his strength to fight Farmire. Not that Ian thought he had a chance at gaining the control over his god he'd once had, but he wasn't going to go without a fight.

Ian glanced down at his kilt and the large red and green plaid covered in mud and muck. He needed a bath as well. Which, in the cold, was going to be grueling.

The freezing temperatures wouldn't kill him because of his immortality, but it might help to keep his god away for a while.

With his first ghost of a grin in days, Ian stepped out of the cave.

# CHAPTER
# THREE

Danielle gripped the steering wheel with both hands. She barely made it out of Inverness before her Mini sputtered and then just died.

It had taken an hour and a call to a mechanic to fix it. There went two hundred pounds of her money.

At least the car was running now, but with the wind and the snowfall, she couldn't make up the lost time by driving faster. Despite her wishing that she could.

At that moment her car hit a patch of ice and fish-tailed. With her heart in her throat, Danielle was able to get control of the car once more.

Maybe she should have taken the mechanic's advice when he suggested she get new tires before traveling. Regardless, it was too late now.

Her more pressing worry was finding a place to stop for the night. The radio station she'd been listening to confirmed Whitney's report of a massive storm coming their way.

Danielle didn't want to be on the roads late at night with such a storm. Yet it was New Year's Eve. Most places would be completely filled.

She hadn't slept in her car in years, and the one time hadn't been a good one. The last thing Danielle wanted to do was repeat that night. But she might not have a choice.

Minutes ticked by, reminding Danielle that she could be having a nice dinner and then dancing the night away until the clock struck midnight.

The quick bite she'd grabbed had tasted so awful she'd only eaten half the sandwich. Now she was starving and in the middle of nowhere.

As the song on the radio finished, she turned up the volume when the announcer began to speak.

"Breaking News Inverness! The YouTube video of those small, yellow creatures that hit the Web almost four months ago is no' a fake. It appears as if these wee beasts are indeed real. They've been spotted all over Scotland in the past few days. And believe it or no', one was caught today. They are vicious wee mongrels, so doona approach one lest they tear you in two with their claws and sharp teeth."

"Wonderful," Danielle said as she turned the volume back down. "Every day more dire predictions and announcements. No wonder everyone thinks the world is coming to an end."

Suddenly, the brake lights from the car in front of her flared. Danielle immediately let off the gas and hoped it slowed her, but as they were going down the mountain, it wasn't enough.

With all the snow and ice, she didn't dare slam on the brakes. But as she drew closer and closer to the car she had no choice.

Danielle slowly pressed on the brakes. The car behind her, however, didn't. It rammed her, which propelled her into the car in front of her.

She swerved the wheel to try and miss the car, but

the screech of metal as her font bumper hit the vehicle told her she'd failed. Before she could register that she'd hit the car, she screamed when her Mini began to spin as it continued its downhill descent. All Danielle could do was hold on to the steering wheel and pray no one else hit her.

It felt as if she spun for an eternity. She closed her eyes, her stomach pitching from the intensity of the spin. Danielle had no idea if she was still on the road or not. Finally, the Mini came to a rest. Danielle opened her eyes just in time to see headlights coming at her entirely too fast.

She lifted her arms and turned her face away an instant before the vehicle plowed into her.

Ian sat with his back against the cave wall and his arms locked around his knees. He thought over the day as he watched the deer slowly cook.

He'd left the cave and ventured to the loch that was down the mountain. Ian had made certain he encountered no one, and in this weather, he knew the possibility was slim.

The loch had been frozen. He'd had to punch through the ice in order to get in to bathe. The water had left him feeling more alert than he could remember, which could be the reason why he'd only blacked out for a few moments that day.

The day had been a good one, he supposed. Except for the blackout. It had happened right after he'd killed the buck and begun to skin the animal.

The sight of all that blood had sent his god into a frenzy. As soon as he'd felt himself slipping into Farmire's control Ian had gotten angry. He'd fought and wrestled hard to keep a grip on his mind and body.

He had won, but barely. Every time he battled Farmire

it became more and more difficult to win, each time more exhausting and the blackouts lasting longer.

How much time did he have before he didn't awaken from a blackout? Before Farmire took over completely?

Ian didn't want to think of it, but it was the reality of his life now and he needed to face the facts. His time was short, that he knew.

Somehow he'd been more himself this day than he had in months. His god would return with a vengeance, and though Ian knew his time was limited, he wouldn't go without a fight. He owed that much, at least, to his brother. If it meant Ian needed to dive into the frigid loch every day he would do so.

He held out his hand and watched as a pale blue claw lengthened from the tip of his finger. Ian used it to slice off some meat and began to eat.

Ian ate until he couldn't take another bite. He couldn't remember ever being so full, but then he had no idea how long he'd gone without food.

Already he could feel his strength returning, and with it his mind seemed clearer. He turned his head toward the entrance of the cave wishing he would hear a wolf howl. Ever since he had been taken from MacLeod Castle he couldn't remember seeing or hearing a wolf.

*"You always loved the dangerous beasts, Ian."*

Ian snorted. He had always loved the wolves. They were majestic and wild, untamed and ferocious, a lot like Warriors. And just like Warriors, wolves were misunderstood.

People feared them and hunted them when a pack ventured too close to their land. The wolves were only doing what was in their nature.

"Just as I am," Ian murmured.

Maybe all Warriors were destined to fall under the control of their god.

Ian thought of the MacLeods and how much tragedy they had borne. He thought of Quinn and how he'd lost his wife and son to Deirdre's massacre of the clan. Though Quinn had been on the edge of losing himself to his god, he'd pulled through it.

Marcail's love had had a lot to do with it, Ian was sure, but there had been something else as well. A drive within Quinn to not give in and become what Deirdre wanted.

Quinn had spoken often of his brothers while they'd been held prisoner. He'd always known Lucan and Fallon would come for him. No matter how much time had passed, his belief had never wavered.

Ian had understood Quinn. Always he and Duncan had been there for each other. Whatever trials life had thrown at them, he and Duncan had survived them together.

*"Not this time, brother. This time, you must do it on your own."*

Ian wasn't sure he could. He wanted to believe he could, but the simple truth was his god was much more powerful than he'd ever known.

He'd taken it for granted that he'd not had Farmire's full strength and rage to contend with alone. Duncan had borne half of it all.

How Ian wished he'd been the one to die instead of Duncan. Not that he'd want Duncan to have to battle Farmire alone, but knowing he'd never look upon his twin again or share a meal with him again made Ian's chest ache with a fierceness that would never diminish.

The anguish that filled him was as strong as it had been the moment Ian had felt his brother's connection fade. Ian had known Duncan was gone, but before he could face it, Farmire's complete power and rage slammed into Ian.

He'd been in the great hall of MacLeod Castle when it happened. He didn't remember much after that. Only the fury and the need to kill.

Now the only sounds Ian heard were of the falling snow, the wind, and the profound silence. No laughter, no conversation, no friendship.

*"You need more."*

At one time Ian might have thought he did, but not anymore. The moon-drenched, snow-covered mountain was his home now.

*"And the MacLeods? The other Warriors? What about them and their fight against Deirdre? I canno' believe you doona want revenge for her killing me."*

Ian shook his head slowly. "I want to help the MacLeods, Duncan. You know that. But I'm a danger to the Druids in the state I'm in."

*"Then fight Farmire!"*

"I'm trying."

*"No' hard enough, brother."*

At one time Ian wouldn't have had a conversation with himself as he was doing now. Though the voice sounded like Duncan, Ian knew it was his own mind he was speaking with.

"If I get near Deirdre in this state, I doona think I could stop my god from taking over."

*"You can. You were always the strongest, Ian. This hiding away in a cave away from friends who could help isn't you."*

"Ah, but it is, brother. And the mere fact I'm having this conversation tells me it's a good thing I'm alone."

*"You doona think this is me?"*

Ian rolled his eyes and turned to lie on his back. "I know it's no'. I'm going daft."

*"Nay, Ian. It's me. I doona know how or why, but it's me."*

How Ian wanted to believe the voice, needed to believe. He'd seen some spectacular things done with magic, but there was no way Duncan could be speaking with him, none at all.

No matter how much Ian wished it were otherwise.


Danielle came awake with a moan. She pushed away from the steering wheel and leaned against her seat. Tentatively, she touched her head and winced when she came in contact with a large bump on her forehead. Then she saw the blood on her fingers and groaned.

Through the haze of pain she looked around her Mini to see the window busted into thousands of cracks that somehow held together.

Her door was another matter. The SUV that had rammed her had bowed the door inward. When Danielle tried to move her leg, it wouldn't budge.

For a moment, dread made her fret that her leg was broken, but when she was able to move her toes, she let out a long breath.

She spent the next few moments working her leg free so she could crawl out of her seat. Her dress was torn, and somehow she had managed to lose one of her gloves.

Since she couldn't get out through her door, Danielle shifted into the passenger seat. But that proved more difficult than she had first thought.

Every time she moved, her body screamed in agony. She wasn't sure what she had hurt when she was hit. All she knew was that she wanted to lie down and sleep for the next twenty years.

But in the cold, Danielle couldn't chance it. She made herself keep moving no matter how slowly she did so.

When she got to the passenger seat, the door wouldn't open either. She swallowed and pushed her shoulder into the door. And was rewarded with agony that blinded her.

Danielle took a deep breath and wiped the fog off the window. And found the reason the door wouldn't open. Snow.

"This just isn't my night," she muttered.

With no other recourse, she rolled down the window. A blast of frigid air filled her car, making her teeth chatter. Danielle shouldered her way through the open window, and then turned so that she sat on the door.

But as she was trying to move one leg out of the car to put on the ground, her stiletto got caught on the seat and sent her sprawling backward.

Fortunately, the thick snow cushioned her fall. Even though her coat was soaking up the moisture, Danielle didn't want to move.

She looked up at the sky to see that the clouds blocked out all trace of stars or the moon. All she could see for miles around her was falling snow.

Danielle forced herself to stand. Using her car to steady her, she walked to the SUV to see if anyone was hurt.

"Hello," Danielle called as she reached the large vehicle. "Is everyone all right?"

She knocked on the driver's window and tried to look inside the tinted windows. When there was no answer, she tried the door, but just as she expected, it was locked.

Danielle walked around the SUV to the passenger side. And stopped cold.

"Oh, dear God."

She covered her mouth with her hand as she looked at the woman lying dead in the snow, a shard of glass sticking out of her neck. The snow around the woman was stained red from all the blood.

Danielle stumbled backward, her heart pounding

wildly. She looked up to find the passenger door window completely shattered. There was glass everywhere.

Reluctantly, Danielle leaned to the side and peered into the SUV. The driver's eyes were empty as he stared at her.

"I've got to call someone," Danielle said to herself as she half ran, half stumbled her way back to the passenger side of her Mini.

Her purse had been thrown to the floorboard, and most of its contents had fallen out. Danielle got what she could see and reach as she leaned through the window.

"Aha!" she cried when she found her iPhone.

Yet one look at the cracked glass and she wondered if it would work. No matter how hard she tried, the phone wouldn't come on.

Danielle looked around. She couldn't get her bearings. She wasn't sure if she was facing the way she had come, or still going east.

She had always been directionally challenged, but with the bump on her head, she was more disoriented than usual. And it hurt her head to think.

"Where is the other car?" she asked, a hand pressed against her pounding head. She had rear-ended a car. She was sure of it.

Was someone out there hurt? Or had they fled the scene?

Danielle glanced at her watch to see that three hours had passed since the accident. And no one had come to help them. That wasn't a good sign.

With the wind howling and the snow falling faster, she had to find shelter from the weather. She would freeze to death if she stayed in her car.

As much as she didn't want to, Danielle looked through the SUV for another mobile phone. She tried to ignore the two dead people, but after looking for ten minutes, she found that it it got too eerie and she gave up.

Danielle reached into her pocket and touched the key with her bare hand. "Which way? Which way do I go?"

Oddly, the key told her nothing.

She'd always trusted her instincts before, and she had no other choice now. Her iPhone didn't work, and there was no other way to reach anyone. She would have to walk.

Danielle looked around her until she found what she thought was the road. It was difficult to tell with all the snow that had fallen so quickly. She would travel it. Sooner or later she was bound to come across someone or some town.

At least she hoped she would.

# CHAPTER
# FOUR

Danielle burrowed beneath her coat and scarf and trudged through the snow. She had no idea how far she had walked when she realized she wasn't on any type of road.

She halted, tears stinging her eyes. Her breath clouded white in front of her as she stared over the landscape. With her sense of direction always off, she had no idea where she was going.

Danielle gripped the key in her hand. "Which way?" she asked it for the twentieth time.

The object stayed silent. She didn't understand it. In the past, the objects had always been adamant about where she needed to go and how soon she had to get there. The only time an object was silent was when she reached her destination.

A hysterical laugh escaped Danielle. "This can't be where MacLeod Castle is. Where is the bloody castle?!" she hollered into the night.

She looked over her shoulder as she considered re-tracing her steps to her car, but the snowfall was wiping away all traces of her footprints. It was either stay put and freeze or go forward and hopefully find some help.

"Onward it is," she mumbled.

She had taken a dozen or so steps when the eerie shriek rent the air. Danielle froze in her tracks, the hair on the back of her neck rising in fear.

Every fiber of her being told her to run. Fast.

She didn't think twice as she ignored the thick snow and the ascent up the mountain as she ran.

How many days had passed? How many trips to the loch? Ian had lost track. He stood in the dark, cold depths of the loch and felt his god stir.

"Nay," he growled.

The freezing water helped. It had kept Farmire away. But it seemed his god was only growing stronger instead of weaker.

"Nay," Ian said again.

He looked into the water and watched as his reflection changed before his eyes. His tanned skin faded, replaced by the pale blue of his god.

Lethal blue claws sprouted from his fingers, and when he peeled back his lips, he saw the fangs that filled his mouth. He could only shake his head in shame as his brown eyes faded away and pale blue filled them completely, including the whites.

He'd seen Duncan in his Warrior form, but Ian had never seen himself. He looked . . . fearsome. Angry. Vengeful.

He was all those things and more.

Farmire's voice was insistent, demanding, as he called for blood, for death. Ian had always denied him, but his god was becoming louder, more powerful.

Ian didn't think he had many more weeks, or even days, before he would fall to Farmire completely. He had to end it all before then. It was the only way. Under no circumstances would he tumble under Deirdre's reign again.

*"Fight, Ian!"* Duncan's voice yelled in his head. *"You are strong enough to overcome our god. I know you can."*

Ian squeezed his eyes shut. Daft or not, Ian would rather listen to Duncan's voice than Farmire's. Without another thought Ian dove beneath the surface. He swam with fast, sure strokes into the middle of the loch, bursting through ice as he did.

When he reached the middle, Ian treaded water. He wouldn't leave until he had his god under control. The water would kill mortals, and though Ian could feel the cold, his immortality kept him from dying.

Only when he was able to make his claws retract and his fangs disappear did Ian start toward shore. By the time he stood in the shallow water, the blue skin of his god had faded as well.

*"You did it, brother. I knew you could."*

"But for how much longer?"

*"As long as it takes."*

Ian snorted. "I have plenty of time."

*"You need something that will give you the motivation to overpower Farmire as you once did."*

"Fighting against Deirdre should be reason enough. Avenging your death should be reason enough."

*"Doona blame Malcolm for killing me. He's under Deirdre's control. And my death wasna Logan's fault either. We all knew the dangers in fighting Deirdre. We all risk our lives each time we confront her."*

Ian knew it was true, but he didn't have to like it. "I miss you, Duncan."

*"I've not left. And I willna until you no longer need me."*

Ian drew in a deep breath of the cold air and felt a thread of satisfaction at knowing Duncan would always be there, because there would never be a time he didn't need his brother.

*"You should return to MacLeod Castle so they can help you."*

"I'm a danger to the Druids. Farmire's desire for blood and death grows each day. Sometimes I think about giving in. I miss the satisfaction of killing wyrran and Deirdre's Warriors."

*"Then go looking for wyrran. If you need to ease the lust for battle, they are the perfect targets."*

Ian smirked and began the long journey back to his cave. Not even his wet kilt that began to ice over could distract him. "Ah, that's a tempting thought. Verra tempting indeed."

*"It could be the answer. You know as well as I that our gods need battle. It helps to control their desire for death."*

Ian's god, Farmire, was the father of battle. His desire to fight, to end someone's life, was very strong and only grew stronger each day Ian suppressed him.

*"Inside Cairn Toul we had Deirdre's Warriors to fight. At MacLeod Castle, there were wyrran and others who sided with Deirdre."*

"Aye," Ian murmured.

All Duncan said was the truth. Maybe he did need to find wyrran to battle, but that meant letting Deirdre know he was no longer with the MacLeods. Except for all he knew, she had been the one to pull him into the future.

But why? And where was she? Why hadn't she come for him yet?

Ian paused when he reached the top of a foothill and stared out over the landscape. The only things breaking up the white of the snow were the boulders sticking out of the ground and the pine trees standing tall and proud.

In the distance, above one of the mountains, there was a break in the dreary gray sky where a shaft of sunlight shove through.

The approaching clouds signaled more snow, but Ian didn't care. He was in his mountains and had a spectacular view to look at every day no matter the weather.

He glanced down to the narrow valley below and the loch. Mountains rose steep and colossal on either side. The thick covering of snow hid the treacherous crags and cliff edges, but Ian had never seen anything that could rival the beauty that was Scotland.

Reluctantly, Ian turned away and continued on to his cave. His mind was clear for the moment, and it allowed him to think on Duncan's words.

Should he go in search of wyrran? Ian knew he'd like nothing better than to kill the diminutive, hairless, yellow creatures created by Deirdre.

They did Deirdre's bidding without question, and they were rarely seen alone. They traveled in packs. Or at least they used to.

Many things could have changed since he'd been at MacLeod Castle. He no longer knew Deirdre's whereabouts or what her next plan of attack was. Nor did he know how his fellow Warriors fared.

But if there was one thing Ian could be sure of, it was that Deirdre would still be hunting Druids. Those Druids supplied Deirdre's ever-growing black magic. And the more powerful Deirdre was, the harder she was to kill.

It was why Ian and the others at the castle had vowed to protect all Druids, *mie* and *drough* alike. Scotland had magic in her soil, and the only ones who could feel it, use it, were the Druids.

Without the Druids, the magic would die. And Ian didn't want to think about how that would affect his beloved land.

He walked into his cave and down the narrow entrance until it opened to the large space he called his. Ian glanced down at his hand, remembering the last time he had severed a wyrran's head from its body.

It had felt good to destroy something so evil. It had felt *right*.

# CHAPTER FIVE

Danielle stumbled in the snow. She had been fighting to keep on her feet for hours, but this time, she didn't bother. She turned as she fell and lay on her back in the snow.

When the sun had crested the mountains that morning, she had seen just where she was. And it terrified her. She was deep in the mountains.

With no roads or towns in sight. She kept telling herself she'd find something over the next rise, but every time there was nothing.

Just more snow. More mountains.

Warmth was a distant memory.

The dampness penetrated her coat, making her shiver even more. She was starving and wanted nothing more than to curl up on her couch and turn on the telly while sipping some hot tea.

To her horror, several hours ago the key had spoken to her. It had urged Danielle to continue going deeper into the mountains.

Maybe she had been going east the entire time and hadn't known it. One thing she was sure about was that she would be carrying a compass with her from now on.

Exhaustion weighed heavily upon her, and the cold only hampered things. It took more effort than she wanted to admit just to keep putting one foot in front of the other.

Twice already she'd had to backtrack and find another trail because she'd been so intent on staying upright she hadn't realized she almost walked off a cliff or into a boulder.

Since she was alone, she needed to be vigilant. She needed to be aware of her surroundings. If she wasn't careful, she'd find herself frozen to death or falling off a mountain. And neither sounded very appealing.

Danielle let out a loud sigh and climbed wearily to her feet. She looked around, wondering, waiting to hear the inhuman shrieks she had heard last night.

Her stomach growled. Danielle lifted a handful of snow and munched on it as she had the entire day. It might help quench her thirst, but it was doing nothing for her hunger.

"Over the next rise," she said to herself. "I'll find a road or a village over the next rise."

At least she hoped she would since the sun was sinking on another day. Danielle had walked nonstop since the accident. Her feet would probably hurt if she could actually feel them. Which was probably a good thing since she had never walked so long or far in stilettos before.

She needed to rest, to eat a hot meal. But that could be a long time coming.

"They're going to find me in the spring. I'll have frozen to death because either my magic isn't working or the stupid key got me lost on purpose."

She lifted one foot in front of the other and started walking.

"I hope the MacLeods are the friendly sort," she said to herself. "If I survive this and discover they aren't, I'll scream. Loud. And long."

This is what she had come to, talking to herself. But the quiet had begun to weigh on her earlier. With no one else around, Danielle didn't see the harm in speaking to herself.

She snorted, then wiped at her nose. "At least no harm yet. Who knows if I'll be sane by the time I get out of the mountains."

Danielle scratched her cheek and stilled. She could have sworn she saw movement out of the corner of her eye. The trees were thick, and the snow concealed footsteps, but she'd been sure she'd seen a shape that had moved quickly and quietly.

She turned her head and peered through the trees. The snow had lessened, the flakes swirling in their dance upon the air. It was eerily quiet on the mountain, more so than before. As if the woods knew there was a predator near.

Again, just out of the corner of her eye she saw movement. Danielle whirled around, and this time she caught a spot of pale yellow.

Her heart pounded in her chest. Yellow?

She recalled the radio announcer talking about yellow creatures before her wreck. He'd called them dangerous. Teeth and claws, he'd said.

Danielle inhaled deeply, and remembered everything Aunt Josie had told her about being a Druid. Danielle had never used her magic in defense before, but she was about to learn.

She called to her magic. Instantly, she felt it move and expand within her. She was surprised it had answered her so swiftly. Surprised and gratified.

She moved in a circle, her eyes looking for the creatures. Always they were just on the edge of her vision. It was as if they were toying with her.

"Find other prey," she commanded, and let a small amount of her magic shoot from her hand.

Her magic filled the silence, but there was no hiss of hurt or other sound to let her know she had hit her target. Was she so tired she was seeing things? Was her mind playing tricks on her as it used to as a child?

Danielle lowered her hand and adjusted her purse on her shoulder. She was thankful no one else had seen her act so foolishly. With a sigh, she started walking again.

She'd taken two steps when she heard the first shriek.

It was unnatural and caused the hairs on her arms and neck to stand on end. Just like the night before, Danielle didn't hesitate as she began to run. It didn't matter that she had no idea what made that sound. All she knew was that it was strange and sinister.

The knee-high snow hampered her from moving as fast as she wanted. To make matters worse, the shrieks continued louder and longer. And they grew closer.

What kind of creature made that sound? And how many were there? Two? Three? Or more? Danielle didn't want to find out. All she could think of was the yellow creatures everyone was talking about.

She kept running, kept moving. A chance look over her shoulder showed her the nightmare was coming true. Small yellow creatures were jumping from tree to tree as they chased her.

Danielle's blood pounded in her ears, her heart thumping wildly in her chest. She gripped the trees and rocks to make it to the top of the mountain, sliding on the ice on several occasions. With the cold air stinging her lungs, Danielle started down the other side of the mountain with barely a glance at it. She spotted a valley below with a frozen loch. Maybe she could find a place to hide there.

Her knee crumpled underneath her as she started down the mountain, causing her to roll a couple of times in the snow. She managed to right herself and get back on her feet. Then her foot hit a patch of ice, and she was tumbling again.

Danielle's arm slammed into a boulder hidden by the snow. Pain exploded throughout her body. She wrapped her arms around her head and tried to use her body to slide down the mountain feet first.

The snow and the ice weren't slowing the yellow creatures, however. They continued after her, their shrieks causing her ears to ring from the unholy sound.

The snow was packed so hard that it cut her hands and face whenever she had the misfortune of connecting with it. She would have preferred to make the trip down on her feet, but at least she was moving fast. It might give her an advantage over the beasts.

It was because she was moving so quickly that she couldn't stop herself when she saw the edge of the cliff coming at her. A scream lodged in Danielle's throat as she slid off the cliff and hung in midair for a moment before plummeting.

Her arms and legs flailed around as she sought some kind of hold. She barely had time to register she was falling before she landed with a small tumble in a thick patch of snow.

Danielle had no time to make sure she was unhurt as she climbed out of the snow and began to run. The shrieks continued, and if she lived through this, she knew she would recall the sound until the day she died.

She made for the loch, her lungs seizing and her body protesting such abuse. She was halfway to the loch when one of the yellow beasts landed in front of her.

Danielle screamed and skidded to a halt, the heel of one of her boots twisting beneath her foot and causing her to roll her ankle. The creature's huge yellow eyes glared maliciously at her while it snapped its mouthful of teeth. It couldn't close its lips around its teeth, which gave it a menacing, ugly look.

And then more yellow creatures surrounded her.

Danielle directed a blast of magic at them. It sent the creatures tumbling back and shaking their heads as if to clear them, but they rose and came at her again.

If her magic couldn't help her, then she was doomed. But Danielle wasn't about to give up without a fight. She sent another, more powerful blast at them. This time all but one got up. With each step they took toward her, Danielle retreated.

Their long claws snapped as if they wanted to slice her open. They began running at her one at a time to see how close they could get to her.

For magic she hadn't used in quite a while, Danielle was happy with how quickly it was responding to her. But she couldn't keep the beasts away no matter what.

One got close enough to grab the strap of her purse, sending it flying through the air to land ten paces away from her. Danielle tried to reach for her purse, but the creatures kept coming at her, preventing her from doing anything other than using her magic.

Then the sound of a roar, loud and vicious, echoed through the valley.

The creatures quieted and lifted their heads, their eyes darting about. Danielle could feel their trepidation. Whatever had just made that roar was something that gave the creatures pause. The only question was, would it help Danielle or come after her as well?

Danielle used the interruption to try and slink away.

She was almost past one of the beasts when it turned its evil eyes to her and let out a vicious shriek right before it raised its claws at her face.

Ian had awoken to the sound of wyrran. He'd tracked and killed four the day before. Maybe they'd come to him this time. It had felt good to kill evil again, felt right to use his Warrior abilities to help those at MacLeod Castle in the only way he could.

Then he felt the magic. He'd never felt anything so . . . glorious, so amazing in all his days. It took just a moment to realize the wyrran were chasing a Druid.

Ian had loosened his god before he'd reached the entrance to his cave. He used his speed to follow the Druid's magic. As he ran he saw the trail in the snow as well as the wyrran tracks.

When he crested the hill and saw the wyrran surrounding her, Ian had titled back his head and let loose a roar. He started toward them wanting, needing . . . craving to kill the wyrran.

Then one of them cut the Druid. Her scream of pain sent him barreling into the wyrran. He decapitated one as he ran past it. Another he impaled on his claws and tossed it into the air as he put himself between the Druid and the wyrran.

Ian turned and faced the remaining seven wyrran. He bared his fangs as he bent his legs and flexed his claws. Farmire roared with approval inside him.

This was what Ian needed. Battle. Death. Blood.

He wanted the wyrrans' blood to coat the ground until the snow was no longer white. He sought to wipe the creatures from existence, just as he desired to erase any evidence of Deirdre.

Ian was prepared when the wyrran attacked him at

once. Even while slashing at the wyrran and evading their claws he noticed two had gone after the Druid, pushing her farther and farther onto the loch.

"Nay," Ian bellowed to try and stop her.

She had no way of knowing the ice was very thin in places because he broke through it every day, and she was nearing a spot he had used just the day before.

Ian snapped the neck of a wyrran, and slammed two of the others' heads together. He used his claws and sank them through the other two wyrrans' hearts.

Then he turned to the Druid. "Doona move!" he shouted.

But she was too intent on the wyrran coming after her. She kept her gaze on the wyrran and one of her hands in the pocket of the cloaklike garment she wore.

Ian stepped onto the ice, but it groaned under his weight. Normally he didn't care because he wanted to go into the water, but the Druid wouldn't survive the temperatures.

"The ice is too thin," he said again.

The Druid's eyes lifted to his. Ian found himself staring into eyes as bright as emeralds a heartbeat before there was a loud crack and the ice split beneath her feet.

# CHAPTER
# SIX

With the ice now broken, Ian ran toward where the Druid and the wyrran had fallen into the loch, the ice cracking beneath his weight. But his Warrior speed allowed him to move so fast that he didn't break through.

He was surprised to find worry and anxiety filling him now when before he'd felt nothing but fury and despondency.

Rage swelled in him when he saw the two wyrran climbing onto the Druid and pushing her under the water as they attempted to scramble out.

The Druid's eyes met his a moment before she went under. And didn't come back up.

Ian severed the wyrrans' heads as he reached the Druid and jumped into the water. He dove beneath the surface and grasped the edge of her clothes as she drifted away.

She wasn't moving. Her long silvery blond hair stretched behind her as he pulled her to the surface. Ian lifted her above the water and set her atop the ice. Then he climbed back out of the water, careful not to crack the fragile ice. He lifted the Druid's limp body in his arms and used his incredible speed to get to shore.

He was about to pass up her bag, but then he remembered how she had desperately tried to reach it. With a curse, Ian once more set her down and stuffed the spilled contents back into her bag before he looped it over his head.

Ian pressed her body against his and scowled at how cool she felt against him. He didn't stop again until he was in his cave.

A growl tore from his throat as he looked around the cave. There was no soft place to lay her, no place for a woman among the sparse, harsh rocks.

But if he didn't get her warm soon, she would die.

Ian used his feet to arrange the furs from the animals he'd killed into a pile before he placed the Druid upon them. He jerked her bag off him and pulled another fur over her shivering body. Then he set about adding wood to the fire.

Once that was done, he sat back and waited.

Long locks of her silvery blonde hair were stuck to her neck and face. Her skin was as pale as her hair, and her lips were a faint shade of blue.

To make matters worse, Ian could feel her magic ebbing away, taking her life force with it.

"Nay," Ian growled, and rose to pace the cave.

He'd rescued her from the icy depths of the loch. She was before a fire and covered. What else was there to do?

"Shite," he said and whirled toward her.

He tossed the fur off her and reached to pull off her boots. The strange way the boots fit over her legs made him frown. He'd never seen anything like it, nor her clothes for that matter.

His claw touched the small silver thing at the top of her boot. After a moment's hesitation, he pulled down.

And to his surprise, it opened her boot so he could pull it off her feet.

She wore something black under the boots as well. It wasn't anything like the woolen hose he was used to seeing women wear, but they had a similar purpose, he suspected.

Once he had removed both the boots and the hose-like things covering her feet he looked at her clothes.

They were soaked, but he was able to get the heavy cloak off her. And then he stared at the black gown that clung to every curve, every mouthwatering swell of her body.

Ian swallowed, wholly unprepared for such a sight. Or the way his blood rushed to his cock to make it swell.

To get his hands moving again, he had to remind himself she needed warmth. It didn't take long to unbutton the row of tiny buttons that went from her breasts to the edge of the gown that stopped above her knees.

Ian shook his head, befuddled at the change in clothing. But liking it. "Just where am I?"

When he removed the gown and caught a glimpse of deep red lace that covered her glorious breasts and wrapped around her hips to hide her sex, Ian forgot to breathe.

"By the saints," he whispered, and reverently ran a finger over the lace at her hip.

He hissed in a breath when his hands touched her bare skin and felt the chill. His light blue claws gleamed in the firelight. Ian urged his god back down, but Farmire wouldn't listen.

Ian concentrated, demanded. And to his surprise, Farmire retreated. As soon as his claws disappeared Ian rubbed his hands up and down her legs and arms to help warm her.

But that wasn't enough. It was going to take more

than a single blanket and a fire. It was going to take
him.

With his jaw clenched, Ian removed his sporran,
boots, kilt, and shirt and lay next to the Druid. It had
been many moons since he'd touched a woman. As wonderful as her lithe body felt against his, Ian pushed aside
all thoughts save warming her.

He refused to notice the softness of her skin, refused
to look at the gentle swell of her hips or the indent of her
waist. But he did note the many cuts and bruises over her
body. He pulled the blanket around them so he wouldn't
see the pale pink tips of her nipples through the red lace
or the fullness of those bountiful breasts.

Ian turned her onto her side and wrapped himself
around her. She fit perfectly against his large frame, almost as if she'd been made for him.

He lifted his head while he tugged loose the strands
of her hair stuck to her neck and face. He couldn't help
but run the tips of his fingers along her neck and over
her jaw to her high cheekbones.

His cock ached where it pressed against her soft bottom. He longed to lift her leg and slide within her. The
need, the yearning was so powerful that he almost gave
in. Somehow, he managed to keep himself in check.

But it didn't stop him from being aware of the way
her soft skin felt against him. Or the way she gravitated
to his warmth by pressing back against him.

He wanted to lift the fur and look more at her long
legs and the lace that covered her softness. He'd never
seen anything so erotic, and that brief, tantalizing view
only made him hunger for more of her.

Whoever the Druid was, she was stunning. He just
prayed she lived.

He laid his head down, his gaze on the wall of the
cave. Warmth that had nothing to do with the fire touched

his skin. It was the Druid's magic. It caressed him like a lover, learning him, studying him.

The magic was heady. Invigorating. Seductive.

Longing swept through Ian, but also peace. His soul calmed, his god quieted, and for once his mind was silenced. As the Druid's magic enveloped him, Ian found his eyes closing.

Not in sleep, but in rest. He didn't sleep, hadn't slept in months. But the serenity surrounding him felt too fine to ignore.

How long had it been since he'd slept more than a few moments at a time? Suddenly, he couldn't keep his eyes open, nor did he want to.

Ian took a deep, slow breath and heard the fire crackle as if from a great distance.

MacLeod Castle

"We've got a visitor," Arran MacCarrick said from his place on the battlements.

Camdyn MacKenna came to stand next to him and flattened his lips as he saw the man walking toward the castle before his skin changed to an orange color. "Aye. It appears we do."

"He's a Warrior."

Camdyn glanced at Arran. Arran's honey-colored eyes were narrowed on the newcomer. Camdyn didn't blame Arran for his suspicions. When battling an evil like Deirdre, it was better to be safe than dead.

"So he is," Camdyn said. "I'll alert Fallon and the others."

Arran gave a nod, and then whistled long and high. A few heartbeats later a large indigo form flew from one of the windows of a tower.

Camdyn watched as Broc spread his great wings and

climbed high into the sky. He was their eyes from above, and with his power to find anyone anywhere, he was one of their greatest assets.

Camdyn jumped from the battlement to the bailey and ran into the castle. He found Lucan, Ramsey, and Galen seated at the table. Their heads turned as one to him.

"A Warrior is approaching," he told them.

Lucan rose swiftly. "I'll let my brothers know."

"I'll find the others," Ramsey said.

Galen hurried into the kitchen as he said, "I'll collect the Druids."

As leader, Fallon MacLeod had made sure they were prepared for any event. They all knew their places and who was to do what. The Druids would be guarded by Larena, the female Warrior.

Since she could turn invisible, any threats to the Druids never knew what hit them. It was the perfect way to keep the Druids safe from any harm.

Camdyn had the ability to call up the earth in whatever way he needed. He let loose his god, Sculel, the god of the underworld, as he raced to his position atop one of the towers.

When Camdyn reached the tower, he climbed out the window and onto the top. The wind whipped around him from the sea to his back. He inhaled deeply and breathed in the salt air.

To his right he saw Hayden with his deep red Warrior skin help his wife, Isla, out of another tower. Isla used her magic to cloak the castle to keep other unwanted people from finding it.

Those not looking for MacLeod Castle would only see the land thanks to Isla's magic. It had kept them for four hundred years as those inside the castle walls waited until he, Logan, Arran, and Ramsey had returned to them. It had been the Druids who had tossed them into the future to find Deirdre as well as Ian. But none of them had expected a new evil to rival that of Deirdre. Declan Wallace was a menace, and he would be dealt with accordingly.

Hayden wrapped an arm around Isla to hold her close as he leaped from the tower down to another part of the castle. Once there Hayden moved behind Isla, the small red horns visible through his blond hair.

To Camdyn's left was Logan Hamilton. The silver-skinned Warrior had the ability to control water, and since the sea was behind them, it could come in handy.

Arran, Galen, and Ramsey were outside the castle walls, hidden and waiting. Broc continued to fly overhead while the Macleods—Fallon, Lucan, and Quinn—stood in the gatehouse.

The MacLeods shared a god, and when they fought together, they were unstoppable. Much as Ian and Duncan had been. But Duncan was gone, his life taken by Deirdre. Ian had been pulled into the future not long after Deirdre had been.

Whether Ian had learned to control his god or not was another matter. One they hoped to discover soon, along with Ian.

Camdyn wondered where his friend was. They could use Ian now. It had been too quiet. No one knew what Deirdre was about or why she hadn't attacked again.

Declan, they knew, would attack soon. After all, they had rescued the Seer he had kept chained in his dungeon.

Camdyn knew he likely wouldn't survive this war with Deirdre. He didn't mind dying, but the thought of being captured by Deirdre again and turned to her side made him ill.

Broc flew over the bailey and held up one finger, letting all know the Warrior had come alone.

"I seek the MacLeods!" the Warrior bellowed. He looked around and lifted his hands as he touched the barrier to Isla's shield. A moment later he stepped through the shield and smiled as he caught sight of the castle.

No one moved as the Warrior made his way through the village toward the castle. When he neared the gates, Broc dove from the sky causing the Warrior to pause.

"Who are you?" Fallon demanded, his deep voice carrying clearly in the wind.

"I am Charlie," the Warrior answered. "I'm here to help you battle Deirdre."

Camdyn frowned. The MacLeods had welcomed him and others into the castle without hesitation, but that was before Malcolm had left and had his god unbound by Deirdre, before Malcolm had killed Duncan.

Now, Camdyn was suspicious of everyone. Even though they needed Warriors to fight Deirdre, Camdyn wasn't sure about this Warrior.

Logan lifted a brow in question to Camdyn. Camdyn gave a single shake of his head. Logan clenched his jaw and flexed his silver claws.

So, Camdyn wasn't the only one who had doubts about the Warrior.

"How did you find us?" Lucan asked.

Charlie chuckled. "Deirdre. She's on the hunt for new Warriors. I was turned some time ago and managed to escape. I knew if anyone could help me learn to control my god, it was the MacLeods."

Quinn leaned forward, his face set in hard lines. "If you doona want me to kill you where you stand, you will give us the answers we seek."

Charlie let out a loud sigh and shook his head. "Charon should have told me I wouldna get in so easily."

Camdyn didn't know Charon, but he'd heard Arran, Quinn, Ian, and Duncan speak of their time together in

Deirdre's mountain. Camdyn had been a wee bit surprised the Warrior hadn't joined them in their fight, but then again, Quinn had said Charon was a tad hard around the edges.

"Charon?" Quinn repeated. "What do you know of him?"

"I know that he said the MacLeods would welcome me," Charlie said. "He found me wandering the mountains. I asked for his help, but he said he had none to give. He sent me here."

Camdyn dug his claws into the stones as he crouched down. He trusted the MacLeods, he trusted everyone in the castle, but that had come from fighting—and surviving—alongside each other.

There was no debate among the brothers. Fallon looked first at Lucan, then to Quinn before he said, "We welcome you to MacLeod Castle, Charlie."

Galen swung open the gates as everyone came out of their hiding places. Camdyn jumped from the tower and landed beside Ramsey in the bailey.

One by one the Warriors gathered around Charlie. The newcomer looked at them with a smile and laughing blue eyes. His black hair was cut short and spiky on top.

"Thank you," Charlie said. "I've been thrust into a world I know nothing about. Charon said there are those who fight Deirdre. I want revenge for what she has done to me."

Fallon moved to stand directly in front of Charlie. "You will be welcome here. But you must earn our trust. If you do anything to jeopardize the castle or anyone within it, I will sever your head from your body myself."

Charlie bowed his head. "You've nothing to worry about. I only want to kill Deirdre for what she's done to me."

Camdyn watched Charlie as he strode past and into the castle.

"What is it?" Logan asked.

Camdyn shrugged. "I'm no' sure."

Arran walked to the other side of Logan. "I doona like him."

"We need Warriors," Ramsey said. "Especially with Duncan dead and Ian missing."

Hayden blew out a breath. "True enough, old friend. This new fellow will take some getting used to."

"It's his eyes," Broc said as he landed and folded his massive leathery wings behind him. "There's something . . . wrong about his eyes."

Galen clapped Broc on the shoulder. "You were in Deirdre's mountain too long. You're suspicious of everyone."

"That isn't always a bad thing," Arran murmured.

Camdyn had to agree.

# CHAPTER
# SEVEN

Ian was pulled from the dark depths of sleep by the feel of silky skin and a soft, tempting body. Awareness came to him slowly, his unconscious battling against waking.

But when he did open his eyes, he found himself frozen in place. Afraid to move. Afraid not to.

He was on his back, the generous curves of a female pressed against him, her bare leg thrown over his hips. And his rod hard and aching.

Her deep, steady breaths fanned over his chest as she snuggled deeper against him. Her head rested on his shoulder while one of her arms draped across his chest. Ian discovered his arm wrapped around her, holding her tightly against him while his hand grasped the ends of her silvery blond hair.

His arousal lengthened and grew as her leg brushed against him. He closed his eyes as he felt her nipple harden where it pressed alongside him. His hands ached to cup her breasts, longed to fondle her nipples until they were hard as pebbles.

He shifted his hips to ease the ache in his cock, but it

only caused him to touch her leg once more. Ian sucked in a breath as she rubbed her hips against him.

Need, pure and bright, burst through him. Desperate desire. Frantic longing. Wild hunger.

It felt . . . right . . . to be as they were. Yet Ian knew it was far from right. He hadn't thought of losing control to his god when he'd been trying to save her. But he should have. He could have hurt her during the night. He could have had a blackout and killed her.

Ian needed some distance between them before he gave in to his urge and took her. Again and again. His breath lodged in his throat as he recalled her gorgeous emerald-green eyes. Her delicate face and stunning body would be imprinted on his mine for eternity.

Slowly, all the while trying not to touch her more than he had to, Ian extracted himself. She moaned softly when the fur fell away from her. Ian quickly covered her, but allowed his fingers to brush against the supple skin of her shoulder.

Then he stood looking down at her.

Her silvery hair lay in waves around her, one lock stretching toward his feet. Ian found himself enthralled with her.

Her milky skin was flawless. Brows, a darker blond than her hair, arched regally over her eyes. Her lips were wide and full. Kissable. Seductive. Erotic.

Who was she? And what had she been doing in the mountains alone?

Ian scratched his chin. He was surprised to find a new day dawning. Had he slept through yesterday afternoon and the night? He couldn't remember the last time he had slept so soundly.

Could the Druid's magic have had something to do with that? Ian shrugged, assuming that's what it was.

He glanced at the Druid again. While they had slept, the fire had died. Needing something to do, Ian dressed and set about building another fire.

Next, he picked up her clothing and spread it out so it could finish drying. He was curious about her. About her strange clothes. And about how the wyrran had found her.

He wanted to wake her to gain the answers he sought, but the thought of his god taking control made him pause. He paced the cave as he waited, his mind searching for any way to keep her safe.

From him. And the wyrran.

Ian sat across the fire from her. She drew his gaze again and again. He wanted to see her eyes once more. He wanted to hear her voice and know her name. But he feared all those things at the same time.

With his god vying for control, Ian could snap at any moment. How could he protect the Druid if Farmire had him? Yet, he couldn't leave the Druid alone. Who knew when she would awaken?

At least the danger of her dying had passed. Her magic was as strong as it had been when he'd first felt it. As soon as she woke, he would see that she was on her way.

*"And if she needs your help, brother?"*

Ian ran a hand down his face and wished he hadn't heard Duncan's question, because he didn't have an answer. Ian had made a vow to protect Druids. If this one needed his help, he couldn't refuse her.

But being near her in his state could put her in even more danger.

Ian rose and left the cave. He needed to hunt. Oddly enough, his god had been quiet, almost content, since he had encountered the Druid.

There would be time enough to test his control later. Ian glanced into the cave before he called up his god and stepped into the snow.


Danielle couldn't remember ever being so warm. She snuggled deeper into the furs.

*Furs?*

Her eyes flew open as she lay perfectly still. A fire blazed before her, but she could detect no one around her. The odd thing was she could have sworn someone had been near her, warming her, holding her.

And it had felt heavenly. Even if her body ached.

It took half a heartbeat for her to realize she only had on her bra and panties beneath the fur. She rolled onto her back and looked at the rocks around her. Was she in a cave? She licked her lips as she tried to remember what had happened before.

She recalled running. From those awful yellow creatures. An image of a tall man with shoulder-length wavy hair and pale blue skin flashed in her mind. She had seen the darker blue claws and his fangs as he roared.

He had fought the wee beasts.

Danielle then remembered the sound of the ice cracking beneath her feet a heartbeat before the glacial water swallowed her.

Everything had gone black after that. She had thought for sure she was dead. Who had saved her? The man who wasn't a man at all?

The fire popped, and a moment later Danielle smelled meat. She held the fur against her chest with her hand and slowly sat up.

"Hello?" Danielle called. "Is anybody there?"

When no one answered her, she let out a sigh and bent her legs so that her feet were tucked against her. She spotted her coat, dress, socks, and boots spread out among the rocks.

Someone had pulled her from the water. Someone had brought her to this cave. And someone had undressed her.

Where were they?

The cave held many shadows. The fire was large and the light danced upon the walls and ceiling where she could see deep gouges in the rock as if a blade of some kind had struck it. But the light didn't reach into all the shadows.

She swallowed past the fear lumped in her throat and looked around the cave. The area was large, with the fire built in the middle. A few paces away she could see where the cave narrowed so that only one person could walk to the entrance, where she caught a glimpse of the darkening sky. And more falling snow.

How many days had passed since she had fallen into the loch? One? Two? More?

"If I get out of this I'm taking a holiday. Somewhere tropical like Jamaica or the Bahamas. No. Tahiti. For a month," she said as she gently touched her hand to the injury on her head from the accident.

She sat up straight and stretched her back. Instantly pain ran through her, causing her to wince. She looked at her arms and shoulders to see bruises everywhere.

"Dear God, I'm a sight. And still talking to myself." She rolled her eyes. "I've gone daft. That's the only explanation. I wandered the mountains too long. The lack of food and warmth has done me in."

She laughed as she thought of what Whitney and Clair might say to that statement. How she wished she weren't alone. She should have stayed at home instead of wanting to celebrate New Year's.

Then she wouldn't have found the key, wouldn't have hurt Mitchell, wouldn't have gotten into the accident, and certainly wouldn't have gotten lost.

Her stomach gave a long, low growl. Danielle laughed as she shook her head. The smell of the meat was too tempting to resist.

She inched closer to the fire and reached for the meat. Only to realize she had nothing with which to cut off a piece.

"I was never one for camping," Danielle said with a sigh. "I should have gone with Aunt Sophie and Uncle Henry more often. Maybe then I'd know what to do in this situation."

But her hunger was too great to be ignored. She reached for the meat and tried to pull off a piece, but the heat from the flames and the meat itself only burned her fingers.

"Bugger," she said with a yelp and stuck her injured fingers in her mouth.

Nothing had moved in the cave, but suddenly she knew she wasn't alone. Danielle looked around carefully, noting several places someone could hide in the deep shadows.

"Are you the one who saved me?" she asked. "Thank you."

She had to wonder why the person was hiding. Did they not want to show themselves to her? Or was it that they didn't want her to know who they were?

Long moments passed with no answer. Then a shadow to her right shifted, moved. And came toward her.

Danielle recognized the man instantly. He was the same one she had seen fighting the creatures. But his skin was no longer pale blue. It was tanned a deep bronze that set off his sherry-colored eyes.

She was struck speechless at the rugged, untamed

handsomeness of the man. The man was tall and held himself stiffly, as if he were on guard. Through the torn saffron shirt she saw the corded muscles of his arms, chest, and shoulders. His light brown hair was long and wild about his shoulders.

There was a dark intensity about the man, a coiled violence that seemed ready to explode at any moment. Though his face was hidden by a thick beard, she could still make out the hard planes of his face, his wide, thin lips, and hollowed, angled cheeks. He had deep-set eyes that pierced her to her soul, and an aquiline nose that spoke of his heritage.

"Hi," she said with a smile.

He didn't reply, just looked at her. He studied her as one did an insect they had never seen before.

Danielle grew uncomfortable in the silence. She shifted back to her position on the furs and looked anywhere but into the man's all too seductive eyes.

She couldn't take her eyes off him. He was incredibly handsome. Even if he did wear a kilt that looked to be several hundred years old and in need of throwing away.

"Hell . . . o."

She jerked her gaze to him and smiled. "So you can talk. I was beginning to worry."

He frowned as if he were struggling to understand her. Danielle was beginning to wonder if he was a half-wit who had taken to living in the mountains.

Regardless, he had saved her life and she owed him.

The man knelt before the fire in one smooth movement. She was so entranced with the way the firelight danced upon his face and highlighted his light brown hair that she wasn't aware of what he was doing until he held out a piece of meat to her.

"Thank you," she said as she accepted it. She bit into

the meat and closed her eyes on a groan. "This is most excellent."

She tried to be polite and take small bites, but she was ravenous. The moment she stuffed the last bite into her mouth, he held another piece out to her.

Danielle ate and ate. And ate. She had missed a meal or two before, but she had never missed a day or more. When he offered yet another piece, Danielle waved it away and wiped her mouth with the back of her hand.

"I don't think I could eat another bite for at least an hour." She chuckled at her own joke.

When he didn't say anything, Danielle looked at her clothes. She was tired of sitting half naked in front of him. She needed something more than the fur between them.

She rose to her knees, careful to keep the fur against her, and bit her lip to keep from crying out. Her knee must have hit something in her fall down the mountain.

Undaunted, Danielle climbed to her feet, but had to reach for the wall behind her to keep her balance. Out of the corner of her eye, she saw the man rise and begin to reach out a hand to her.

She turned her head to him and saw concern in his eyes. Danielle gave him a soft smile.

"I'll be all right."

His raised brow said he questioned her statement.

Danielle didn't blame him. She questioned it herself. Lying and sitting down had been one thing. Standing and walking was something else entirely.

It took her several minutes, but she made it over to her clothes. To her relief, they were dry. She lifted her dress and looked at her savior.

"You might have undressed me, but you won't watch me dress. Turn around."

When he only frowned at her words, Danielle sighed

and shook her head. She had to release her dress since her other hand held the fur against her. She lifted her arm, her finger down, and twirled it.

Realization dawned, and the man turned his back to her. But not before she saw his grin.

"Men," Danielle grumbled.

She dropped the fur and slid her arms into her dress. She had to lean against the wall in order to button it, but when she was finished, she felt much better.

"All right. You can turn back now."

The man glanced over his shoulder, then faced her fully.

"Do you talk at all?"

He cocked his head to the side.

Danielle rolled her eyes and grabbed her socks and boots. She made her way back to the pallet of furs. The heat of the fire warded off most of the chill, and the long sleeves of her dress helped to keep her warm.

She sank down to the furs and began to put on her socks. When she saw him staring at her socks strangely, she held up one.

"Socks. They come in all colors and heights. I like the short ones that barely reach my ankle, myself." She glanced at his well-worn boots, boots that looked like they were made in medieval times. Boots that looked very authentic.

"Socks," he repeated.

Danielle laughed as she put on her second sock. "Exactly. I wish I had a few more pair to put on. My feet are still frozen."

The man pointed to her boots.

Danielle picked up one and put it on her foot. "It's a boot. Different than yours, however. Mine has a heel," she said and showed him. "They're called stilettos. Very fashionable. I love them, but they hurt like Hell."

She grabbed the zipper and paused. Why the questions? It was obvious he had no idea what the items were, but why? How could anyone living in the twenty-first century not know something so basic?

"This is a zipper," she said. "They're used on boots, pants, coats, dresses, and well, just about anything."

She slowly pulled the zipper up, then down, showing him how it worked. Obviously he had been able to unzip her boots in order to get them off her, but his rapt attention told her he hadn't known what it was.

After she zipped her second boot, Danielle tucked her legs to the side and regarded him. She touched her dress. "This is a dress. They come in different lengths. Some have long sleeves like this one. Others have short sleeves, and some are sleeveless or even strapless—which are my favorite."

"Strap-less."

She pointed to her coat. "That's a coat. Again, different lengths, different colors, different weights. That's a pretty thick wool coat."

He nodded, as if he understood. He then pointed to her arm.

Danielle looked down, amazed to find she had a couple of her bangles still on her wrist. "My bracelets."

"Bracelets."

The way he said it, as if the word were foreign, as if he were learning how to move his lips just right, caused Danielle to raise her gaze to him.

"Who are you?"

He lowered his sherry gaze to the flames for a moment. When he looked at her again, his expression had hardened. "Ian Kerr."

# CHAPTER
# EIGHT

"Ian," Danielle repeated. It suited him. A strong Scottish name for a strong Highlander. "I'm Danielle Buchanan."

"Hello, Danielle."

The sound of her name on his lips sent a thrill rushing through her. His voice was deep and smooth, and altogether sexy.

"Why did you not speak earlier?"

He shrugged, a small frown marring his face. "I was learning your speech."

"Learning . . . ? I'm sorry. I'm confused. What do you mean?"

"You speak differently. I had to learn it."

Danielle could see he spoke the truth. There was intelligence in his gaze. No half-wit would be able to pull that off.

"Where are you from that we speak so differently?"

He stiffened, a look of affront on his face. "Scotland, of course."

"Of course," she said, the sarcasm heavy. "Everyone in Scotland speaks as I do. Have you been hiding up here?"

"For some time, aye."

"That doesn't explain all of it though," she said.

Ian scratched his chin. "What year is it?"

There was something in his voice that gave her pause. Something that told her once she answered him everything would change. "It's 2012."

"Shite," he said, and slammed his hand on his knees. "Four hundred years."

Danielle blinked. "Did you just say four hundred years? As in, four centuries?"

"Aye, lass."

"What does that mean? Did you time-travel?" she asked with a nervous laugh.

When Ian's sherry gaze met hers, her stomach dropped to her feet. She'd been joking, but apparently he wasn't.

"That's not possible."

Ian lifted a shoulder in a shrug. "You're a Druid. You know as well as I that anything is possible."

She gaped at him. "How did you know I was a Druid?"

"I feel your magic."

Danielle opened her mouth to tell him that was impossible, but she thought better of it. "What are you? I saw your skin at the loch. It was pale blue. And the claws. I saw those as well."

"Are you sure you really want to know?" he asked as he ran a hand through his hair.

"I'm sure."

Ian didn't want to tell her. He was still too shaken up to learn he had been jerked forward in time. By four centuries!

Instead of walking out as he had intended to do before she woke, he found himself wanting to talk to her. Her speech hadn't been difficult to learn. The fact she had continued to talk to herself had helped him grasp it even faster thanks to the powers of his god.

"Ian," Danielle urged.

"Were you raised as a Druid? Did you learn how to use your magic?"

She nodded. "Yes. By my aunt."

"Did she tell you anything of the history of the Druids?"

"She told me that magic is in the land, that it makes Britain what it is."

"Anything else?" Ian prompted.

Danielle shrugged. "She told me that I'm descended from a long line of Druids dating back to the Celts."

Now they were getting somewhere. "Did she mention anything about the Celts and the Romans?"

"No."

Ian rubbed a hand over his face. He was uncomfortable sitting across from Danielle as if he were a normal man. He wasn't. Farmire could rear his head at any moment.

There was no doubt Ian knew he should leave Danielle. He couldn't bear the thought of being the one to harm a Druid. But she was injured. The weather hampered her from going anywhere herself, especially in those boots she wore.

He looked at Danielle to find her watching him. "Do you know why Rome left our shores?"

"Of course. The Saxons were invading and Rome was tired of holding on to a land on the fringes of their empire. Though Rome conquered England, they never were able to conquer past Hadrian's Wall."

Ian chuckled. "Who told you that nonsense?"

"We're taught that in school," she said with a lift of her chin. "Why? What were you taught?"

"The truth."

"Which is?"

Ian liked her spirit. Maybe a little too much. "You

were correct in that the Romans never conquered past the wall. The Romans were kept at bay by the Celts. And the Druids."

Danielle sat up straighter. "Tell me more."

"Though the Celts won most of their battles, they couldn't get Rome to leave. So they turned to the Druids."

"Rome said the Druids were pagans that sacrificed women and children."

Ian shrugged. "If Rome wrote that part of history, then they controlled it."

"True enough."

"The Druids of old had their own way of doing things. Their magic came to them naturally. Those who were content to derive their magic from nature were called *mies*. Those who craved more power, stronger magic, found another way to get it. They turned to Satan and offered their blood and soul to him. In exchange they were given very powerful magic."

"And these Druids were called?"

"*Droughs*. It was the *droughs* who had an answer for the Celtic problem with Rome. With the strongest warriors of each family present, the *droughs* called up primeval gods locked away in Hell. These gods inhabited these Warriors, taking over their bodies."

Danielle swallowed and ran her thumb over one of her bracelets.

"These men were now Warriors. They attacked the Romans. And Rome had no answer. In a matter of weeks Rome was leaving Britain. However, the gods didn't stop their fighting. They turned against anyone who got in their way. The *droughs* tried to pull the gods out, but they refused to leave their hosts. It took the combined magic of the *mies* and the *droughs* to bind the gods inside the men."

"Bind? How exactly?"

"The gods were still inside the men, but the men didna know it. The gods passed through the bloodline to the strongest, most powerful warrior each time. The Druids knew they had no' solved the problem, and so they stayed near these families in case the gods were somehow unbound."

"What were these . . . Warriors exactly?" Danielle asked.

Ian took a deep breath and let himself drown in her emerald depths. "They took on the characteristics of their god. Each god had a power and a color they favored. These Warriors' skin and eyes would change. They would have claws and fangs. And be able to wield a power."

"You are one of these Warriors?"

Ian had expected her to recoil, to run away. But she asked the question bluntly. He gave a small nod. "I'm no' one of the original Warriors. When the Druids bound the gods, the spells they had used were burned. Or at least they thought they were. One was kept hidden. A very powerful *drough* found the scroll. Deirdre is her name, and she wants to rule the world."

"You make it sound like she's still alive."

"Because she is. In the scroll it listed one clan. The MacLeods. Deirdre found the three brothers of the clan who had been mentioned to her by her Seer. Deirdre wiped out the entire MacLeod clan in one day and trapped the brothers. She unbound the god the three brothers shared. Awakening the Warriors once again."

"MacLeod," Danielle mumbled. She rose and walked to her coat where she fumbled in the pocket. She took something out and returned to her seat. "None of what you are telling me is in our history."

"Nay. Deirdre set about finding as many Warriors as she could. The MacLeods escaped and returned to their

castle where they hid for three centuries. Others, like
me, were found by Deirdre and taken to her mountain."

Danielle leaned forward. "What mountain?"

"Cairn Toul Mountain. Her magic is to control stone,
so the inside of the mountain is her castle. She kept it
full of prisoners. Druids who she killed and stole their
magic to make herself more powerful. And men she
captured in the hopes they were Warriors."

"Like you."

"Like me and my twin, Duncan. We shared a god as
well. We were inside the mountain for far too long, but
we never gave in and sided with her. Many Warriors did."

"I don't understand. Why would they do that?"

"The god inside us, Danielle. It's evil. Its rage is . . .
overwhelming sometimes. Weak men are unable to fight
for control of their own bodies."

Danielle smiled. "That's obviously not you."

Ian couldn't meet her eyes.

"So how did you time-travel?"

"I'm no' sure," he answered. "There were nine Warriors who had gathered at MacLeod Castle with the
MacLeod brothers to fight Deirdre. We had several Druids who had taken safety within the castle as well. In the
process of saving a Druid we learned Deirdre was searching for artifacts that could make her stronger."

Danielle snorted. "How am I not surprised?"

Ian hid a smile. "One of these artifacts happened to
be a Druid who told us the artifacts would awaken
Deirdre's twin, who was the only one who could defeat
Deirdre once and for all."

"Did you find all the artifacts?"

"Logan and my brother, Duncan, had gone to the Isle
of Eigg to search for an artifact. That's when Deirdre had
Duncan killed. I knew the moment he was murdered.
With Duncan gone, the god we shared was no longer

split. It was all mine. I was mired in misery and anguish. One moment I was in the castle, the next I was in the mountains."

"Oh, God, Ian. I'm so sorry about Duncan."

Ian tossed another stick onto the fire. "He will be avenged."

"You don't know how you came to this time?"

"I assume it was Deirdre. She knew I would be vulnerable with Duncan gone. I would be contending with my god for control. A perfect opportunity for her to capture me."

Danielle's emerald eyes narrowed. "Do you have control of your god?"

Ian looked her dead in the eye. "Nay."

# CHAPTER
NINE

Danielle let out the breath she'd been holding. "Why tell me the truth? You could have lied."

"I could have, but you need to understand what I am. I shouldna be with you now, but I canno' leave you either."

"Because of those yellow beasts?"

"They're wyrran," he said, and leaned to the side, his weight on his hand. "They are made by Deirdre. Their one goal is to do whatever will make her happy."

Danielle rubbed her hands up and down her arms. "They're hideous, and I sensed the evil in them."

"As a Druid you probably would. They hunt Druids for Deirdre. If the wyrran are here, then so is she."

"Why would she come forward in time? That doesn't make sense."

"Nothing about Deirdre makes sense," Ian said with a snort. "You must stay away from her at all costs."

Danielle looked at Ian's kilt. "Everything you've told me seems so far-fetched. I shouldn't believe it, and in fact I wouldn't. Except I was chased by those wyrran. And I saw you."

"Are you afraid of me?"

His voice was soft, but his gaze pinned her. Danielle slowly shook her head. "You pulled me from the water and saved my life. You had ample opportunity to harm me while I slept. You didn't."

"I still could."

"Possibly. You have no idea how much magic I have."

"Oh, but I do." His eyes seemed to darken as he inhaled. "Warriors can feel the magic of Druids. We sense how much magic a Druid has. With yours, it's . . . potent. I've never felt magic like it before."

Danielle reached down to the key she had hidden beneath her thigh and wrapped her fingers around it. "You mentioned you had stayed at MacLeod Castle."

"Aye."

"Can you take me there?"

For several tense minutes Ian simply stared at her as he slowly sat up straight. She didn't know what was going through his mind, but she wished she did.

"It's important," she said.

"Why?"

She touched the key, wondering if she should tell him. "I must deliver something to the MacLeods."

"What something? Those people are my family. I willna see them harmed."

"If they're your family, why aren't you with them?"

Ian looked away, his hands fisting at his knees. "I would no' put them in harm's way."

"You mean while you're battling your god?"

He turned his gaze to her and gave a single nod.

"You've done very well with me so far."

His brow furrowed at her words. "I doona understand why. Before I sensed your magic, my god was taking control often."

Danielle wanted to believe she could protect herself with her magic, but since she knew nothing about Warriors, she wasn't sure if her magic could stop them or not.

"Please, Ian. I need to reach MacLeod Castle. You know the way. I don't want to freeze anymore."

"All right," he said after a lengthy pause. "I'll do it."

Danielle smiled and squeezed the key. "Thank you."

"Doona thank me yet," he cautioned. "We'll be traveling fast, and through harsh weather."

"I won't slow you down."

The doubtful expression on his face told her he believed otherwise. "We leave at first light. The storm should be over by then."

"I'll be ready."

He glanced at her boots. "No' in those."

"We'll have to find a town. There I can buy more suitable clothing and rent us a car."

"A what?"

Danielle smiled. "Oh, Ian. So much has changed in the four hundred years since you've seen the world."

"Like what?" he asked, and leaned forward.

"The cars I speak of are what we use to get from one place to the next."

"No' horses?"

She considered that a moment. "Horses are kept for pleasure, but not as a mode of transportation anymore. There are also airplanes that fly in the sky."

"That I canno' believe."

Danielle laughed. She was getting a lot of pleasure out of trying to shock him.

"Your accent. I hear a bit of brogue in it, but something else as well."

The smile died on Danielle's lips. "My father was Scottish. He went to the U.S. on business and fell in love with my mother."

"The U.S.? What's that?"

"Another country. The United States of America. Britain had control for a bit, but the U.S. had a revolution in 1776 and kicked Britain's butt back home."

"The English always did think they could rule everything," Ian muttered.

"They controlled a lot of countries for a while."

"As interesting as that might be, I'd rather learn more about you."

Danielle picked at her dress. "I'm nothing special, Ian."

"You're a Druid. That makes you more than special."

She wouldn't tell him how much his words meant to her. She'd never thought herself unique in any way.

"How many Druids do you know?" he asked.

"I only knew of my aunt Josie. Her sister, Aunt Sophie, didn't have any magic that I knew of."

"So your father was Scottish and your mother . . . ?"

"American," Danielle supplied as she recalled the laughter she had shared with her parents. "My father chose to stay in the States once they got married. They had me, and we lived quite happily."

"Until?"

She looked at Ian and gave a shake of her head. "My parents were killed in a car crash when they went out one night. It took them both. Aunt Sophie came and packed up everything I had and brought me to Scotland."

"How old were you?"

"Twelve."

"Such a young age for such an awful tragedy."

She nodded. "My aunts were good to me. This is my home now. Just as Aunt Sophie told me I would feel one day."

"Tell me of your magic."

Danielle was jarred by the quick change of subject. "I'd rather learn more about you. Tell me of your god."

Ian relaxed against a boulder. "What do you want to know?"

"Everything."

His chuckle was soft, hoarse. "My god's name is Farmire. He's the father of battle."

"What does that mean?"

"It means he likes battles. I can hear him in my head urging me to join a battle. Or create one."

"So I gather when you fought the wyrran he was happy."

"Verra much so."

"What kind of power do you have?"

"I have the ability to absorb another Warrior's power and use it as my own for a short amount of time. Duncan used to be able to cancel another Warrior's power."

Danielle saw the sadness in Ian's eyes when he spoke about his brother. "Do you have both powers now?"

"I doona know. I've no' tried to use them."

"With Duncan gone, it stands to reason that if you got the full rage of your god, you would also get its full power."

Ian shrugged. "Perhaps."

"How does it feel to have that power?"

"When I'm fighting Deirdre, the wyrran, or defending others against her, it feels glorious. Knowing I could verra well fall to Farmire makes me wish I never knew any of this."

"How long have you been a Warrior?"

"I had been a Warrior for two hundred years before I was taken from my time."

Danielle choked and coughed. "So you're six centuries old? You didn't say anything about immortality?"

"We have enhanced speed, hearing, and other abilities as well."

"Like what?"

"We used to jump from the top of the cliffs at MacLeod Castle to the bottom and back up again."

Danielle could only imagine how high the cliffs were. Immortality. Time travel. Powers. Warriors. Deirdre. It was almost too much.

"You doona believe anything I've told you, do you?" Ian asked, his sherry eyes studying her.

"It's not that. It's just so much to take in and believe all at once."

"Unfortunately, I have a feeling I'll be proving a lot of it to you on our way to MacLeod Castle."

"What if Deirdre has gotten to them already?"

Ian started shaking his head before she finished her sentence. "We had fought Deirdre several times at the castle and defeated her each time. We attacked her in her mountain in order to free the youngest MacLeod, and managed to kill her. Only we didn't realize it was going to take much more than beheading her to end her for good."

"You beheaded her?"

"Aye."

He said it so matter-of-factly, as if they were speaking of the weather. "And she didn't die?"

"Her body died, but no' her soul. She was able to create another body."

"I'm beginning to really dislike this woman."

"She's no' a woman, Danielle. She's a monster."

"I may have run into her on the street and never known it."

Ian's brows drew together. "No' possible. No' only would Deirdre have sensed your magic, but you would

have known if you'd seen her. She has long white hair
that reaches to the ground. She uses it as a weapon, killing and torturing with it. And her eyes are the same white
as her hair."

"White? Was she born that way?"

"It's the use of the black magic that has turned her
hair and eyes white. Believe me, when you see Deirdre,
there's no mistaking who and what she is."

Danielle shuddered at the thought of meeting up with
something so evil. She hoped she would never have such
an encounter, but if Ian was correct and Deirdre had
brought him forward in time with her then it was inevi-
table that Deirdre would find him eventually.

When that moment would come was the real question.

# CHAPTER
# TEN

With his arms crossed and one fist beneath his chin, Declan Wallace stared at the empty cell that had held his greatest prize—Saffron. He hadn't believed his luck when he had found a Seer.

Saffron had fought him. She hadn't wanted to accept she was his prisoner. So, he had taken away her sight. That had curbed her need to try and escape every ten minutes.

But it hadn't stopped her from fighting.

Declan had been raised to never hit a woman. That's why he had his cousin, and captain, Robbie, do it for him. No matter how many times Robbie hit her, she never stopped struggling.

With no other choice, Declan had had her chained in the dungeon. She could have had riches, could have been showered in jewels had Saffron but agreed to help him.

But the interfering MacLeods had somehow found Saffron and freed her.

The fury that welled inside Declan made his vision run red. He would take his vengeance on the MacLeods.

He would wipe them from the earth, but first, he would make them suffer. Terribly.

"Declan."

He turned his head slightly and raised a brow at Robbie. "What is it?"

"More wyrran have been spotted."

Declan dropped his arms and let out a resigned sigh. He had more than Saffron and the MacLeods to deal with. There was also Deirdre. "She's gone back to Cairn Toul as I knew she would."

"Do we go after her?"

"Nay. We lure her to us. She's been after the Mac-Leods from the beginning. I'm going to get them, and when I do, Deirdre will come to me."

Robbie looked down, his jaw tight as he hooked his thumbs in the front pockets of his black fatigues.

"What is it?" Declan demanded.

Robbie's lips tightened for a moment before he answered. "Declan, I've seen your power. I know what you can do. But I also know Deirdre's magic."

"You've heard about Deirdre's power," Declan corrected.

"Same difference. You know how powerful she is."

Declan rolled his eyes. "Your point, Robbie?"

"If she attacked the MacLeods and was never able to take them, what makes you think you can?"

Declan walked over to his cousin and slapped him on the shoulder. "Is that what your concern is?"

"Aye. We lost several men when the wyrran and Deirdre's Warriors broke her out of here. We lost more when you tried to take Gwynn and the Warrior Logan. There were additional men lost when we were attacked."

"Do you fear the MacLeods?"

Robbie's gaze narrowed. "I'm no' afraid of anyone."

"You should be afraid of me," Declan said as he took a step closer. "I could end you now, cousin. You may be able to find more mercenaries because there are plenty to choose from, but there is only one of me. I captured a Seer. I brought Deirdre forward in time. I can do anything."

"Then how do we get into MacLeod Castle?"

Declan smiled. "A Druid, of course."

"Why no' a Warrior?"

"First, we'd have to find one, and I suspect that will be rather difficult, especially since I doona have the spell to unbind the gods. Second, the MacLeods willna expect a Druid to betray them."

Robbie chuckled. "I like the plan, Declan. How soon can you find a Druid?"

"Verra soon."

Declan took one last look at Saffron's cell and followed Robbie out of the dungeon. Declan needed to focus his attention on finding a Druid.

And he knew just the one he was looking for. One who had no idea of her magic. One who would be easy to mold and manipulate to do exactly what he wanted.

She wouldn't survive, but then again, Declan didn't care. All he needed was for her to get into MacLeod Castle and he could do the rest.


Ian glared at the thick newly fallen snow from the entrance of his cave. Their journey was made even more difficult now.

"Oh," Danielle murmured as she came to stand beside him. "The snow is deep."

"Possibly too deep. We should wait another day."

"Nay." Her eyes were wide and filled with anxiety. "I need to go now."

There was something in her voice that drew Ian's gaze. He watched her carefully, noting how pale her face was. "Are you ill? Do your wounds hurt you?"

He had seen the cut on her forehead, but she had assured him she was all right. Now, he wasn't so sure.

"I . . . I'm fine." Danielle answered. "I just need to get to the MacLeods."

"I'm no' taking you anywhere until you tell me what is going on. I'm no' a fool. I can see that you're in pain."

"And I will stay in pain until I get to the MacLeods. It's part of my magic, Ian."

That's when he realized she had no intention of telling him about her magic. "You doona trust me."

Danielle sighed and leaned against the stone wall. "If I didn't trust you, I wouldn't have asked you to take me to the castle."

"You would if you didna know the way."

"Why do you want to know what my magic is?"

"Because those people at MacLeod Castle are my family. I willna see them harmed in any way."

"Oh," she said softly. "You want to make sure I'm not going to betray them."

"Aye."

Danielle looked at the snow and took a deep breath. When she raised her gaze to his, her emerald eyes were open and honest. "I'll begin by telling you I don't care for the power my magic gives me."

"It causes you harm?"

"When I don't do as it asks."

Ian was more confused than ever. "Explain."

She shivered as her fingers rolled something in the pocket of her coat. "I will find something. A scarf, money, a locket, a wallet, anything. Once I see it, the object tells me who its owner is. If I don't return the object, I feel tremendous pain throughout my body. So, I'm compelled to follow the directions given to me by the object. As long as I am going toward its owner, I won't feel any pain."

"You have something that tells you to go to the Mac-Leods?"

"I do," she answered.

"Will you no' tell me what it is?" He knew he was asking a lot. He had no right to ask either, but he wanted to know not just in order to keep those at the castle safe, but because he wanted her to trust him completely.

It was important to him. More important than anything had been in a long, long time.

Lengthy moments passed while Danielle did nothing but look at him. Ian was beginning to think she wouldn't tell him but then she withdrew her hand from her pocket.

She held her hand out, fist up, and slowly opened her fingers.

Ian kept his gaze on her face until her lips tilted upward in a small smile. Only then did he look down to see a key resting in the middle of her palm.

"I found it the other night. Sometimes I'm able to wait to take the object to its owner. This time, it made me set out immediately in the middle of a storm."

Ian put one of his hands under hers while with his other he closed her fingers over the key. "Thank you for showing me. It must be verra important for you to need to go to the castle so quickly."

She took a step toward him, their hands between their bodies. "I wanted you to know I trust you," she said.

Ian's body flared to life at her nearness. As if she too felt the desire, the overwhelming need to get closer, her emerald eyes darkened and her lips parted.

He wanted to press his mouth against hers, to sweep

his tongue through her luscious lips and taste her sweetness. The need was so great, so powerful, that Ian found his head lowering.

Danielle leaned into him, the pulse at the base of her throat as erratic as her breathing.

How easy it would be to close the small distance and get his first taste of her. How simple it would be to take what she was freely offering.

But then he remembered why he was alone in a cave.

It was Ian who looked away first. When he returned his gaze to Danielle, she had dropped her head and taken a step back. Reluctantly, Ian released her hand.

"I'll walk in front of you to help move aside the snow," he said and stepped out of the cave.

He didn't wait to see if she followed. He knew she would. The snow came up to his thighs it was so thick. He trudged several steps and glanced over his shoulder to find Danielle using the trail he had made.

The sun continued its ascent into the sky while Ian walked onward. He looked behind him every few steps to make sure Danielle was there.

She met his gaze with a direct look every time. She kept her shoulders back and her head high. How she managed to walk in the snow with such heels on her boots he'd never know, but she did it with grace and a skill he couldn't help but admire.

She did trip a few times, but not once did she fall. Her emerald eyes were bright, and her nose and cheeks red, but she kept pace with him, telling him of this new time he found himself in and all its wonders. And many wars.

They paused at noon to eat some of the leftover meat from the night before and for Danielle to rest. She'd told him she was fine, but he could see the fatigue in the way she held her mouth.

Ian had wanted to rest longer, but Danielle would have none of it. So onward they moved. As the day wore on, Ian was thankful the storms that had wreaked havoc on the mountains in the days and weeks before had seemed to dissipate. At least for a while.

The sun had been bright and the sky a vivid blue with thick clouds rolling past. But with his advanced eyesight, he could see another storm gathering in the distance. If they were lucky they would reach the Mac-Leods before it hit.

"The sun feels good," Danielle said.

They had walked most of the day in silence. Ian had been quiet because he couldn't stop thinking about their near kiss and how her tempting body had felt against his.

He knew it had been a while since he'd had a woman, but the need, the sheer yearning he had to pull her into his arms, was distracting and impossible to ignore.

She seemed content to be with her thoughts, which had suited Ian just fine since he was satisfied recalling how soft her skin had been, how plentiful her curves. And how nicely she had fit against him.

"Aye," he answered.

She chuckled. "I think you've been alone too long. You've forgotten how to have a conversation."

Ian smiled as he kept looking straight ahead. "Aye, but you talk enough for both of us."

"Oh. Now that was just wrong," she said in mock horror. "So where are we exactly?"

"We're in the Monadhliath Mountains."

"I wonder if we're close to a village?"

"There used to be one no' far from here. I'm heading there now in the hopes we can find lodging for the night and something else for you to wear."

"Why? Is my cocktail dress not fancy enough for a

hike through the mountains in the middle of winter?" she asked sweetly.

Ian shook his head. He liked her sarcasm and the way she teased. Despite their situation, she smiled and kept going. A trait that made the Highland people who they were. She also had valor befitting the bravest of warriors.

"What is a cocktail dress?" he asked.

"A dress meant for a party, but not a formal get-together. It's usually reserved for nighttime."

"Ah, I see." All too well. "Who is the man you were meeting?"

Danielle gave a bark of laughter. "Ian, I hate to be the one to tell you, but dating in the twenty-first century is a spectacular joke. Men don't know how to be men, and then you have the ones who just won't take a hint and go away."

"Which was it for your party?"

"The one who wouldn't take a hint. Me and my flatmates, Whitney and Clair, were supposed to go out and ring in the New Year together."

He paused and turned to look at her. "What?"

She laughed, her smile brightening her face. "People usually get together when one year ends and another begins. It's called ringing in the New Year. I was going to such a party."

"Hm," Ian said and resumed his walking. "What happened?"

"Wouldn't you know, my flatmates' boyfriends finally stepped up and acted like gentlemen? Since it was a large group going out, I kept my plans with the others. Then one by one people began to back out until it was just me and Mitchell left."

Ian already didn't like this Mitchell. "What did he do?"

"Nothing. I knew he wanted more than friendship. He had for over a year now, and he'd made it known several times."

"Was there something wrong with him?"

"No, actually, he's a good-looking guy with a great job."

"Job?" Ian asked with a frown. He had so much to catch up on in this new time.

"It's what one does to earn money."

Ian had a little coin, but it was at the castle. "Mitchell was handsome with a good job. What was wrong with him?"

"There was no spark," she said with a sigh. "I tried to make one, I tried to talk myself into dating him. But Mitchell is the kind of guy you don't just date. He's the kind of guy you marry, and I knew I wouldn't be marrying him. So, I never let it get beyond friendship."

Ian listened attentively. He was learning a lot about Danielle that he might not otherwise know. "How did Mitchell react?"

"Badly. Since it was just the two of us going out he had set up a nice dinner. I knew I had to tell him no before the night began or he'd never let up. He was disappointed and a tad angry. I suppose I would be as well."

Ian crested a mountain and paused to help Danielle up beside him.

"Wow," she said with awe. "This is stunning."

Ian looked over the vista and smiled. "There's no' another place like it on earth. I doona think I could live anywhere else."

With his enhanced eyesight he caught a glimpse of a town. Ian continued on, and Danielle paused a moment longer before she followed him.

Ian knew he should be focusing all his concentration on keeping Farmire in check. There had been a few times

that day when he'd felt Farmire shift inside him, his voice
loud in Ian's mind. But Ian had focused on Danielle and
what he needed to do. It had kept Farmire at bay. For the
time being.

That wouldn't last.

Danielle's safety was paramount. Ian would never
forgive himself if he harmed her because he'd been too
weak to control his god.

Somehow she allowed him a measure of power over
Farmire. How long his god would let that continue, Ian
wasn't sure. Farmire had gotten a foothold in Ian's mind,
and he wouldn't be content until Ian had fallen to him.

Ian looked up and found the sky had begun to darken.

"Did you spend the evening with Mitchell?" Ian was
a fool to ask, but he had to know.

"No. He said he couldn't go out if I only wanted to be
friends. I left his flat and was on my way to my car when
I fell and found the key."

"You didna go to your . . . flat . . . and change?"

"The key wouldn't let me, remember? I started out
right then with only the knowledge that I had to go east
to find MacLeod Castle."

"How did you end up in the mountains?"

She sighed and moved up beside him when the snow
grew more packed. "There was a wreck. That's how I
got the cut on my head. The people who hit my car both
died, and in the collision my mobile phone was broken.
I thought the key would tell me which way to go, but it
was strangely quiet."

"So you just set out?"

"No," she said with a short laugh. "I have an awful
time with direction, and after the accident I wasn't sure
where anything was. When I hit my head I passed out
for a while and the snow covered everything. I thought I

took the road, but apparently I didn't because I ended up in the mountains."

"It's a good thing I found you. Those wyrran would have taken you to Deirdre."

She shuddered and blew out a breath. "It's almost like it was fate."

Ian nodded, unsure if he believed in anything like destiny. He'd always thought a man made his own way in the world, but maybe he'd been wrong all those years. Maybe there was such a thing as fate.

# CHAPTER
# ELEVEN

"Look," Danielle said as she pointed. "I see lights from a village."

"We'll be there by nightfall."

Ian hid a smile when Danielle quickened her pace. He knew she was cold, and despite her not saying anything, he knew her feet had to be hurting.

Not only were the boots not well insulated, the heels made it difficult to climb the rocky slopes of the mountains. He knew she had twisted her ankle several times along the way.

He couldn't wait to throw away the boots as soon as he could. If she continued to wear them she was likely to break her ankle.

Though he did have to admit he liked the way her legs looked in the high heels. Stilettos, she had called them. It was no wonder women wore them then. They certainly caught men's attention.

They reached the small village almost an hour after the sun had set.

"An inn," Danielle said with a tired smile. "Let's get our rooms first."

Ian followed her to the inn that looked as if it had indeed been around for four hundred years. There were traces of something new, but whoever owned it had gone to great pains to keep the original look.

When they entered the inn Ian scanned the front room and the dining room within. He didn't detect anything that might put Danielle at risk of harm.

"We need two rooms," Danielle told the woman behind the counter.

"One," Ian said without glancing at her.

Danielle leaned away from the counter until she caught his eye. "One?" she asked, a blond brow raised.

"One."

She sighed but said, "We'll need one room."

"Just fill this out," the woman said.

Ian peered through the windows and surveyed everything around him. He needed to get outside and take a look around.

"Ian? Are you ready?"

He turned at Danielle's voice to find her at the foot of the stairs. With a nod to the woman behind the counter, he followed Danielle.

"I've coin."

She shook her head. "I'm afraid to ask what type of coin it is. Don't worry. I've enough money."

"I doona like a woman paying for me."

She put the key in the door and laughed as it unlocked. "Welcome to my time, Ian. Get used to it, because quite a bit has changed."

He wasn't sure he liked hearing that, but there was nothing he could do as they stepped into the room. The door shut behind him and he watched Danielle walk to the bed and fall backward on it.

"We should get you some clothes and food."

Danielle rose up on her elbows. "We should probably get you some clothes as well."

Ian glanced down at his kilt. "It's a wee bit dirty, but it's my kilt."

"I know." She spoke softly as she sat up. "There are many who still wear kilts. It is Scotland after all."

Ian took a step toward her and paused when something flashed in the corner of his eye. There was a light shining above him that was not fire, and as amazing as that was, it was nothing compared to the huge mirror he looked into.

And what he saw made him grimace. Maybe Danielle was right. Maybe he did need new clothes. He had caught a glimpse of what others had been wearing in the dining room. It wasn't exactly what he wanted to wear, but it was needed.

"Is there a place we can get new clothes?"

Danielle raised a brow at his words. She hadn't expected him to give in, and after the look on his face when she mentioned it, she hadn't planned on pushing the issue. "Yes. The receptionist told me there's a store just up the road."

"Do you want to go later?"

She rose from the bed and grabbed her purse. "Let's go now."

As they left the room, she looped her arm through his and saw his start of surprise. She had forgotten how old-fashioned he was. "Sorry," she said and dropped her arm.

"Nay," Ian said as he took her arm and looped it back around his. "I just didna expect your touch."

The feel of his large, warm hand over hers sent chills racing over her skin. How could such a simple touch turn her stomach to jelly?

She found herself walking next to him, wanting and needing his heat. Not because she was cold. But because of him. There was something altogether fascinating about Ian Kerr. And she liked it.

Part of it could be because he was an immortal Warrior who had time-traveled to her time.

But she suspected a lot of it was because of who Ian was as a man. He exuded confidence in a way she had never seen before. He wasn't cocky or self-absorbed. He knew what he could do without question.

And other men noticed it as well.

She'd seen the looks he got when they walked into the inn. The men had sized him up and immediately knew not to mess with Ian.

While the women had all begun to drool over his physique.

Not that she could blame them. She'd looked her fair share at his nice backside the entire journey from his cave. It was the reason she had tripped so many times.

Ian commanded attention. He defied temptation with his sultry sherry gaze that warmed her from the inside out.

If he knew what he did to her, she'd be completely at his mercy. Because she couldn't deny the attraction she felt for him, nor did she want to.

She had waited so long to feel *something* for a man. Now that she had, it most likely would never work. But at least she knew she could feel something. She wasn't the cold person Mitchell and other men thought her to be.

"Are you all right?" Ian asked.

Danielle nodded and tried to keep her eyes away from his toned arm muscles. "Just a wee tired."

They walked out of the inn and to the right where the receptionist had told her the store was. Just as Danielle had expected, it wasn't much more than a sporting goods store.

Yet, they sold exactly what she would need.

"Ready for this?" she asked Ian with a grin.

"It can no' be as bad as fighting Deirdre, can it?"

Danielle laughed as she pulled open the door and stepped inside. She watched as Ian looked over everything, his brow furrowing in either confusion or bewilderment. Or both.

Ian stayed close as she pulled out jeans for both her and him.

"Why so many?" he asked as they piled up in his arms.

"Are you kidding? Jeans are all made differently. I know my size, but depending on how these are made, they'll fit differently. I hate buying jeans for just this reason. And not to mention, I can take five pairs of the same size into the dressing room and all of them will fit differently."

"It was easier in my time," Ian mumbled.

Danielle chuckled as she pulled one last pair out and put it into his arms. Next they moved to the sweaters. She found a navy cable knit that she liked, but when she looked at men's sweaters for Ian he stopped her.

"I doona want something that heavy."

She looked away from him and glanced outside. "It's snowing. Aren't you cold?"

He shook his head. "I'm a Warrior, remember."

They settled for a plaid flannel button-down in a pattern similar to his kilt. However, it wasn't until they were heading to the dressing rooms that she noticed Ian's clenched jaw.

She put a hand on his arm to halt him. "What is it?"

"Remember when I told you I didna have control of my god?" he asked between clenched teeth.

Danielle dropped her arm. "Yes."

"He's wanting free."

"Oh." What did she say to that? "What can I do?"

He hastily looked around. "I need away. Somewhere safe."

"There is nowhere safe, Ian. You're in the middle of town. Do you think you can make it back to your cave in time?"

"Nay."

"Then you'll have to learn to control your god." Danielle couldn't believe the words came out of her mouth. She could see by the way Ian's lips were flattened that he was obviously distressed.

His sherry gaze swung to her. "Do you think I'm jesting?"

"Not at all. I know what you can become. But I also know you came to protect me. You cannot do that if you allow your god to take control."

Danielle winced at the harshness of her words. She wasn't sure if her trick would work, but she had to try. Ian had had control of his god before. He could do it again.

"Danielle, you doona know what you're asking of me."

"I'm asking as a Druid. I'm asking because I don't care to know what Deirdre's mountain looks like or to get another glimpse of the wyrran. I'm asking because I have to get to the MacLeods."

He swore under his breath and growled.

Danielle should have been startled or even wary at the sound of that growl, but she knew Ian wouldn't harm her. She wasn't sure, but she suspected the key might have led her to him somehow.

"You can try on your clothes in there," she said, and pointed to the one dressing room.

He turned on his heel and entered the small room. He reached for the clasp over his heart to unpin his kilt, and as much as Danielle wouldn't have minded seeing his glorious muscles for herself, she didn't want the clerk to.

Danielle quickly yanked the curtain closed between them as she shook her head and smiled.

The smile died however when she realized just what could happen if Ian did lose control of his god.

"I won't let that happen," she murmured to herself. "I'll do whatever it takes."

"Who are you talking to?" Ian asked from behind the curtain.

"Myself. You know how I love to talk to myself."

A snort was her only answer.

Danielle saw his boots hit the floor one at a time as he removed them. She expected to see his kilt next, and when she did it was folded neatly and laid gently on the floor.

Tears stung her eyes. His kilt meant everything to him. It was probably his only connection to the clan he'd once belonged to. And to his family.

The saffron shirt didn't get the same attention. It was tossed to the floor carelessly. That's when Danielle realized she hadn't gotten Ian any underwear.

"Ah . . . Ian?"

"Aye?"

"I . . . um . . . I didn't get you any undies."

"Undies?" he repeated. The curtain shifted and he poked his head around it. "What are you talking about?"

"Underwear. Men—and women—wear them beneath clothes. Men can wear briefs that . . . um . . . hug the body. There's also boxers."

Danielle ran over to a rack and grabbed a pack to show him. Ian's eyes crinkled at the corners when he saw the picture of the naked man wearing nothing but tight-fitting briefs.

"I prefer to go without," Ian said.

The thought of Ian naked beneath his kilt, and now whatever clothes he bought, made her body heat up and her heart thud in her chest.

"Danielle?"

She jerked, startled to hear Ian's voice so close to her. She dropped the package of briefs as she lifted her gaze to him. He caught the package before it hit the ground and put it back in her hands.

"How is this?" he asked.

Danielle let her eyes roam over the flannel shirt that fit snuggly across his broad muscled chest. He hadn't tucked the shirt in, but it didn't distract from his long legs encased in black denim.

"Is it that bad?"

She shook her head. "Not at all. It's just taken me a moment to see you in anything but the kilt. Turn and let me see how the jeans fit in the back."

"I doona think I like these jeans," he said. He turned as she asked and shifted from one foot to the other. "I'm no' used to my legs being so bound."

But Danielle could certainly get used to it. "Try the next size smaller."

"Smaller?" Ian asked as he looked at her over his shoulder. "Lass, I may no' get them on."

"Trust me, Ian."

He went back behind the curtain, and a moment later returned in the next pair of jeans. They were another black pair, and they fit him to perfection.

"Wow. The girls are going to be drooling over you."

He lifted a brow. "I take it that is good?"

"That's what every man wants. I'll go pick up some more jeans and a few more shirts. Want to look at the boots?"

"I've had enough change for one day," he muttered.

Danielle smiled as he turned to walk back into the dressing room. "Oh, Ian? By the way, how is that control with your god coming?"

# CHAPTER
# TWELVE

Ian blinked and realized he had managed to maintain control over Farmire as he tried on the clothes. He wished he knew how he had done it so he could do it again, but it was enough that he had control right now.

He grabbed his boots and sat in a nearby chair to put them on. The jeans were going to take some getting used to. He wasn't sure he liked how they felt rubbing against his legs. But everywhere he looked, men, women, and even children had some form of trousers on.

Once his boots were on, he gathered his kilt and shirt and turned to find Danielle before him.

"You can set those on the counter with the other things I picked up for you. I'll just be a moment."

He nodded and walked to the counter to see a young brunette lift her gaze and give him a dazzling smile. Ian laid his items on the counter while the girl continued to bat her lashes at him.

"I'll put this in a separate bag," she said, still smiling.

Ian turned his back to the girl and kept his eyes on the curtain Danielle had disappeared behind. It was a tiny room. Too tiny for someone to get in with her.

Yet she had been in there a while.

"It takes women longer," the girl said as if reading his thoughts.

Ian shifted so he could look at her. "Why?"

"Because we want to look good for our men. Your lady took a bundle of clothes in with her. It will take her some time to try them on. I've also gotten out the boots she asked to try on."

Ian couldn't believe how much the world had changed. Never in his wildest dreams had he imagined a place where a person could come and buy clothing already made in every size conceivable.

It boggled his mind.

Another fifteen minutes passed before Danielle came out in her same dress and boots.

"Did you no' find anything?" Ian asked.

She laughed and set several items on the counter. "I did, but after our little adventure, I want a bath before I put anything new on."

Before he could utter another word Danielle went to where the clerk had set aside a couple of pairs of boots for her to try on.

Ian let out a sigh and braced a hand on the counter. His finger snagged something, and he looked down to see a white bra and some panties nearly hidden beneath the clothes.

An image of Danielle's pale skin and the dark red lace of her bra and panties in the firelight flashed in his mind. Instantly he hardened, need pounding inside him.

Danielle looked up then, their gazes locking. Ian wanted to go to her, to pull her into his arms and kiss her until nothing else existed but them.

She rose and walked to him, her eyes never leaving his. When she reached him, she put her hand over his on the counter.

"You two are so hot for each other," the clerk blurted.

Danielle smiled shyly and looked away. Ian turned his head to the girl to find her giggling at him. He paid her no more attention as she began to tally their items.

It wasn't until Danielle pulled something out of her purse that Ian leaned close to her ear and said, "I doona like you paying."

"Get used to it," she whispered back. "Until you have money, I'll be buying."

He frowned and looked down at her. "You're enjoying this, are you no'?"

"Actually, I am," she said, surprise on her face. "I need you to take me to the castle. You need me for this. It only seems fair we need each other."

But Ian needed her for so much more. The hunger, the yearning was unbearable, and he didn't know how much longer he could go without touching her.

*"Then touch her, brother,"* Duncan said. *"Take her. You've seen the desire in her eyes."*

Ian had seen the desire, but did he dare to touch her? Could he?

"Ready?" Danielle said as she reached for the packages.

Ian hurried to take them before Danielle did and headed to the door. He shouldered it open and waited for her to walk through.

She smiled up at him. They walked in silence back to the hotel. Once inside the room, Ian set their packages on the bed and watched as Danielle shed her high-heeled boots and coat. Her two silver bracelets came next.

Just when her fingers landed on the top button of her dress, her gaze lifted to his. "Would you rather take a shower first?"

Since Ian had no idea what a shower was, and he knew how much Danielle wanted one, he shook his head. "You go."

"Thank you." She grabbed some items out of the bag and disappeared into a small room.

The door shut and a moment later the sound of running water reached him. Ian paced the small chamber while Danielle took her shower.

Ian gathered she was bathing. He was curious to see how the water ran, but more than that, he was interested to see Danielle in the shower.

His already hard rod swelled even more.

Ian gritted his teeth and laid his head against the cool pane of glass on the window. It was going to take a great amount of effort to keep his hands off Danielle.

If he could.

He didn't want to. He desired her, all of her. He wanted to touch her, taste her, feel her. And the longer he was with her, the more he craved her.

Ian had no idea how much time passed before the door opened and Danielle stepped out of the room. Her hair was wet and she wore a sleeveless white cotton nightgown that reached her knees.

"The shower is all yours. Oh," she said and bit her lip. "I need to show you."

For the next five minutes Ian listened as she explained the shower, the sink, and the toilet. He was about to dismiss her when she held up what she called a razor. He'd always used his claws to shave, but the more he looked at the razor, the more intrigued he became.

Ian was in for another surprise when she showed him the soap and shampoo to wash his hair. He was stripping out of his clothes before she left the bathroom.

He heard her soft laugh as he turned on the water and

felt the warm spray hit his hand. Ian stepped into the shower and closed his eyes as the hot water rushed over him.

He washed his body four times and his hair six. Reluctantly, Ian shut off the water and stepped out of the shower to the feel of a soft towel.

It took him a few tries, but he got the hang of the razor and quickly shed his beard. A look in the mirror at his long hair had him considering trimming it.

Never again would he cut it to his scalp. He would leave it long in honor of Duncan.

Ian pulled his jeans back on and walked out of the bathroom. Danielle was looking at the key in her palm when she raised her eyes to him.

Her gaze widened and her lips fell open.

Ian couldn't remember a time when he'd been nervous around woman, but he was now. He cleared his throat and rubbed his face. "No' what you expected."

"No. Exactly what I expected and more," she said. "You're a very handsome man, Ian."

Ian tugged his shirt back on and buttoned it up. He sat down on the lone chair in the room and began to put on his boots.

"Going somewhere?" Danielle asked.

"I want to have a look around. I doona know this town." He finished and stood. "I willna be long. Doona leave this room."

"You think Deirdre could find me here?"

"Without a doubt."

Ian was loath to leave Danielle, but he had to make a few rounds of the village. He had to find the nearest exits, the places that would trap them, and more importantly the places where an attack might come.

His first step would be to have a look around the inn.

Imagine his surprise when he walked out of the inn

to find himself face-to-face with Charon, a Warrior who had been imprisoned with him in Deirdre's mountain.

"Well, well. What brings you to my village?" Charon asked slyly.

# CHAPTER
# THIRTEEN

Ian wanted to punch the smirk on Charon's face. After Charon had helped them kill Deirdre and escape Cairn Toul, Ian had thought he would return with them to Mac-Leod Castle.

Instead, Charon had disappeared. No one had heard from him again. Though Ian hadn't particularly liked the Warrior, Charon was a strong fighter, and the more of them against Deirdre the better.

"What, no response?" Charon said with a chuckle. Then his dark eyes narrowed. "You are no' Duncan."

Ian inwardly winced at the reminder that he and Duncan had looked exactly alike.

"Nay," Charon continued. "You are no' Duncan. But Ian always kept his hair shorn."

Ian clenched his fists, eager to get away from Charon and back to his task at hand and Danielle.

The smile gradually fell from Charon's lips. His gaze was sharp, knowing, as he said, "Ian."

Ian gave a nod of acknowledgment. "Charon."

"You look . . . different. You look . . ." His voice trailed off as realization dawned. "Duncan is gone, is he no'?"

"Aye."

"When?"

Ian shrugged. "I doona know."

"How could you no' know?"

"I was somehow transported from the seventeenth century to this one."

Charon's nostrils flared as he looked away. "I'm sorry. I know how close you were to Duncan. I saw the link myself when Deirdre was torturing you and Duncan experienced every pain you were put through. I take it Deirdre is to blame for Duncan's death?"

"She is."

"And bringing you to this time?"

Ian gave a single nod. "Before you ask, I doona know the reason. I've been hiding from her and everyone for countless weeks."

"You doona have full control of your god, do you?" Charon asked, his knowing eyes hard and demanding.

"I do no'." Ian swallowed and looked around him. "I take it this is your village?"

"In a way. The laird was old and dying when I came here four hundred years ago. I've made it my home, leaving when I needed to and reinventing myself."

"So you control everything?"

Charon grinned. "I grew up here, Ian. My father walked into that tavern every night for a drink. This village used to thrive, but so much had changed by the time I returned. I brought order back to them as well as ensuring that if the wyrran do attack, they willna do much damage."

Ian had never dreamed of returning to his clan, and the mere idea that Charon had not only done it but had made it his home once more left Ian in awe. "Are you sure all of this is wise?"

"With Deirdre? Most certainly. For centuries there

was no sign of her or the wyrran. Then, three months ago wyrran were spotted again."

"Aye, they've returned. And so has Deirdre. I believe she came forward in time with me."

"Interesting."

Ian kept his attention from the inn in the hopes Charon wouldn't know of Danielle. "Now, if you will excuse me I need to return to the inn."

"To the Druid, you mean," Charon said. He crossed his arms over his chest and lifted a brow when Ian glared. "My men alerted me of two visitors. It was no' until I was on my way here that I felt the Druid's magic."

"I'm helping her," Ian said. "She was being attacked by wyrran when I came upon her."

Charon frowned. "You're bringing her to MacLeod Castle?"

"It's where she belongs, as well as where she wants to go."

Charon motioned with his hand and six men walked past them to the inn. "My guards will watch over her while we talk. They know of the wyrran and Deirdre. If any wyrran are spotted they'll sound the alarm."

"Do they know what you are?" Ian asked in a low voice as he watched the men set up guard at the inn. "Do they know of the other Druids?"

"I've told them of the Druids, aye. As for what we are? Nay. They sense there is something different about me. They sensed the same about you. These men are intelligent, Ian."

Ian wiped a hand down his face. "You play a dangerous game."

"Nay," Charon ground out. "I'm merely balancing the odds. It's time the mortals knew what Deirdre is about, time they understood how perilously they hang in the scheme of things. They may no' have any magic, but the more that stands against Deirdre the better."

"If you felt that way, why didn't you come to Mac-Leod Castle?" Ian asked.

Charon turned his head away and shrugged. "I've always been a loner even before my god was unbound. Once Deirdre had me and blackmailed me to spy for her, it ruined any chance I had at finding a place with the MacLeods."

"You'd have had a place."

Charon's dark eyes swung to him. "I think you believe that, but I know the truth. I sense the battle within you, Ian. Your god is winning."

"He is. Slowly, but he is."

"Is that why you have no' gone to the MacLeods sooner?"

Ian let out a long breath. "I would no' be going now except for Danielle."

"And the Druid at the inn? Are you sure you willna be harming her?"

Ian looked at the inn and the window to Danielle's chamber. "When I'm with her, I'm able to gain more control over my god. It's something about her magic."

"You and your Druid will be safe here," Charon said after a moment. "My men and I will patrol the village and surrounding mountain. If there are wyrran or any Warriors who attack, I'll sound the alarm so you can get the Druid out."

Ian looked at Charon and saw the same loneliness within himself. "You are a good man."

Charon snorted. "No' hardly. Now, return to your Druid. Oh," Charon said before Ian could walk away. "Just so you know, Deirdre has begun to gather more Warriors."

The same rage Ian always felt when he thought of Deirdre began to surface, and with it, Farmire's voice demanding battle.

Ian struggled to gain control, but Farmire wouldn't be denied. Ian felt his claws extend from his fingers and his fangs fill his mouth.

"Ian," Charon ground out. "Control yourself."

Ian squeezed his eyes shut and desperately thought of anything that could hold back Farmire. Ian thought of Danielle and her easy smile, her emerald eyes, and her silvery blonde hair.

As if his thoughts had called her up, he felt her magic pulse and grow stronger as she neared. Ian's eyes snapped open when she came running out of the inn in nothing but her white nightgown to stand between him and Charon.

"Get away from him," Danielle ordered Charon. "I won't allow you to harm him."

Charon lifted a brow. "Harm him? He's a Warrior, Druid. There are only two ways he can die. Beheading and by *drough* blood. If I had wanted to harm him, I wouldna be standing here talking with him."

"Danielle," Ian said on a gasp as he laid his hands on her shoulders. Instantly Farmire's rage backed away so Ian could gain control once more. "Charon is a . . ."

"Friend?" she supplied.

"Acquaintance," Ian finished. "He was locked in Cairn Toul with me."

Danielle looked over her shoulder at Ian then at Charon. "So you're a Warrior?" she asked Charon.

Charon bowed his head. "I am."

"Do you fight Deirdre?"

"I do."

She frowned. "Then why aren't you at MacLeod Castle?"

Ian pulled her back so that she stood beside him, his

arm around her shoulder. "Charon has his own way of doing things. This is his town."

"And I have promised your safety while you are here. My men and I will keep guard so that no wyrran or Deirdre gets near either of you."

Danielle let her shoulders droop. "Thank you. But what of yourself? Will the wyrran not attack you?"

"They can certainly try," Charon said with a wicked gleam in his eyes. "I'd relish the battle."

Ian knew exactly how the Warrior felt. "How up to date are you on the MacLeods?"

"No' very," Charon said with a shrug. "There has no' been a need."

"Then let me tell you what I know. Fallon married a female Warrior."

Charon's eyes widened. "A female Warrior? Is that who I saw in the battle? Her color was iridescent?"

"That's her. She had a cousin helping her hide from Deirdre. Deirdre had Malcolm attacked, but Broc managed to save him before the Warriors could finish him. Malcolm was to be laird of his clan, but he was maimed and scarred."

Charon blew out a harsh breath. "There's more, is there no'?"

"Malcolm left MacLeod Castle. Deirdre caught him and unbound his god."

"He's a Warrior?" Charon asked in shock.

"Apparently Larena and the MacLeods knew he could be carrying a god inside him. Now, he is Deirdre's. He leads her Warriors. And he is the one who killed Duncan."

Charon dropped his arms to his side as a muscle in his jaw ticked. "I've felt other magic besides Deirdre's, Ian. Strong *drough* magic. I doona know who it belongs to, but I suspect we'll find out soon enough."

"Because of us." Charon might not have aligned with the MacLeods, but he hadn't returned to Deirdre. That in itself told Ian all he needed to know about Charon's intentions. "There are artifacts, Charon. Artifacts that the MacLeods are gathering to find a powerful tool that can end Deirdre once and for all."

Charon's dark eyes searched Ian's. "Are the MacLeods finding the artifacts?"

"They are. Duncan and Logan were in search of one when Duncan was killed. I was pulled here right after my brother was murdered so I doona know if they've found more."

"You should return to the MacLeods," Charon said. "They've need of you."

Ian looked at his hands and the claws that had begun to lengthen as he thought of Deirdre. Danielle placed her hand on his, and he instantly calmed. "Until I have control of my god, I'm a liability."

"So you'll deliver the Druid to them and leave?"

"No," Danielle said before he could respond. "He's going to learn to control his god, because as you said, Charon, the MacLeods will have need of him."

Charon smiled and shook his head. "I like her, Ian."

Ian narrowed his eyes at him.

Charon clapped him on the shoulder. "If you find you can no' stay at the MacLeods', return here. There's no reason for you to battle your god alone, Ian. I could use another Warrior at my side, and I'll do all I can to help you fight your god."

"And if my god wins?" Ian demanded.

Charon glanced away before he said, "Then I'll be the one to take your life."

It was all Ian could ask for. And when Charon held out his arm, Ian didn't hesitate to clasp his forearm. "I wish you would reconsider joining the MacLeods. They need Warriors like you."

"Keep Danielle safe," Charon said, instead of responding to Ian's comment.

Ian released his arm and turned to walk to the inn with Danielle on his left. Charon fell into step beside him on his right.

"We'll be departing at dawn," Ian said. "Danielle's need to get to MacLeod Castle is great."

Charon looked to Danielle. "What is your magic?"

Danielle glanced at Ian before she looked at Charon. "Ian may trust you, but I don't know you. Just know that getting to the castle is very important."

"Fair enough," Charon said as they reached the door to the inn. "Until next time."

"Until next time," Ian repeated and watched Charon walk away.

"You like him," Danielle said.

Ian frowned. "He could be a friend, but he chooses to keep himself apart. While we were in the Pit, a last resort Deirdre used to turn the Warriors to her side, we suspected Charon was a spy for Deirdre. It was Marcail, Quinn's wife, who had gotten him to admit the truth."

But none of them had been prepared to learn that Deirdre was using something against him. Hatred burned bright in Charon's eyes each time he spoke of Deirdre.

Whatever Deirdre had used to get him to spy must have been great. Ian had no doubt Charon would help the MacLeods when the time came to battle Deirdre.

It was enough that the Warrior would battle against Deirdre. If he was setting up men in the village to learn about the wyrran in order to combat them, then whatever hold Deirdre had on Charon was long gone.

A wave of magic engulfed Ian. He inhaled deeply at the calming, peaceful, seductive feel of Danielle's magic.

And Ian enjoyed it. Entirely too much.

He looked down at Danielle as they entered the inn and made their way to their chamber. Once inside the room, he bolted the door and let out a sigh.

Ian leaned his head against the door and simply listened to her and let her magic envelop him. With every breath he could feel Farmire begin to calm and the need for battle and blood ease from within him.

He placed his palms flat on the door as he remembered holding Danielle's naked body next to his as he warmed her. He recalled the way she fit against him. He remembered the touch of her skin and the way his body had responded to her.

Even now he hungered to touch her. Craved to feel her against him. Yearned to taste her lips.

And he would do it all in a heartbeat if he had control of his god.

Ian closed his eyes and sighed. He'd never wanted something as desperately as he did Danielle.

# CHAPTER
# FOURTEEN

Camdyn leaned against a wall in the great hall, his arms crossed over his chest as he watched Charlie talking to the Druids. It was Reaghan Camdyn watched the closest however.

One thing her magic could do was detect when someone was lying. There had been a few times the Druid had frowned at something Charlie said. But in order for Reaghan to fully use her magic, she had to see into a person's eyes.

Charlie managed to look anywhere but directly into Reaghan's eyes. It was as if he knew what Reaghan's magic was.

"Still think there's something wrong with him?" Hayden asked as he came to stand next to Camdyn.

"I have no explanation for it, I know. But I have a bad feeling about him."

"Now, if you were a Druid and told me that, I'd believe you," Hayden said with a chuckle. "But we doona have those kinds of powers. Or do you?"

Camdyn rolled his eyes and looked at Hayden. The

big blond Warrior leaned one hand against the wall and watched Camdyn with laughing black eyes.

"Nay, my god doesna give me that kind of power. Just the ability to move the earth if I see fit."

Hayden threw back his head and laughed. "And everyone thought you didna have a sense a humor, with you always frowning."

"I doona always frown." Camdyn was taken aback by Hayden's words.

Hayden raised a blond brow. "Aye, my friend, you do. I was once like you." Hayden then turned his gaze to his black-haired, blue-eyed wife. "Until I found something that made me smile."

"You are a lucky man to have Isla."

"Aye. Verra. I nearly lost her because I was so stubborn. All I'm saying, Camdyn, is that sometimes there is nothing to be suspicious of. We've been waiting for months for Deirdre to make a move, and she hasna. It's left us all on edge."

Camdyn flattened his lips as he realized the truth in Hayden's words.

"And we have another Warrior for our fight. You should be rejoicing. If nothing else, you should get to know Charlie," Hayden said, and clapped Camdyn on the shoulder before he walked away.

Camdyn rubbed the back of his neck and pushed off from the wall. Hayden was right. He did need to get to know Charlie. Because if there was something to find out that Charlie wanted kept hidden or something that could harm those at the castle, Camdyn was going to discover it.

He had barely taken two steps toward Charlie when he stopped in his tracks and looked to the stairs. Magic, gentle yet powerful, soft yet strong, mysterious yet unguarded, washed over him.

Saffron.

In less than a heartbeat, she appeared at the top of the stairs. If he hadn't known for himself that she was blind, he would never have been able to guess it by looking at her.

She was slowly descending the stairs with one hand always on the stone wall next to her. Her walnut-colored hair was pulled away from her face at her temples, but hung straight and glossy to her shoulderblades.

Camdyn had been the one to carry her out of Declan's dungeon. He'd also been the one to hear her screams in the middle of the night.

Try as he might, he'd been unable to stay unaffected by her. He'd gone into her chamber the night before when her screams from her nightmares grew too much for him to listen to. Her body had been drenched in sweat as she shivered from the hold the nightmare had on her.

Upon Camdyn touching her shoulder, she had begun to calm. Only when she slept soundly once more did he leave her room.

Thankfully, no one had spotted him in her chamber. He knew how Cara and the others liked to play matchmaker, and Camdyn wanted no part of their schemes.

Besides, he would make a poor husband. He had demons of his own that invaded far more of his life than just in nightmares.

Danielle's stomach fluttered when she saw the hungry look on Ian's face that had nothing to do with food. When his lids opened and his sherry eyes focused on her, Danielle's breath left her in a whoosh.

She'd never seen such desire, such *yearning* before. It made her feel alive. Aware. Vibrant.

As if she had been waiting her entire life for Ian so

she could be who she was meant to be. It didn't make sense, but then it didn't need to. Not to her.

What she felt when she was around Ian was what she had been looking for. She'd thought it was something she'd only find in her dreams.

Instead, he stood before her like a mythical warrior, brave and strong and full of longing so deep she felt it to her very soul.

"You shouldna have left the inn," Ian said.

Danielle shrugged and took a step toward him. "I saw you struggling with your god, and I didn't know who Charon was."

"So you would have protected me?"

"Yes."

"Even though I have evil inside me? Even though my god could overtake me?"

"Even then."

Ian looked away and swallowed. "Why?"

The fact he couldn't look her in the eye and ask that question nearly broke Danielle's heart. She closed the distance between them and laid her hand upon his heart. "Because of this."

His gaze swung back to her. "What?"

"Because of your heart, Ian. You may have evil inside you, but you aren't evil. Despite battling your god, you have promised to take me to MacLeod Castle. You've put my needs and everyone else's above your own."

"I'm doing what I think is right."

She smiled. "Exactly."

"Charon could have killed you," Ian said, his brow puckered in a frown.

"He could have tried. You wouldn't have let him."

Heat spread over Danielle's body when Ian's hands rose to lightly grasp her arms. She had never been tempted so by a man before. Oh, she'd given in to desire before, but no man had ever made her . . . burn . . . as Ian did.

And did she ever burn.

Ian's gaze held hers, smoldering with a dark intensity that took her breath away. Time stood still, their hearts beating as one. Danielle's breath quickened when his head tilted toward her, slowly, gradually.

Her lips parted and her heart leaped when his gaze dropped to her mouth. Of their own accord, her eyes slid shut as she waited to feel his mouth on hers.

His cheek brushed hers, smooth from the recent shave. She lifted her face, anxious to taste him, to know the Ian she sensed was locked away.

And then his lips found hers.

Danielle leaned into him as his hands slid around her back and his arms held her in a tight embrace while his lips brushed hers once, twice.

She held her breath waiting for more. And he didn't disappoint.

Ian tilted his head and took her mouth in a kiss meant to savor, to explore. A kiss that began soft and eager turned hungry and demanding. Ravenous.

A shudder of pleasure deep and true raced through her to settle between her legs. No one had ever kissed her so thoroughly or with such yearning.

He deepened the kiss while their tongues continued to duel. Urging her desire onward, compelling her body to open for him. Danielle had no thoughts of turning him away. She wanted all of Ian.

A gasp tore from her lips as Ian spun them so that Danielle was against the door, the hard sinew of his body pressed against her front.

Her breasts swelled, her nipples tightened when his hand moved to her side and his finger grazed the bottom of her breast. Danielle had held on to the front of his shirt, but now her hands drifted upward and around his neck.

He moaned when her fingernails gently scraped his scalp. Danielle was consumed by his frantic kisses full of sensuality and need that matched her own.

When his hand shifted to cup her breast through the thin cotton of her gown, Danielle moaned into Ian's mouth. But that moan became a gasp when his thumb brushed over her nipple.

"By all that's holy I want more of you," Ian said as he kissed down her jaw to her neck.

Danielle leaned her head back, her eyes closed, while his mouth and tongue left a trail of heat to her collarbone. She clutched his shoulder tighter when he turned her away from the door and bent her back over his arm.

She opened her eyes to find him watching her, his mouth hovering over her breast. "Yes," she said, her voice breathy and low. "Please."

A slow, masculine smile graced his mouth a heartbeat before his lips clamped over her nipple.

Danielle cried out from the exquisite pleasure. His tongue dampened the cotton, but not even the thin material could take away from the delight he was giving her.

Her hips rubbed against his as the desire pooled low in her belly and steadily grew to a blaze that consumed her. Devoured her.

Engulfed her.

Ian knew he should release Danielle, but he couldn't. After one taste of her he'd been powerless to walk away. He had to have her now. She was in his blood, in his soul.

Her hands jerked at the buttons on his shirt as she struggled to get it off him. Ian smiled at how her hands shook, because his did as well.

And then her soft hands touched his bare chest.

Ian moaned and suckled her turgid nipple even harder. Her breaths were coming quicker, her cries of pleasure louder.

Ian raised his head for another kiss as he lifted her in his arms. He groaned in torment when her legs wrapped around him so that the heat of her pressed against his aching arousal.

He walked to the bed, amazed to find such a beautiful, special woman in his arms. A woman who had opened up a new world for him. A woman who had brought him out of his seclusion and his cave to a new time.

Ian stopped when his knees hit the bed. Danielle dropped her legs from around his waist so that she was kneeling on the mattress.

She pulled back from the kiss and let her hands caress his wide chest exposed by the open shirt. Need and lust pounded through Ian in such a rush he could barely stand.

But the desire darkening her emerald eyes caused his heart to pound faster.

He didn't know how he kept his hands from her when she pushed his shirt off his shoulders and to the floor. Ian closed his eyes and bit back a groan when Danielle's fingers grasped the waist of his jeans and unbuttoned them.

Ian grabbed his pants to pull them down himself, but she stopped him. His eyes flew open to find her smiling seductively.

"Let me," was all she said before she placed a kiss over his heart and climbed off the bed.

She turned him and gave him a slight push until he sank down on the mattress. Then she proceeded to remove his boots. When the second one hit the floor, she took his hands and pulled him back to his feet.

Danielle would never grow tired of watching him. Ian was perfection in every sense of the word. Every muscle in his body was honed, sculpted. He was a work of art, something men spent hours a day in gyms trying to achieve came naturally to Ian.

She leaned up on her tiptoes and placed her lips on his while her hands grasped the waist of his jeans. The kiss was quick, and when she moved away, she pulled his pants down with her.

He jerked off the jeans before she could, and Danielle smiled as she ran her hands up his muscular legs. His chest narrowed to a V with a tight waist and a bum she had discovered for herself looked perfect in a pair of jeans.

The sinew of his arms matched the rest of him, toned and powerful. He took a deep breath and watched her, his sherry eyes darkened by desire. His large hands gently caressed down her back, a small smile playing upon his wide lips.

Ian could only watch her in amazement. A woman had never tended to him with such care or attention before. Every stroke of her flesh against his only made him crave her more, his hunger deepening until he ached with a need so great he shook with it.

Ian could stand it no more. He took Danielle into his arms for another hard, demanding kiss. She opened for him, welcomed him. When he asked for more, she gave it willingly, as if she were as ready as he. As if her need were as great as his.

Ian grasped the hem of her gown and began to gather the material in his hands. He broke the kiss long enough to pull the nightgown over her head and toss it on the floor along with his own clothes.

He'd seen her with naught but her bra and panties before, but now she stood before him bare and beautiful. For a moment, he couldn't find words to express what he thought of the stunning woman before him.

"My God, you are the loveliest thing I've ever seen."

Danielle's shy smile told him he'd said the right thing. He pushed her against the bed until she fell back with a startled laugh, her knees dangling from the side.

He had her just where he wanted her. Ian gazed down at her with her silver hair spread around her and her body flushed with desire.

His hands caressed up her legs to her hips and then to her breasts. He fondled her nipples, pinching and rolling the turgid peaks until her hips were rising from the bed seeking him.

"Ian, please," Danielle begged.

It had been a long time since he'd had a woman, and though need burned bright within him, he had no wish to hurry. He wanted to savor every moment, to prolong the ecstasy he knew would take them both.

But more than that, he wanted to burn Danielle's image into his mind. Her every smile, every look, every sound.

Ian knelt down on the floor between her legs. With a soft nudge, he pulled her thighs wider so he could see her sex. Danielle's legs fell open to expose the silvery curls, and Ian's cock twitched when he saw how wet she was for him.

He groaned, needing to taste her essence, to hear her scream in pleasure. Ian gripped her hips and pressed his mouth to her softness.

Danielle's hands fisted in the bedspread when she felt Ian's tongue on her sex. She had barely pulled a ragged breath into her lungs before that wicked tongue of his began to tease her clitoris.

He was merciless, ruthless, as he licked and sucked and excited her. The need humming through Danielle coalesced in a raging inferno that burned bright and fiery. Her nerves were stretched taut, her body shuddering from the sweet torment.

The pleasure was intense. Ian swept her away on a tide of unending pleasure. The bliss was almost too much to take, but it never entered her mind to turn away.

This, this wondrous, incredible desire was what she had always hoped to experience. What she had always thought she never would.

Ian lifted her hips and moved his tongue back and forth over her clitoris. Danielle whimpered as the desire intensified within her, drawing tighter and tighter until she thought she would burst from it.

With one flick of Ian's tongue, he sent her over the edge.

Danielle screamed as the pleasure rocked her, shook her . . . consumed her. She rode the waves of ecstasy as they pulled her deeper into the flames of desire.

Dimly, she was aware of Ian's weight shifting the bed. Danielle opened her eyes to see Ian's hard body braced over her. His sherry eyes burned bright with need, and his arousal stood thick and heavy between them.

She reached for him, a contented smile on her face she knew she had never experienced before. Ian brushed his lips over hers and settled between her legs. She inhaled deeply as the wonderful weight of him sank atop her. He hooked an arm beneath one of her knees before he leaned down.

A groan tore from her lips when his chest rubbed against her aching nipples. Then the broad head of his cock pushed against her softness.

She was eager to feel him inside her, impatient for him to fill her. She shifted her hips forward, urging him to push inside her.

But he held back. She opened her eyes and watched as he bent and wrapped his lips around her nipple once again, this time without her gown. His tongue swirled around the peak before he suckled it deep.

Her back arched off the bed, a cry locked in her throat. His tongue teased and tormented, suckled and licked. Each flick of his hot tongue felt as if it were on her sex, pushing her higher, urging her to give him more.

She lifted her hips, seeking him, any part of him that she could rub against. When she came in contact with his rod, she ground her hips against him, his name a whisper as she groaned with need.

Danielle rubbed against him again, her nails digging into his side as she urged him to her.

With a soft curse, Ian lifted his head and held her gaze. The desire she saw in his eyes, the yearning that she saw there, made Danielle's breath lock in her chest. "Ian," she whispered.

He positioned himself at her entrance, and slowly entered her. Danielle bit her lip as he stretched her while pushing farther and farther inside her. And it felt glorious.

He filled her, and then he pulled out until only the tip of him remained.

Only to thrust hard and fast.

Danielle sank her nails into his back and cried out at the magnificent feel of him inside her and his weight atop her.

The way he held her leg up helped him go deeper, harder, as he plunged inside her again and again. Danielle was powerless to do anything but hang on as Ian took control of her body, seized her need and took them both higher.

She closed her eyes and felt the desire building toward another climax. Her body was attuned to his every breath, every beat of his heart. As she clung to him, she offered him everything she had, everything she was.

And everything she wanted.

She met him thrust for thrust, their bodies sliding

against each other from the sheen of sweat covering them. Once more she found her body tightening, her nerves taut. He drove into her hard, rocking her.

The climax took her, pulled her. It was more powerful than before. And it swept her away into an abyss of pleasure so profound, so earth-shattering Danielle knew she would never be the same.

Ian continued to rock against her, prolonging her pleasure, even as his body strained over her as he fought against his own orgasm.

Danielle lifted her other leg and wrapped it around his waist. He looked at her, and their eyes held. Her body clenched around his thick arousal, urging him toward his own release.

He drove into her hard and quick, and with one last thrust, his body stiffened above her. He threw back his head, his neck muscles straining against his skin.

Danielle held him as he poured his seed inside her, his body convulsing atop her. Pleasure wrapped tightly around them, cocooning them in a haven of rapture and satisfaction.

# CHAPTER
# FIFTEEN

Ian held Danielle in his arms in the aftermath of their lovemaking. Their breathing had calmed, but he knew he'd never be the same again.

Being with Danielle had changed him. He'd felt it, though he couldn't pinpoint how or why. Only that he wasn't the same man as before.

She lay with her head pillowed on his shoulder and her arm thrown over his chest. Their legs were tangled together, as if neither of them wanted to stop touching the other.

"When do we leave?" she asked, her finger making designs on his stomach.

"At first light."

She lifted her head and sighed. "That's just six hours from now."

"Ah, the clock," he said after a moment. "It will take me some time to get used to things in this time."

"You're learning fast, which will help. Are you anxious to see your friends again?"

"Aye. And then nay."

Her fingers lightly stroked his chest. "I'd feel the

same, I think. You called them your family. They'll welcome you."

"Will they? They didna look for me." He hadn't realized how much that bothered him until he'd said it.

"Scotland isn't a small place, Ian."

"Broc's power is to find anyone anywhere. Why did they no' look for me?"

"Maybe they couldn't. God forbid, but maybe something happened to Broc."

Ian shook his head. "We will find out soon enough."

"Do you think you'll be able to convince Charon to come with us?"

"Nay," Ian said with a frown. He grasped a strand of hair that fell over her face and tucked it behind her ear. "I'm glad he's here though, which is odd to say. I never trusted Charon while we were in the Pit."

"People change. He's had four centuries."

"I suppose."

She looked away, causing him to frown. "What is it? Are you worried about meeting the MacLeods?"

"A castle full of Warriors and Druids? Why would I be nervous?"

Ian laughed at her sarcasm and kissed her. "It will be a few days yet before you'll have to meet them."

"A few days?" she said with a brow raised. "I'm not walking to the castle. I talked to the owner of the inn and rented us a car."

It was Ian's turn to raise a brow. She actually wanted him to ride in one of those . . . cars. It would get them there faster and keep her warm. It would also make it more difficult for the wyrran to track them if the car went as fast as Danielle said it would.

"All right. We'll take this vehicle you told me about. But tell me, Danielle, is there anything else bothering you?"

She sighed and shrugged. "I forgot to tell you to put on a condom."

"A what?" he asked softly. Obviously it was important to her, but he had no idea what she was talking about.

"It's protection from disease and getting me pregnant."

Ah. Now he understood. "I can tell you I have no diseases, or any that I could pass on to you. My god controls that. As for getting you with child, I didna think of that either."

"I've never been so into the moment that I forgot something so vital."

"I know the Druids at MacLeod Castle used to make a potion every month that would prevent them from getting with child. Once we're there, ask them to show you how it's done."

Neither spoke about the chance of his seed already taking root. The idea thrilled him, but Ian knew he was in no condition to be a father, much less anything else, with his god vying for control.

"There's a store I want to stop at before we leave to buy us mobile phones in case we get separated," Danielle said into the silence.

Mobile phones, cars, hotels, jeans. The world he had known and loved had changed drastically. Some things he liked, others not so much. But he was in this time whether he wanted to be or not.

At least he had Danielle.

"You don't agree with Charon having returned to this village, do you?"

Ian stared at the ceiling and considered her words. "I envy him that he was able to return. But I doona think it wise."

"Did you ever go back to your clan?"

"Nay. Neither Duncan nor I thought it a prudent choice. We wanted to. Never doubt that."

Danielle was silent a moment before she asked, "Does anyone know that Charon is a Warrior?"

"No' yet." Ian blew out a breath and held Danielle closer. He liked her against him, enjoyed the feel of her bare skin against his. "It's just a matter of time, however. His men, I watched them. They are loyal, so they may stand by him once they discover what he is."

"But you don't think they will."

"Some will be too frightened. They'll forget they've known him for years and only see the monster we become."

"Monster?" Danielle said as she sat up and turned so that she faced him. "You think yourself a monster?"

"Aye. I do. You saw me, Danielle. Do you deny it?"

She looked down at his chest where her hand lay. "I only saw you for a moment. I want a closer look."

Ian frowned as he realized she was asking him to transform for her. "You can no' mean that."

"I do."

"Danielle, nay."

"You won't hurt me. I want to see you in your Warrior form."

He knew it was a bad idea, but the way her emerald eyes pleaded with him made him waver.

"Please, Ian. Let me see you."

Ian slowly sat up until his back was against the headboard. "I willna be angry if you run away."

"I won't run."

And somehow he knew she wouldn't. Her bravery was astounding.

Ian prayed he would be able to tamp his god back down when it was time. If not, things could get bad. He took a deep breath and released Farmire.

Danielle sucked in her breath as she watched Ian's sun-bronzed skin disappear to be replaced with cool, pale blue. Long claws, a darker blue, extended from his fingers.

She ran her finger over the back of his hand and down a finger to his claw.

"Careful," Ian said, and pulled back his hand before she could touch the talon.

Danielle then looked into his face. She leaned forward and tucked her legs beneath her. "I didn't realize your eyes changed as well."

"What do they look like to you?"

"They are endless. Like pools of the lightest blue. I could almost drown in them."

"You are no' . . . revolted?"

She blinked away tears when she heard the wariness in his voice. "No. Not at all, Ian. It's different to no longer see an iris surrounded by white. Instead, the blue colors your entire eyeball. Can you see differently like this?"

"Nay," he said with a small shake of his head. "My eyesight increased when Farmire was unbound."

"Amazing."

And she was amazed. Truly. Genuinely.

"I remember seeing fangs," she said. "Did I dream that?"

Ian shook his head and then peeled back his lips so she could see the ferocious teeth.

"You would make an excellent vampire."

"Vampire?" Ian repeated with a small frown. "What is that?"

"A monster that drinks a human's blood in order to survive. He uses his fangs to puncture the skin to drink."

Ian's face scrunched up in revulsion. "That is most certainly a monster. Is he real?"

"Some say they are. Others believe they're nothing but make-believe. Yet, they say vampires are immortal. So who knows?"

"I've never encountered one," Ian said.

Danielle rested her hand on his cheek and smiled. "Thank you for showing me."

He covered her hand with his as his Warrior form faded. "You need to sleep. Dawn will come early."

Danielle didn't hesitate to move against him when he lifted the covers for her. Her head rested on Ian's strong shoulder while his arm held her close. She would sleep deeply knowing someone like Ian was with her keeping her safe.

Cairn Toul Mountain

Deirdre ran her fingers over the beloved stones of her mountain. They soothed her as nothing else could. They also fed her black magic in ways she had never understood. But she was a part of them just as they were a part of her. Bound. United.

For all eternity.

She turned her attention away from the stones and looked at her slave, Toby. He was a hulky man with obscene bulging muscles and a very tiny brain. She had hoped he had a god inside him, but to her disappointment he'd been without.

Instead of killing him, she used her magic to invade his mind. Now he was hers to command just as her wyrran were. And just like the wyrran, Toby would never think of betraying her.

Toby stood next to her overlooking the huge cavern that used to house dozens of Warriors.

"What do you see?" she asked her slave.

"I see an empty mountain," he answered, his voice flat, dead. "Except for wyrran."

She cocked an eyebrow and grinned. "Only for a short time. I'm not going to concern myself with gathering Warriors this time. Nay, this time my attack will be different."

"As you say, mistress."

Deirdre rolled her eyes at Toby's meekness. It was what she demanded of him, but she found herself missing Malcolm's unwavering stare and hard-edged words.

But she had sent him on a mission, a mission that would ensure he was hers. She sensed the war inside Malcolm, though he hid it well.

If it weren't for his cousin, Larena, who was married to one of the MacLeods, Deirdre wouldn't think twice about Malcolm being loyal to her.

Being betrayed by Broc had changed everything.

No longer did she take a Warrior's word that he was hers to command. Now, they would not only have to prove it, but seal their fates as well.

Charlie, her newest Warrior, was at MacLeod Castle already. She hadn't released his god as much as she had with the other Warriors, which allowed him to think he had more control than he did. But that was because she needed him sooner than she could allow him the time to achieve that control.

He would gain the trust of those at the castle, then destroy them. While Malcolm was on his way to kill a school full of children and find the Druid hiding there.

People needed to fear her again. Time had erased the power she'd had over everyone. The evil that had once been felt was gone. Now was her time. And she wouldn't fail.

At one time Deirdre had wanted to kill the MacLeods

herself. She had yearned to be the one to end their miserable, interfering lives once and for all.

But Declan Wallace had changed all that when he pulled her forward in time. Declan wanted to join forces with her so they could rule together.

But Deirdre didn't rule with anyone.

Declan had not only pulled her from her time, he had held her prisoner in his mansion for months before Malcolm and her wyrran had freed her.

It was no longer just the MacLeods whom she turned her anger against. Declan now had that honor, and with it would come the attack that would end his life no matter how much black magic he had. Or who favored him.

Deirdre hated that she no longer had the sword she had taken from the ancient Celtic burial mound. The MacLeods had found it during the centuries she was gone. They had the artifacts that could awaken Laria, her twin, to kill her.

But Deirdre wouldn't sit back and do nothing. Even if Charlie failed to kill the MacLeods, Deirdre wouldn't allow them to awaken Laria.

She would discover where Laria was hidden, and she would be there to stop the MacLeods. Deirdre had an advantage too, because none of the Warriors would want to battle with Malcolm. They considered him their friend, and to Larena, he was family.

Unlike the others who had served her before Malcolm, he didn't show the fear or desire to bed her as she was used to. Nay, Malcolm showed nothing.

But she could call forth the rage she knew was inside him if she wanted to. The occasion had arisen before. She could turn him into the monster she would need.

Until then she allowed him to function as he was. His

lack of emotion meant he wasn't plotting to kill her, or trying to get back to someone he cared about.

Part of that was due to the fact Deirdre had promised Larena, Malcolm's cousin and the only female Warrior, would live as long as Malcolm served her. So far, Malcolm had kept his end of the bargain.

In all her thousand years of ruling, she had never had a Warrior as dedicated and intelligent as Malcolm. He was the perfect Warrior.

*Her* perfect Warrior.

She'd had her reservations about unbinding his god because of his hatred for her. Deirdre thought it would take months or years even to break him.

But Malcolm had done it all on his own.

She drew in a deep breath and once more looked at the cavern that served as her great hall. Her mountain was quiet now, except for a lone cry from a Druid Charlie had found before he left for the MacLeods.

Soon, however, Cairn Toul would teem with Warriors and wyrran again. Screams would rise up from the dungeons. Blood would flow from the Druids she killed for their magic.

And the MacLeods would be no more.

Deirdre smiled. Everyone who helped the MacLeods would die horrible, painful deaths. At her hands.

Already her plan was in motion. She'd been impatient and greedy before. She'd learned her lesson though. Now, she would wait until her plan came to fruition.

Because when it did, she would have all she wanted.

"And then I will rule this land."

She fell to her knees and closed her eyes as her magic swelled within her. She needed to know if Ian had gained control over his god, because if he hadn't, he was going to be hers.

Flames leaped from the stones before her, burning orange and pale yellow. She began to chant the spell that would find Ian so she could bring him back to her mountain where he belonged.

It didn't take long for the answer to her spell to show itself in the flames. Deirdre smiled as she gained her feet and looked down at the wyrran waiting to do her bidding.

"I want you to bring me Ian Kerr!"

# CHAPTER
# SIXTEEN

Ian didn't allow himself to sleep. He didn't trust Charon completely to protect Danielle's life. Ian dozed in the hour after Danielle had finally fallen asleep.

As much as he longed to stay next to her, he rose from the bed without disturbing her. She sighed and rolled onto her other side before snuggling beneath the heavy blankets.

Ian pulled the covers up around her shoulders and stared down at her. He still couldn't believe she had wanted to see his Warrior form.

She hadn't run from him, nor had there been any fear in her eyes. Surprise, yes, but no fear. She'd touched him, the wonder in her gaze had made him take another look at himself.

He'd always considered himself a monster. Yet Danielle saw something else entirely.

Even if she wasn't afraid of Farmire, Ian knew the damage his god could cause. Farmire's thirst for battle, his need for death and blood, was immense. And he would only be denied for so long. Losing control to his god just once could kill her.

"Duncan?" Ian whispered.

He hadn't heard his brother's voice in hours. He'd been concerned the first time he'd heard it, but now that Duncan wasn't there, Ian didn't know what to do.

*"Aye, brother. I'm here."*

"Where have you been?"

*"You've no' needed me."*

But Ian knew that wasn't true. He did need Duncan. He'd never lived apart from his twin until Malcolm had killed Duncan.

*"Follow your heart, brother."*

Ian lifted a lock of Danielle's silvery blonde hair in his fingers. It was cool to the touch and as smooth as silk. He knew the rest of her felt just as good, better even.

His cock throbbed as he recalled how tight and wet she had been when he slid inside her. She'd been wanton and eager while they'd made love.

Ian dropped the strand of hair and sighed. Whether he'd wanted it or not, he was now tangled securely in Danielle's life. And he found he didn't mind it.

He'd probably be overjoyed if he wasn't battling his god or running from wyrran.

Just the thought of the ugly creatures had Ian walking to the window. With his superior eyesight he saw three of Charon's men in the dark.

Farmire had begun to push against his mind, steadily and solidly. That normally happened right before a battle. All seemed quiet and normal in the night, yet Ian had a sense something was off.

Ian's blood went cold. A battle was coming.

Farmire bellowed inside his head, as if in agreement.

Ian spun on his heel and looked at the bed where Danielle lay asleep. The wyrran wouldn't get her. He'd make sure of that.

He stalked to the door and soundlessly opened it. He hurried to the front of the hotel and grabbed one of Charon's men by his shirt.

"Stand guard outside Danielle's door. Doona let anyone but me enter."

The man narrowed his eyes, but nodded. "Are we expectin' someone?"

"Aye." Ian turned to the second man. "Alert the others. There's something coming."

Ian kept his back to the inn and faced the bare expanse of valley before him. There was no movement, but he knew something was out there.

"What is it?" Charon asked as he strode up.

Ian shrugged. "A feeling."

"I've learned to trust my feelings. Do you want to try to get the Druid out before whatever is coming gets here?"

Ian was surprised Charon would offer, and even though Ian had considered it, he shook his head. "This town and its people will fare better with two Warriors."

Charon smiled, his dark eyes filled with excitement. "I was hoping you'd say that. And Danielle?"

"I will no' allow anything to happen to her."

Danielle wasn't sure what woke her. She sat up in bed, alert and on edge. A glance to Ian's side of the bed showed she was alone.

She touched the bed and found his spot cool. He'd been gone for some time, but where? Ian wouldn't leave her, of that she was sure. He could be with Charon.

Danielle threw back the covers and swung her legs over the bed. She winced when her bare feet touched the icy, wooden floor. Ignoring the biting cold and creaking floors, Danielle wrapped a blanket around her and hurried to the window to look out.

For the briefest of moments, fear spiked within her. Then she remembered Ian's words, the solemn vow she had seen in his beautiful eyes that he wouldn't leave her.

She spotted Ian as well as Charon as they directed men about the town. The men moved in the shadows, their legs bent and bodies hunched.

Something was going on.

Danielle desperately wanted to run to Ian, but maybe she'd be safer in the hotel. It could be Deirdre out there for all she knew.

Then she remembered she was a Druid. She had magic she could use. She could aid Ian, even from a distance.

As if sensing her gaze, Ian turned and looked up at her. For several moments they stared at each other before Charon said something in Ian's ear.

Ian glanced away a moment before he started toward the inn. Danielle tossed aside the blanket and reached for her new clothes. She had her new bra, panties, and socks on in less then a heartbeat.

She ripped the tags off her jeans and jerked her legs into them in a matter of seconds. She had just buttoned them when the door to her room opened and Ian entered.

Danielle pulled on the tight-fitting long-sleeved shirt before she tugged the thick sweater over her head.

"Who is out there?" she asked when he didn't say anything.

Ian quietly shut the door and leaned his back against it as he watched her. Danielle finished putting on her hiking boots and grabbed a ponytail holder.

"Tell me," she urged as she gathered her hair at the back of her head and quickly worked the ponytail holder in place.

When she was finished she slapped her hands on her legs and lifted a brow at Ian.

"I sense something is coming. I doona know what," he finally answered.

"I assumed that much when I saw you and Charon directing the men. I want to help. I can help with my magic."

Ian dropped his chin to his chest and blew out a harsh breath. "Danielle, I've seen the wyrran destroy villages in a matter of moments. They leave no one alive and burn everything."

"Just another reason to have me aid you."

He lifted his gaze to her as one side of his mouth lifted in a half smile. "Charon said you'd say that."

"Then he's a smart man. An even shrewder man would allow me to help."

Danielle looked at the man standing before her. Ian had changed. Before her stood not just the protector, but the warrior. His masculinity. The unadulterated virility that promised pleasure, satisfaction.

And sin.

She knew the strength of his hands and arms. She knew the gentleness he could exhibit. But she had also seen him fight the wyrran. It had been brutal, and that's exactly the type of man she wanted protecting her.

"Are you going to let me help?" she asked.

Ian pushed off the door and stalked toward her with long strides. He stopped before her and wrapped his large hands around her arms. "Is there nothing I can say that will keep you in this chamber?"

"Nothing."

"As I feared." Ian dropped his arms from her and ran a hand through his light brown locks. "Have you ever battled someone with your magic before?"

"Just the wyrran that attacked."

"So you doona know how long your magic will last."

Danielle lifted her chin. "My magic will last as long as you need me."

"I know you think so, but you've no' been in battle, Danielle. You doona know how hard your heart will beat or how fast the blood will pump through your body. Fear will take hold, and your magic may no' come."

She took one of his hands in both of hers. "If my magic came to me when I was chased by creatures I didn't know with my blood pumping and my heart pounding, and fear swallowing me, I know I can do this."

"I just want one promise from you."

"All right. What is it?"

"If your magic falters, hide. Doona wait for me. Return here and do whatever you can to keep the wyrran out until I can get to you."

Danielle could see her vow was important to him by the way his sherry gaze held hers. "I promise, Ian."

"Good," he said, and briefly closed his eyes. "I want you somewhere out of the heat of things."

"You don't even know where the wyrran are attacking, or if it is them attacking."

"Precisely. Which is why I want you on the roof."

Danielle blinked. It made sense. She would be able to see well no matter where they were being attacked from and use it to her advantage. It would also keep her out of the fighting.

"One of Charon's men will be with you," Ian continued. "He'll be using a weapon. A rifle Charon showed me."

She nodded. "They're effective. The ammunition they use can be shot from a great distance."

"Good. Now, come. I'll take you to the roof."

A smile formed when his hand grasped her. They left after she had grabbed her jacket and scarf and made their way to the roof. The night was cold with light flurries beginning to fall.

They were alone on the roof, and Danielle took that time to voice a worry that had been niggling at her. "You said Charon's men might react differently when they realize what he is. What do you think they'll do when they see you?"

"I'm hoping they'll be too occupied fighting whatever is coming to pay much attention," Ian said as he stood still as a statue.

Danielle knew his words were meant to calm her, reassure her. And they did to an extent. The fact she knew Ian didn't fully trust Charon gave her pause.

Ian turned to her and cupped her face with both his hands. "If anyone, and I mean anyone, attacks you, use your magic. Promise me."

"I promise," she said, shaking, and not just from the cold.

Ian leaned down and gave her a quick, hard kiss. He pulled back and stepped away. "Remember your promises."

"I will, but I have one as well."

His head cocked to the side. "What is it you would ask of me?"

"Don't die or get captured."

His face softened for a brief moment. "I give you my word to stay as safe as I can, but I also promise I'll do what I must to keep you from Deirdre."

Before she could say more Ian leaped over the side of the roof. She leaned over the railing and saw him land softly, his legs bent, before he straightened and walked to Charon.

Danielle was left alone for just a moment before a short, stocky man came into view. He gave her a nod before he melded into the shadows to await the attack.

Danielle stuffed her hands in her coat pockets and wrapped her fingers around the key.

"MacLeod."

"I know," she whispered. "I'm a little busy at the moment trying to stay alive."

"MacLeod Castle. East!"

Danielle rolled her eyes and released the key, praying she wouldn't feel any pain. She was taking the key to the castle, just not fast enough for its satisfaction.

Not that she could help it at the moment. If Ian was correct, an attack would come that night.

No sooner had the thought crossed her mind than she heard the deep, fearsome growl of a Warrior. Danielle rushed to the edge of the hotel and looked down to find Charon with his hand around a wyrran's neck.

The wyrran was scratching at Charon's copper-colored skin. Charon had thick horns sprouting from the side of his head and wrapping around to his forehead where the points curled upward.

With a sickening snap, Charon broke the wyrran's neck and tossed the creature to the ground.

That's when the battle began.

Wyrran poured into the small town. their shrieks piercing the night. Charon and Ian, both in their Warrior forms, were fighting multiple wyrran at once while Charon's men were using guns and swords to kill them.

There was a boom from beside her as the man fired his rifle. It put Danielle into action. She called up her magic, felt it rise and swirl within her. The power of it was heady, intoxicating.

She gathered it inside her, and propelled it through her hands to a wyrran who ran toward one of the houses.

Her magic drove the beast backward, and before he could rise, the man beside her fired a shot into the middle of the wyrran's head.

The man lifted his head from his rifle and smiled at her. "Keep it going."

She didn't need to be told twice. Danielle used her magic again and again to blast wyrran away from homes and businesses. The commotion had woken everyone, but fortunately, only a few dared to look outside.

Just a look was all it took to make anyone want to stay away.

Danielle glanced over to where she had last seen Ian. He and Charon were leaving a trail of dead wyrran in their wake, but there were still many more. Too many.

She faced forward to find that a wyrran had climbed up the outside of the hotel and reached the roof. Danielle lifted her hands, and with barely a thought sent magic blasting toward the wyrran.

When she looked over the edge of the roof, the wyrran was on the ground, his arms and legs at awkward angles. And he wasn't moving.

She could no longer afford to look for Ian. There were simply too many wyrran running about. Everywhere she looked there were wyrran.

There was a strangled scream as one of Charon's men was taken down by three wyrran. Danielle was disgusted by how the creatures ripped the man to shreds. She added more power to her magic and lunged forward as she pushed the magic from her hands.

Her magic barreled into the three wyrran, leaving two dead. But the damage was already done. Charon's man was dead.

Time slowed to a crawl as Danielle blasted her magic time and again into wyrran. Beside her, the rifle fired nearly as often as she used her magic.

Dimly, she heard the roars of Warriors and prayed Ian was unharmed.

Finally, the number of live wyrran dwindled. Danielle caught a glimpse of Charon chasing one as it ran from the village.

But no matter how hard she looked, she couldn't find Ian.

"Danielle."

Her shoulders drooped when she heard his voice. She turned to find him walking toward her bare-chested with long gashes on both arms and over his chest. She knew there would be others on his back as well.

A glance down at his legs showed his jeans hadn't come out unscathed either. There were slashes all along his pants.

"Are you all right?" Ian asked as he reached her.

She nodded, barely able to keep her eyes open from the exhaustion of using so much of her magic. "Is it over?"

"Nearly."

"You're wounded."

He shook his head. "Look again."

When she looked down she saw his wounds close and heal right before her eyes.

"Fuck me," came a voice beside her.

Danielle and Ian turned to the man as he stood and slung his rifle over his shoulder.

"What are you?" the man asked Ian.

"I'm a Warrior. Men like me and Charon are here to protect innocents from the creatures we fought tonight."

"Well then," the man said and sniffed. "I suppose that's all right."

"And I'm a Druid," Danielle said.

He smiled. "I thought ye might be. I gotta tell me

wife I met a Druid and a Warrior. She'll never believe it. I bet she slept through the entire battle."

He continued talking to himself as he walked away. Danielle turned her head to Ian. "Were the wyrran after me?"

"They came for me, which means Deirdre has discovered where I am. We need to leave. Now."

# CHAPTER
# SEVENTEEN

Ian turned back to Danielle when he felt her sway toward him. She was shivering, and her hands were like ice. He looked down at her to find her face as white as the snow falling.

"Danielle?"

"So tired," she whispered.

Without another word Ian lifted her in his arms and strode from the roof. He reached their room but before he could get inside, another of Charon's men rushed out with their belongings.

"Come," the man beckoned Ian.

Ian followed him out of the hotel to a car parked at the entrance. The man tossed their belongings into the back then shut the trunk. He opened the door and moved the seat forward to allow Ian to get into the cramped backseat. With a nod, the man walked away.

Cursing, Ian stared at the automobile. He had no idea how to drive one, and Danielle was in no condition to do it. But they couldn't stay in the village. They had to get moving.

"Get in," Charon shouted as he ran toward the car.

Ian laid Danielle in the back, pushed the seat back into place, and slid inside by the time Charon had gotten behind the wheel. Ian barely had time to close the door before Charon had them moving at a speed Ian couldn't fathom.

"I'm sorry, Ian. I couldna catch the last of the wyrran. The four buggers set off in different directions."

Ian braced an elbow on the door and ran a hand down his face. "Deirdre will know then."

"Bloody Hell," Charon shouted and slammed his hand on the wheel.

"I doona blame you," Ian told him. "We saved your town and the people."

"Did we?" Charon's lip curled in disgust. "Deirdre will retaliate. I have no doubt of that."

"Then why are you coming with me? Should you no' be with them?"

Charon glanced into the backseat then lifted a dark brow. "Were you going to drive, mate?"

Ian felt the warm air shooting from the vents. He pointed them back toward Danielle. "She used too much magic."

"She helped save everyone, just as I knew she would. Her magic is strong. I've no' felt magic like that in centuries."

"Are there many Druids about?"

Charon shook his head. "Verra few. They are nearly gone. Only a small handful still practice. I suspect Deirdre will discover them soon."

"And the others?"

"They doona know of the magic within them. Much has changed since you've been gone."

"So I see," Ian muttered. He turned his head to Charon. "Why are you helping me?"

Charon's fingers tightened on the wheel so that his

knuckles turned white. "I know you doona trust me, and you have every right to that mistrust. I never served Deirdre willingly."

"I assumed as much when you broke her neck."

Charon smiled. "God, that felt good. I want to do it again. I want her gone forever, Ian." Charon glanced at him, his brow furrowed. "Life was good these past four hundred years without her. I doona know why Danielle needs to get to the MacLeods. It matters no' to me. If it will help end Deirdre, that is enough."

Ian blew out a deep breath. "Thank you."

"Thank me when we reach the castle."


Declan buttoned his coat as he got out of his car. He didn't bother to thank the chauffeur for opening his door.

It had taken the simplest of spells to find the Druid nearest him, thanks to his help from Satan. He was short on time after all. Now, all Declan had to do was convince her to do as he wanted.

And if he couldn't convince her, he had another way of forcing her to do as he commanded.

Declan walked into the tiny café and straight past the counter into what passed for a kitchen.

"Excuse me," the heavyset woman at the register called.

But Declan ignored her, his focus on Kirstin. She was tall with an athletic build. Her dark blond hair was short, barely brushing the lobes of her ears.

She turned and gasped to find him behind her. "Can I help you?" Kirstin asked.

"Kirstin Maxwell?"

"Aye. That's me. What do you want?" she asked, and tried to move past him.

Declan stepped to the side and stopped her. "I'm here for you."

"Me?"

"Aye. I've a job offer I doona believe you'll pass up."

She looked him up and down then shook her head. "Sorry, mister. I don't know you."

This time Declan grabbed her arm as she tried to pass. "Oh, but you do. I know how you've dabbled in the occult. I know how you go out with the small group of supposed Druids to the stone circle and dance naked in the moonlight."

Her brown eyes widened. "How do you know?"

Declan smiled. "I have magic, Kirstin. I'm here to tell you that you do as well. Come with me now, and all you ever wanted can be yours."

"I'm a Druid?" she whispered.

"Aye. With real magic."

"Shit. I always thought, but—"

"Come," Declan urged, and pushed a small measure of magic into her to make her more biddable. "We need to leave. Now."

Kirstin allowed him to lead her out of the café to his car. "Where are we going?"

"To my home."

"I don't even know your name," she argued, but climbed into the car anyway.

"Declan Wallace."

She gasped. "*The* Declan Wallace? Oh, my God. I'm in heaven."

Declan smiled. It had all gone so easily.

Once in the backseat of his Jaguar with her, he turned to Kirstin and said, "Listen carefully. I've a story to tell you about Druids, Warriors, and Romans. The story is about where you came from. And where you are going."

"I'm listening," she said and leaned toward him.

By the time Declan was finished with the story Kirstin was practically eating out of his hands. Of course he altered the telling some. The MacLeods weren't the good guys they pretended to be, and Deirdre wasn't as bad as everyone made her out to be.

As for himself, Declan had led her to believe he was trying to save them all.

"So I need to get into MacLeod Castle," Kirstin said thoughtfully. "There are other Druids there? And these things you call Warriors?"

"Aye. The only way you'll know they are Warriors are when they release their gods. They are immortal, but remember what I told you, Druids can use their magic against them."

"But I've never used my magic."

"It willna matter. Warriors can sense the magic in Druids. That will be enough to gain you entrance. Once that is done, I want you to get friendly with the Druids. They will show you the artifacts they are going to use to end Deirdre. I want those artifacts."

Kirstin frowned. "What are the artifacts?"

"The Druids will show you."

"But—"

"Enough," Declan said, his nerves on edge with her endless questions. "I've thought of everything. Including how to get you inside the castle. If you do exactly as I tell you, everything will be fine."

For the next two hours they went over every detail again and again until Kirstin was able to repeat everything without hesitation. She sounded convincing even to his own ears.

Declan was more than pleased with his work. "You'll do fine, Kirstin."

"Thank you," she said, turning away from the window. "When do I get to learn magic?"

"Never." Declan raised his hands, his magic freezing

her in place as he began to chant the spell that would
make her sleep. And forget all about him.

"We're nearly there, sir," his driver said.

"Good. I'm ready to get her out of the car."

In a matter of moments the driver had pulled the car to
the side of the road. Declan blew out an impatient breath
as his driver tugged the unconscious Kirstin from the car
and half carried, half dragged her away from the road
where she couldn't be seen.

"It's done," his driver said as he settled behind the
wheel and put the car in drive.

Declan drummed his fingers on his knee. It wouldn't
take long for his plan to begin to work, and once it did,
he would have the MacLeods, the artifacts, and then he
would have Deirdre.


Kirstin woke with her head pounding. She sat up and
looked around. Where was she? She remembered quit-
ting her job at the café and setting out to find . . .
something.

She knew there was something out there waiting for
her, but she didn't know what it was.

A glance at her watch told her it was just after eight
in the morning, and if she didn't find shelter soon, she'd
be buried under the snow.

Kirstin looked around for her purse, but couldn't find
it. Had she left it? Or had someone stolen it? With no
money for food or lodging, things had certainly gone
pear shaped.

"Great. It's just what me mum always said would happen to me," Kirstin said as she got to her feet. At least her
thick coat insulated her from the snow.

The same couldn't be said for her jeans.

Kirstin looked first one way then the other, trying to

decide where to go. Something pulled her to the left, so she began walking.

Few cars passed her, but she didn't bother to wave them down. It wasn't until a car passed her, then skidded to a halt that she looked up.

The black Range Rover's reverse lights came on as it rolled back toward her. It pulled off the road and the driver's side door opened. Kirstin could only blink at the man who emerged. He was gorgeous with his black hair and silver eyes.

"Hello." He spoke calmly, his voice deep and rich. "Are you lost?"

Kirstin shook her head. She knew better than to talk to strange men. "Nay."

"My name is Ramsey MacDonald." He took a couple of slow steps toward her. "I'm no' trying to frighten you, but when I felt your magic I had to stop."

"Felt my magic?" Kirstin repeated, her ears ringing in disbelief. "You can feel it?"

"So you know you're a Druid?"

"I've always wanted to be. I had hoped."

Ramsey smiled and held out his hand. "I can take you to other Druids if you'll allow me."

He paused, his brows lifted. Kirstin laughed. "Sorry. I'm Kirstin Maxwell."

"Hello, Kirstin."

She looked at his offered hand. It went against everything she knew to get into his SUV, but she desperately wanted to be a Druid. He had said he felt her magic.

*Warriors sense a Druid's magic.*

Where had that thought come from? And how did she know about Warriors?

"Kirstin?" Ramsey called, concern marring his strong, angular face. A face that she could stare at for all eternity.

There were things coming into her head, things she

hadn't known before. She didn't know how she knew them now, but it frightened her.

Every fiber of her being told her not to get in the SUV, but a stronger sense urged her to get inside quickly.

But why? What was going on?

"We willna harm you," Ramsey said patiently. "We protect Druids."

Unable to walk away no matter how much she wanted to, Kirstin found her hand in his without knowing how it happened.

"You're shaking," Ramsey commented as he led her to the Range Rover.

"I'm frightened."

"Donna be. Everything will be all right now. You'll be with others who can help you with your magic."

Yet, even as they drove away Kirstin felt it was wrong to go with him. Not because she thought he might hurt her, but because some unknown force was making her.

She swallowed, her fear growing as the miles were eaten up by the tires.

# CHAPTER
# EIGHTEEN

Deirdre stared at the four wyrran in front of her. Of all the ones she had sent to find Ian Kerr, only four returned. She seethed, but she kept her anger in check. For the moment.

"What happened?" she demanded of the four.

"Warriors," one hissed.

Warriors? That wasn't possible. "There should only have been one. Ian. There were fifty of you. You should have had no trouble subduing him and bringing him to me."

"A Druid," another answered.

Warriors and a Druid. Deirdre took a slow, measured breath. "Who was the other Warrior?"

The wyrran closest to her blinked its large pale yellow eyes at her. "Charon."

Deirdre whirled around and sent a blast of magic into the rock, which shattered at the impact. The stone screamed its rage at her for harming it, and Deirdre hastened to the spot to soothe it.

She looked at the wyrran. "Charon will pay for interfering. I need Ian though. If he hasn't yet gained control over his god, he could easily become mine. The power of his god to either absorb another Warrior's power or cancel it is one I will need when the MacLeods try to awaken Laria. Find Ian!"

Then she recalled the Druid. "Wait," she called after them. "Bring the Druid with Ian. I always have need of more magic," she said with a smile.

The wyrran grinned back at her, saliva dripping from their lips that couldn't close over their mouthful of teeth.

With the wyrran gone. Deirdre sank to her knees and caressed the stone. She knew better than to take out her anger on the rocks. They were all she had, and she needed to remember that in the future.

Danielle opened her eyes to find herself in a car. A very luxurious car if the black leather seats said anything. A glance to the dashboard showed the well-known Mercedes emblem.

She shifted her gaze to the two seats in front of her and smiled when she saw Ian. His head swiveled toward her, and his sherry eyes warmed when they noticed she was awake.

"I was getting worried," he said.

Danielle pulled herself into a sitting position and smothered a yawn. "I don't know why I fainted."

"It was the use of your magic. I warned you it would drain you."

"But I didn't fail you."

"Nay," Ian said with a grin. "You were amazing."

"Aye, you were." Charon said from the other seat. "I thank you for helping us."

Danielle leaned over to see him. "You're welcome. I didn't expect you to come with us."

"Someone had to drive," Charon said with a smirk at Ian.

Danielle laughed and settled back in her seat. "Did we get all of the wyrran?"

The smiles faded from the men's lips.

"Nay," Ian said. "Some got away."

"To tell Deirdre they no' only found Ian but a Druid as well," Charon finished.

"Wonderful," Danielle muttered.

Ian reached back and took her hand. "It will be fine. We'll be at the MacLeods' soon. Deirdre can try to get us there, but she'll fail as she has the times before."

Danielle grabbed the key in her pocket. "Will Deirdre or the wyrran be able to get to the castle?"

"Aye," Ian said, but his smile was confident and eager. "But they willna get you, Danielle. There are plenty of Druids and Warriors there to stop her."

"Her Warriors were killed," Charon said. "So that gives you an advantage."

"No' all her Warriors," Ian corrected him. "There was one she had locked far below the mountain. His name is Phelan."

"And he didna side with you and the MacLeods?"

Ian shook his head. "It was Isla that tricked him into coming to the mountain when he was just a lad. Deirdre kept him there until he reached a score of years."

"Then she released his god," Charon said with a curse. "Who freed him?"

"Isla. Phelan helped Broc and Sonya against Deirdre, but as far as I know, he never joined the MacLeods."

Charon snorted. "Anything could have happened in four hundred years. He may be there now."

"Where you should be," Danielle told him.

Charon looked at her through the rearview mirror.

She shrugged. "I'm only speaking the truth. You know they will need you. And as you've said, four centuries is a long time. Let the past go, Charon. Help us end Deirdre."

He frowned, but he didn't respond.

Ian squeezed her hand. He gave her a small nod as well.

Danielle still felt weak, but no longer did she feel as if she might pass out as she had on the roof. She'd tried to tell Ian, but by that time it had been too late.

When he'd said her magic could drain her, she hadn't really believed him. Now she knew exactly what he meant. And it wasn't a good feeling.

She could feel her magic swirl inside her though. And that was enough to put her at ease.

"We're here," Charon said as he slowed the car and turned off the main road.

He drove over raw land for about fifteen minutes before he stopped the car and put it in park. There were no words spoken as both he and Ian got out of the car.

It was Ian who moved the seat so she could climb out of the back. Danielle walked to the front of the dark gray two-door CL65 AMG where Charon stood.

Charon faced toward the ocean, a peculiar look on his face as if he weren't sure he wanted to be there or not.

"You know they would welcome you," Ian said.

Charon looked down, a half smile on his face. "Would they? After what I've done? I think no'."

"They would, and you know it."

Charon ignored Ian and turned to Danielle. "Guard yourself well, Druid. If Deirdre ever feels the strength of your magic she'll stop at nothing to get you."

"I don't plan to ever meet her," Danielle said. She walked to Charon and hugged him. "Thank you. For everything."

He awkwardly patted her back and quickly stepped

away. He cleared his throat and glanced toward the sea again. "I need to get back to my village."

Ian held out his arm, and Charon hesitated but a moment before they clasped forearms. "You are a good man," Ian said. "Remember that."

"Be careful. And vigilant," Charon said in answer. "If Deirdre did bring you forward in time it's because she has a plan for you. A plan you'll want no part of."

They released each other, and as Charon walked away Danielle stepped closer to Ian.

"Charon." Ian stopped him. "What did Deirdre do to make you spy on her?"

Charon lowered his eyes, but not before Danielle saw the torment in their dark depths.

"Do you recall how crazed you were when your god was first released? All the fury and the power? It was too much to take at times."

"Aye," Ian answered softly.

"Even through all of that I denied Deirdre. During a particularly rough bout with my god, she put my father in the dungeon with me. I didn't recognize him, Ian. I thought he was one of Deirdre's men. Only too late did I realize who he was."

Danielle turned her head and pressed her face into Ian's arm.

"You killed him," Ian said. It wasn't a question.

Charon nodded. "She had the rest of my family as well. If I didna do as she said, she threatened to put the others in with me as well."

"But you had control of your god."

Finally Charon lifted his eyes to Ian. "Barely. Deirdre knew what to say to send me into a rage. I feared she would do it just to make me suffer."

"Had I been in the same situation I'd have spied as

well," Ian said. "I would've, and did, do anything for my family."

Charon visibly swallowed and forced a smile. "Good luck to both of you."

Danielle waved as Charon got back in the car and drove away. She had been wary of him at first, but her heart ached for the anguish she heard in his voice.

"I wish we had known what Deirdre had done to him while we were in the Pit," Ian said.

"It's in the past. Let it go."

His sherry eyes looked down at her. "As Charon has?"

"Charon has to live with what he's done. Until he forgives himself, he'll carry it with him always."

Ian waited until Charon's car drove out of sight. It felt odd being back on MacLeod land, especially when he knew Duncan wouldn't be waiting for him.

"How do you feel?" Danielle asked.

"Hard to say."

"And your god? Do you have control?"

Ian rubbed his jaw. "He still fights me, but I've no' blacked out since I met you."

"That's good then."

"Is it? Or is it because I've had wyrran to fight. It felt good to kill them, Danielle. It felt right."

"Because it was. They are evil, and they meant to murder innocents. They would have taken you to Deirdre."

He shook his head. "I will no' ever be in her hold again."

Farmire was strong, and he continued to try and break through, but somehow Ian managed to stay in control. Mostly.

He still wasn't sure how, but it was enough that he did. He suspected it had something to do with Danielle's magic, because when he was around her his chaotic world filled with agony and grief righted itself.

Everything came into focus again, as if he were the man he had been before Duncan's death.

"Ian?"

He turned and gestured to the rolling landscape before him and the sea beyond. "You are on MacLeod land now. Have been for some time, I imagine."

"Where is the castle?"

Ian chuckled. "It's hidden by Isla's shield. It keeps others away, making them feel as if they need to leave."

"And the ones who belong here?"

"They will feel the magic of the shield," Ian said as he looked at her. "Do you feel it?"

"I feel . . . something. It's hard to put into words."

Ian took her hand and walked her through the trees that had once been a thick forest. When they reached the other side of the trees he paused.

Danielle's eyes were closed and a bright smile lit up her face.

"I feel it," she whispered. "It's wonderful. Like a pulse deep in my soul, calling to my magic, waiting for me to answer."

"Step through," Ian urged.

Danielle didn't need to be encouraged twice. She opened her eyes and held up her hand until she reached the shield. For several moments she simply stood against the magic.

And then she stepped through.

Ian watched her disappear into the shield. His smile dropped as he thought of facing the others. It had seemed like only weeks since the last time he had sat at their table, but for them it had been centuries.

They would have changed when he hadn't.

Yet to see the castle that had become his home was a

yearning that had begun on the ride to the castle. The more he thought about seeing his fellow Warriors, the more the ache grew, until he knew he had made the right decision in taking Danielle to them.

Ian took a deep breath and walked into the shield. There was a jolt of magic as the shield engulfed him. The magic swarmed him, making his head buzz. And then he stepped through.

Before him stood the village Deirdre had destroyed numerous times. And farther away, perched on the edge of the cliff, was MacLeod Castle.

Danielle hadn't moved since walking through the shield. She looked around her as if she were in a daze.

"This is unbelievable. Isla's shield hides all of this?"

Ian smiled at the amazement in her voice. "Aye."

"The cottages look as if they came right out of the medieval time. And my God, the castle."

Ian let his eyes drink in the sight of the gray stones. The sun had broken through the thick clouds and shone upon the castle as if it had been waiting for Ian to appear.

"I've seen castles before." Danielle continued talking, unaware of his turmoil. "But this is . . . I cannot find the words."

Ian had felt much the same when he'd seen the castle for the first time. "It's the magic within the land and the castle that makes it so different."

"The magic is potent. Nowhere else have I ever felt so connected to magic before."

Ian put his hand on her back. "Shall we go to the castle?"

"I don't know. I think I need a week or so just to stare at the thing."

Ian laughed at her frank honesty. "You've nothing to be afraid of."

"Neither do you." Danielle said as she looked into his eyes.

Her emerald depths were clear and bright as she gazed at him. Her silvery hair had begun to come loose from the band she'd wrapped around it at the back of her head.

Ian touched a strand that lifted in the soft sea breeze. "You think I'm afraid?"

"I think you want to be here, but you worry. Because Duncan isn't here."

Ian dropped his hand and sighed. "It willna be the same without my brother."

"It's never the same when you lose family."

Ian heard the sorrow in her words. She too had lost family and everything she had known when she'd been uprooted from Florida to live in Scotland.

"We're a pair, aren't we?" Danielle asked with a grin.

He took her hand and started forward when something flew over them. Danielle stifled a scream and latched onto his arm.

"It's all right," Ian said as he spotted Broc flying back toward them. "It's Broc."

"He has wings," Danielle hissed.

This time when Ian laughed he felt it through his entire body. And he thought it might have cracked the casing around his heart.

# CHAPTER
# NINETEEN

Danielle was so taken aback by Ian's laugh that she momentarily forgot the huge Warrior with wings.

But only briefly.

"You should laugh more," she said when she was able to find her voice.

Ian's body tensed for a moment. "I'd forgotten how."

She wanted to kiss him, to soothe the torment she saw in his eyes. She wanted to wrap her arms around him and take all his grief, all his pain, into herself.

And she would have if they'd been alone.

Without taking his eyes from Danielle, Ian said, "Hello, Broc."

Danielle squeezed his fingers to let her know she was all right. Only when Ian's head swung to face Broc did she look at the Warrior.

Broc's Warrior skin was the most stunning shade of indigo. And his wings. Danielle had never seen anything so huge before. They towered over Broc's blond head as he folded them behind his back.

Danielle blinked, and when she did, Broc's god had

faded. He stood before them bare-chested, a smile on his face.

"It's good to see you, Ian," Broc said.

Ian's lips were tight, his jaw clenched. "Is it?"

Danielle winced when she saw Broc's smile falter.

"What does that mean?" Broc demanded. "We've been waiting four centuries for you to return to us."

Ian didn't answer. Instead he turned to Danielle. "Danielle, this is Broc. Broc, Danielle."

Danielle gave a hesitant smile to Broc. "Hi."

"It's good to have another Druid here," Broc said with a bow of his head. "The others are waiting impatiently for you both."

She was glad when Ian threaded his fingers in hers. She was nervous to finally meet the MacLeods and everyone else in the castle. Danielle had meant to ask Ian about everyone, but there hadn't been enough time.

A quick look at Ian showed the man she had glimpsed just a moment ago with his brilliant smile that lit up his face was gone. Beside her was a man with a heart as heavy as lead and demons too plentiful to rid himself of them.

Broc walked on the other side of her seemingly unaffected by the cold. His dark brown eyes met hers fleetingly before he looked at Ian.

She wanted to tell Broc . . . what? That Ian had been getting better? Danielle had thought that Ian returning to the castle would help him. Now that she saw his reaction, she wasn't so sure.

Her mind was briefly taken away from Ian as they walked through the village. She saw ruins that were overgrown with grass and weathered with time.

"It was an abbey where orphaned children were raised," Broc said when he saw her looking.

"What happened to it?"

"Deirdre." That one word from Ian, laced with such hatred, made Danielle's eyes sting with tears.

Broc gave a brisk nod. "She killed all within as she searched for Cara. Deirdre had no idea Lucan had already met Cara and was protecting her at the castle."

Danielle looked at the castle again. It wasn't just any castle. It was a castle that offered protection and a future for those who lived inside. It was a castle that had given the MacLeods hope.

Would it also give Ian hope?

The closer they walked to the castle the more enthralled she was. It was huge. She counted six towers, round and rising to the clouds like ancient stone arms.

"It's beautiful," Danielle murmured.

"Aye," Ian and Broc said in unison.

They weren't far from the castle gates when two men came into view. Once again Danielle felt Ian tense, and then he halted altogether.

Danielle moved closer to Ian to give him as much support as she could. She didn't know what was going on, but she knew Ian wasn't comfortable here.

"Ian? Holy Hell, it is you," said a man with light brown hair and the palest green eyes. He wore dark jeans and a thin long-sleeved pullover that showed off his wide shoulders and muscled arms. The gleam of gold caught her eye as she saw the Celtic torc around his neck.

The second man smiled widely, obviously excited to see Ian. "I can no' believe you're finally back."

The men hadn't noticed her yet, so she took her time looking over the second man with his brown hair so dark it was almost black and his honey-colored eyes. He wore cargos and a deep red tee with a beautiful Celtic design going over his left shoulder and onto the back of the shirt.

The two men's smiles faded when Ian didn't respond.

Danielle licked her lips and released Ian's hand. She'd had a hold on the key in her pocket since they had arrived and it warmed when she looked at the man who had first spoken.

"I'm Danielle Buchanan," she said. "Ian saved my life and graciously offered to bring me here."

The man's pale green eyes grew sad as they looked from Ian to her. "I'm Quinn MacLeod. It has been a long time since another Druid has made it to our castle."

"MacLeod," she repeated. "So I did find you."

Quinn nodded. "You did."

"I'm Arran MacCarrick," the second man said and held out his hand.

Danielle smiled and shook it. "It's nice to meet you, Arran."

"Come," Quinn beckoned. "My wife and the other Druids are wanting to meet you."

"How did they know I was coming?"

Arran chuckled. "Saffron told us. She had a vision of you a week ago, so we knew you were coming, and that you had help, but we had no idea it was Ian."

The men, including Broc, started toward the castle, but Ian didn't move. Danielle faced him and put her hand on his arm. "Ian?"

"I wanted to be here, but . . . I doona think I can stay."

"Why?"

The wind picked up his long light brown hair so she saw strands of gold as well. "They didna search for me."

"You don't know why. Save your anger until you do."

"They were my family, Danielle," he said as his sherry eyes bored into hers. "I trusted them with my life."

She ached for him. "You trusted them enough to bring me here. Trust in them now."

A muscle moved in his jaw but he nodded his head. Danielle turned on her heel and started toward the gates where Quinn waited for them. In two strides Ian had caught up with her.

When Danielle entered the gate her steps slowed as she saw people crowding the steps and doors of the castle.

"They are impatient," Quinn said with a chuckle.

Danielle wasn't exactly a shy person, but she wasn't the kind who opened up easily either. She'd always blamed it on the scars from her parents' deaths and being moved to Scotland.

Yet seeing the friendly, welcoming smiles, Danielle understood why Ian had talked so fondly of the castle and the people he called his family.

There was another man who resembled Quinn who ushered the others back inside. He wore a torc just as Quinn did, and the two small braids on either side of his temples set him apart from the others. That and his sea-green eyes.

With Ian by her side, she followed Quinn into the castle as Broc, Arran, and the other man entered last.

Danielle desperately wanted to turn and look at Ian. She couldn't imagine how difficult it was for him to return, especially since Duncan was gone. She had a memory that was as vivid as if it had happened yesterday of when she walked back into her house in Florida after her parents' death. It had been harder than she could have imagined.

The memories had flooded her, but more than that, the knowledge that her parents were no longer with her made the house seem emptier, stranger. Even cold.

"Ian!" A petite woman with wavy sable hair that reached past her shoulders and dozens of tiny braids at the crown of her head walked to Ian and wrapped her arms around him.

Danielle could only stare as Ian stood frozen, his

arms at his sides. Several moments passed before he slowly, awkwardly lifted his arms and loosely returned her hug.

The woman stepped back, tears in her eyes. "We thought we'd lost you. You have no idea how worried we were."

"Give him some room, my darling," Quinn said as he wrapped an arm around the woman's slim shoulders and pulled her against him. "Danielle, this is my wife, Marcail."

Marcail laughed and wiped at her eyes. "Forgive me. I'm being so rude. I'm delighted to meet you, it's just that Ian and Arran were with us in the Pit."

"You were in the Pit?" Danielle asked, her mouth open in shock.

Quinn growled. "No thanks to Deirdre. It's a long story, and one we'll be happy to tell you once you've met everyone and gotten settled."

"A Druid, Quinn. It's been so long," Marcail whispered.

Danielle's attention was pulled from the couple as the man with braids stepped around her. "I'm the middle MacLeod brother, Lucan. And this"—he motioned a woman with long chestnut hair over to his side—"is my wife, Cara."

"Oh, I heard a little about your adventure when we passed the abbey," Danielle said.

Cara smiled. "We're happy to have you here, Danielle."

"And I'm Fallon, the eldest MacLeod," said another man who stepped beside Cara. He had short golden-brown hair and the darkest green eyes.

She would have known he was a brother to Lucan and Quinn by his smile, but also by the torc around his neck.

"I'm his wife, Larena."

Danielle could only stare in shock at the exquisite beauty of Larena. Before she could utter a word Hayden and Isla were there. Then Galen and Reaghan, Broc and Sonya, Logan and Gwynn, Camdyn, Fiona, Braden, and Charlie.

She was surprised to discover Quinn and Marcail had a grown son, Aiden. And then there was Saffron. She stood off by herself, and when Fallon said her name, she smiled in Danielle's direction.

It was then Danielle realized Saffron was blind.

With her mind in a whirl from all the introductions, Danielle wasn't sure if she should give them the key now or not. The key had gone ice cold when she'd been surrounded by so many.

*"Not yet,"* it whispered in her mind.

"Why don't I show you to your room?" Gwynn said.

Danielle looked at Ian.

"Go on," he urged. He handed over the bag of Danielle's things to Gwynn.

But Danielle didn't want to leave him. She knew he was having trouble coping with everything. He might need her. And she knew she felt more comfortable with him by her side.

As Gwynn and Cara tugged her toward the stairs through the crowd, an uneasy feeling ran down her spine. She glanced back hoping to see who had caused it, but no one was looking at her. All eyes were on Ian.

"Wait," she said when she had walked up two steps. "I'm not leaving Ian."

"You aren't," Marcail said.

Danielle looked behind her to find all the women with her. Only the men remained. Ian's gaze lifted to her, and he gave her a slight nod.

"He isn't going anywhere," Larena said. "Fallon won't

let him now that he's home. Meanwhile, let Sonya heal your wounds. You'll feel much better."

Danielle had no choice but to go with the women as they urged her up the stairs.

Ian watched Danielle go and wanted to call her back, to reach for her hand and hold on to her. He'd been protecting her, keeping her away from danger. And even though he knew she was safe at the castle, he wasn't done watching over her.

*"Will you ever be?"* Duncan asked.

Only when the women had disappeared up the stairs did Ian face the men before him. He knew every face in the crowd but two. Charlie and Aiden.

He'd been slightly surprised to see Braden all grown-up, but he could still see the intelligent lad he remembered.

"Aiden, you, Braden, and Charlie see if you can catch some fish for supper," Quinn told his son.

Son. Ian had looked forward to the birth of Marcail and Quinn's child. When he had last seen them, Marcail had just begun to show. Now, Aiden was a grown man.

There was so much Ian had missed, so many things he hadn't experienced with his brethren. He felt like an outsider now. It was an emotion he hadn't ever experienced at the castle before.

"Where have you been?" Camdyn asked the question Ian knew everyone was curious to know.

"Hiding."

A glass was shoved in his hand. Ian looked down to find amber liquid and the scent of whiskey. He downed it in one swallow then pushed through everyone and walked to the table.

He stopped and stared at the spot where he had been sitting when he felt Duncan's death. He could still remember the pain of their connection being broken, the spike of rage as all of Farmire's power pooled within him.

"We erected a stone cross for Duncan," Quinn said softly from beside him. "It's at the place where he was killed near the Isle of Eigg."

"Isla and the others protected it with magic," Hayden continued. "No one will ever touch it."

"A fitting tribute to a good man and an honored brother," Ian said.

He touched the table before he lowered himself onto the bench. Memories of him and Duncan laughing and arguing assaulted him, of him calming Duncan's vengeance for Deirdre that burned brightly inside his brother.

If he started a sentence, Duncan would finish it. They always knew what the other was thinking. When Deirdre had Ian tortured, Duncan felt every lash, every hit that landed on Ian.

The bond that had bound them as twins had only been strengthened with Farmire's unbinding. And made it all the worse with Duncan's death.

"How long have you been in this time?" Arran asked.

Ian wasn't sure if he was grateful to be pulled out of his memories. He shrugged. "I doona know."

The others took their seats around the table, and Ian felt their eyes on him. He wanted to shout and tell them to go away, but they wouldn't leave him alone until he gave them the answers they sought.

"Please, Ian," Fallon begged. "We want to know what happened."

"You want to know?" Ian bellowed, and slammed the glass on the table. It shattered in his hand, cutting him, but he didn't feel anything. "One moment I was sitting here, then I was ripped to pieces by Duncan's death. The next thing I knew I woke to find myself atop a mountain with my god trying to take control!"

He rose and raked a hand through his hair. It was too much. The memories, the questions. He couldn't take it. He had to leave.

Ian started for the door, but Hayden blocked his path. "Move."

Hayden shook his head, his arms crossed over his muscular chest. "Let us help you."

"Help me?" Ian asked with a snort. "Why were you no' there to help me when I needed it most? Why were any of you no' there to bring me back home when I sat cold and alone in that godawful cave?"

# CHAPTER
# TWENTY

"Because we couldn't find you," Ramsey said from the door.

Ian briefly squeezed his eyes shut and turned away from Hayden and Ramsey. He walked to the wall and leaned against it, weary to his soul. Every fiber of his being wanted to believe them, but he knew Broc could find anyone, anywhere.

They could have found him.

"We couldna find you," Galen repeated. "We tried countless times."

Broc's face was resigned as he nodded. "I tried more than any of them realize, Ian. There was something shielding you so I couldna find you, just as I couldna find Deirdre."

There was no doubt they were telling the truth. Ian had seen the lengths the others had gone to to rescue Quinn from Deirdre. They all would do anything to rescue one of the others. He shouldn't have doubted them.

That thought had barely formed in his head when he felt new magic. It was faint, barely registering as magic, but it was there.

Ramsey closed the door and stepped to the side to reveal a young woman with short, dark blond hair. "I found a Druid," Ramsey said.

"Two in one day?" Lucan said. "What are the odds?"

"Slim," Ian answered uneasily.

Logan nodded. "Verra slim."

A new Warrior and now this new Druid. What was going on? Ian wondered.

"Kirstin, these are the Warriors I told you about," Ramsey said.

Fallon gave a shout, and a moment later Larena appeared at the top of the stairs. She hastily took Kirstin up with the others.

And then Ian found Ramsey standing beside him. "You brought a Druid?"

Ian nodded. "Danielle. She has something that could help us."

"What is it?"

"It is hers to give. I'll let her decide when to tell everyone."

Ramsey had always been a man of few words, but he seemed to see so much more with his silver eyes. "We worried you were lost to us forever. It was devastating to lose Duncan, and then you disappeared. Broc figured out you had been transported to the future though."

Ian looked to where Broc sat to find the Warrior's eyes on them.

"It was Hell," Broc admitted. "But I was no' going to give up searching for you."

Ian swallowed and glanced away, uneasy with the emotions that rose within him.

Logan shifted in his seat and leaned his elbows on the table. "Ramsey, Camdyn, Arran, and I had the Druids time-travel us to this time as well. We left just hours after you disappeared."

"We did it to find you," Camdyn said.

Ian felt like a fool. He dropped his chin to his chest and shook his head. "I didna know."

"How could you?" Ramsey asked.

Hayden blew out a breath. "We knew you would have all of your god's power now, and I realize how difficult that can be. We feared. . . ."

"That I might give in," Ian finished for him. He looked at the men around the great hall. "I doona have control over him. No' yet."

"Which is why you were hiding," Quinn said.

Fallon rubbed his jaw. "How did you find Danielle?"

"She found me actually." Ian took a deep breath and told them how he had found Danielle and saved her from the wyrran and from the loch, of Charon, and the attack.

"Charon?" Arran said with a twist of his lips. "You trusted him?"

"He kept guard, Arran. He left his village without protection to drive me and Danielle here. Aye. I trusted him. I trust him. He also told me why he spied on us. I'd have done the same in his shoes."

"Why did he?" Quinn asked.

Ian wasn't sure if he should tell them. It was Charon's tale to tell, and he hadn't wanted to share it with Ian. But Ian suspected there might be a time when they would need Charon's help. If the others understood what had motivated Charon, they would ask for his help.

"He had just had his god released and was battling for control, but even then he refused to follow Deirdre. So she put his father in the cell with him. Charon, in his rage, killed his father."

"Shite," Ramsey said, his lips flattened.

"Deirdre then threatened to toss every member of his family in with him until he agreed to do as she said."

"Which was spy on us," Arran murmured.

Ian nodded. "He did what any of us would have done to protect our families."

"He should have told us," Quinn said. "We could have helped him."

"I asked him to come with me to the castle, but he declined," Ian said.

"Damn," Fallon said. "We could have used another Warrior who had experience fighting Deirdre."

"Especially now that we know she's found Ian," Lucan stated.

Ian pushed away from the wall. "She willna get her hands on me again."

"She killed Duncan to get to you," Logan said as he gained his feet. "I saw the maliciousness in her eyes, the deadly intent. She knew exactly what she was doing."

"Why bring me to the future then?" Ian asked.

Galen released a loud sigh. "She didna. Declan Wallace brought her to the future, but she was connected to you because of Duncan's death. Somehow you were transported with her."

"Declan Wallace?" Ian repeated the name. "Who is he?"

"A *drough* who is just as evil as Deirdre," Logan answered. "I fought against him and nearly died."

Ian had seen Logan fight. He didn't think there was anything that could bring the Warrior down. "Impossible."

"No' when he has bullets filled with *drough* blood."

Ian had seen what bullets could do to wyrran. To have some filled with *drough* blood would stop a Warrior in his tracks.

"How did you live?" Ian asked.

Logan shrugged. "I still doona know. Gwynn brought me here, and Sonya healed me."

"It was a damned close thing," Hayden said wearily.

Galen rubbed his eyes. "We thought we had lost Logan."

"This has to end," Ramsey said.

Ian turned his head to the quiet one of the group. Ramsey wasn't a talker, but when he did talk, everyone tended to listen.

"What do you propose?" Ian asked.

"We need to unlock the Tablet of Orn. Once we do, I think we'll be able to find where Laria is and awaken her."

Fallon sat back in his chair and folded his hands atop his stomach. "I wish it were that easy, Ramsey, but you forget. We still need a Druid from Torrichilty Forest."

There was something in the way Ramsey stood that caught Ian's attention. It was Ramsey's stillness, the way the mask of calm he always wore shifted for just a moment. And in that moment, Ian saw resignation in Ramsey's silver eyes.

"That willna be a problem," Ramsey said.

"Willna . . ." Arran shook his head in disbelief. "We've been looking in Torrichilty Forest for centuries for a Druid. We have no' found one yet. Why do you think you can?"

"Do you trust me?" Ramsey asked instead.

There was a chorus of "ayes."

"Then leave it be for now. You will have the Druid you need to awaken Laria."

"Do we no' still need the sword Deirdre got from the burial mound?" Ian asked.

Lucan smiled as everyone else chuckled. "We had four hundred years without her, Ian. We were in that damned mountain of hers every week looking for that sword."

"So you found it?"

"We found it," Fallon answered.

Ian pushed away from the wall and crossed his arms over his chest. They had never been this close to awakening Laria before. "Then what are we waiting for?"

"We're no' sure if there is another artifact we need to get," Logan said. "Gwynn found the Tablet of Orn on Eigg, but it's locked. We have no idea what's inside."

Locked. Ian instantly thought of Danielle and her key. That's what the key was for. The sooner the Tablet was opened, the sooner they could discover what was inside.

And possibly end Deirdre in a matter of days.

Urgency filled him, but he held it in check. Ian hadn't lied to Ramsey. It was Danielle's to give, and Danielle's right to tell the reason that brought her to the castle.

But Ian was going to ask her to tell them soon. The idea of Deirdre being gone once and for all was too tempting.

The fact there was another *drough* they were going to have to fight made it all the more urgent to get rid of Deirdre soon. If Declan and Deirdre ever joined forces, Ian wasn't sure he and the others could best them.

Farmire roared inside Ian. He clenched his hands, desperately trying to keep control. Ian had done so well while he had been with Danielle.

He had hoped he was actually gaining ground over his god, but that hope died swiftly and painfully. Ian hadn't gained any ground. It was simply the battles that had saved him over the last few days.

Which meant he was putting Danielle in danger. Something he had sworn not to do.

He needed to leave, to get away as fast as he could. But he was finally back with his brethren. How could he leave now when they might be fighting Deirdre soon?

Ian looked up at the ceiling, wishing he could have one more night in Danielle's sweet arms, to feel the heat of her body and the passion in her kiss. To hear her shout his name as she peaked.

It had been the best few days of his life. And he couldn't believe it was ending.

# CHAPTER
# TWENTY-ONE

Malcolm Monroe had always thought himself a decent man. He'd been a decent man. When he was still mortal.

He'd done what he thought was right and left his clan to be with his cousin Larena after he discovered she was much more than just a woman.

A Warrior.

He could still recall that first time when he'd been just nine summers and he'd seen her transform. Malcolm had been terrified. But he'd also been intrigued and fascinated.

Once Larena had found him spying on her, he'd visited her every day. They had become as close as brother and sister. When he reached manhood and learned she was leaving the clan for Edinburgh Castle to try and find the infamous MacLeods, he'd not hesitated to accompany her.

Not only had Malcolm met the eldest MacLeod, Fallon, but he'd watched his beloved cousin truly smile for the first time on meeting Fallon.

Malcolm had been delighted for her.

Then disaster struck when Deirdre had sent wyrran and Warriors after Larena. *Drough* blood had been used, and Larena had nearly died. It was only Fallon who had saved her.

But Malcolm hadn't known that when he saw Fallon disappear with Larena in his arms. Malcolm had promised Larena he'd return to the clan he was expected to lead. He'd vowed to forget about her and the Warriors and most importantly Deirdre.

But no matter how hard he tried, he couldn't. He had to know if Larena had survived.

Malcolm had only wanted to see for himself that she was all right. He'd planned to return to his clan straightaway. But Deirdre had sent her Warriors after him.

He could still feel their claws sinking into his skin, into his cartilage and muscle. He could still feel the ease with which the Warriors broke bone after bone in his body.

The pain had been more than he thought he could endure. Despite the Warriors' obvious advantage, Malcolm was a Highlander, a laird's son. And he had fought them.

One moment he knew death was coming, and the next he was at MacLeod Castle with Larena beside him. The Druids there had done what they could, but Deirdre's Warriors had already inflicted their damage.

They might not have killed him as Deirdre instructed, but they ruined him, broke him. There were no more dreams about returning to his clan or illusions of being laird.

What man in his right mind would follow a laird with only one good arm and scars so hideous they could make children cry?

No one.

Malcolm had stayed at MacLeod Castle trying to determine what his future could bring him. He was useless to anyone at the castle. He wasn't a Warrior, and so couldn't fight in their battles. He wasn't a Druid so wouldn't be coddled and hidden away.

He was . . . worthless.

Though he'd known it was wrong, Malcolm had walked away from everyone at the castle during one of Deirdre's attacks. He had to find his way in the world somehow. Somewhere. Some way.

He just never expected it to be with Deirdre.

Not that she had given him much choice when he discovered her standing before him. For the second time in his life, he found himself on his knees, bellows of pain ripped from his throat.

Only this time it wasn't because Warriors were trying to kill him. It was because Deirdre had unbound his god, a god Larena had known he held within him but hadn't told him.

Malcolm had wanted to run from Deirdre as fast as he could, but the newness of his god, the rage and the sheer power that ran through his fingertips, was too much.

Deirdre was much more intelligent than Malcolm had ever given her credit for. "Stay with me. Be the leader of my Warriors, and I'll allow Larena to live," she had promised him.

Malcolm couldn't attack her. She was much too powerful for him, and after all Larena had done for him, he wanted to protect her if he could. So he had agreed to Deirdre's terms.

And became the monster Larena and the others at MacLeod Castle hunted.

Deirdre had done more than release his god. She had made his scars from the attack vanish as well as healed his right arm so he could use it once more.

Yet, when he saw himself in the reflection of a loch, he wasn't the same man he'd been just a year earlier. He was something different, something cold.

Something evil.

A horn sounded to his right as a car came up behind him while he leisurely walked along the roadside. Now he wasn't just evil, he was evil that had been transported through time hundreds of years into the future.

It was a world that dazzled him. So much had changed. He had wasted no time in diving into the new culture and language. Thanks to the god within him, he'd caught on very quickly.

Malcolm could see himself with his own flat, sitting on the sofa watching the telly every night. He could see himself fading into the crowds of people in a large city.

A part of him was tempted to run off and do just that. If there was a chance he could do it, he would. But he knew Deirdre would find him. With her black magic, there was very little she couldn't do.

Malcolm tensed when he sensed a car slowing as it neared him. He glanced over his shoulder to find the window of the sleek red sports car being rolled down. The woman within had stunning black hair and the brightest green eyes he had ever seen.

Before he'd been a Warrior or his body ruined, he'd had his share of women. He'd quite forgotten what it felt like to have a woman smile at him with interest.

"Hello," she all but purred.

Malcolm might be interested, but he knew better than to bring a woman into his world. It would mean certain death for her. He might have evil inside him, he might work alongside evil, but he wouldn't kill an innocent.

*You're about to. Nothing gets more innocent than children.*

Malcolm inwardly shook his head to clear it. "Hello," he responded.

"Are you lost?" the woman asked.

He shook his head and continued walking. He'd hoped the woman would take the hint and go away, but she kept the car rolling slowly beside him.

"Can I give you a ride? It's rather cold out."

Malcolm glanced at the sky. It would snow again soon, possibly by nighttime. "I enjoy the weather."

She laughed. "I don't think I've ever met anyone quite like you. There's something different about you."

Malcolm stopped and leaned his hands on the door of her car. "You're a verra beautiful woman. You shouldna talk to men you doona know."

"Is that a threat?" she asked, wariness sharpening her gaze.

"Nay. Just an observation. Thank you for the offer, but I enjoy walking."

He straightened, and the woman took off without another word. Malcolm sighed. He wouldn't have minded her conversation. Or her body.

But if he had gotten in the car, he'd have arrived in Edinburgh too soon.

He still couldn't believe he was going to carry out Deirdre's command to kill a school full of children in order to find a Druid within it. Was Larena's life worth those of a multitude of children?

Malcolm started walking again. There was no doubt that Larena's life wasn't worth more than even one child's, but if he didn't carry out Deirdre's orders she'd send someone else. At least Malcolm would make sure none of the children suffered.

That wasn't a lot, but it was something. If he'd been the man he used to be, the man who had risked his family's ire to help Larena, he would be rushing to Edinburgh and the school to try and save the children and the Druid.

But that man was long dead. The man he'd used to be had died, and in his place stood a cold man. A man without emotion.

A man without a soul.

Danielle puffed her checks and blew out an exhausted breath as she stood in one of the towers overlooking the sea. The day had begun by fighting off wyrran before she had arrived at MacLeod Castle.

But once she was inside the castle, the women had taken over. They had gone over their names with her, and even told her stories of how they'd met their Warriors and came to be at the castle. Even now, recalling the tales of their adventures made her eyes widen.

Then had come a tour of the castle and the surrounding land.

"I was wondering when I'd get to see you again."

With a smile, she whirled around to find Ian leaning casually against the doorway, but not even his nonchalant attitude could hide the unease in his beautiful sherry eyes.

"They've certainly kept me busy. I think it was because they knew the men wanted to talk to you, and they didn't want me to feel left out."

"They did want to talk to me," he said, and pushed away from the door. His light brown hair was disheveled, as if he'd sent his fingers through it multiple times.

Danielle turned her back to the wall, curious about what had occurred. "What happened? Things were tense when I left."

"They didna come find me because they couldna.

There was something that blocked Broc from being able to use his powers to find me. Or Deirdre. Which was a first for him."

"Do you feel better knowing they didn't forget you?"

Ian nodded. "Four others allowed the Druids to move them through time. To search for me."

"It's obvious these people care greatly about you."

"I should no' ever have questioned it."

Danielle closed the distance between them. "Ian, you may be immortal with a powerful god inside you, but you are still just a man. You have feelings and emotions that are normal for anyone."

"I shouldna have questioned them," he repeated, his eyes blazing with self-loathing and a need for comfort that nearly made her knees buckle.

Danielle rose up on her toes and wrapped her arms around his neck. As soon as she touched him, he enveloped her in a crushing embrace.

"I would have questioned it as well," she whispered.

Ian buried his face in her neck and just held her.

"You're home, Ian. You're home," she said.

Many moments passed before he lifted his head and inhaled deeply. He pulled out of her arms, but didn't release her. "There's more. I wasna transported through time by Deirdre."

"Then by whom?"

"Another *drough*. A man named Declan Wallace."

Danielle raised a brow, then burst out laughing. "Declan Wallace? *The* Declan Wallace? He's a playboy, Ian. All he cares about are fast cars, fast money, and fast women."

"Doona be fooled, Danielle. That's the man I was told of. The others fought him and rescued Saffron from him."

"Ah," Danielle muttered. "It makes sense now."

"What does?"

"Saffron. She keeps herself apart from everyone. I thought it was because she was blind, but now I know it's because of Declan. Do any of them know what he did to her?"

"He blinded her and kept her chained in a dungeon."

"Shit." Danielle rubbed her forehead and began to pace the tower. "And I thought my life was bad. What does Declan want?"

"Deirdre, it appears. He's the one who brought her through time. They also think Declan held Deirdre for a while, which is why no one saw much of the wyrran."

Danielle halted. "With the wyrran running loose, that means Deirdre is free of Declan."

"Aye. We doona know if they are working together or no'."

"And the only way to find that out is by getting close to them."

"Doona even think about it," Ian stated, and took her hand before she could pace once more. "Cara said you made a call today?"

Danielle nodded, not surprised Ian changed the subject. "I called my flatmates to let them know I was fine. And to get my car. Whitney told me she got engaged to be married. We were supposed to celebrate, but I've put her off for the moment. They had many questions that I answered as best I could."

"Is that what's bothering you?"

"It's not what is bothering me, Ian, it's what's not."

He frowned. "I doona understand."

"Whitney told me my boss called. She gave my biggest client to another guy at work. I've also been told if I don't come in tomorrow I'm sacked."

"Sacked?"

"I'll lose my job. It's a job I worked years to get."

She saw Ian's face harden a fraction as he released her hand. "Fallon can have you home in a blink."

"That's just it," she said with a smile. "I don't care about that stupid job anymore. What is going on, what we're fighting, is much more important than my job with an architecture firm."

"You're . . . staying?"

"I'm staying."

The smile started slowly, then pulled at the corners of Ian's mouth until it brightened even his eyes. "Just what I wanted to hear," he said before he pulled her against his chest and kissed her.

# CHAPTER
# TWENTY-TWO

Danielle finished blow-drying her hair as she remembered the kiss in the tower. The taste of Ian was more delicious than she remembered. She loved the hard feel of him, the heat of him. And the need driving him.

They'd been interrupted by the arrival of supper, and all through the meal she'd found she couldn't look away from Ian. He'd been seated across from her so that their gazes met constantly.

The small smile she'd seen on his lips had made her stomach feel as if it were full of butterflies. But it was the desire she saw in his eyes that made her clench her legs together.

He'd disappeared while she and the other women cleaned the table. She'd wanted to go looking for him, but he needed time alone in the castle where he'd spent time with his twin.

Danielle shut off the blow-dryer and looked at herself in the mirror in the small bathroom connected to her room. She'd been fascinated to discover the MacLeods had modernized the castle through the years.

The bathroom might not be large or extravagant, but it had everything she needed. And that was enough.

Danielle opened the door to the bureau where she'd unpacked her clothes. Clothes that Larena and Fallon had retrieved from her flat for her.

Whitney and Claire hadn't wanted to pack some of her stuff, but Danielle had managed to convince them. With Fallon's power of teleporting, though they called it jumping, it took him but seconds to get from one place to another.

Danielle touched the white nightgown she'd worn the night before when she and Ian had made love. It had been the only thing at the store other than a flannel one with a high neck and long sleeves that reached to the floor.

The castle was a bit draftier than the inn, so Danielle opted for one of her favorite sets of pj's. She tugged on the red short-sleeved shirt and the long black pants with red, pink, and white hearts all over them.

She was finishing brushing her teeth and combing her hair when she caught what sounded like a scream. The castle stayed quiet, so she didn't fear an attack, but something was obviously going on.

When she heard the faint cry again, Danielle cracked open her door and poked her head outside. She stepped out into the long corridor and looked first one way and then the other.

The sound of the cry again had her jerking her head back around. She started toward Saffron's room, a sneaking suspicion that the Druid was having a more difficult time than she told anyone.

She was just steps away when a hand covered her mouth and pulled her into the shadows and against a hard, warm chest she knew all too well.

"Shh," Ian whispered and jerked his chin toward Saffron's door.

Danielle gripped his hand and pulled it from her mouth as she saw a man appear out of nowhere and silently enter Saffron's room. She looked at Ian.

Before she could ask, he put a finger to her lips. "Come."

They moved quietly down the hall. Danielle leaned her head over and was able to see through the crack in Saffron's door to find Camdyn smoothing his hand over her forehead, soothing away the nightmare that had overwhelmed her.

For long moments she and Ian watched Camdyn. Camdyn said not a word, simply put one hand on Saffron as if he really didn't want to touch her but couldn't help himself. His body was rigid and turned sideways away from her and the bed, as if he couldn't stand to look at her.

That one simple touch helped to calm Saffron, however. Even when she drifted off to a peaceful sleep and Camdyn had removed his hand from her forehead, he didn't leave. There was something in the way he stood by Saffron's bed, still as a statue, silent as the night, that pulled at Danielle's heart.

She didn't want to go when Ian tugged her away from the door, but she'd spied on them enough. Neither said a word until Danielle closed her door and turned to look at Ian.

"How did you know Camdyn would go to her?"

"I didna," Ian admitted. "I heard something and feared it was you. I was on my way to your chamber when I spotted him. So I waited."

"He didn't want to be with her."

Ian sighed and slowly shook his head. "He never faced her. He kept his body sideways to the bed."

"If he didn't want to be there, why did he help her?"

"That is a good question, is it no?" Ian asked. "One I doona believe we'll have answered anytime soon."

"His eyes. They seemed so haunted."

"Lucan told me it was Camdyn who carried Saffron out of Declan's dungeon. That could be the reason he feels he must help her."

"No." Danielle shook her head. "I may not know a lot about men, but it's more than that. Any of the women could have gone to comfort Saffron."

"Is that what you were doing?"

"I was. She didn't speak much today, but I was told she was from America. We have that in common."

"And her family?"

"Reaghan is trying to discover where they are. Apparently Saffron comes from a wealthy family who likes to travel."

Ian looked around her chamber. "Are you comfortable here?"

"I am. I sent my boss, Isabella, a message tonight. I quit my job."

"Will you be able to find another?"

Danielle shrugged as she walked to the bed. She pulled back the covers and fluffed her pillow. "I don't care anymore. I have a little money saved if it's needed. But I need to see what brought me here carried out. Not just delivering the key, but seeing Deirdre's end. And Declan's."

Ian came up behind her and stilled her hands with his. Danielle closed her eyes and let his heat wrap around her. She felt herself grow damp at his nearness. Her breasts swelled and her nipples pebbled.

All because he touched her.

"Have you given the MacLeods the key?" Ian whispered, his breath warm against her neck.

"N-no," she managed as goose bumps rose along her arms.

Ian moved his mouth to her other ear and nibbled along the delicate, sensitive skin. "Why no'?"

"I don't know. It won't let me."

He spun her around so she faced him. With his forehead furrowed and his eyes searching hers, he asked, "And why no'?"

"It's odd really." She sank onto the bed and shrugged. "The key was in such a hurry to get here. It wouldn't even allow me to wait out the storm I got caught it. Even when we reached MacLeod land it was ecstatic to find them."

"Then?" Ian urged.

"Once we were inside the castle, it stopped. It kept telling me 'Not now.' "

"What is that supposed to mean?"

"It doesn't want me to give it to anyone now."

Ian rubbed his hand over his forehead and twisted his lips. "Is it because I'm here?"

"Nay. There's something odd in the castle, Ian. Like an undercurrent of . . . something. I cannot name it, but it's there."

He nodded. "I thought it was just me because I'm fighting Farmire for control still."

"No, I think it's more than that. I wouldn't feel it otherwise. Have any of the other Warriors mentioned it?"

"Nay. The Druids?"

She shook her head. "Not a word. The longer I'm in the castle the more I feel it."

"I'll talk to the MacLeods tomorrow." He leaned over her, causing her to recline back on the bed. "For now, I want a taste of you."

"Just a taste?" she teased.

He smiled again, small, hesitant, but a smile nonetheless. Danielle rejoiced and slid her hands up his well-defined arms to the thick sinew of his shoulders.

"Much more than a taste," he whispered, his voice low and seductive.

He kissed her slowly, languidly, as if he were putting it all to memory. Danielle threaded her fingers in his light brown hair to find it damp and cool to the touch.

Her body melted under his expert mouth. Did the man ever know how to kiss! He deepened the kiss then as his body leisurely lowered atop hers.

Danielle enjoyed the feel of him atop her. She ran her hands over his shoulders, loving the way the muscles in those shoulders and his back moved beneath her hands.

Undulating. Bunching. Straining.

Urgency entered the kiss on the sound of her moan. The hot, hard length of his erection pressed against her stomach, reminding her how good he'd felt inside her.

Danielle slid her bare feet up from his ankles to his jeans-encased knees, urging him for more, needing more. As if sensing her growing desire, Ian rocked his hips against her softness.

She tore her mouth from his and cried out at the utter pleasure that simple movement gave her. Danielle clawed at the white short-sleeved tee he wore. In a heartbeat Ian had it off and thrown to the floor.

Danielle moaned at the feel of his bare skin beneath her fingers. "You have the most beautiful body."

He shook his head, but there was a smile on his lips. "Nay. It's your body that leaves me speechless."

Tears gathered in Danielle's eyes. "No one has ever said anything so sweet to me before."

"They were fools," he whispered as he kissed across her jaw and down her neck. "Complete fools."

Danielle hadn't thought the night before could ever be beaten, but with every touch, every caress, every sensual, delightful kiss, Ian was showing her something so much more.

He was giving her a new world, showing her a new place that belonged just to the two of them. A place where nothing and no one could hurt them.

Danielle rotated her hips against his hardness, seeking more of him. Ian claimed her mouth in a hot, demanding kiss that sent her senses reeling on a ride that took her breath away.

She gasped into his mouth when he cupped her breast and rolled the nipple between his fingers through her thin shirt. Heat instantly filled her. When he pinched her nipple, she felt a flood of wetness between her legs.

"Off," Ian muttered.

Danielle tried to grab her shirt to remove it, but before she could, she saw a blue claw lengthen from his finger. It barely registered in her mind before he had split open her shirt.

She was reeling from it all when his mouth found her nipple and began to suck while his other hand thumbed and rolled the other.

"Ian," she whispered and clung to him as her body spiraled out of control.

Sweat glistened over her skin as he continued to tease and suckle her breasts. Danielle gripped the sheets in her fists and ground her hips against him. She could feel herself peaking, knew she was so close.

She'd always had a hard time reaching orgasm with a man, so for Ian to call forth one so effortlessly left her dazed, her body shaking and oh, so needy.

There was another ripping sound, and then she felt cool air upon her heated skin as her pants were jerked away. Danielle wanted to wrap her legs around Ian, but with one hand upon her thigh he held her still.

She whimpered, needing to move, to have that hardness against her.

Danielle's breath locked in her lungs when his finger

brushed aside her curls to touch her swollen softness. He ran his finger up and down her sex, spreading her wetness.

She rocked against his hand, her climax building so that she wound tighter and tighter inside. He dipped a finger inside her, filling her. He thrust once, twice, then pulled out.

Danielle moaned, her head thrashing from side to side as she sought more. His finger circled her clitoris, wringing a startled cry from her. Again and again he encircled the swollen nub until she shook with need. All the while he rolled first one nipple then the other with his tongue before nipping the hard peak.

Every nerve in her body trembled and shuddered. She was on the edge of a cliff, waiting to go over the side, but Ian held her, wringing more cries of pleasure from her.

Danielle moaned as one finger, then two filled her as his thumb stimulated her clitoris. His fingers pumped inside her as he took her to a new level.

"Come for me," he whispered.

Danielle threw back her head and screamed as her orgasm claimed her, took her spiraling into an abyss of pleasure so profound, so utterly beautiful, she knew she'd never be the same.

# CHAPTER
# TWENTY-THREE

Ian watched the emotion cross Danielle's face as her body clamped down on his fingers and she peaked. She was glorious with her face flushed, her lips swollen from their kisses, and her body open to him.

He was enthralled. Fascinated.

Completely mesmerized.

By a woman with a smile that brought out the sunshine, silver hair, and the most amazing emerald eyes he had ever seen.

Ian had known he was in trouble the moment he held her nearly naked body against his after pulling her from the frozen loch. It had only gotten worse the longer he was with her.

She made him feel like a man again. She made him . . . feel.

It was a dangerous thing for any man, but most especially a Warrior. Deirdre was still out there, and now there was also Declan. How could Ian be the Warrior he needed to be to end them and still look Danielle in the face afterward?

He rose over her, tremors of her climax still racking

her lithe body. She opened her eyes and smiled content-
edly up at him.

Whether she knew it or not, Danielle had given him
a reason to hold Farmire at bay. Being near her soothed
him in ways he couldn't begin to understand, and didn't
care if he ever did.

Ian let his gaze run over her full breasts and pale
pink nipples to her trim waist and flared hips to stop at
the amazing triangle of silvery blond curls between her
legs.

He bent and took her lips in a kiss full of longing and
hope, of desire and need so bright, so intense, Ian thought
he might drown in it.

A moan tore from him when Danielle's arms wrapped
around him and tugged him atop her. He rocked his
arousal against her and smiled when she gasped and dug
her nails into his back.

Ian rolled to his back, bringing Danielle with him
until she sat astride him. She broke the kiss and smiled
wantonly.

"All my life I thought I couldn't feel anything during
sex."

Ian frowned. The idea of her with another man made
his blood boil. She was his. Only his. And he would
prove it to her this night. "What do you mean?"

"No one has ever made me feel so alive, so free," she
said, the last word nothing but a whisper. Her eyes caught
and held his. "I thought there was something wrong with
me."

"There's nothing wrong with you." Ian wanted to find
the men who had dared to touch her, who had dared to
make her feel so inadequate and beat them to a pulp.
"You're perfect."

She framed his face with her hands and kissed him
slowly and softly. "No, Ian Kerr. You are perfect."

Ian could have argued with her, but instead he wanted to show her how much he desired her, how desperately he yearned for more of her.

He slid his fingers into her long, thick hair and held the back of her head as he kissed her. Rough. Demanding. Unrelenting.

And she answered him, their tongues dueling in a dance as old as time.

Ian's hands smoothed down her satiny skin to rest at her hips. He held her still while he lifted his hips and rubbed against her soft, swollen sex.

Her moan was kindling to the fire raging within him.

When she sat up and gazed at him with eyes darkened by desire, his balls tightened in response. He'd never seen a woman so beautiful, so full of life and passion. He didn't know why she was in his arms, but he knew that's where he wanted her to stay.

Forever.

The thought sent a thread of alarm through him, but before he could think more about it, Danielle rose over him, her softness waiting to take his hardness.

Ian watched as the thick, swollen head of his erection brushed against her sex. She was so wet it made his cock jump in anticipation.

He held his breath as she took him inside her inch by agonizing inch. His fingers dug into her flesh as he struggled not to thrust deep while he tugged her down his length.

With a groan he felt his erection stretching her, filling her tightness. When he glanced up at her face he found her head flung back and her eyes closed. And it was all he could do not to spend himself right then.

Ian took in a ragged breath when he was seated inside her fully. He told himself not to move, to let Danielle take charge, but he found it near impossible.

She rose up on her knees, only to lower herself upon him once more. Again and again she impaled herself upon his aching cock, faster, harder each time. Her soft cries filled the chamber as his breath came in great gasps.

He was riveted by the way her hips undulated and her breasts bounced. He was transfixed by the pleasure on her face.

And he was captivated to see his rod slide in and out of her slick heat.

Ian cupped her breasts and squeezed her nipples. Danielle cried out and rocked her hips back and forth. He thumbed her nipples, hardening even more when her lips parted and soft cries echoed in the chamber.

He sat up and held her tight as he kissed her. Her arms locked around him as their bodies continued to move against each other sensuously, delightfully.

Her nails dug into his back as she suddenly stiffened in his arms. Ian loved the feel of her clamping down on him, loved feeling her climax sweep through her body. But the orgasm he'd been holding off surged forward.

Ian pushed Danielle onto her back. He pulled out of her and then flipped her onto her stomach. With his jaw clenched, he lifted her hips and slid back inside her with one solid thrust.

She moaned into the blanket, her hands fisting the covers. Ian began to pump his hips, sliding in and out of her quick and hard. The faster he thrust inside her, the louder her moans became.

Ian held her hips still as he set up a driving rhythm. Harder, faster he plunged inside her. And when he heard her scream his name a heartbeat before she peaked again, he gave himself up to his climax.

With one last thrust, he threw back his head and shouted as he poured himself inside her. Waves upon waves of pleasure rolled through them, taking them, carrying them higher than ever before.

Ian wrapped his arms around Danielle and brought her against him as he fell to his side. She lay with her back to his front, their breathing harsh in the silence of the room.

Slowly their heartbeats and their breathing calmed once more. With their limbs tangled together, they lay in the safety of each other's arms.

Deirdre looked dispassionately at the Druid Toby held in his grasp.

"You've done very well, Toby," Deirdre complimented her slave. He was as willing to serve her as her wyrran were. Some men had incredible mental strength, but most, like Toby, were weak and that allowed Deirdre to take over their minds.

"A Druid. Just as you asked for, mistress."

The Druid paled when Deirdre neared. Deirdre had to give the Druid credit for hiding the fear she sensed in her so well.

"I'm not a Druid," the woman said.

Deirdre glanced at the Druid's soft brown hair. "You may be plain, but I sense your magic. There's no use lying to me."

Still, the Druid held her head high. Fury radiated from her light brown eyes, fury and . . . death. Ah, so the Druid wanted her death. Deirdre smiled inwardly.

Deirdre looked over the Druid at her leisure before she said, "You have no idea what I went through to find you."

The Druid spat at her. "I hope you rot in Hell."

Deirdre wiped the spittle from her face. "Why would I rot when I do His bidding?" she asked. "You are right to fear me, Druid. I may have been away for several centuries, but I'm back. And I need your magic."

"I won't give it to you," the Druid said through clenched teeth.

Deirdre merely smiled. "Everyone says that. Be original for once. Respond differently."

"Everyone refuses because they know the evil inside you. And no matter how strong you think you are, you'll be defeated."

"You know who I am, don't you?" Deirdre asked.

The Druid refused to answer, but Deirdre saw a flash of panic in the woman's eyes.

"I've killed so many Druids for their magic. I've lived for over a thousand years. There is nothing you can do to stop me, nothing you can do to keep yourself safe."

And to prove it, Deirdre jerked her chin toward the huge slab of rock behind her. The Druid began to scream as Toby tossed her roughly onto the rock.

Toby might just be one man, and the Druid desperate to get free, but Deirdre had given Toby extra strength when she'd taken over his mind. The Druid wasn't going anywhere Deirdre didn't want her to go.

"Finished," Toby said and took a step back.

Deirdre turned to see the Druid strapped to the table by her wrists and ankles. "Perfect," Deirdre said as she reached for the knife.

She'd done this ceremony countless times over the millennia as she killed Druids and took their magic. Each time was a thrill, a rush so heady it made her sway.

Deirdre slashed the Druid's wrists and watched as the blood, thick and dark red, leaked from the cuts onto the hollowed grooves of the table. Those grooves spilled the blood into the four corners of the table where it was collected into goblets.

While the blood flowed, Deirdre began to chant the

ancient spell that called up Satan and all his evil. A black cloud rose up from beneath the stone slab and hovered over the Druid.

The Druid tried to scream, but she was weak from loss of blood and could only whimper. Deirdre watched as the cloud, an evil spirit from Hell, descended onto the Druid.

The Druid thrashed on the table, her pitiful half screams filling the high-ceilinged room as the spirit took the Druid's soul.

"I am yours!" Deirdre screamed and plunged the dagger through the spirit and into the Druid's stomach.

The ghoul vanished, and the girl's lifeless eyes stared above her. But the ceremony was far from over.

At one time Deirdre's servants would have handed her the goblets to drink. Now, it was Toby in his awkward and clumsy way.

Deirdre drained each goblet, and as the last drop of the last goblet hit her lips, she threw her arms wide as the wind began to howl and swirl. As the new magic mixed with hers she threw back her head, her long white hair lifting above and around her.

The power that filled her wasn't as great as she had once experienced, but it was still magic.

When the wind died, Deirdre faced Toby. "Get rid of the body and clean up."

"Aye, mistress."

# CHAPTER
# TWENTY-FOUR

Danielle had never slept so well as she did in Ian's arms. The only thing that could have been better was if he'd still been in her bed when she woke that morning.

The slow, sensuous smile he gave her when she descended the stairs into the great hall made her stomach flip before falling to her feet.

"I hope you slept well," Marcail said as she walked past Danielle.

"I did," Danielle responded.

Marcail winked and said, "I'm glad you asked for the spell yesterday. I had a feeling you would need it soon."

Danielle licked her lips to try and hide her grin. "Is it so obvious I was with Ian?"

"Aye, but I think it's fabulous. The spell will keep you from getting with child."

"And if I conceived before?"

Marcail frowned. "The babe will not last."

Danielle bit her lip, wondering if she'd done the right thing. Yet, she had just had her menstrual cycle a few days before meeting Ian, so she should be safe. She looked around the hall and saw a few people were missing. "Where is Kirstin?"

The Druid had been silent and withdrawn ever since she had arrived with Ramsey just moments after Danielle and Ian.

"Still in her chamber," Reaghan answered on her way to the kitchen.

Danielle started to follow her until she spotted Saffron sitting at the table. Danielle recalled the previous night and Saffron's nightmare. She wondered if Saffron remembered it as well, or if she knew of the Warrior who had gone to soothe her.

"She won't talk much," Cara whispered as she came to stand by Danielle. "We know she suffered at Declan's hands, but she won't talk about it."

"Sometimes it's easier to try to forget than to talk about it."

Cara shrugged. "We want to help her, but she won't let us."

"She's scared."

"She has every reason to be based on what I've been told about Declan."

Danielle rubbed her hands up and down her arms. "First Deirdre, now Declan. Will there be more?"

Cara sighed. "Most likely."

"Has there been any word on Saffron's family? Ian told me she wanted to go home and that her family was trying to be located."

Cara's lips flattened as she looked away. "Gwynn got news this morning about it."

"I take that to mean it isn't good news."

"Nay," Cara murmured and walked away.

Danielle took a deep breath and walked to Saffron. She was steps away when Saffron's head turned toward her.

"Hello, Danielle."

Danielle paused.

Saffron smiled. "My apologies. When the eyesight is taken, other senses become more alert. You have a distinct cadence to your walk."

"Ah," Danielle said, unsure of what to say.

Saffron's head cocked to the side. "I heard it yesterday, and then again today. Your accent, it's a mix, isn't it?"

"Yes. I spent the first twelve years of my life in Florida."

Saffron smiled and motioned to the spot beside her on the bench. "Please, sit. Tell me more."

"There's not much to tell. My father was Scottish and my mother American. He came to the U.S. for work, and fell in love."

"How did you end up back in Scotland?"

"My parents died in a car accident. The only family left was my father's sisters, so they took me in."

Saffron's hand reached for her, and after a moment of searching, she rested her hand atop Danielle's. "I'm sorry."

"I am too."

"Do you miss Florida?"

"A little. Where are you from?"

"Colorado Springs," Saffron said with a bright smile. "I've always loved it there. Gwynn is from Texas."

Danielle chuckled. "I know. I could peg that accent of hers anywhere."

They shared a quick laugh. Danielle noticed how everyone in the hall, especially Camdyn, looked at Saffron.

Saffron ducked her head and ran her finger up the leg of her faded blue jeans. "My mother hated it when I wore jeans. She said they were for the lower class."

"What do you think about them?"

"At first I wore them to piss her off. Now I wear them because I think they're comfortable. Don't get me wrong, I still love wearing dresses and heels, but there's just something so . . ."

"Comforting?" Danielle offered.

"Yes," Saffron said with another smile. "There is definitely something comforting about jeans. Tell me, what is your magic?"

Danielle glanced around, but found only Ian watching her. She scooted closer to Saffron since she remembered how well the Warriors could hear. "Objects find me and let me know who they belong to."

"Objects? Like rings and such?"

"Anything really. I've found money before and it told me who it belonged to."

"What if you don't want to bring the item to its owner?"

Danielle blew out a breath and tucked a strand of hair behind her ear. "I'm not given a choice. If I refuse or hesitate, an unbearable pain assaults me."

"What brought you to the castle?"

It wasn't that Danielle didn't want to tell her, it's that the key had asked her not to speak of it yet.

"Never mind," Saffron said. "I shouldn't have asked."

"Does your magic work the other way?" Isla asked.

Danielle jerked as she turned to find Isla beside her. "You heard?"

"Aye," Isla said with a sheepish smile. "I'm sorry. I shouldn't have eavesdropped."

"It's all right," Danielle told her.

"But can it work the other way?" Isla asked again. "Can you search for something?"

Danielle soon found the entire hall looking at her. Her gaze met Ian's, and he gave a small nod of encouragement. "I don't know. I've never tried it," she finally answered.

"What do you want her to do?" Hayden asked Isla.

Isla licked her lips. "I thought maybe Danielle could discover the spell Declan used to take Saffron's sight since we've had no luck reversing it."

Danielle felt as if she'd been punched in the stomach. She wanted to help Saffron, but what they were asking seemed impossible. She'd never tried anything like it before.

"Please," Saffron said. "Just one try."

Danielle swallowed and took Saffron's hands in hers. "I don't think this will work, but I'll try."

All conversation ceased when Danielle took a deep breath and closed her eyes. She had no idea where to begin. She hadn't pushed her magic away, but neither had she worked at it much.

"Let your magic surround you," Isla said. "Feel it beating inside you."

Almost as if it had been waiting for her, Danielle's magic swelled inside her. She let it fill her, soaking up every fiber of it into her being.

"Listen for the chanting," Reaghan whispered in her ear.

Danielle was too busy floating along with her magic to care about chanting. She'd never heard chanting before, so why would she now?

It was as if time ceased as her magic continued to grow. It was all around her, through her, in her. And then, distantly, she heard something.

She strained, begging her magic to let her hear it. And then . . . *chanting*.

Danielle smiled when she heard it. It was so faint she couldn't hear the words, but she knew what it was. She wanted to draw closer to it, to learn what they were saying.

"Now search Saffron for the spell," Isla urged. "Forget the chanting for now. Look for the spell Declan used."

Danielle didn't want to leave the chanting, but Isla's insistent voice wouldn't let her be until she did. Danielle thought of Saffron, of sweet, quiet, forlorn Saffron.

Suddenly, Danielle's hands began to warm. Long, slim fingers tightened around her hands.

*Saffron. I have had a hold of Saffron.*

Danielle had only used very basic spells, and had just learned bigger ones when Aunt Josie had died. How was she supposed to know what spell Declan had used?

Despite not having a clue what to look for, Danielle continued to let her magic peer around Saffron, seeking, searching.

When she came to something that felt wrong, her magic recoiled. Danielle leaned forward, seeking it once more. And when the full cloud of evil assaulted her, she released Saffron and fell off the bench in her effort to get away.

"Danielle?" Ian whispered as his arms came around her.

She clung to him and opened her eyes to look at Saffron.

Saffron slowly stood. When she reached to steady herself on the table, Danielle saw how her hand shook.

"You felt it, didn't you?" Saffron asked.

Danielle didn't have to ask what Saffron meant. "I did."

"Felt what?" Ian demanded to know.

Saffron shifted her head to the sound of Ian's voice. "Declan. She felt Declan's malice, his evil. He used his magic on me, and because of it, a part of him is inside me."

Danielle lifted her head from Ian's chest. "Yes, I felt him."

Saffron walked away, and Danielle ached for the re-signation she saw in her eyes. She wanted to help Saf-fron, but she'd been wholly unprepared for such evil.

"What happened?" Reaghan asked.

Danielle shrugged. "I'm not sure. One moment I was searching, and the next it was if I were surrounded by sludge, a darkness so deep, so overwhelming, I knew it would swallow me. It kept trying to pull me under."

"Damn," Isla said. She rubbed a finger on her temple and slowly shook her head. "I had thought it might work."

Hayden pulled his wife into his arms and rubbed her back with his large hand. "It was worth a try, love."

"I'll try again." Danielle looked up to find Ian study-ing her. "I know what to expect now, and the spell needs to be reversed. She's hurting, Ian."

"Aye, I know," Ian said with a sigh. "I just doona want you harmed."

Reaghan folded her hands in front of her and smiled. "That's why Isla and I are here. We won't let her get pulled into the chanting or Declan's evil."

"Chanting?" Ian repeated. "She can get pulled into it?"

Reaghan shrugged and Isla didn't respond. Danielle found Ian's eyes once more on her.

"Do you trust Isla and Reaghan?" Danielle asked.

Ian gave a firm nod. "Of course."

"Then so I do."

"My family," Saffron said, her voice clear and high in the great hall as she stood by the hearth. "Have you found them?"

Danielle turned with Ian to watch as Gwynn rose from her seat at the table. "Saffron, we can do this later."

"Now," Saffron demanded.

Gwynn linked fingers with Logan and took a deep breath before she said, "I couldn't track down your mother and stepfather exactly. They were in Switzerland last week skiing, but their flight plan had them heading to the Bahamas."

Though Saffron's face never changed, Danielle saw the way her breath hitched.

"The rest," Saffron said.

Gwynn looked at Fallon, who stood with his arms crossed over his chest. At Fallon's nod Gwynn cleared her throat. "I, ah . . . I found where your mother had petitioned to have you declared dead."

Danielle could have heard a pin drop, the great hall was so quiet. She wished she could help Saffron. Danielle recalled how it felt to think she was alone in the world. She'd felt as if she were in the middle of the ocean, tossed around in a massive storm with no land or ship in sight.

It had been terrifying. All these years later, Danielle could still feel that same terror, that same sinking feeling of loneliness that settled like a cold weight in her belly.

Danielle pulled out of Ian's arms and started toward Saffron. She would try to find the spell inside Saffron again. Danielle might be the only one who could help the Druid, and she wouldn't rest until she could.

She was just strides away from Saffron when Saffron went to take a step back that would put her inside the massive hearth. In a blink, Camdyn was behind her.

"Easy," Danielle heard him murmur to Saffron.

Danielle took Saffron's hands then and pulled her into one of the empty chairs placed around the hearth.

"I didn't mean to do that," Saffron whispered, her face ashen.

Danielle squatted next to the chair. "What can I do for you?"

"Remove this spell blinding me so I can be the one to kill Declan."

Saffron's words were spoken softly, like a lady of

society, but they were said with such heat and rage that it had Danielle leaning away from her.

"I'll keep trying," Danielle vowed. "I'll keep searching until I find it."

Saffron smiled as a lone tear trailed down her cheek. "You should stay away from me, Danielle. The more you touch his evil, the more it will seep into you. All of you should . . ."

Her voice trailed off. Danielle watched as her eyes went milky white. In an instant everyone was around her, but it was Camdyn who caught her before she fell out of the chair.

Saffron's chest heaved as she blinked and her honey-colored eyes stared sightlessly at those around her. "The children," she whispered, her tears flowing freely now. "He's going to kill the children."

"What children?" Danielle asked. "Saffron, tell us. What children? Where are they?"

"Edinburgh. Deirdre is sending him to kill the children."

"God help us," Sonya said and turned away.

Larena shook her head. "Nay. I won't let him."

Danielle didn't brush Ian's hand away when he helped her to rise. "Malcolm," he whispered in her ear. "It's Larena's cousin. Deirdre found him and released his god. He's now Deirdre's to command."

Malcolm. Danielle had heard that name before. She turned to look at Ian. "He's the one who killed Duncan."

"He is."

# CHAPTER
# TWENTY-FIVE

Ian was surprised that he felt so little anger at Malcolm. Malcolm might have been the one who killed Duncan, but ultimately it was Deirdre's fault.

Deirdre was the one Ian wanted to kill.

"I need to see to Saffron," Danielle said as she pulled out of his arms.

Ian didn't want to let her go. His arms dropped to his sides and he fisted his hands. The hall had erupted in chaos when Saffron announced her vision.

Fallon was trying his best to calm Larena while Quinn, Marcail, Lucan, and Cara stood ready to help if needed.

The others were all speaking of what had happened. All expect two. Kirstin and Charlie.

Ian eyed the new Warrior. He'd asked Quinn about Charlie, but Quinn hadn't had much to say on the matter. It was apparent, however, that the other Warriors didn't care for Charlie one bit.

Kirstin, on the other hand, looked ill. She reminded Ian of a rabbit about to be snared. It knew it was a trap, but it wanted the carrot. Kirstin acted the same way.

Danielle had said there was something wrong because the key refused to be given to the MacLeods. Could it be Kirstin or Charlie? Or both?

The MacLeods had always welcomed any Druid or Warrior into their fold. They had been betrayed but once, and it hadn't been the Druid's fault. Deirdre had gotten into her mind and controlled her.

It was no wonder the MacLeods were as trusting as they were. But Ian had a suspicion the MacLeods' luck was about to run out. The question was, which one was it? Charlie or Kirstin?

The only way for Ian to discover who was disturbing the tranquil peace of the castle was to follow both of them. It wasn't going to be easy, but when it came to those at the castle, especially Danielle, he'd do what he had to do.

He hadn't been there to help Duncan. But he was here now, and he could do something.

"What is it?" Camdyn murmured as he came to stand beside Ian.

"What do you know of Charlie?"

Camdyn snorted. "I doona like him. He's always around, but he never does anything."

"You suspect him of something?" Ian asked as he looked at Camdyn.

Camdyn shrugged and crossed his arms over his chest. "I've watched him. He does nothing that would bring my suspicion. Or at least nothing I can bring to Fallon. Why? What is it?"

If he was going to find out what was amiss in the castle he was going to need help. "Danielle said something was wrong."

Camdyn's brow furrowed. "Wrong how? She's never been to the castle before."

"Something brought her here. It demanded she get

here as soon as she could, but once she was here, it doesn't want to be seen."

Camdyn took a deep breath. "It sounds to me like she is the problem. Is she working for Deirdre?"

"I've seen what she brought to the castle, Camdyn. I know why it's here. It has nothing to do with Deirdre. She was supposed to give it to the MacLeods as soon as she arrived, but she said the . . . thing refused to leave her. It told her not yet."

"Interesting," Camdyn said as he rubbed his chin. "Have you spoken to the MacLeods?"

"Nay. Only you. Look at Charlie and Kirstin. Everyone is trying to decide what to do about Saffron's vision except those two."

"It could be because they're outsiders."

"You know that's a lie. Look at how easily the other Druids fit in here when they arrived."

Camdyn let out a deep breath. "I admit, there seems to be something wrong with Kirstin. It's almost as if she can no' decide if she wants to be here or no'."

"My thoughts exactly."

"What do you want to do?"

Ian lifted his gaze to see Isla and Danielle leading a visibly shaken Saffron up the stairs to her chamber. "I'm going to get to know Charlie better."

"I can no' stand to be near him, so better you than me. I'll spend some time with Kirstin."

"Watch yourself. It could be Deirdre or Declan doing this."

"Or both."

Ian hoped it wasn't, but they couldn't rule out anything. The hall was beginning to calm once more as he made his way to where Charlie sat at the table.

"Is it always like this, mate?" Charlie asked him with a wide smile.

There was something in that smile that made Ian take offense instantly. It wasn't Charlie's good looks, or his overconfident attitude. It was something that went much deeper. "We deal with problems swiftly."

"You seem rather calm about it."

Ian took the seat across from Charlie and rested his forearms on the table. "I hear you escaped Deirdre."

"I did. She's a crazy bitch," Charlie said with a laugh.

"How did you escape her?"

Charlie shrugged and continued eating his breakfast of toast and poached eggs. "I doona know. I knew I couldna stay, so I made a run for it. As I already told Fallon there were verra few wyrran and no other Warriors about."

"And Deirdre's magic didna stop you?"

"I took her by surprise." Charlie finished chewing and swallowing his bit of food. "I expected that hair of hers to grab me, but I got away."

There had been some who had managed to escape Deirdre, but none of them with the ease of which Charlie spoke. Deirdre might not have as many wyrran or Warriors as before, but she was just as powerful. And now she would be furious, which would only fuel her power.

"I'm no' sure I believe you."

Charlie stopped chewing and slowly lowered his fork. "I doona give a bloody damn if you do or doona, mate. The MacLeods do, and they'll be the ones making the decisions."

With that Charlie pushed back his plate and rose from the table to stalk away. Ian stood, and as he started to follow Charlie Arran blocked his path.

"What was that about?" Arran asked.

Ian shrugged. "A hunch."

"Be careful."

"You mean because I doona have control of my god?" Ian asked him.

Arran looked away for a moment before meeting Ian's gaze. "Aye. You say you doona have control, but you look as if you do."

"I'm good at hiding it, Arran."

Ian walked away wondering why Farmire hadn't tried to take control of him as he had when Ian had been in the cave. Was it because he was with people he cared about? Or was it something more?

*Danielle.*

That had been Ian's first thought. As soon as Danielle came into his life everything had changed. Farmire had tried a few times to get the upper hand, but Ian had managed to remain in control both times.

He hadn't cared to know how at the time, but he did now. What if he let his guard down and Farmire seized the moment to take control?

Ian took the stairs three at a time as he followed the path Charlie had taken. He was so lost in his own thoughts he didn't see Charlie until he was nearly upon him.

But it was Danielle pressed against the wall with Charlie's hand by her head that sent Ian over the edge. He growled, and in a blink, released his god.

Danielle's gaze met his. Ian didn't see fear there, but it didn't lessen his rage.

"Easy," Charlie said when he caught sight of Ian. Charlie lifted his hands, palms out, and took a step away from Danielle. "I simply wanted to know if Saffron was all right."

Ian flexed his hands, his claws eager to feel Charlie's blood on them.

"I'll talk to you later, Dani," Charlie said before he turned and walked away.

Only when Charlie had turned the corner did Ian try

to rein in his god. Farmire refused to listen on the first and second try. He demanded Charlie's blood, and it was only because Danielle was near that Ian was able to focus on her and gain the upper hand on his god. He turned to Danielle to see her staring at him, one brow raised.

"Dani?" he repeated.

She shrugged. "It's always been my nickname. So what was all that about?"

Ian opened his mouth to tell her, but he didn't want to worry her until he had more proof. "Nothing."

"I don't like being lied to," she said and reached for the handle of the door near her.

Ian used his speed to get to her before her hand touched the door. "Wait."

"Dammit, Ian," she growled. "Don't scare me like that."

"Sorry." He was mucking up everything. "What did Charlie want?"

"To see how Saffron was. He's worried. I think he likes her."

Ian hadn't seen that one coming. "Is that all he wanted?"

"Yes. Why the interest in Charlie?"

"I doona trust him," Ian whispered as he pulled Danielle into his arms. He breathed in the clean scent of her. "Be careful around him."

Danielle leaned back. "You're frightening me."

She kept her voice low, which told Ian she knew there was more to his curiosity about Charlie than he was telling her.

"Please," he said. "Just be careful. Doona ever be alone with him."

"Ian, just tell me what it is you're thinking."

"I want proof first, Danielle. If I go to them now they'll think it's because I doona have control of my god."

Her fingers were playing with the hem of her sweater. "Are you sure that isn't the reason?"

"Nay. I doona. Which is why I want to know if it's just my imagination, or if it's something more."

Danielle smiled and leaned up to place a quick kiss on his lips. "Then I'll be careful."

Ian didn't let out his breath until she was in Saffron's chamber. He started after Charlie once again. It bothered him that Danielle questioned his motives, but he had seen the worry in her eyes.

She had seen for herself his struggle to remain in control of his god. He was grateful he hadn't lost consciousness around her or, worse, killed her on the occasions when Farmire did take over.

Ian came to a halt when he couldn't figure out if Charlie had gone down the corridor or up to one of the towers. But as Ian listened, he heard footsteps on the winding stairs of the tower.

Without hesitation he followed Charlie, careful to keep at a distance and be very quiet. By the time Ian reached the top of the tower, the door stood slightly ajar.

The last time Ian had been in this tower was when they'd had to restrain Hayden when he'd woken to find Isla gone and had flown into a rage.

It had taken every Warrior in the castle to pin Hayden to the ground. And when Ian had heard the soulful mourning in Hayden's voice when he'd told them Isla was gone, it had taken him aback.

Ian had known there was something going on between Hayden and Isla. He'd even suspected it might be love. But those few words whispered with such anguish and desperation from Hayden's mouth had confirmed it was love. The kind of love that pierced all the way to the soul.

Slowly, Ian leaned forward to peek into the tower. He saw no sign of Charlie, but still he waited, listening for anything. Minutes ticked by until finally Ian poked his head into the tower.

To find it empty.

# CHAPTER
# TWENTY-SIX

Charlie waited at the top of the tower for Ian to follow him. He'd known the moment the Warrior began asking questions that he would be a problem.

There was no way Charlie was going to let down Deirdre.

But now Charlie had the perfect plan. With a little eavesdropping on Danielle and Ian's conversation, Charlie would ensure his place at MacLeod Castle while having Ian asked to leave or possibly killed.

Charlie rubbed his hands together. He was eager to begin, and he'd already set his plan in motion. Too bad no one at the castle had bothered to make him prove what his power was. If they had, they'd have learned he'd lied about being able to control wind.

A laugh nearly escaped him at the thought of seeing everyone's expressions when he began to kill them. Charlie could hardly wait to carry out his deed and return to Deirdre triumphant.

Charlie stood atop the tower and braced himself against the rising wind. He didn't bother to look into the tower as he jumped and landed at the beach below.

He did look up at the castle and give Ian a wave when the Warrior stuck his head out of the window.

"We need to go now," Larena stated for the third time to all those gathered in the great hall.

Danielle felt uncomfortable being included in the meeting, but Fallon had told her she was part of things now, which meant she needed to be in on the decisions.

She found it refreshing, and a bit odd, at how easily they trusted her as well as Charlie and Kirstin. Danielle had tried to talk to Kirstin earlier but had only gotten a few monosyllabic answers before Kirstin walked away.

There was definitely something wrong with Kirstin.

"We have no idea when Saffron's vision will take place," Fallon said in response to Larena's demand.

Larena slammed her hand on the table. "That's my cousin out there!"

"And our friend," Lucan added.

Larena put her head in her hands.

Danielle cleared her throat. "There are also a number of schools in Edinburgh. Saffron, did you see anything that stood out about the school?"

"No," Saffron said softly. "Just death. Lots of death."

Broc shook his head. "I doona understand why Malcolm would kill children. What has this to do with Deirdre?"

"Maybe nothing," Ramsey said.

Galen said, "Maybe his god is in full control of him now."

"Then why no' kill everyone as he travels to Edinburgh?" Hayden asked.

"He's right," Ian added. "If Malcolm's god were in

control there would be a slaughter in every village Malcolm passed through."

"Which brings us to what?" Lucan asked.

Fallon blew out a breath and reached for Larena's hand. "What my wife knew all along. Malcolm is going to this school because Deirdre sent him."

"Again, why?" Camdyn asked.

Logan braced an elbow on the table and looked around him. "What is the one thing Deirdre covets above all else?"

"Druids," the Warriors said in unison.

"Holy Hell," Quinn muttered and raked a hand through his hair.

Larena lifted her head. "Then that's how we find the school. We search until we feel the Druid's magic."

"What happens if we do save the Druid and the children? What do we do about Malcolm?" Ramsey asked.

Larena slowly stood. "Nothing. He's my cousin, my family."

"And mine," Fallon added.

Lucan kissed the back of Cara's hand. "He's part of our family, Larena. But more than that, he was part of this castle."

"You can no' honestly think he'll come willingly," Charlie said. "He's been under Deirdre's influence all this time."

Danielle felt Ian stiffen beside her. She reached under the table and put her hand on Ian's leg in an effort to calm him. He tensed for a moment, then began to relax.

"Tell me, Charlie, where was Malcolm when you escaped Deirdre?" Ian asked.

Charlie laughed easily and shrugged. "I doona know, Ian. I didna stick around to find out."

Danielle noticed how Camdyn and Arran watched Charlie closely. It was obvious from Ian's question that he didn't believe Charlie.

"What do we do about Malcolm?" Danielle asked to turn the attention away from Charlie.

It wasn't that she didn't want to know what was going on, but saving the children and the unknown Druid seemed more important at the moment.

"Broc," Fallon said. "See if you can locate Malcolm. Doona speak to him. I just want to know if he's close to Edinburgh yet."

Broc nodded, then leaned over to kiss Sonya before he rose to his feet. As he headed toward the door, he took off his shirt and tossed it on a nearby chair.

He'd taken just two more steps before his skin turned an indigo blue and huge wings sprouted from his back. Within another heartbeat, he was gone.

"Broc will find Malcolm," Fallon said to the hall at large, but his eyes were on Larena's.

"I have to save him," Larena said.

Fallon briefly closed his eyes. "You may have to face the fact that you can no'."

Gwynn suddenly got to her feet. "I'm going to do some research on how many schools are in Edinburgh. Dani? You want to help?"

"Sure." Danielle looked at Ian, wanting desperately to wrap her arms around him and kiss him.

Ian winked at her and squeezed her hand. It was enough. She rose from the table and hurried after Gwynn who was already up the stairs.

For the next few hours Gwynn and Danielle did search after search, jotting down their findings and the locations.

"At least Broc will be able to find Malcolm," Gwynn said.

Danielle laid aside her pencil. "But soon enough? What I mean is, will everyone be at the right place when it happens?"

"Damn. I didn't think of that." Gwynn tucked her dark hair behind her ears and leaned against the headboard of her bed, her legs crossed. "I saw Malcolm."

"When?"

"On Eigg when Logan and I were retrieving the artifact."

Danielle nodded. She'd been filled in on the artifacts, but none of them had trusted her enough to tell her what the artifacts were or where they were kept. Not that she could blame them. She'd be wary as well.

"So what happened?" Danielle asked.

"They tried to talk to him. Larena wanted him to return to the castle, but he said he couldn't. He didn't talk long. One moment he was there, and the next gone."

"So he can teleport like Fallon?"

Gwynn shook her head. "No, I don't think so. Lightning flashed behind us, so I'm thinking he had something to do with that. We all looked at it, and when we turned back he was gone."

"Does Larena actually think she can convince Malcolm to return here?"

Gwynn looked down at her hands and shrugged. "Logan doesn't seem to think so, but Larena is determined. Malcolm blamed her for Deirdre having him."

"I don't understand."

Gwynn straightened from the headboard and rested her elbows on her legs. "Larena had discovered a scroll that listed all the surnames of those first turned into Warriors. She saw Malcolm's surname."

"Why didn't they tell him?"

"Logan said if given the choice he wouldn't have told Malcolm either. He said Malcolm was a broken, scarred man and all any of them wanted to do was make him feel at home."

Danielle took a deep breath as understanding dawned. "Larena was protecting him."

"Yes, but in doing so she omitted the very thing that could have kept him at the castle and out of Deirdre's hands. She captured him, Dani. Captured him and unbound his god."

Danielle picked her pencil back up and rolled it between her fingers. "What do you think of Charlie?"

"Not much. He's friendly and always there with a smile. Why?"

"It seems that some of the Warriors may not like him."

Gwynn chuckled. "I haven't been here long myself. A few days later Charlie shows up, then you and Ian, and then Kirstin. It's a lot of change. I can see where others might be hesitant to trust."

"Precisely. But what I'm really wanting to know is what kind of . . . vibe . . . do you get from Charlie?"

Gwynn's smile died. "Do you feel something about him, Dani? Is he bothering you?"

"No," she hastily said. "I'm just curious to know why the others might not trust him."

"Fallon wouldn't have allowed him in the castle if they didn't trust or believe his reasons."

Danielle nodded as she realized Gwynn wouldn't give her an answer.

"Although I will admit to getting an odd feeling sometimes," Gwynn said.

Danielle's head snapped up. "What kind of feeling?"

"I can't explain it. It comes and goes so that I feel as if I'm losing my mind."

"Do you know who it's coming from?"

Gwynn shook her head, her black hair moving back

and forth over her shoulders. "It didn't start until you arrived."

Danielle blinked. "Oh." It had never occurred to her that she could be the reason something felt off in the castle.

"I don't think it's you." Gwynn hurried to reassure her. "But it started then."

"When me, Ian, and then Kirstin arrived."

Gwynn bit her lip.

Danielle tapped the eraser on the notepad in front of her. "I didn't feel it until I got to the castle, so I don't think it's Ian."

"Are you sure?"

Danielle thought of the gentle way Ian had held her that first night they made love. Of how his passion had only made hers burn hotter, higher. She recalled how his kiss could make her forget her name and everything around her.

"Yes."

Gwynn smiled. "Maybe it's just that he's still battling for control of his god. Logan said it looked as though he were winning the battle."

"He fights it constantly."

"Not constantly," Gwynn said, a knowing look in her eyes. "I've seen the way he watches you. There's no denying the desire I see in his eyes or in yours for him."

Danielle shifted uneasily on the bed. "So much has changed in my life in just a matter of days. I know how dangerous Ian is. I saw it firsthand when he saved me from the wyrran, and then again when the wyrran attacked Charon's village."

"But?" Gwynn urged.

Danielle smiled. "But the way I feel when I'm with him is like . . ."

"Magic."

"Yes. Magic," Danielle said with a nod. "Ian didn't have to help me get to the castle. He could have left me to die. He could have killed me any number of times since I've been with him. He's made sure I know just how lethal he is, but when I see him here with everyone he considers family, I see there is no way the evil inside him will take over."

Gwynn put her hand on top of Danielle's. "Logan has told me the rage and power that comes with the unbinding of the god is a heady experience. Ian isn't just dealing with the full force of his god, but the death of his twin. The combination might be too much for him."

"No." Danielle rose from the bed. "I won't allow Ian to give in."

"Dani—"

"No," she repeated. "I know Ian. He'd never hurt me."

# CHAPTER
## TWENTY-SEVEN

Charlie smiled as he leaned against the wall outside Gwynn's chamber. What he had just overheard solidified his plans. By the end of the day Ian would be either locked away or banished.

And the beginning of the end of the MacLeods could commence.

Charlie rubbed his hands together in anticipation and walked away, his mind racing with plans.

When he returned to Deirdre she'd praise him for all he had accomplished. He'd be the one she turned to instead of Malcolm. He'd be the one who led her Warriors into battle conquering the world.

How could have he been so foolish as to fear her? Her magic was potent. No one could resist her. They shouldn't even try. He'd struggled, but she had shown him the way to immortality and a future where he stood atop the world.

This was only the beginning.

Danielle left Gwynn's room more upset than she liked. The thought of anyone thinking Ian couldn't control his god infuriated her.

She knew Gwynn was only worrying, but Danielle couldn't help it. Ian had shown his true self to her, and she knew he would never harm her. Nor would she sit by and allow Farmire to take him. She would fight for Ian, even if he didn't fight for himself.

Danielle pulled her hair out of her face to gather it at the back of her head and quickly wrapped the ponytail holder around it.

She rubbed her hands together, her two remaining bangle bracelets clinking together. The need to find Ian, to have his arms envelop her against his hard body, made her feet walk faster.

Yet, as she entered the great hall, Ian was nowhere to be seen. No one was. The hall was empty, the only sound that of the crackling fire.

Danielle rubbed her forehead and touched the key through the front pocket of her jeans. She kept it with her always just in case it told her it was time to hand it over. And because the key refused to be left alone.

She even slept with it under her pillow, which wasn't an easy thing to do. Especially when Ian was in the bed with her.

Danielle smiled as she sank into one of the chairs near the fire and recalled her night with Ian. Every time they were together was more intense, more passionate. With every touch, each kiss, she wanted him more, needed him more.

Though she'd been searching for someone like Ian for so long, it frightened her how much she had become attached to him in such a short time.

But being put in danger and having him save her had certainly accelerated things.

Danielle's life had never been in jeopardy before. In the span of just days, the wyrran had come after her twice. As scary as that was, it was nothing compared to the fact that Deirdre had killed Duncan so she could have Ian for her own.

If she had gone to that much trouble to have Ian, then there was nothing she wouldn't do to have him.

Danielle was glad she had never encountered Deirdre, but how could she fight someone she knew little about? Ian had told her the story. But stories were altogether different from meeting the real person.

She let out a sigh and stared into the orange and yellow flames. Just a few days ago she'd despaired of ever being truly happy. She missed her friends and her flat, but within MacLeod Castle and the magic surrounding the stones, Danielle felt as if she had found her place.

There was a sound behind her a moment before Charlie came into view as he strode to the hearth. He grabbed the poker and nudged the dying wood around before he placed two new pieces atop them.

He replaced the poker, and then turned. Charlie paused when he caught sight of her. "Apologies. I didna realize you were here."

"The castle is quiet when the hall is empty." She forced a smile and tried to relax. Ian didn't trust Charlie, and if Ian didn't trust him then neither would she. But maybe if she spoke with Charlie she could learn something for Ian.

Charlie leaned a hand against the fireplace and returned her smile. "Where is everyone?"

"I have no idea. They showed me around, but I'm afraid if I go looking I might get lost."

He laughed heartily, the corners of his eyes crinkling. "I heard the tale about how Ian came upon you and saved you from wyrran. They're nasty little buggers."

"I couldn't agree more. I was very fortunate that Ian was nearby."

"Where was this exactly?"

Danielle shrugged, though his question made her stomach clench. "With the blizzard and just trying to stay alive I couldn't begin to say. Ian led us out of there. Maybe you should ask him."

"Maybe I should."

It was the way Charlie said it that sent a warning tingle up her spine. In that instant, Danielle knew Charlie had already asked Ian, and Ian had refused to answer. Why did it matter to Charlie where Ian's cave was?

Unless Charlie worked for Deirdre. Or Declan.

Danielle silently swore. There were too many evils they had to battle. How could anyone possibly win with the odds so stacked against them?

"Actually, I'm glad I found you alone," Charlie said as he straightened and took a step toward her.

"Why is that?"

"There is some concern among the others about Ian. They're afraid for you."

"For me?" Danielle repeated. "Ian saved me. Twice. Why would he do that only to turn around and hurt me now?"

Charlie shrugged. "I doubt it will be on purpose. Unless you have a god inside you, you cannot begin to fathom how difficult it is to control."

The more she spoke with Charlie the more she agreed with Ian. "Ian won't hurt me."

"Are you saying that for my benefit or yours?"

Danielle gasped as Charlie seized her arms and hauled her to her feet. His fingers dug into her upper arms painfully as he shook her slightly.

"Tell me, Dani," Charlie said as a malicious light came into his eyes. "Do you fear Ian?"

"No."

Charlie laughed. "Oh, but you will."

*   *   *

Ian was with Arran, Quinn, and Hayden as they stood in the center of the village. Even though only Ramsey, Arran, and Camdyn lived in the cottages, everyone kept the others clean and repaired regularly. With the snowfall, they were getting as much off the roofs as they could.

"Tell me again where Ramsey is?" Hayden asked as he pushed a mound of snow off one of the cottage roofs that landed next to Quinn.

Quinn took a quick step back and laughed. "He's with Fallon talking about Torrichilty Forest and the Druids there."

"Fallon is determined to get Ramsey to tell him the name of the Druid, is he no'?" Arran asked.

Quinn nodded. "My brother is nothing if no' hardheaded."

"Just Fallon?" Ian asked as he jumped from one roof to the next and began to move the snow.

"Ah, a jest," Arran said with a laugh.

Ian hid his smile, and in doing so missed the ball of snow Arran threw at him.

It hit Ian square in the chest. Not to be outdone, Ian balled up his own snow and threw it. It sailed through the air and hit Arran so brutally in the head that it knocked him off his feet.

Quinn laughed so hard he had his hands on his knees as he bent over. Ian found himself chuckling as well. That chuckle turned into a full-on laugh as Hayden also threw snow at Arran.

"Verra funny," Arran said as he ducked more snowballs thrown by both Ian and Hayden.

Ian was readying another ball of snow when Danielle's magic slammed into him. The smile died on his lips as her panic and distress swirled around him, urging him to find her.

Without a word to the others he leaped from the roof and ran toward the castle.

"Ian!" Hayden shouted behind him.

But Ian didn't have time to stop. Danielle's fear cut through him like a blade, sharp and true. He had to get to her, had to protect her.

Ian bounded over the castle wall and landed in the bailey. He didn't pause, but continued up the stairs and through the main castle doors.

The doors banged against the wall as he rushed into the great hall to find Charlie's hands on Danielle.

Whatever control Ian had snapped. He roared his fury as his god rose to the surface. Farmire demanded death, demanded blood. And Ian was more than happy to have Charlie's blood spilled.

Ian flexed his hands, his claws eager and ready for blood. He peeled back his lips and growled at Charlie. "Release her," Ian demanded.

Charlie merely smiled. "Nay."

Ian's vow to Danielle drummed over and over in his mind. He refused to allow her to be harmed in the one place she should be safe.

He knew he should wait for the others to arrive, but when Charlie shook Danielle and Ian heard her inhale there was no waiting.

Ian roared and launched himself at Charlie. He wrapped his arms around Charlie as he drove the Warrior into the floor. Dimly, Ian heard Danielle cry out. But with his hands now around Charlie's throat, all Ian could think about was killing the bastard.

Time and again Ian slashed his claws across Charlie's chest. He pounded his fists into Charlie's nose until he heard the crunch of bone. Ian pulled back his arm, readying to take Charlie's head when several pairs of hands grabbed him and pulled him off Charlie.

Ian bellowed and fought, desperate to get back to Charlie and take his miserable life for harming Danielle.

"Ian! Enough!" Arran yelled.

Ian heard him, but his fury was too great. Just the memory of Danielle being held by Charlie sent another wave of rage rushing through Ian.

"Bloody Hell," Hayden said as they continued to hold Ian.

"Dammit, Ian. Calm yourself!" Quinn bellowed.

It wasn't until Ian's gaze found Danielle huddled near the fire that he was able to tamp down his rage and his god. Still, the others held him.

"What was that about?" Hayden asked.

Ian no longer fought his friends, but it was difficult. They held him, kept him away from Danielle. "Charlie had a hold of Danielle," Ian ground out. "He shook her. Hurt her."

"What?" Quinn asked as his head swiveled to Charlie, who had risen to his elbows on the floor.

Charlie wiped at the blood from his nose that had already healed. "Ian saw me and Dani together. About to kiss."

"Nay," Ian said with a growl.

Quinn looked at Ian. "Are you in control?"

Ian gave a nod and glared furiously at Charlie.

Hayden's and Arran's hands released him as Quinn walked to Danielle. Ian clenched his jaw together when he saw Quinn gently help her to her feet.

When Ian caught sight of the blood dripping from her arm and the five long slashes through her sweater and into the skin underneath, he felt sick to his stomach.

He swung his gaze back to Charlie. He would kill Charlie. Slowly. Painfully.

"What happened?" Quinn asked Danielle.

She lifted her gaze still full of apprehension and

unease to flicker over Charlie before she looked at Ian. "I . . . I remember talking to Charlie."

"Who cut you?"

She looked down at her arm, her face losing what little color it had had. "I don't know."

"I never released my god," Charlie said. He gained his feet slowly. "I'm newly made and no match for Ian."

Ian felt every eye in the hall turn to him. He couldn't take his gaze away from the cuts on Danielle's arm. Surely he hadn't done that. Had he?

In his rage to make Charlie release Danielle he could have accidently cut her. But surely he hadn't. He'd been so careful with her.

Ian briefly squeezed his eyes shut before he looked at Danielle. "I'm sorry."

He strode from the hall before he could hurt her more.

# CHAPTER
# TWENTY-EIGHT

Danielle felt her heart jump to her throat when Ian walked out of the castle. She followed him with her eyes, wanting to tell him everything would be all right.

But she couldn't.

She recalled the fear, the feel of the claws ripping into her flesh. The Godawful pain.

All this time she had been telling everyone Ian would never hurt her, yet he had. How could she have been so wrong about him?

"Dani," Hayden said as he walked to her side. "Tell me what happened?"

She shook her head. "I'm trying to remember. It's all so fuzzy."

"Fuzzy?" Arran repeated.

"Yes. As I said, I remember being in here with Charlie. I remember him pulling me from the chair, and then . . . the roar."

"Were you and Charlie about to kiss?" Hayden asked.

Danielle blinked at him, unsure if she'd heard correctly. "Kiss? No."

"It's what he alluded to," Arran said.

Danielle looked across the hall where Quinn had taken Charlie. Even with his clothes ripped and bloody, Charlie looked calm and unruffled.

"No. I wouldn't kiss Charlie. Ian doesn't trust him."

Hayden ran a hand down his face. "Who cut you?"

She shrugged, wishing she could give them answers because she wanted to know herself.

"Something is no' right here," Arran said. "I know Ian. He wouldna hurt her."

"No, no' on purpose," Hayden admitted.

"But he was in a rage."

Hayden nodded. "As soon as I heard his roar I raced into the castle to find him on top of Charlie beating the crap out of him."

Danielle swallowed and felt her stomach begin to churn. She breathed through her mouth as she sank into the chair between Hayden and Arran.

"I'll get Sonya," Hayden said and raced off.

Arran squatted beside Danielle. "This doesna look good for Ian."

"I know," she said, and wrapped her arms around her stomach. She knew all too well. "What will he do?"

"I need to find him."

"Go. And tell him I don't blame him."

Arran smiled sadly before he rose and followed the path Ian had taken moments before.

Danielle wanted to go after Ian herself, but she didn't think he'd listen to her now. And a minute later it didn't matter because Sonya and Isla were suddenly before her.

While Sonya healed her, all Danielle could think of was the few seconds where her memory was unclear. Nothing like that had ever happened to her before. Was it because it had been Ian who had cut her, but she didn't want to believe it?

Or was it because of something else?

If Charlie had lied about them almost kissing, what else had he lied about? And more importantly why?

Danielle had to get to the bottom of it for Ian's sake. She knew how desperately he had wanted to return to the castle. And how much he feared it.

If any doubt entered Ian's mind that he couldn't be in control of his god around others, Dani knew he would leave. Without a backward glance or a word to her.

"You need to hold still," Sonya told her.

Danielle grabbed hold of Isla's hand and pulled her closer. "I need help from both of you."

Sonya and Isla exchanged a look before Sonya's amber eyes locked with Dani's. "What do you need?"

"Help with Ian. I can't believe he'd do this to me."

Isla sighed and patted Danielle's hand. "When I first came to the castle, Hayden was struggling with his god. His years of rage against his family's slaughter ate away at him. When he lost control and let his anger take him, he would forget himself and just who was around him."

"You think that happened to Ian," Danielle said.

Sonya shrugged. "It's a theory. The fact you can't remember and Charlie's and Ian's stories are so different casts doubt."

"On Ian." Dani shook her head. "Why doesn't it also cast doubt on Charlie?"

Isla cut her eyes to Charlie and flattened her lips. "A very good question."

Danielle took each of their hands into hers. "I know there have been a lot of additions to the castle lately. You don't know me, but I have to ask, have you felt anything . . . off?"

"Off?" Sonya asked.

"Yes. Off? Odd? Strange? Anything?"

Isla gave a slight nod. "I don't feel it often, but sometimes, there is a hint of something. I feel it through the shield I have surrounding the castle."

Sonya pulled at the end of her strand of red hair. "Why haven't you said anything?"

"I wasn't sure," Isla said. She then turned her gaze to Dani. "Ian told Hayden you were sent here. By who?"

Danielle knew if she were going to gain their trust, she would have to tell them the truth. "Not by who, but a 'what.'"

Sonya pulled Danielle to her feet. "Come. I have a feeling this will require privacy."

Danielle didn't miss the look that passed between Isla and Hayden as the three of them walked out of the hall and up the stairs.

"Hayden will keep Charlie busy until I return," Isla said.

Dani soon found herself in Sonya's chamber. Isla shut and barred the door, then turned to face her.

Danielle twisted her hands together as she began to pace. "Remember when I told Saffron what my magic was?"

"Aye, objects tell you who they belong to," Sonya said.

"Exactly. Well, that's what happened. I found an object, and it demanded I bring it to the MacLeods with all haste."

Isla took a step to her. "What is it?"

"That's just it," Danielle said with a frown. "It doesn't want me to give it to the MacLeods yet. As soon as I walked into the castle, it stopped bellowing to be given to the MacLeods and instead started begging me to wait."

"I don't understand," Sonya said.

Danielle lifted a shoulder in a shrug. "When the . . . object . . . began to urge me to keep it hidden and safe, that's when I started to feel there was something off in the castle."

"Is the object evil?" Isla asked.

Sonya gave a firm shake of her head. "Reaghan looked into Dani's eyes and saw the truth of how she came to be with Ian."

Danielle still couldn't believe there was a Druid who could know if she spoke the truth or not. "Has Reaghan looked into Charlie's or Kirstin's?"

"She couldn't get any type of reading on Kirstin, and with Charlie he wouldn't hold eye contact," Sonya said.

"Which doesn't necessarily mean he's lying," Isla pointed out.

Danielle lifted a brow. "It sure is suspicious to me."

"Will you show us the object that brought you to the castle?" Sonya asked.

Danielle thrust her hand into the front pocket of her jeans and wrapped her fingers around the key. "I want to show all of you. I want to give it to you now."

"But it won't let you."

"What if you just tell us?" Isla asked.

Dani let out a deep breath. Ian trusted these people, and so must she. Slowly, Danielle withdrew her hand from her pocket and held her arm out in front of her.

She turned her fist toward the ceiling and unfurled her fingers so that the key lay visible in the middle of her palm.

"By the saints," Sonya whispered.

Isla reached out a finger and carefully traced the top of the key. "We've been looking for a key."

"I know. It fits into a cylinder-shaped object with Celtic engravings."

"How—" Sonya began.

"The key showed me," Danielle answered.

Isla dropped her hand. "The others need to know."

"No," Dani said louder than she intended. She tucked the key back into her pocket. "There is someone here preventing the key from being known. Until we find that someone, I must keep the key to myself."

"Why tell us then?" Isla asked.

Dani thought of Ian's laughter, of his sherry eyes as he looked down at her right before he kissed her. "Because Ian trusts you."

"You think Charlie had something to do with your cuts, don't you?" Sonya asked.

Danielle nodded. "I can't prove it, but I feel it in my gut. Twice Ian was in the midst of battle and saved me, and neither time did he so much as nick my skin."

Isla's lips twisted sardonically. "Aye, but Warriors can be insanely protective of their women. Ian might have lost control because he believed Charlie was either going to hurt you, or going to try and take advantage of you."

Fear. Danielle remembered she had felt fear while Charlie had held her. "What power does Charlie have?"

Sonya shifted. "He can control wind, why?"

"Could he be lying about it?"

Isla's ice blue eyes narrowed. "We took him at his word."

"Be vigilant around him," Danielle said. "It was something Ian asked of me, and I didn't take heed. Now, I need to find Ian and get this sorted out before he does something stupid like leave the castle."

"Which could be just what Deirdre wanted," Isla said.

The three of them left the chamber together. Dani to go in search of Ian, and Sonya and Isla to find their husbands and let them know what they had discovered.

* * *

Ian stood facing the stone wall damp from the earth just on the outside of it. The ground beneath him was nothing but dirt and rock, hard from the cold.

"Ian, you can no' be serious," Fallon said from behind him.

Ian had known Fallon would object to what he wanted, but there was no other way. "I willna put Danielle's, or anyone else's, life in danger. Close the door, Fallon."

"Nay," Quinn said as he ran into the dungeon. "Ian, get out."

Ian turned to face Quinn who stood next to his two brothers. Lucan hadn't been happy with Ian's request, but out of the three of them, he seemed to understand why Ian would want to be locked in the dungeon.

"After all the time you spent locked in Deirdre's prison you'll willingly put yourself back in one?" Quinn asked.

Ian took a deep breath and released it slowly. "For Danielle, aye."

"You care for her," Lucan stated.

"She is . . . different than any woman I've met in my two hundred"—he paused and recalculated—"well, six hundred years of existence."

"Putting yourself behind these bars will no' help her," Quinn said.

Ian and Quinn had shared several months in Deirdre's mountain. Along with Arran and Duncan, the four of them had bonded, their trust in each other absolute.

"I swore I wouldna hurt anyone while gaining control of Farmire," Ian said. "And I harmed the very person I swore to protect."

"There has to be another way," Fallon said.

Ian grabbed the iron bars of the door and slammed it shut. He looked at the MacLeod brothers. "I beg of you to watch over Danielle while I'm in here. As soon as I have control, I'll ask to be released. But if Farmire takes over . . ."

Quinn nodded, his face full of sadness and regret. "I'll see it done. I willna allow Deirdre to get you."

Ian gripped the bars once the brothers were gone and rested his head against the cold metal. The last thing he wanted was to be locked away again, but for Danielle, he would do it.

To keep Danielle safe, he would endure anything.

# CHAPTER
# TWENTY-NINE

"Where is Ian?" Dani demanded. She was fast losing patience as the MacLeods continued to evade her question.

"He's fine," Fallon answered.

Danielle took a deep breath and tried to count to ten. She only made it to three. "I didn't ask if he was fine. I asked where he was."

They'd been going through this for over fifteen minutes and Dani was about to pull her hair out. When neither Isla nor Sonya was told anything different, Danielle began to get a sinking feeling in her gut.

She knew Ian had been closest to Quinn because of their confinement in Cairn Toul together, so she turned to the youngest MacLeod. "Please. I need to know where Ian is."

Quinn ran a hand through his hair and murmured, "Holy Hell."

"Doona say it," Lucan cautioned.

Danielle glared at Lucan, then faced Quinn. "Ian and I gave each other promises. He vowed to bring me here, and I swore to help him gain control of his god."

"He's still here," Quinn finally answered.

"But where? I've searched all over. I need to speak with him."

Lucan shook his head. "That wouldna be a good idea."

"Dammit," Dani shouted and buried her face in her hands. Why wouldn't they tell her where he was? The idea of not seeing Ian, not touching him left her . . . cold.

She had just begun to feel. She didn't want to be that cold, lonely person again.

Danielle lifted her head and blinked away her tears as she faced the brothers. "If you've hurt him . . ."

"Hurt him?" Fallon said with a snort. "Ian did it for you!"

"Shite, Fallon," Lucan said, and kicked the leg of the table.

Dani frowned and turned to Quinn. "Where is he?"

Quinn swallowed, a muscle in his jaw working as he clenched his teeth together. "Understand that this was Ian's idea. He did it because of you."

"Did what?" She took a step closer to Quinn, silently begging him to give her the information she so desperately needed.

"He locked himself in the dungeon."

The room tilted as Danielle reached out to grab hold of anything to keep her upright. It was Isla who steadied her.

"Nay," Dani whispered.

Isla blew out a breath. "Why? Why would he willingly lock himself away after all he had endured in Deirdre's mountain?"

"Do you really need us to answer that?" Lucan asked.

Danielle looked at Isla. "What does he mean?"

"He means Ian cares a great deal for you," Isla answered softly.

Dani shook her head. "He barely knows me. I know how much he hated being locked away. He shouldn't have put himself in a cell again. It's not right. We need to get him out," she said as she surged toward the doorway that led down to the dungeons.

Quinn's arm snaked out and snagged her before she could rush past him. "Nay," Quinn said as he held her.

Dani continued to struggle as images of Ian confined in a cell flashed in her mind.

"Nay," Quinn said again. "He willna want you to see him like that."

Danielle stopped fighting against Quinn's hold as his words sank in. "He doesn't want to see me?"

"I've no doubt he wants to see you," Fallon said. "It's more he doesna want you to see him caged as he is."

"Then let him out."

Lucan glanced at the floor before he said, "We promised him we wouldna let him loose until he had control of his god."

Dani jerked out of Quinn's arms and looked at the brothers with fury mixed with distress. "Did none of you think that being restrained could very well give Farmire the advantage he wants over Ian?"

The silence that greeted her question was answer enough.

"Since you won't let me see Ian, I'll tell you what we've discovered. Ian didn't trust Charlie."

Fallon shrugged. "That's no' a surprise. Neither does Camdyn."

Isla sighed as she leaned her hands on the table. "Fallon, you've always been a good leader. We've always trusted you, but I think you're overlooking two very important things."

"And they are?" Fallon asked.

"Two of your Warriors don't trust Charlie," Sonya answered.

Lucan squeezed the bridge of his nose between his

thumb and forefinger. "And Quinn was adamant about no' allowing Hayden, Ramsey, and Logan into the castle because he didna trust them."

"Why does Ian no' trust Charlie?" Quinn asked.

Danielle shrugged. "I don't know, but I do know something is off in the castle. When I first felt the magic it was strong and pure. Now, it . . . falters, for lack of a better word, at times."

Lucan's green eyes narrowed. "Falters?"

"Maybe that's the wrong word," Isla said. "There is an undercurrent that hasn't been here before. Like Dani, I don't feel it all the time. Just on occasions, and it's brief."

"Sonya? Do you feel it as well?" Fallon asked.

Sonya shifted from one foot to the other. "I hadn't until Dani mentioned it. I've been feeling the magic since then, and there is something wrong."

"I think it's Charlie," Danielle said.

Quinn crossed his arms over his chest. "Why? Because Ian thinks it is?"

"That's partly why. The other reason is because I don't remember what happened earlier. I know Charlie grabbed me, and I know I wasn't happy about it. I remember hearing Ian's roar. Then there's nothing until I found myself sitting with my arm slashed open."

"The trauma of it maybe. Of it being Ian who hurt you," Lucan suggested.

Danielle shook her head. "As I told Isla and Sonya, Ian had plenty of opportunity while we were alone to harm me. He never did. Yes, I saw him struggle with his god, but he always managed to get it under control. It wasn't easy, but Ian did it."

Fallon let out a deep breath, his pale green eyes intense as he stared at Danielle. "We've had several new people come into the castle."

"Yes. And I was one of them," Dani said.

Lucan's brows drew together. "You doona mind that we're suspicious of you?"

"I would expect nothing less. You need to protect your families. I understand why you welcome Druids and Warriors into these walls, but with Deirdre, and now Declan, you must be cautious of everyone."

"She sounds like Cara," Lucan muttered.

Fallon nodded. "Larena said much the same thing."

Danielle wanted to tell them about the key, just as she desperately wanted to hand it over to them, but as she put her hand in her pocket to grab the key it yelled *"No!"* over and over in her head.

She might not be able to give them the key yet, but she could tell the brothers a little about why she was there. "I came here because I was sent to help you."

"How?" Quinn asked.

"I can't say yet." Danielle waited for Sonya or Isla to say more, but the two Druids remained quiet.

Fallon asked, "How can we trust you if you doona tell us everything?"

"You can't. And I can't tell you everything because of what is wrong at the castle."

Lucan began to pace. "This isna what we need now, Fallon. We've got Deirdre and Declan, and now this."

"The list of suspicious people can be narrowed down to just a few," Sonya said.

Isla glanced at Dani and nodded. "Aye. Charlie, Kirstin, Dani, and Ian."

"No' Ian." Quinn said the words softly, but there was a hard edge to his voice.

Fallon turned to his brother. "Ian has been gone a long time. We have no idea if Deirdre got to him or no'."

"Which, I believe, is another reason he put himself in the dungeon," Lucan pointed out.

"And where you should put me," Danielle said.

Fallon gave a shake of his head. "Absolutely no'. Ian would have my head if I did."

"You don't know me," she argued. "You need to take precautions."

Isla moved to stand beside Danielle. "Look to Charlie first. He told us his power was over wind, but we never made him prove it."

"That's a good place to begin," Quinn said.

Sonya walked to the other side of Danielle. "Meanwhile, we'll keep Dani and Kirstin with us. Between all the Druids here, we'll be able to determine if they are a threat."

It seemed everything was settled, but Danielle still hadn't got what she had come for. "I want to see Ian first."

Lucan stopped pacing and ran a hand down his face as he turned his back to her. Quinn wouldn't meet her eyes, but by the way he clenched and unclenched his fists Dani knew he was fighting how to respond.

It was Fallon who finally answered. "No' now. I'll take you to see him tomorrow."

Tomorrow. Danielle would have to wait until then, even though it would kill her. And she couldn't imagine what it was doing to Ian.

He hadn't spoken in much detail of his time in Cairn Toul, but Marcail had when she'd told Danielle the story of how she and Quinn had met.

Marcail's words had painted a vivid, terrifying picture of what life had been like for Ian in the Pit. The descriptions of the torture Ian had gone through at Deirdre's orders, and of how Duncan had felt every lash and strike until Marcail had taken away his pain made Dani's heart clutch in her chest.

Those memories and more would assault Ian while he was alone in the dark dungeon. Danielle knew it just as she knew she belonged in this new world of magic and Warriors.

"Don't let him be alone." Dani said.

Quinn met her gaze. "I willna."

"Thank you."

Sonya tugged at Danielle, and with nothing left to say, she allowed Sonya and Isla to take her back up the stairs to the chamber she had shared with Ian.

The door closed behind Danielle with a soft thud, yet in her mind it was as loud as the tolling of the church bells in Inverness.

"Quinn will watch out for Ian," Isla said.

Dani looked over her shoulder to see it was just her and Isla. "Would you let Hayden stay down there by himself?"

"Absolutely not. However, I do know he would do his best to keep me out so I wouldn't see him."

Danielle walked to the hearth and tossed logs on the long-dead fire. She worked at lighting it again while she went over all that had happened in her mind.

When the fire popped with new life, Danielle took the chair closest to her and drummed her fingers on the wood. "I can't just sit and wait."

"I don't think you're going to have to wait long." Isla said. "Sonya has gone to tell the other women, minus Kirstin, what is going on. We are a close family here, Dani. We will find who is responsible for the disturbance at the castle."

Danielle touched the outside of her pocket and the key beneath the denim. "What if it's me?"

Isla's head cocked to the side. "You think it's you?"

"No. I know I'm not a bad person. I know I'm not *drough*, but what if the key is evil? What if the key used me to bring me here?"

Isla took the chair opposite her. "Do you trust your magic?"

"I do."

"Has it ever led you wrong before?"

Danielle thought back over the years and shook her head.

"Then trust your magic now. You may have found the key, but it showed you what it was for. Evil wasn't a part of that."

"But evil wants it. I think that's why it won't allow me to give it to the MacLeods yet."

"It's a secret Sonya and I will keep from the others for now. We don't like doing it, but it's a necessity until we straighten all this out."

"Ian said I would like it here," Danielle said with a sigh. "He wasn't wrong. When I first mentioned Mac-Leod Castle I could tell he didn't want to come, but the closer we got, the more he looked forward to it. He missed all of you terribly."

"And we missed him. It pains us all that he has suffered alone these months."

"Now he's suffering again."

Isla laid a hand on Danielle's arm. "You will go to him tomorrow. Talk to him. Convince him to come out of the dungeon, because you're going to need him."

Isla's words chilled Danielle because she knew they were the truth.

# CHAPTER
# THIRTY

"This is Deirdre's doing," Larena said as she paced the small kitchen where Fallon, Quinn, Marcail, Lucan, and Cara stood with her as she raged about Malcolm.

"No doubt," Cara mumbled.

Larena paused in front of Fallon. "We have to find Malcolm and stop him before he kills those children. If he murders those innocents . . ."

"I know," Fallon said and pulled her into his arms.

Larena clung to him. Ever since she had seen the Monroe name on the scroll she had known Malcolm housed a god. She should have told him, but she had wanted to protect him.

All she had done was driven him away from the castle and straight to Deirdre.

More tears gathered when Larena recalled seeing Malcolm on the Isle of Eigg. She almost hadn't recognized her beloved cousin. It wasn't because of his Warrior form and the dark burgundy color of his god. It was the deadness in Malcolm's blue eyes that haunted her.

"If we go to find Malcolm, we'll leave the castle weak," Quinn said.

Larena lifted her head. "We have to take care of both. If what Dani said is true, then one of the newcomers is to blame for the disturbance, as they called it."

Marcail rubbed her hands up and down her arms. "Dani repeated everything to Reaghan just a few moments ago. She's not lying about any of it."

"So we can rule her out as the cause, aye?" Lucan asked.

Fallon shrugged, his arm still around Larena. "I'd like to say aye, but until we know for sure, we keep watch on all of our newest arrivals."

"You doona think it's Ian, do you?" Quinn asked Fallon.

Lucan leaned a hip against the large worktable in the middle of the kitchen. "He was gone for a long time, and Deirdre's connection with him after killing Duncan is what pulled him into the future."

"So let Reaghan see if he's telling the truth," Cara said.

Fallon shook his head. "I willna do that to one I consider a brother. I doona like him locked in the dungeon, but maybe that's where he needs to be."

"And if Dani is attacked again?" Larena asked.

"Ian will move Heaven and Earth to get to her," Quinn answered.

Cara raised her brows. "You think he cares for her that much?"

"Marcail is the only reason I'd put myself in a dungeon again."

Lucan scratched his chin as he looked at each of them. "We need to keep an eye on Dani since Ian can no' at the moment."

"But who?" Larena asked. "We need to get moving on Malcolm."

Fallon kissed her forehead as he squeezed her. "And

we will as soon as Broc returns with Malcolm's location."

"Until then, we need to see what we can learn about Kirstin and Charlie." Marcail stated.

Quinn winked at his wife. "Who is with Dani?"

"Isla," Larena answered.

"And Kirstin?"

Cara sighed and said, "Reaghan. She's trying to get whatever she can out of Kirstin, but the girl seems confused about everything. Reaghan has had a difficult time of it, but she's not giving up."

"Galen and Braden are also with Reaghan." Lucan added. "I think Braden has taken an interest in Kirstin."

Fallon glanced out of the kitchen door into the great hall before he said, "It is time Braden found a wife. Camdyn and Arran are with Charlie as I requested."

"Perfect," Quinn said with a smile.

Larena took a deep breath and squared her shoulders. "Now we wait for Broc's return."

She just hoped they would have enough time to combat the attacks that were happening all around them. Everyone knew it wasn't coincidence that Kirstin, Charlie, and Danielle arrived so close together. But who was to blame? Deirdre? Declan? Or both?

Larena liked Dani, but that wouldn't stop her from killing Dani if she was a threat to all Larena held dear. As for Kirstin, Larena felt as the rest of them did—confused.

Kirstin was timid and shy one moment, then aggressive and forward the next. Who was the real Kirstin?

As for Charlie, Larena had thought him semicharming at first, but the longer he was at the castle, the more he grated on her nerves.

Which one of them was the cause for the disruption of the magic inside the castle?

   "Fallon," Larena said as the others left the kitchen. "This could be a ruse by Deirdre or Declan, or both, to get us out of the castle."

   Fallon nodded as he allowed her to see just how worried he was. "Quinn, Lucan, and I have already thought of that. Only a few of us will go to Malcolm."

   "A few includes me," she said in warning.

   "As much as I'd prefer you to stay here, I think Malcolm will respond better to you."

   "Who is coming with us?"

   "Broc and Isla, because both spent a great deal of time in Deirdre's control. Maybe the two of them will be able to convince him to return with us if you cannot."

   Larena blew out a pent-up breath. "I had gotten used to the peace. Four centuries without looking over our shoulders or worrying if there was some trap waiting for us."

   Fallon slid his hands through her golden hair to cup either side of her face. "We're going to end this, Larena. Soon. We're so close. All we need is the key to open the Tablet of Orn, which will hopefully lead us to where Laria has been hidden. Then Deirdre will be gone."

   "It's not going to be that simple."

   "Nay, and we'll have to watch for Declan as well, but we've never been this close, my love. I refuse to accept defeat."

   She closed her eyes as his lips found hers. Fallon's head tilted to the side as he deepened the kiss. Larena clung to him as she melted against his heat and the promise of tomorrow.


Danielle stared at the minutes ticking by on her watch in the chair she had curled up in beside the fireplace. She turned her mind away from Ian for a short while when she once more tried to reach the spell in Saffron's mind.

She had gotten farther into Saffron's mind, but the choking evil had promptly made Dani back away.

That had been over an hour ago, and as soon as she left Saffron's room, her thoughts had returned to Ian. She couldn't stop thinking of him and how he was coping being locked away again.

"They won't keep you away from him forever," Isla said.

Danielle raised her eyes to find Isla smiling at her over the top of her iPad. Dani had been mildly surprised at how everyone at the castle had stayed up to date on the latest technology and styles. It seemed being immortal and held within a shield that blocked the world from finding them didn't stop them from living.

"I hope not, because if they do I'll simply sneak down there myself."

Isla smiled. "Any one of us would do the same. Fallon is just doing as Ian asked, but I think Ian needs to see you. Maybe you can talk some sense into him."

For the first time since learning what Ian had done, Danielle grinned. "Thank you."

"There's one thing you'll learn quickly around here, and that is we stick together. We fight and quarrel, but at the end of the day we're family, and we'd die for each other."

Danielle thought back over Isla's story of how she came to be at the castle and united with Hayden. "Is it hard to be immortal?"

Isla set aside the iPad and clasped her hands in her lap. "While I was under Deirdre's control it was Hell. Every hour was like a lifetime. I watched helplessly as she put my sister into the black flames so she could never live again but Deirdre would be able to continue to get her visions.

"Then there was my sweet, darling niece. She was

life for me. Deirdre ruined that as well. When the Mac-Leods came for Quinn and everyone attacked Deirdre, I thought my chance at freedom had come. I cannot begin to tell you how angry I was to wake up in this castle. But the magic here, the love, it changes a person. I no longer feel the time passing as I once did."

"Yet you have no idea if you're still immortal or not outside of your shield."

Isla shook her head. "It was Deirdre's magic which kept me immortal all those centuries. With her link to me gone, I assume I'm mortal once again."

"Do you long to live a normal life?"

"More than you can imagine," she whispered and glanced down at her hands.

Danielle caught the glimmer of tears in Isla's ice blue eyes. "I'm sorry. I didn't mean to pry."

"You didn't," Isla hurried to say. "Hayden and I speak of children often. It can never be until Deirdre and now Declan are both dead. We struggle to stay alive and keep the evil at bay. I refuse to bring a child into this world who could end up in Deirdre's hands."

For long moments they sat in silence. Danielle rose from the chair and walked to the bed where Isla reclined. Dani sat and crossed her legs. "I've been wondering something since I first learned of the shield."

"What is it?"

"The shield can never be lowered. No one knows of this castle. In this day and age of technology and instant news, the castle can't just suddenly appear."

Isla's smile was a little sad. "No. The castle must forever stay hidden."

"That doesn't seem right. After everything that has happened here, it seems the world should get to see it. The MacLeods should be able to live in it."

"The land is theirs. They have kept up the documentation to prove that it is theirs."

"Passing it down through the centuries," Dani said as understanding dawned.

Isla nodded. "I've heard them speak of building a home on their land."

"Did none of you ever think of lowering the shield during all those centuries Deirdre was gone?"

"All the time," Isla confessed. "A week rarely went by that we didn't debate the issue. However, I also used the shield to keep everyone immortal inside it."

"Couldn't you have done that without hiding the castle or the village?"

"Of course. Deirdre knows where the castle is, but we weren't keeping it hidden from her. We were keeping it hidden from any other evil that might try and come here."

"I've only been in this battle for a few days and already I'm anxious for Deirdre to be gone forever."

Isla chuckled and moved her hair over one shoulder to begin braiding it. "It's a wish we all desire greatly. Soon, Dani, very soon I suspect it will happen. Just be lucky you haven't met Deirdre yourself."

Danielle shivered at the thought of facing Deirdre. As much as she wanted to finish Deirdre, Danielle had a feeling she would get to meet the *drough* before all this was over.

And Dani didn't look forward to it.

# CHAPTER
# THIRTY-ONE

Ian heard a commotion in the great hall above him. He longed to rush up the stairs and discover what it was, but then he recalled the five slashes on Danielle's arm and he knew he had to stay where he was.

The sound of footsteps rushing down the stairs made Ian lean toward the door and peer through the iron bars to see who was coming.

Relief flooded him when he saw it was Arran and not Danielle.

"What's going on?" he asked.

Arran raked a hand through his hair and leaned against the cell opposite Ian. "Broc found Malcolm. Malcolm is a day and a half outside of Edinburgh."

"A day and a half," Ian repeated and frowned. "Why is it taking him so long to get there?"

"He's walking."

"Walking? Why in God's name is he doing that?"

Arran shrugged. "I've no idea. Broc didna talk to him, but he said Malcolm didna look to be in a hurry."

"That could be good news. Do you think Malcolm is having second thoughts about killing the children?"

"No' in the least. He could have taken the train or the bus to Edinburgh. He could have even hired someone to drive him, but he's walking. There's a reason for that, but I've no idea what it is."

Ian rubbed his jaw, his mind racing with possibilities. "When is Larena going after him?"

"She wants to leave immediately, but Fallon has bade her to wait."

"Tell me he's no' leaving the castle defenseless."

Arran rolled his eyes. "You know he's no'. Charlie asked to be one of the Warriors to stay behind and guard the Druids and the castle."

"I doona like the sound of that."

"Neither did any of us. Fallon agreed, but Ian, you doona need to worry. We are all going to be watching him."

"Doona watch just him. Keep your eye on Kirstin as well. I have a bad feeling about this."

Arran raised his hand and let his long white claws extend from his fingers. "It's been a long while since I've seen battle. I'm more than ready for it."

"We doona know if Deirdre and Declan are working together. Be wary, my friend."

Arran's claws disappeared, and he dropped his hand as he raised his eyes to Ian. "I will. I have no' waited this long to kill Deirdre to make a mistake."

"Who all is staying behind?"

Arran pushed off the wall, his gaze on the floor. "Fallon asked that I no' tell you."

Ian gripped the bars in his hands and squeezed. He wanted to throw back his head and bellow his frustration.

Instead, he held his gaze steady on Arran. "Fallon doesna trust me."

It wasn't a question.

Arran's brows snapped together as he jerked his eyes to Ian. "You know that isna the case."

Ian knew no such thing, but then again, he couldn't blame Fallon for not wanting him to know. Ian had locked himself in the dungeon because of his god.

"I'll return when I can," Arran said as he sprinted to the stairs.

Ian blew out a breath and turned his back to the bars. Slowly, he lowered himself to the cold, damp ground. He'd thought being in a dungeon once again would drive him daft, but the knowledge that his friends were around him helped to calm the anxiety that threatened to take hold.

It was the silence, the long intervals with nothing but the darkness for company once again, that was the worst.

*"You can do this, Ian,"* Duncan's voice sounded in his head.

Ian closed his eyes, comforted more than he cared to admit by hearing Duncan's voice. It only proved how close to madness he was, however.

"Duncan. I thought you'd left me."

*"I will soon, when you need me no more."*

"I'll always have need of you, brother."

*"There are others who will be brother to you. They already are."*

"Aye, but they are no' you."

Duncan chuckled. *"It's my sour disposition you miss so much."*

It was much more than that, so much that Ian couldn't put into words. "I doona know how to get control of Farmire."

*"Aye. You do. Listen to your heart. You conquered him once, you can do it again."*

"I conquered half of him. The other half you had."

*"Exactly. We conquered him. You were the calm one, Ian, the one who looked for logical ways to any problem. There is a way in this. Find it."*

"How?"

*"You know how."*

"A little help would be appreciated."

Instead of an answer, Ian had only more silence.

"In all the months I spent by myself in the cave, I never spoke to myself. I spoke to Duncan, which could be just as bad, but never to myself. It seems Danielle has rubbed off on me."

The thought of Danielle with her silver hair and emerald eyes sent his balls tightening. Ian longed to hold her in his arms once again, to kiss her, caress her. Love her.

His nights with her had shaken him to his core. She was passionate, open, and so very giving. Danielle was everything he had wanted in a woman and more. He didn't deserve her, but he wanted her more than life itself.

Ian leaned his head back against the iron bars and sighed wearily. Maybe he hadn't made such a good decision in locking himself in the dungeon.

He squeezed his eyes closed when Danielle's wound flashed in his mind. He had vowed to keep her safe from any harm. The possibility that he had hurt her made him sick to his stomach.

Ian put his fists to his head when Farmire began ordering Ian to give him control, demanding a battle filled with blood and carnage.

"Nay," Ian said. "Nay! Nay!"

He shouted it over and over until his voice was hoarse

and his throat was raw. Only then did he realize Farmire had quieted.

But for how long?

It had been over twenty-four hours since Ian had cast himself in the dungeons. And it had been the longest, roughest twenty-four hours Danielle had endured since her parents' deaths.

She had stopped begging to see Ian. Fallon had given his word he would allow her to see Ian on his return. Danielle, however, had no intention of waiting that long.

As Fallon, Larena, Broc, and Sonya prepared to depart in an effort to stop Malcolm from killing innocent children, Dani stood in the great hall with everyone else.

Kirstin had found a friend with Reaghan. The tall, auburn-haired Druid was rarely seen without Kirsten. Danielle was glad of that. Maybe Reaghan would be able to discover if Kirstin was the threat or just a messed-up girl.

Danielle herself hadn't been left alone except to sleep. She knew part of the reason was because of Ian, but the other part was that they didn't fully trust her either.

"Good luck," Hayden said as the four readied to leave. He grabbed Isla and gave her a long, heated kiss before they said quiet words to each other.

Broc and Hayden exchanged a look that didn't go unnoticed by Danielle. She wondered what it was all about. Her attention was soon diverted as Larena placed her hand on Isla's shoulder who placed her hand on Broc's, who in turn placed his hand on Fallon's shoulder.

"Ready?" Fallon asked them.

"Ready," the three answered in unison.

With a nod Fallon placed his hand on Larena's shoulder and they were gone. Danielle stared at the spot for several moments. She didn't know what she had expected upon learning that Fallon could teleport, but she hadn't expected it to be so quiet.

"I bet I had that same look on my face," Gwynn said with a laugh.

Danielle chuckled and slowly shook her head. "All the things we see in movies that were never supposed to be real."

"You mean like magic? And Druids?"

"Yes," Danielle agreed with a smile.

Gwynn looped her arm with Dani's and steered her away from the others. "How long are you going to wait?" she whispered.

"Wait?" Danielle repeated and cut a glance at her.

"To see Ian."

Danielle sighed. "Only until no one is looking."

"No one is looking." When Danielle eyed her, Gwynn smiled and gave her a nod. "Go on."

Dani didn't need to be told twice. She inwardly laughed when she realized Gwynn had walked her to the door which led down to the dungeon.

She squeezed Gwynn's arm in thanks and hurried to the door. It squeaked a little as she opened it and slipped through. When the heavy oak door closed behind her, Danielle found herself in the dark.

After all these years she thought the Warriors would remember the Druids couldn't see in the dark. Then Dani caught the faint glow of a light at the bottom of the stairs.

She began her descent slowly, reaching for each step carefully. Her hand never left the railing. The closer she came to the bottom of the stairs the more the light shone until she could take the rest of the steps with ease.

When her feet touched the ground, Danielle paused. The dungeon was much larger than she had expected.

She looked to the left and found several sets of open doors. To the right she found a path with barred cells on either side.

Danielle turned to the right and started down the center. As she walked she recalled Cara's tale of hiding here in the first attack by Deirdre and how Cara had nearly been taken by an ash-colored Warrior.

As she passed every cell Danielle looked inside to find them empty. She wasn't surprised to discover Ian toward the end on the left side. He sat in the corner against the stone wall with his feet resting on the ground and his arms draped casually over his knees.

"Ian?"

She licked her lips when he refused to answer.

"Please, Ian. Talk to me."

"You shouldna be here."

Danielle sighed, overjoyed to hear his voice again. "No. You shouldn't be here. How could you think you hurt me? You would never hurt me."

"I saw the marks."

"Marks I think were made by Charlie." She gripped the iron bars and gave them a shake.

"You think."

Danielle rolled her eyes. Ian's voice was flat, emotionless, and he refused to look at her, his attention focused elsewhere. "Yes, I think. I've gone over and over it in my head. That's the only part of the entire day that is fuzzy. Why is it so hazy?"

"Because I injured you."

"No!" she yelled. "Dammit, Ian. Listen to me, please. Charlie told the others his power is over the wind, yet no one made him prove it. What if he lied? What if he was able to confuse me and he was the one who cut me?"

Ian pulled in a long breath and slowly blinked. "Those are a lot of ifs."

"I need you, Ian," she whispered, and put her head on the bars.

A tear fell from her eye when she squeezed them closed. He didn't respond, but she was undeterred. He might not want to hear what she had to say but she was going to say it regardless.

"I missed you in bed beside me last night. How is that possible? We've shared two nights together, yet it feels as if I've known you my entire life. I've come to rely on you when I swore I would never do that again. I don't want to feel the pain of losing someone again, but at the same time, you've made me feel things I didn't think were possible."

Danielle opened her eyes hoping to find Ian at least looking at her. Now, he sat with his head back and his eyes closed.

She wiped at her eyes and straightened. "There's no doubt in my mind that you weren't the one who cut me. You've locked yourself in here, Ian. Who is going to protect me from Charlie?"

# CHAPTER
# THIRTY-TWO

It took everything Ian had not to respond to Danielle. He'd felt her glorious, astonishing magic as soon as she'd entered the dungeon. The excitement and urgency that had filled him rocked him to his very core.

He had hoped she'd come to him and prayed she wouldn't. He wanted to hold her sweet body against his, but he didn't want her to see him locked away.

When she stopped in front of his cell, her words had reverberated through him. He'd refused to look at her, because if he had, he'd have gone to her. Until he knew for certain he had control of his god, he didn't want to be near her.

Her words cut through him sharper than any blade. He wanted to believe her, needed to believe her. But there was so much doubt in his mind.

Ian had felt her defeat and her resolve through her magic. He never expected to find someone who believed in him as much as she did, regardless of how much danger he posed to her.

He hadn't been able to keep up the façade of uncaring bastard. Every instinct demanded he go to her, that he hold her and promise everything would be all right.

Instead, he sat there, his eyes closed and head back against the damn stones.

Eons passed before he heard Danielle exhale and walk away.

Her question had been valid. What was he going to do from the dungeons if Charlie attacked her? Ian opened his eyes and launched to his feet to pace the small confines of his cell.

His only option was to gain control of Farmire. Quickly.

Ian stopped in the middle of the cell and called for his god. Farmire answered swiftly. Ian glanced down at his skin to find it pale blue.

Farmire had always answered his call with haste, but since Ian had taken all his power, forcing Farmire back down took more time than before. Which proved how much Farmire fought him.

Ian urged his god back down, and as expected, Farmire battled to stay. Again and again Ian wrestled for control. Sweat broke out over his skin, and his entire body shook by the time Farmire relented and retreated.

After just a few moments' rest, Ian repeated the process again. His thoughts were on Danielle, of holding her, of kissing her, of falling asleep beside her.

He would do this for her, for Duncan, and for all those he called family.

Those were his last thoughts moments before he blacked out as Farmire took complete control.

Declan swirled the dark red wine in his glass. He brought the glass to his nose and inhaled the aroma of oak, black cherries, and a light citrus flavor. With a tip of his hand, he sipped the expensive wine and closed his eyes as the flavors exploded on his tongue.

His life was good, albeit not complete. Yet. He still had to get Deirdre, but he knew that was simply a matter of time.

The sound of his office door opening had Declan lifting the lids of his eyes. "Ah, Robbie. Care for a glass of wine?"

"I prefer whiskey, as you know."

"I do know, but it wouldna hurt for you to refine your tastes a wee bit."

Robbie drew in a long breath and slowly released it.

"What is it?" Declan asked wearily.

Robbie rested his hand on the hilt of the dagger he wore at his waist. "It's been two days. Should we no' have heard from your little Druid?"

"Kirstin?" Declan asked with a laugh. "Nay, cousin. She wasna sent there to do a quick job. She will worm her way into their hearts and give me everything I need to know."

"And if Deirdre is plotting something sooner?"

Declan sat forward and lowered his wine glass to the table. He regarded his cousin silently for a moment. "I've no doubt Deirdre does have something planned. It isna in her nature to sit back and wait. I, however, have more patience. Kirstin will take care of whatever threat Deirdre may throw at the MacLeods."

A slow smile spread over Robbie's face. "Verra smart."

"I am the brains of this operation."

"How soon until we hear from Kirstin?"

Declan shrugged and ran his finger over the edge of his wine glass. "It depends on how soon they let her into their trust. Until then, we sit back and wait."

"I'd rather take action."

"Then tell me, is there movement out of Cairn Toul?"

Robbie crossed his arms over his chest. "A few comings and goings from that blighter I spoke about before."

"Ah, the muscle man Deirdre captured. He's no' a Warrior though."

"Nay. He just does her bidding. The burgundy Warrior, however, has no' returned yet."

Declan rubbed his chin. "Interesting. Deirdre would only send him away for so long if she had some mission for him to do. I've no doubt we'll hear of it soon. I would love to see Deirdre's face when she discovers Druids are no' as plentiful as they used to be. That will put a wrinkle in her plan."

"She had to know Druids would one day be no more."

"I've no doubt she did, but she'll have expected to have had much more magic by then."

Robbie walked to the sideboard and reached for the crystal decanter of whiskey. He poured himself a glass and lifted it toward Declan before he tilted his head back and drained it in one swallow.

"Tell me, Declan, how does it feel to sell your soul to Satan?"

Declan smiled. "Would you like to find out?"

"He's already got my soul after the things I've done. But he gave you magic."

"And he gives me information," Declan added. "He no longer trusts Deirdre to take over the world as he had planned. It's why he brought me into the fold."

"You'll get the job done," Robbie said with a chuckle.

Declan took another swallow of his wine. "Most certainly. I'm in a position no' to fail. Deirdre was as well, but she took her eye off the prize. She's more worried about the artifacts."

"And are you no' getting those artifacts for her?"

"Aye. A man likes to make his woman happy."

Robbie set down his glass and strode to the door.

"Watch yourself, cousin. Remember who you're working for now."

Declan snorted. As if he needed Robbie to tell him the Devil held his soul. One day Declan would have to pay for his sins, but that time was thousands of years in the future. Until then, he would live in luxury like a god.

Supper was not the usual boisterous affair it had been days before. Danielle, like the others, kept the conversation flowing, but there was no doubt that worry and apprehension filled the castle.

She had told Gwynn and Sonya what had happened with Ian, but neither thought his actions odd. They kept telling her it was just like a Warrior to act as he had.

Danielle, however, wasn't buying it. She had always been the kind who faced reality. If Ian really cared for her, he would have shown it when she went to see him.

She knew how much it bothered him that he didn't have control of his god. She had seen his surprise and dread when he caught sight of her wound. Because of those things she understood why Ian was in the dungeon.

But to not talk to her? To not listen to what she had to say?

Dani pushed her baked scallops around on her plate for several more minutes before she rose and took her plate to the kitchen. She needed something to do, something to occupy her hands and her mind.

She caught sight of the sink and immediately started washing all the pots and pans from the meal. Shortly Marcail was drying the dishes while Cara put them away.

All too soon everything was cleaned, but Danielle wasn't ready to leave. She found other things to wash, even as the others urged her to retire to the great hall with them.

Danielle's hands were all pruny when she rinsed off

the last dish and set it to drain. She then dried the remaining dishes she had washed. Still not ready to leave, she put those dishes away.

Only then did Dani lean back against the worktable and close her eyes. She would spend another night alone. That shouldn't matter after all her years by herself, but somehow it did. After Ian, it did.

They might be in the middle of the most dangerous situation she'd ever known, but she felt alive. For the first time in her life she felt as if she were living instead of just existing.

Being at the castle was part of it, but the one who had awoken her, the one who had shown her passion and pleasure and ecstasy was Ian.

Ian.

He might not want her near him, but she needed him. She needed to see him, hear him.

Danielle left the kitchen and went straight to the door to the dungeon. Talk in the hall lowered, but no one stopped her. This time when she walked down the stairs she wasn't scared.

She went straight to Ian's cell and looked inside to find him flat on his back, his arms spread out beside him. It looked as if he'd collapsed.

"Ian?" Danielle called as she squatted down. "Ian, can you hear me?"

She reached an arm through the cell in order to touch him. She was just breaths away, and no amount of squeezing more of her shoulder through the bars would get her closer.

Danielle huffed and tried again, shifting her body so that she lay at an angle. This time her fingernail was able to graze his shirt but nothing more.

She sat up and called to him again. "Ian. Come on. Talk to me. Tell me you're all right."

He groaned.

Danielle gripped the bars and rose to her knees. "Ian?"
"Danielle?"

She smiled and held the bars tighter. "It's me. Open
your eyes. Let me see you."

He rolled to his side facing her and opened his eyes.
His sherry eyes stole her heart as he gazed at her a moment before he lifted himself to his hands and knees and
scooted back to the corner she'd found him in earlier.

"What happened?" she asked.

He shook his head and rested it in the palm of his
hands. "What do you think?"

His voice was muffled, but she heard the anger in his
words. "All the while you were with me Farmire never
took control.

"I fought. Danielle. I had wyrran to kill. It kept
Farmire content."

She sat sideways against the door and leaned her head
on the iron. "He tried to gain control while we were shop-
ping, remember? You didn't let him. I know you have the
willpower to stop him."

"Do I?" Ian asked, and lifted his head to pin her with
his stare. "Do I really? I'm lost, Danielle. I doona know
who I am anymore."

"I do," she whispered. "You're the man who saved
me from creatures I didn't know. You're the man who
pulled me from a frozen loch and warmed me so I
wouldn't die. You're the man who promised to bring me
to the MacLeods even though you didn't want to go.
You're the man who stood with Charon against dozens
of wyrran intent on killing innocents. You're the man
who fought even though you knew there was a possibility Deirdre would take you. You're the man who has
kept me safe no matter what. And you're the man who

makes sweet love to me and holds me in the cold, dark hours of the night."

"Maybe that man is gone."

Dani smiled. "No. I'm looking at him. I have faith in you, Ian. Have faith in yourself."

# CHAPTER
# THIRTY-THREE

Ian wanted to believe her. He longed to believe her. There had been times in his life he'd known exactly who he was. Now wasn't one of those times.

He knew what he wanted, and he knew how he wanted to live. Getting there was the problem.

His silence didn't deter Danielle. She began talking. telling him stories of her parents before their death and the fun the three of them had had together and their many trips. She spoke of how terrified she had been on leaving her home and coming to Scotland.

Her words never faltered, but Ian heard the tremor in her voice nonetheless. After all these years, that part of her life still affected her. But it didn't rule her.

Ian found himself smiling as she told stories of her time in school and the pranks she and her friends would play on some of her teachers.

She had been an excellent learner, and for the most part a good girl. She played it safe a lot of the time. Ian could see a pattern begin to emerge from hearing about her life.

His heart ached for the woman who sat on the other side of the iron bars. That woman longed to find love, yearned to belong to someone. Yet, at the same time, she feared losing that person as she had lost her parents.

Ian heard the love in her voice as she spoke of her aunts, especially Josie who had been the one to show her magic.

Danielle might have played it safe her entire life, but all that had changed when she had met him. Ian thought about how much danger she had been in since he had discovered her being chased by wyrran.

She seemed fragile, but inside she was made of steel. She had suffered terrible loss, and instead of shutting out the world, she had looked at it with different eyes.

Ian was so lost in his thoughts, going over all the stories Danielle had told him, that it took a few moments for him to realize she had stopped speaking.

He found her head resting against the bars, and one arm hanging inside his cell. Her eyes were closed and her lips parted slightly as she slept.

Ian couldn't stay away from her another moment. It had been pure torture to keep his distance from her when all he had wanted to do was pull her into his arms.

Now, he crawled toward her soundlessly. She didn't move or utter a sound as he settled next to her. The only things separating them were the iron bars.

Ian linked his fingers with hers and softly kissed the top of her hand. She shouldn't be in a dungeon with the damp and the cold. She could become sick.

A cold chill settled in his chest as he felt how cool Danielle's skin was. There was no way he would allow her to become ill. She could die.

And that thought left his chest aching as if a thousand daggers had plunged into his heart.

The sound of the door to the dungeon opening had Ian on his feet and away from Danielle in less than a heartbeat. He stood in the shadows and watched as Logan and Gwynn stopped next to Danielle.

"Get her to her chamber." Ian beseeched Logan.

Logan sighed, his lips flattening. "I'd like nothing better, but Gwynn willna allow it."

"You want Danielle to become ill?" Ian asked Gwynn.

Gwynn rolled her eyes and spread the blanket she held in her arms. "Of course not. She needs you, and whether you want to believe it or not, you need her."

"She's no' safe here."

Logan braced a hand on the bars. "I doona know what's going on in the castle, but I know something isna right. Dani wants to be with you. I see no reason to keep her from you."

Ian liked how easily Danielle had fit in with everyone at the castle. They even called her Dani, which had been what her parents called her.

He dragged a deep breath into his lungs and released it. "Spread the blanket on the ground and lay her upon it," Ian instructed. "But doona wake her."

Logan smiled as Gwynn spread the blanket, and Logan carefully extracted Dani's arm from around the bars and laid her on the thick blanket.

To Ian's relief Gwynn had brought a second blanket which she covered Danielle with.

"Thank you," Ian said to both of them.

Gwynn tucked the blanket under Dani's chin and stood. "She's an amazing woman, Ian. You'd be a fool not to see what you have."

"Danielle isn't mine."

"She could be," Gwynn said and walked away.

Logan watched his woman for a moment before he looked at Ian. "Listen to Gwynn, my friend. What kind of woman would willingly put herself in this place if she didna care for you?"

"I'm all that she knows."

"Are you trying to convince me or yourself? You were the one who found her, protected her. You were the one who brought her here and vowed to keep her safe. How will you do that behind those bars?"

Ian clenched his fists. He had told himself everything Logan was voicing. It didn't change anything.

"What if I was the one who cut her?"

Logan chuckled. "She doesna believe you did. The fact she can no' remember is making me believe her more and more."

"I need to be sure," Ian said.

"I know what it felt like to think Gwynn was gone from my life forever. That feeling . . ." Logan paused and visibly swallowed. "You've lost Duncan, but you've found us again. And in doing so you found a woman who has stood by your side. She's a rare breed, Ian, and no' just because she's a Druid."

With one last look, Logan walked away.

Ian walked back to the bars to be near Danielle. She had dark circles under her eyes, which only proved to him she hadn't been resting well.

He sank to the ground and stuck his hand through the bars and under the blanket in order to find hers. Only then did he allow himself to close his eyes.

What kind of woman would willingly stay with a man who could have hurt her?

*The forever kind.*

Ian had always expected to get married and have children. When his god had been unbound and he'd been imprisoned in Cairn Toul, thoughts of a wife and family were the farthest thing from his mind.

Then he'd come to MacLeod Castle. He'd seen

Lucan's and Fallon's love for their wives. He'd watched
Quinn fall in love in Cairn Toul. Then he'd seen Hayden,
Galen, and Broc find love.

The idea of a wife wasn't so far-fetched anymore. It
hadn't been for a while, but he hadn't allowed himself to
think on it with Deirdre still alive.

He knew firsthand how much his brethren worried
over their mortal wives. Thoughts of the Druids being
taken by Deirdre caused those Warriors many sleepless
nights.

Ian looked down at Danielle. Yet, he could see the
allure. To hold a woman in his arms as he fell asleep
and wake next to her every morning. To have her stand
beside him through the trials of life, to see her smile
and hear her laugh.

Aye, he could definitely see the attraction.

If he was the man he'd been before. Now, he would
spend his time worrying about being the one who had
hurt Danielle. What kind of life would that be?

*"Then fight Farmire!"* Duncan bellowed in his head.

Ian was so taken aback by the shout that he jerked.
"Duncan," he whispered. "I'm trying."

*"No' hard enough."*

"What else can I do?"

*"Remember, Ian. Remember what we did . . ."*

"Duncan," Ian called. But there was no response.

Ian searched his mind for what he and Duncan had
done when they had first had Farmire released within
them. No matter how hard he tried to remember, Ian
couldn't recall anything that might help.

They had been inside Cairn Toul, lonely and cold
and hungry. And more than a little frightened. They had
had each other though, while others were alone.

Deirdre had separated them, locking them in different cells far from each other. What she hadn't known was that no matter the distance, Ian and Duncan had always been able to communicate with each other.

They knew what the other was thinking, what the other was doing.

Ian shook his head and tightened his fingers around Danielle's hand. To his surprise, she squeezed in response. Ian jerked his gaze to her, but she was still asleep. He lightly caressed a finger down her cheek, wishing with all his might he could kiss her.

She had the most amazing lips. They made him hot. Hard. Hungry.

His balls tightened as he recalled how her pert breasts filled his hands, how her pale pink nipples hardened against his fingers and mouth.

Ian shifted, his cock thickened just thinking of tasting the sweet nectar of her sex, of stroking his tongue along her softness then against the pebble of her clitoris.

He longed to hear her cries of pleasure, her scream of fulfillment. He yearned to have her legs wrap around him as he sank into her wet heat. He craved another touch, another kiss. Always more.

There would never be a time he couldn't get enough of Danielle. She had said he had awoken her, but in truth, she was the one who had awoken him. She had helped him to remember what it was to be a man.

A man he was proud to see staring back at him in the mirror.

He wanted to be that man again. Not just for Danielle, but for the others in the castle. For Duncan. For himself.

Ian closed his eyes and struggled to forget the desire that ran rampant through him. There was no way he would allow himself to do more than hold Danielle's hand, and even that was probably too much.

The feel of a hand on his aching cock made his eyes fly open. He found himself staring into Danielle's face just breaths away from him.

She squeezed his arousal through his jeans, which caused him to moan. The feel of the rough material against him only heightened his need.

"Danielle," he whispered.

She put a finger to his lips. "No more words."

He couldn't form a coherent sentence with her touching him. Ian hadn't heard her move, hadn't felt anything until she had touched his rod. He should have heard her. He should have known she moved.

Why hadn't he? Was he so lost in his thoughts that he hadn't realized anything?

Suddenly, none of it mattered as Danielle unbuttoned his jeans and slowly unzipped them. Ian sighed when his cock sprang free.

His breath came out in a whoosh when her hand closed around his flesh. Ian lifted his hips. All he could do was lean back and give in to Danielle and the inferno that consumed him.

Ian moaned when she used both hands to skillfully move up and down his length with just the right amount of pressure. And when she smeared the bead of precum that had formed over him, Ian's fingers curved into the hard ground.

She cupped his balls, which made him hiss in a breath. But it was when she seductively massaged him while pumping up and down his hard length that he found himself reaching for her.

Ian forgot the bars, forgot he was trying to keep his distance from her. All he wanted was a taste of her lips. He pulled her head toward him and took her mouth in a kiss that ravished, a kiss that demanded.

A kiss full of everything he longed for.

# CHAPTER
# THIRTY-FOUR

Danielle didn't loosen her hold on Ian as he kissed her. And what a kiss it was. He swept her away, devoured her. And she loved every moment of it.

When she had woken to find Ian next to her with his hand under the covers on hers, she hadn't thought. She'd just acted. She wanted him with a fierceness that should have frightened her. But all it did was fortify her. Strengthen her.

"Need you," Ian said between kisses.

Not nearly as much as she needed him. But she understood the desire driving him, the longing burning through his veins.

She shrugged off the blanket and rose to her knees so she could reach him better. He deepened the kiss, his tongue sliding sensuously against hers. Danielle moaned, her breasts swelling and her nipples hardening as they waited for his touch.

Begged for his touch.

Danielle arched her back when his hands slid from her neck down her back to rest on her waist. Then, finally, he cupped her aching breast.

She moaned into his mouth and pressed her breasts into his hand. He squeezed before his thumb brushed over her sensitive nipple.

Danielle concentrated on pumping her hands up and down his thick arousal when she felt a brush of cool air against her stomach. Ian had lifted her sweater in an effort to reach her breasts.

She heard his growl a heartbeat before he ended the kiss. She was getting ready to argue with him, expecting Ian to tell her to go to her room.

Instead, he held his hand in front of him and lengthened his claws. Then, with barely a flick of his wrist, he had cut her sweater down the middle before his claws disappeared.

Danielle shrugged out of it and eagerly went back into his arms. When she tried to remove his shirt, he dodged her hands until she had no choice but to take his rod back into her grasp.

She loved the moan that sounded from deep within his chest when she tightened her fist as she moved her hand from the tip of his cock to the base.

Suddenly, he had her on her feet, kissing her and fumbling with the latch of her jeans. Danielle took off her shoes and her jeans all without breaking the kiss.

They shared a smile as he wrapped his arms around her and brought her against him. The feel of the cold metal against her skin made her wince.

And reminded both of them just where they were.

"No," she said when she saw he was about to pull back. "Don't you dare pull away from me."

There was a moment when she thought she had lost him, then he kissed her again. He held her head, the kiss deep and thorough, while his other hand ripped off her panties. He cupped her sex, pressing the palm of his hand against her clitoris.

Danielle felt herself grow even wetter at his touch. He parted her curls with a finger and slowly ran it up and down her softness, fondling her clit in light, teasing caresses all the while kissing her.

She was doing some teasing of her own as she held his cock in one hand and his balls in the other. She squeezed and stroked until he was panting and thrusting into her hand.

Danielle had every intention of taking him into her mouth and sucking until he came. But she should have known Ian had other thoughts.

He abruptly ended the kiss and whirled her around until her back was pressed to the bars. He cupped both her breasts in his hands, his mouth near her ear as he pressed his arousal into her buttocks. Danielle cried out when he squeezed both her nipples before nipping at the lobe of her ear.

She reached behind her and grabbed onto the bars to help herself stay upright. Her body was on fire, each nerve ending strung tight as a bow, ready—and oh so willing—to have Ian's hands on her.

Decadently, decidedly wickedly, he traced a finger around her areola once, twice. Then that finger dipped between her breasts and meandered lazily down her stomach, around her navel, and over her hips before stopping just seconds from touching her sex.

Danielle cried out and shifted her hips, hoping to move his hand so that he touched her. He chuckled behind her and rolled a nipple between the fingers of his other hand still on her breast.

Ian liked to torment her, loved to see her body respond to him. She was primed and ready for whatever he wanted to do to her body. And that trust brought him to his knees.

A woman like Danielle was special and should be

treasured. She should be given gems and every luxury
known. A woman like Danielle could make the world
shine with a simple smile.

Ian gripped her hip to steady himself and hold off his
need to drive into her, to pound into her tight sheath and
lose himself in the world the two of them created.

It was a world Ian desperately wanted, a world he
needed to be in.

He flattened his hand on her stomach. She quivered
beneath him. The pulse at her throat was as erratic as her
breathing. And it only set Ian's desire pounding higher.

With measured slowness he moved his hand into her
curls. A moan tore from his throat when he felt how wet
she was, how ready for him she was.

"Ian," she whispered, her back arching as he pinched
her nipple again.

His finger dipped into her and smoothed her wetness
over her sex. He rubbed slowly, lightly from her clitoris
down and then up again.

Her hips moved with him, her breathing hitching
when he would swirl his finger around her swollen clit.
Ian smiled when he heard her breath lodge in her throat.
He enjoyed making her burn.

Just as he burned for her.

Ian dipped a finger inside her and thrust deep. She
moaned, her head tilted back so that her glorious silver
locks were spread over his chest. He wanted to see her
hair against his skin, but in order to take his shirt off
he'd have to remove his hands from her. And that wasn't
going to happen.

He pulled out his finger and added a second as he
pushed inside her. Sweat glistened over her flushed skin.
Ian had never seen a more beautiful sight than Danielle
in his arms shaking with pleasure.

Ian wanted her to peak, he wanted to see her scream

as her orgasm claimed her. But his own need was too great. He ground his cock against her bottom and groaned at the feel of her skin against him.

He rubbed her clit as he continued to stroke in and out of her sex. Her cries rose higher and came quicker. He knew she was close to climaxing by the way her body tightened around his fingers.

Ian added a third finger inside her at the same time he pressed against her swollen nub. Danielle screamed his name as her body clamped down on his fingers.

He held her up with his other arm while he continued to thrust inside her, prolonging the orgasm. Her body still jerked with spasms from the climax as Ian slowly lowered her to her knees.

Reluctantly he released her to shed his own clothes. When he turned back to her it was to find Danielle staring at him, a soft, pleased smile on her face.

"That was fun, but it would be a lot more comfortable with you out of that cell."

He shook his head. "No' happening tonight. I want to be sure of myself before I put you in harm's way again."

Danielle had leaned to the side, her mane of glorious silver hair hanging over her shoulder. Ian reached between the bars and grabbed a handful as he pulled Danielle to him. He rubbed the locks between his fingers.

"You have the softest hair."

"And you have the most beautiful eyes," she murmured as she rested her palms flat on his chest. "They're the exact color of sherry. Sometimes I think I can see straight into your soul when I look at you."

His heart skipped a beat at her words. "And what do you see?"

A slow smile pulled at her kiss-swollen lips. "A good man. A man I'm proud to know."

Ian kissed her, hating how the iron bars blocked him

from getting too close to her. Her hands glided up to his
neck, over his shoulders and around his back.

He grabbed her buttocks and pulled her against him as
he ground his throbbing arousal into her sex still swollen
from his touch.

He could feel the heat of her, the slick wetness. Ian
thrust his hips forward and rubbed against her curls.

"Yes," she murmured.

With both of them on their knees, he lifted her up
until she was able to slide her legs between the bars and
around his waist.

Danielle looked down into Ian's eyes and saw the desire, the longing in his beautiful eyes. She thrust her fingers into his light brown locks and held him as he lowered
her. She felt the blunt head of his arousal against her flesh
and shivered.

His fingers had felt wonderful, but nothing was as
good as the real thing.

She held her breath, waiting for him to push inside her.
His arms shook, but not from holding her. They shook
because he was waiting until he could stand it no more.
She saw it in his eyes, in the way he looked at her.

Her heart clutched in her chest. With a grin, she leaned
down and kissed him through the bars. When their lips
touched, the head of his cock slipped inside her.

Danielle gasped at the pleasure of having him stretch
her and fill her. She closed her eyes and leaned her head
back as inch by inch he lowered her until he was fully
seated.

And almost immediately he pulled out until just the
head of him remained. Only to thrust hard and deep.

Danielle dug her fingernails into Ian's shoulders as
pleasure stole her voice. He was in complete control of
her, and she loved it.

He moved her up and down his length. Slowly with short thrusts. Then harder, plunging deep within her. He rotated her hips so that her clitoris pressed against him, sending thrills rushing through her.

With her heels locked at his back she could feel his butt and hips move as he continued to thrust, his big hands shifting her up and down at the same time.

Danielle gripped the bars to help hold herself, and when she did, Ian held her hips and rocked hard against her. She could feel herself begin to tighten inside. Each glide of his cock in her sheath sent her winding tighter and tighter, reaching for the sweet bliss only Ian could give her.

Their eyes met, and when he leaned down and softly nipped at her nipple, she screamed his name. Danielle's back bowed toward Ian as the sweet waves of her climax engulfed her. They pulled her, took her over the precipice and into an abyss of pleasure like she had never known.

She had barely gotten her breathing under control before Ian pulled out of her. Danielle felt bereft, but before she could argue, he had her on her hands and knees facing away from him.

He ran his hand over her buttocks and groaned. Danielle looked at him over her shoulder to find him smiling. He winked at her as he caressed from her shoulder down over her spine to her hips.

That's when she felt him against her. He was still impossibly hard. With one thrust, he was seated inside her.

Danielle bit her lip at the feel of him from behind, the way his balls brushed against the back of her legs. She dug her fingers into the blanket and closed her eyes as he began to pound into her.

He set up a compelling rhythm that was relentless as he pulled her once more into the flames of desire. He was unyielding in allowing her to move against him as he held her hips steady. Yet he gave her pleasure with each thrust of his hips.

Time stood still as their bodies joined, united in an act as old as time itself. Desire and pleasure wound around them, holding them firm. Binding them.

Unbelievably, Danielle could feel her body tightening again. Her nerves stretched taut, her skin was all that was holding her together.

"Come for me," Ian whispered.

That's all it took for Danielle to peak. She screamed, her body stiffening as the climax seized her, took her. Swept her.

Ian pumped desperately into her, his breathing harsh to her ears. His fingers bit into her flesh. Danielle tipped back just a fraction, then clamped down when he surged inside her.

He thrust once more and bellowed her name. Danielle smiled at the feel of his climax inside her. He slumped against her, the glow of their lovemaking, of the bond that had found them, lightening the gloom of the dungeon.

# CHAPTER
# THIRTY-FIVE

Ian watched Danielle sleep for what was left of the night. He never released his hold on her hand. It was awkward the way she slept, but no amount of urging by him would make her seek out her own bed.

He shouldn't have been surprised. Danielle was surprisingly strong and stubborn when she wanted to be. Ian knew he shouldn't have made love to her in the dungeon, but his need had been too great, his hunger for her too vast.

It was always too great when it came to Danielle.

He wondered what it was that drew him to her. She was beautiful, but it was more than that. Her magic was strong, but again, it was more than that.

Could it be the strength he sensed within her? Or could it be that she was able to look to her future and not allow her past to rule her? Not that it mattered. Ian would never find another woman like her if he searched the earth for the rest of time.

Ian knew dawn had come when he heard movement above in the great hall. He was loath to wake Danielle.

The dark circles were nearly gone, and she was sleeping deeply.

But a new day had begun. And with it, the constant threat that needed to be discovered.

"Danielle," Ian called as he smoothed a strand of her silky silver hair away from her face.

She moaned and cracked open her eyes. "Morning already?"

"Aye. I'm afraid it is."

"Damn," she muttered, and rolled to her back where she stretched her arms over her head.

It caused the blanket to shift down and expose one luscious breast. Ian grew instantly hard.

Danielle chuckled and sat up, letting the blanket drop to her waist. "I'm all yours, but you'll have to leave that prison if you want more of me."

At that moment Ian would have offered her the sun and moon if he could have but another taste of her. "Have you no' learned already it's no' good to tempt a Warrior?"

"Oh, but I want to tempt you," she whispered seductively.

Ian's cock throbbed painfully. He palmed himself and adjusted his arousal inside his jeans.

"It's ridiculous for you to stay in there," Danielle said as she began to gather her ruined clothes into a pile.

"You know my reasons."

"And how long will you keep yourself in there? You have no idea how long it will take you to gain control."

"Nay, I doona. But if it will keep you from harm, then I will gladly do it."

Danielle threw down her boot and glared at him with her hands on her hips. Ian ran an appreciative eye over her naked form, even if she was staring at him with daggers in her eyes.

"You're impossible." Danielle stated.

"I will gain control, and when I do, I'm locking us in your chamber for at least a month. I'm going to make love to you every way possible. Twice. I'll keep you so content you willna want to leave the bed."

Danielle gathered the blanket around her and walked to the bars separating them. "Don't you realize, you foolish man, that you already make me content?"

Ian was at a loss for words as she walked away, her torn clothing forgotten. He had thought his words would pacify her until he could be with her as he longed to be. Yet she had completely surprised him.

Which shouldn't have happened. He should have known by now that Danielle was nothing if not unexpected.

Ian paced his square prison, his thoughts going over all that Danielle had said, as well as what Duncan had told him. Ian knew how imperative it was that he gain control over Farmire and soon.

There was no doubt something was going to happen, whether it was Fallon bringing back Malcolm to the castle, or Deirdre or Declan attacking in some way.

Regardless, Ian needed to be there to protect Danielle.

Ian tried to imagine his life without her in it, and he couldn't. She had become as important to him as breath. Keeping her safe, keeping her alive was the most important thing to him.

It took a moment for him to realize how his priorities had changed. Just weeks ago the most critical thing for him to do had been to kill Deirdre.

When Danielle had come into his life and he had

sensed her magic and felt the way it touched every fiber of his being, everything had changed. He hadn't recognized it until that moment, but now that he had, it seemed only right.

Ian took a deep breath and called up his god. Then, he began the process of tamping down Farmire. To Ian's surprise, Farmire didn't fight too hard.

Again and again Ian repeated the procedure, and each time Farmire fought for only a moment.

Ian smiled as he watched the pale blue fade from his skin. He was gaining control.

Broc peered around the corner of the building. "I see him," he told the others who were behind him.

"Is he alone?" Fallon asked.

Broc nodded. "For now. He looks as if he . . ."

"What?" Larena urged.

Broc shrugged. "It looks as if he's sightseeing."

Beside him Isla smothered a laugh. "Surely not."

Broc slowly moved back into the shadows and looked at the other three. "I'm no' jesting. He's walking around looking at everything. I even see a flyer of some kind in his hand."

"Let me go to him," Larena begged Fallon.

Fallon shook his head. "No' yet, love. We need to know where he is going and why. If Deirdre sent him and Malcolm doesna carry out her orders, she'll only send someone else."

"Fallon's right," Broc agreed. "We must wait."

"I can't." Larena shook her head and turned away.

Broc licked his lips. "Let me follow him alone, Fallon. I'll see where he's going. He willna know I'm there."

"Aye," Fallon said. "We'll wait at the hotel."

"Be careful," Isla said.

Broc took a baseball cap from his back pocket and placed it on his head. "Always."

He stepped into the crowded street full of tourists and easily spotted Malcolm a hundred yards in front of him. Broc kept far enough back that Malcolm never saw him. The few times Malcolm's gaze passed him, he didn't recognize Broc from the baseball cap he wore low over his head.

For hours they meandered the city, stopping for food and to gaze at churches and monuments. Malcolm even went to Edinburgh Castle, but he didn't go in.

Broc wondered if Malcolm was remembering the last time he had been at the castle. That's when Fallon had met Larena. Deirdre had sent Broc and another Warrior to bring Larena to her, but the other Warrior hadn't liked the idea of a female having a god inside her.

He'd used *drough* blood on his claws and stabbed Larena. Broc had still been spying on Deirdre at the time, so he couldn't help Larena other than to tell her that the *drough* blood was killing her.

As Broc expected, Fallon took Larena to MacLeod Castle. Days later Deirdre had sent Warriors to attack Malcolm as he traveled to MacLeod Castle.

Broc frowned as he recalled the mangled, bloody mess that had been Malcolm when he fought off the Warriors. He hadn't expected Malcolm to live, and there was only one person who Broc knew could save him. Sonya.

She had saved Malcolm's body, but not his soul. Broc wondered if he shouldn't have allowed Malcolm to die that day. Never had he expected Malcolm to become a Warrior who aligned himself with Deirdre.

Broc saw Larena's pain every time Malcolm's name was mentioned. Everyone knew he was the one who had killed Duncan. And now, Malcolm was set to murder a school full of children.

Although Broc thought of him as a friend, he would not allow Malcolm to kill anyone else.

It was just after noon when Malcolm's wandering brought him to a primary school. Broc kept himself hidden as Malcolm watched the children run and play, their screams and laughter eaten up by the noise of the city.

Broc didn't waste another moment as he ran back to the hotel on the other side of the city. It would have been much easier to fly there, but he didn't think the tourists would appreciate seeing him transform and take flight above them.

By the time he reached the hotel Fallon was outside.

"Get the girls," Broc said.

Fallon teleported out, and a heartbeat later, he was standing in front of Broc with both Larena and Isla.

"You found the school," Larena said, her voice flat.

Broc nodded. "We need to get there now."

Fallon turned and walked into the alley next to the hotel. It was quiet and deserted. A perfect place for Fallon to jump them to the school.

"Which school?" Fallon asked.

He had studied all of them and their locations the day before since he couldn't teleport to a place he hadn't been before.

"The one next to the old theater," Broc answered.

Once they were all touching, Fallon jumped them to an alley near the school.

"There," Broc said as he jerked his chin to where Malcolm still stood.

Isla squinted into the sun. "What is he doing?"

"Watching the children," Larena said softly. "He always had a way with children. I used to tease him that they liked him so because they knew he was nothing but a big child."

Fallon linked his hand with hers. "We willna allow him to kill the children."

"Bloody Hell," Isla said, her voice catching.

"What is it?" Broc asked as he looked around.

"Phelan."

Isla's softly spoken word had Broc scanning the people for a glimpse of the Warrior Isla had tricked into Cairn Toul Mountain.

"I doona see him," Broc said.

Fallon growled. "I doona know what he looks like."

Isla stepped forward. Broc followed where her eyes were trained and saw the dark-headed man staring at Isla. Broc recognized the Warrior instantly.

"It is Phelan."

"I need to talk to him," Isla said, but Fallon held her back.

"No' now. We need Malcolm first."

By the time Broc looked back to where Phelan had been, the Warrior was gone. "I can find him later, Isla. I promise."

Isla nodded and took a deep breath as she turned her head back to where Malcolm stood.

Larena looked at Fallon. "I'm going to talk to Malcolm. You be ready to take him to the castle."

Broc was uneasy with their plan. He wanted to surprise Malcolm and give him no choice but to return to the castle with them. Larena, however, wanted to talk to him first.

They watched as Larena walked to Malcolm. She was twenty paces from him when he suddenly turned and looked at her. Malcolm's body jerked in surprise.

"He's going to run," Broc muttered.

To his disbelief, Malcolm sighed and waited for Larena to reach him.

Malcolm somehow wasn't shocked to find Larena in Edinburgh. He looked at the tight black jeans she wore tucked into black boots that reached her knees. It made her legs look longer, but then as a Warrior, she had begun to wear trousers long before it was acceptable for women to be seen in them.

He had always admired her fearless outlook on life, the way she rushed into things headstrong and courageous.

"You look good," he said when she reached him. Her cream coat was buttoned and belted, but it hugged her frame, causing many men to do a double take.

With her golden waves flowing free about her face and reaching her shoulders, she stared at him. "So do you."

Malcolm glanced down at the faded jeans, chocolate sweater, and scuffed boots he had stolen from some man's home. It had been easier than he expected to set aside his kilt. After all, he was as good as banished from the clan.

He shrugged. "I'm learning to fit in."

"What are you doing here?"

Malcolm scanned the area. He knew Larena wasn't alone. The question was, how many Warriors had she brought with her? "I'm touring Edinburgh. It's amazing how much it has changed in the four centuries I've been gone."

"Many things have changed."

"And many things have no'."

"You don't have to side with Deirdre."

Malcolm barked with laughter. "Oh, but I do. You have no idea how persuasive she can be, cousin."

"Please don't kill the children," Larena beseeched.

Malcolm stilled and narrowed his gaze on her. "Why would you think I would do something like that?"

"We have a Seer at the castle. She saw it. The children are innocents. Look at them. Hear their sweet laughter, see their trusting eyes. Please. I'm begging you. Don't do this."

"If I doona do it, Deirdre will send another." There was no use lying to Larena, especially since a Seer had seen the vision of him killing.

It made him ill to think of all those innocents dying. He was searching for a way to find the Druid without killing the children. It was why he had been standing outside the school.

"If you do this, you'll be lost to me forever."

Malcolm looked at her. How he'd missed seeing her, missed everyone at the castle. But his path had split from them. He could never return there.

"I'm already lost to you."

# CHAPTER
# THIRTY-SIX

The next morning after a long, hot shower, Danielle had dried her hair and even put on makeup. She wanted to look good for Ian when she went down to see him later. After their passionate night together, there was no denying she had it bad for him.

Really bad.

In all her years of dating she had never met a man as enigmatic, dangerous, or seductive as Ian. He drove her wild with his kisses and smoldering looks. He was stubborn to a fault, but loyal and braver than any man she knew.

The world she was in now was more than dangerous. It was deadly. The war raging was one that would soon spill over into the rest of the world if Deirdre wasn't stopped. Danielle knew she would risk her life to keep Deirdre from ruling the world.

Dani also knew she would risk everything to stay with Ian.

She had only known him a few days, but in those days she had learned more about him and herself than she had in the year she'd known Mitchell.

Silly or not, she knew her growing feelings for Ian were stronger than anything she had felt before. She didn't have much experience with love. There had been only two relationships in her life when she had thought she might love a man, and both had failed miserably.

In neither of those relationships had she ever felt anything even remotely as strong as she did for Ian. With Ian, she wasn't afraid to look into her past and revisit memories of her parents.

Now she wasn't afraid to face Deirdre or Declan or whatever else came her way because she knew Ian would be there with her.

Was it love she felt for Ian? If it wasn't, it soon would be if the past few days were any indication.

She wore a smile when she left her chamber and walked down to the great hall. Everyone else had already eaten, so Danielle found a bagel and a glass of orange juice in the kitchen.

Not wanting to dirty anything, she sat on the counter and began to eat. She had taken three bites when Gwynn walked into the kitchen with a tray of dirty dishes.

She smiled at Danielle. "Ian's appetite is improving."

"Uh-huh," Danielle muttered as she finished chewing, suddenly embarrassed. She'd left her clothes in the dungeon when she'd stormed off angry. Had Gwynn seen them?

"Oh," Gwynn said as she began to wash the dishes. "Your sweater and bra are destroyed, but I've got your jeans set to wash and your boots are in the hall."

Danielle choked on her bagel and took a drink to wash it down. "Thank you," she said when she could talk.

"Did the blankets keep you warm?"

Danielle's brow furrowed. "Are you the one who brought the blankets?"

"I did. I saw you go down and knew it would get cold.

You were asleep when Logan and I brought the blankets." She wiped off her hands and faced Danielle. "I'm glad you stayed with Ian. He needed that."

"He's obstinate."

Gwynn laughed loudly. "Oh, but Dani, they all are. Warriors are the worst at being pigheaded individuals. You're seeing just the beginning of it."

"I tried to convince him to come out of that cell."

"He's in there for you."

"I know, and it's silly."

"No," Gwynn said softly. "It shows you how much he cares."

Danielle sighed, knowing Gwynn was right. It caused a warmth to spread over her chest. "It's insane how my life has changed so drastically. You'd think I'd be upset, yet I'm not. I'm excited and scared. Through it all, Ian was always there to guide me."

"He'll gain control of his god. You've given him a reason, Dani. For that, we all owe you a great debt. We thought we had lost Ian."

Danielle thought back on that conversation later that afternoon as she was helping to clean the castle. Reaghan was again with Kirstin, who had been quiet and more withdrawn than usual. Braden was never far from Kirstin either.

As anxious as Danielle was, she couldn't sit and wait. So, when Cara had mentioned cleaning, Danielle was the first to jump up and get started. The castle was huge, so it took all of them to keep it in order.

Even the men helped, though Danielle noticed Quinn and Arran never let Charlie out of their sight. Danielle was thankful of that when she looked up to find Charlie watching her. She thought she caught a brief glimpse of malevolence in his eyes, but it was gone before she could be sure. She left the area he was in shortly there-after.

Danielle stretched her back from dusting in the tower. She had been dusting most of the day and had only done a dozen or so rooms.

She picked up her rag and turned to leave the tower when she found Charlie standing in the doorway. A thread of fear spiraled up from her stomach.

"Hello, Dani," he said, his smile a little too bright.

"Charlie. The tower is cleaned. Maybe Cara needs you for something."

"Oh, no one will be looking for me for some time."

Danielle lifted her chin, refusing to be frightened. "Why is that?"

"You needn't worry." He pushed away from the door and walked toward her. "Tell me, Dani, are you scared?"

"Of you? No."

"You should be," he whispered. His eyes were bright with malice, his smile promising pain as he began to circle her. "You think you're so smart, do you no'? You think you have me figured out."

Danielle kept facing him, tracking him step for step. "You mean because I know it was you who scratched me? Because I know your power isn't wind as you told the others?"

"You and Ian made it too easy for me. I thought I was going to have a difficult time worming my way into the MacLeods' trust, but you've given me all that I need."

"The others know. I've told them."

"By the time I'm finished with them, they willna even remember you existed."

Danielle knew real trepidation then. The door was right behind her. If she was quick enough she might make it out of the tower, but would she make it down the winding stairs? Anything was better than staying in the tower with Charlie.

"Ian will remember, and you won't be able to kill him."

"Kill him?" Charlie asked with a laugh. "He'll be Deirdre's before night has fallen."

*No*, Danielle screamed in her mind. She wouldn't allow that to happen. Before she could think on it more, she made a dash for the door. Just as she was going through it, Charlie slammed it against her. Danielle cried out as she was crushed between the thick wood and the stone. He let loose the door and she fell on the small landing of the stairs.

She never saw Charlie's foot coming at her until he connected with her ribs. She screamed, silently begging for Ian.

Ian jerked awake as he felt a scream resounding in his head, a scream that sounded remarkably like Danielle. He took a deep breath and felt for her magic. What hit him was a wall of icy terror and distress that had him on his feet and racing for the cell door.

He pulled at the metal. "Hayden! Quinn! Let me out!" he bellowed.

The dungeon was made so no one in the castle could hear the cries of those being held, but a Warrior had extra sensitive hearing. He just prayed someone was close enough to hear him.

The more he struggled against the iron and his inability to get to Danielle the more his rage grew until he was in a frenzy. Which only allowed Farmire to grow louder in his mind.

Ian knew he was so very close to losing control. For good, he feared.

Danielle meant too much to him, and the fact he couldn't help her just as he hadn't been able to aid Duncan before his death left Ian feeling helpless and power-less. He hated the feeling.

And Farmire fed his fury and need for vengeance.

Ian threw back his head and bellowed as his fangs filled his mouth. His claws scraped against the iron. With his strength, he should easily bend the bars, but too late he realized they had been enforced with magic.

"Danielle!" he roared.

Through the haze of pain and struggling to draw breath, somehow Danielle called up her power and sent a blast of it toward Charlie. He flew back into the tower.

Danielle pulled herself to her feet, holding her ribs, and half ran half fell down the stairs. She had to make it to Ian.

"It'll take more than that wee bit of magic to keep me down," Charlie said menacingly from behind her.

Danielle didn't look over her shoulder as she kept moving. The stairs seemed to go on forever, and she could hear Charlie gaining on her. She was able to dodge his first attempt to grab her, but on the second try he snagged her hair and jerked her to a stop.

She reached back to try and lessen the pain on her scalp as he continued to yank on her hair.

"You're so pathetic. By tomorrow everyone in the castle will be dead. I'll have the artifacts and Deirdre will have Ian."

"No!" Danielle yelled, and threw her elbow into Char-lie's gut at the same time she pushed her magic into him. She heard something metallic clank on the stairs, but she couldn't look to find out what it was.

He grunted from the hit, but he didn't release his hold on her.

"When they find you, you'll be just barely alive enough to tell them Ian did this to you."

"Never," she swore, and turned so she could face him and try to kick him.

Charlie laughed. "I'm going to release Ian. He'll find you, and it'll be what breaks him, allowing his god control."

Danielle fought with all her might and all her magic. Somehow she managed to free herself and turned to race down the rest of the stairs.

She had just reached the corridor when Charlie's hand wrapped around her throat and began to squeeze.

"Does it hurt?" he asked, his eyes blazing with hatred. "Try and scream for help, Dani. Call out to Ian."

She slapped at his face and desperately tried to move his hand from her throat as her air began to diminish. He held her above him, her feet dangling from the floor.

The edge of her vision was dotted with black while her lungs burned for air.

Danielle couldn't believe she was going to die. And Ian would blame himself. She had thought she'd have a future, maybe even a future with Ian.

"Tell me where the artifacts are," Charlie demanded.

All her strength was leaving her as her body screamed for air, but she had just enough left in her to kick Charlie in the balls.

He doubled over, his squeal of pain music to her ears.

But then he gave one final squeeze.

# CHAPTER
# THIRTY-SEVEN

Ian clawed at the stones and the bars, anything that might get him out of the dungeon and to Danielle. He could feel her magic lessen, feel its panic along with hers.

Farmire urged him to give in, his words persuasive and convincing. Farmire promised Ian the means to get out of the dungeon if he just gave over control.

The thought of Danielle in danger nearly had him agreeing, but then Ian remembered even if Farmire got him out, he wouldn't be there to help Danielle. He wouldn't be at all. It would be Farmire.

"Nay," Ian bellowed, and swiped his claws down the stone.

He clawed at himself and the deep, resonating ache in his chest where his heart was, at the helplessness that consumed him. Devoured him.

Destroyed him.

His madness raged, his fury grew, and all the while Farmire howled his pleasure.

Ian was losing the battle. He knew it in his bones, felt it in his soul. But with Duncan gone, and now Danielle, Ian couldn't find a reason to keep fighting.

An image of Danielle smiling flashed in Ian's mind. Her emerald eyes stared at him, darkened by desire right before she cried out in pleasure as he entered her.

He saw her laughing, pictured her in his arms. It was the only thing that kept him hanging on to himself, by a thread that was swiftly unraveling.

Arran rounded the corner of the hallway and saw Charlie with his hand around Danielle's throat. In less than a heartbeat Arran had called up his god and raced toward Charlie.

Behind him, Arran heard Quinn and Hayden running fast. But it was Arran's claws that severed Charlie's head from his body. The widening of Charlie's eyes as he spotted Arran seconds before his head was decapitated left Arran with a smile on his face.

Charlie's head bounced and rolled down the hallway as his body collapsed at Arran's feet.

"Holy Hell," Quinn said as he slid to a halt beside Arran.

It was Hayden who gathered Danielle's unconscious form in his arms from where she had fallen to the floor.

"I wish you would have let me have a go at him, Arran," Hayden said.

Arran looked from Charlie's body to Hayden then Quinn. "This is my fault."

"Nay, it's mine," Hayden interjected. "I watched Charlie walk to Quinn. I assumed he'd stay there."

"And I assumed Charlie was returning to help Arran as he said he was," Quinn stated. "The blame doesna lie on just one person."

Arran looked at Danielle and the bruises forming on her throat. "Damn."

"Ian," Hayden said with a frown.

Quinn slowly let out a breath. "If he's as attuned to Dani as I think he is, he had to have felt her fear."

"I'll tell Ian," Arran offered.

Hayden grunted. "It might be wise for all of us to go."

"My fear is that he willna be able to listen," Quinn added.

Hayden nodded and said, "He's going to need to see Dani for himself, but first, we take her to Sonya."

"He asked Danielle about the artifacts," Arran said as he clutched the hair on Charlie's head and lifted it in his hand. "The bastard was after the artifacts."

"Ian and Dani knew the entire time. They tried to tell us," Quinn said.

Hayden said, "They were no' the only ones. Camdyn and Arran both had reservations about him."

"It doesna matter now," Arran said. "Get Dani to Sonya while I clean up this mess."

"I'll help," Quinn offered.

Arran and Quinn worked wordlessly to remove all evidence of Charlie in the castle, but no amount of scrubbing would allow Arran to forget he had nearly caused Dani's death.

He found the key on one of the lower steps leading to the tower. Arran had never seen anything like it before, so he put it in his pocket until he could ask about it later.

Arran could be to blame if Ian had given in to his god. He wanted to go to Ian immediately, but once they reached the great hall and heard his bellows, all of Arran's fears for his friend flooded his mind.

"He's strong," Quinn said. "He willna give in easily to Farmire."

Arran swallowed and proceeded out of the castle,

Ian's roars ringing in his ears. "I pray to God you're right, Quinn."

Quinn glanced at the door down to the dungeon and briefly closed his eyes. "So do I," he whispered.

Larena stood next to Malcolm and refused to believe he wasn't the same caring, helpful man who had been willing to stand with her against Deirdre.

"I'm sorry," Larena said. "I should have told you the Monroe name was on the scroll I carry. I wanted to protect you."

Malcolm shrugged. "If I had told you I was leaving, you would have let me know it was on the list and that I could have the god inside me."

"We all knew you had it inside you, Malcolm. None of the Warriors wanted you to endure what they had gone through. We thought as long as you were at the castle you could be kept from it. I knew you were miserable. I just didn't know how much."

He looked down at his right arm and held it up to her. "Deirdre healed me. She took away the scars. They're gone from the outside, but they're still there inside, Larena. They'll always be there."

She put her hand on his cheek and smiled into his blue eyes. A laugh escaped her when a lock of his blond hair fell into his eyes. "I've missed you terribly. I'll do anything you ask, but please come back with us. Stand with us against Deirdre."

"I wish I could, but I didna lie. I'm lost to you. Save your words, Larena, because I willna be swayed."

"Why?" she demanded and dropped her hand. "I know you, dammit. I know what a good man you are. There is nothing besides family that would make you agree to align with Deirdre."

And then it hit her.

"Oh, God," she muttered and covered her mouth with her hand. Tears gathered in her eyes as she shook her head. She dropped her hand and said, "It's because of me, isn't it? You're staying to protect me."

Malcolm looked away from her, but it was all the answer she needed.

"I can take care of myself. You of all people should know this," Larena argued.

Malcolm snorted. "I seem to recall you dying in my arms after having *drough* blood put inside your wounds."

"I'm stronger now. I'm also more prepared. There are Warriors at the castle ready and waiting to attack Deirdre."

"And to awaken her twin, Laria." Malcolm glanced at her and nodded. "Deirdre knows. She gets visits from the Devil, if you can believe that. He told her about the artifacts and what they could do. He also told her to forget them, but she's obsessed. She will stop at nothing to keep you from awakening her sister."

"So she sends you to kill children."

Malcolm shifted uneasily. "I'm here to find a Druid, as I'm sure you've deduced by now."

Larena didn't see any point in keeping it from him. "We have. We also knew it was Deirdre who sent you and not Declan."

At the mention of Declan, Malcolm's lips twisted in a sneer. "That obscene man? He kept Deirdre trapped in his mansion for over a month. He has delusions of having her as his own and ruling with her. You know she willna share with anyone."

Larena was absorbing all the information and filing it away in her mind. "Deirdre will fall, Malcolm. I don't want to fight you."

"Then keep away." He turned his head toward her. "Have one of the others kill me, and quickly. Even if I returned with you, my soul is black now. And dead."

She watched him walk away toward the school. Larena knew she should go after him, but his words had pierced her too deeply.

"Larena?" Fallon asked as he pulled her into his arms. "We got close enough to hear most of what was said."

"We need to go after him," Broc said.

Larena pulled out of Fallon's arms and wiped at her eyes. "No. I saw into his eyes. Somewhere, deep inside, he's still the same man I knew. He doesn't want to kill the children."

"But he will do so to keep you safe," Isla said softly.

They turned as one to the school where the children were lining up to return to their classrooms. Most of the teachers were together, but off to the side stood three women.

"The Druid is there," Broc said as he pointed to the three women.

Fallon nodded in agreement. "Aye, and Malcolm has seen her."

"We aren't seriously going to allow him to take the Druid, are we?" Isla asked.

Before Larena could respond Malcolm disappeared behind one of the buildings. A moment later there was an explosion. Chaos ensued as everyone screamed and tried to run away.

Larena ran toward the Druid with Fallon right beside her. They leaped over the tall fence that separated the school from the street and dodged the kids and adults running away.

When they looked up, the Druid was gone.

"Here," Broc called from across the way.

Larena and Fallon dodged more people until they

found the narrow doorway where the Druid must have disappeared. They ducked through it and found themselves in a small courtyard where Malcolm and the sandy-haired Druid had faced off.

"Malcolm, stand down," Fallon demanded.

"You know I can no'."

The Druid flashed her blue eyes from Malcolm to Fallon. Out of the corner of her eye, Larena spotted Broc and Isla as they approached from the opposite side.

Isla took a step toward the Druid, but the Druid held up her hand, a pulse of magic vibrating around her.

"Stay back," the Druid said.

"We're here to help," Larena spoke slowly. "We know you're a Druid. We can feel your magic."

The Druid's brows furrowed. "I won't hesitate to kill all of you if anyone takes another step closer."

Malcolm chuckled. "Your magic is strong, Druid. But it will take much more than your magic to kill me."

"No," the Druid said as she shook her head, her short sandy hair just reaching to her chin. "The only ones I wouldn't be able to kill are Warriors."

Malcolm clapped his hands slowly. "The Druid knows her history."

"Enough, Malcolm," Larena said, and started for him.

In an instant Malcolm released his god, his skin shifting to dark burgundy. "I asked you no' to fight me, cousin."

"And I'm begging you to remember the boy who found me in the woods, the boy who brought me food and befriended me when my own clan banished me. I'm begging you to remember that boy who grew into a man and forsook his own father's orders to stand by my side even when you were mortal."

A muscle in Malcolm's jaw jumped as he clenched his teeth. He squeezed his eyes closed. "Larena."

His voice so full of desperation and despair brought more tears to her eyes. She took a step toward Malcolm, but before she reached him, his eyes snapped open, and he rushed the Druid.

"No!" Larena screamed at the same moment the Druid threw her magic into Malcolm.

Malcolm went tumbling backward head over heels and slammed against the brick of the building behind him where he slumped unconscious.

Fallon held up his hands when the Druid turned to him. "I'm Fallon MacLeod. If you know what Warriors are, then you must know my name."

"You cannot possibly exist. There's been no word of you in . . ."

"Centuries," he offered. "I know, but it is me. We can protect you from Deirdre if you come with us to the castle."

She shook her head. "No."

"He'll only find you again," Broc said. "Deirdre sent Malcolm because she needs a Druid. He was supposed to kill all the children in order to draw you out. Next time, you willna be so lucky."

The Druid looked behind her at the school. "I'll make it on my own."

The sound of sirens fast approaching took their attention off the Druid. In that instant, she was gone.

"I can find her," Broc offered. "She couldna have gone far."

"We'll keep an eye on her, but for now, we need to leave," Fallon said.

Larena hurried to Malcolm. He lay unmoving, but he was still alive and his god clearly visible. "We can't leave him like this."

Fallon gave a great sigh and hefted Malcolm on his

shoulders before he teleported away. In an instant, he had returned and took the three of them back to MacLeod Castle.

Only to find the castle in an uproar.

# CHAPTER
# THIRTY-EIGHT

The first thing that popped into Danielle's mind when she opened her eyes was Ian.

"Easy," Saffron said with a hand on her shoulder. "You've just been healed."

Danielle shrugged off Saffron's hand and threw back the blankets. "I need to see Ian."

"I doona think that's a good idea."

Danielle turned her head to the doorway to find Ramsey standing there. Her stomach fell to her feet as she realized just what his words implied. "I can reach him, Ramsey. I know I can."

Ramsey moved from the doorway farther into the chamber. "Arran and Quinn have been with him for hours. He's no' even showing he knows they're there, Dani."

Danielle rose to her feet, her legs shaky beneath her weight. "I'm going to him."

She walked past Ramsey and out of her chamber. The cold stones penetrated her wool socks as she walked silently down the corridor then descended the stairs.

The great hall was filled with every member of the

castle. She paused as she saw them sitting still as stones, the Warriors wincing every once in a while. But no one said a word. There was no sound other than the wind from the sea.

Danielle proceeded to the doorway down to the dungeon, and the closer she got, the more she caught a faint sound from below. But when she opened the door and heard Ian's roars, her knees buckled.

She caught hold of the doorway to keep herself standing. Then, after taking a deep breath, she walked through the door and shut it behind her.

Each step down into the dungeon was like a knife through her heart as she heard Ian's bellows and his claws scraping on the stone.

Her feet became as heavy as stone the closer to Ian's cell she walked. When she finally saw him, she took a step back, her hand over her mouth.

"Oh, Ian," she whispered, tears blurring her vision.

He had shredded his shirt, which hung in tatters around his broad shoulders. Blood stained his chest from wounds he had inflicted on himself but had already healed. The stones along the back of his cell were scoured with claw marks, evidence of how badly his fury raged.

She winced when he punched the wall and she heard the snap of bone.

"Ian!" she called as she walked to the bars. "Ian, stop this!"

He continued on as if he hadn't heard her. Danielle wiped her tears away. Ian didn't need tears. He needed strength. She was more afraid than she had been when her parents had died, but for Ian, she would find that strength.

For him, she would walk into Hell itself to bring him back.

Because she loved him.

Danielle bit her lip as the truth of it filled her. She loved him with every fiber of her being, and she would fight for him.

"Ian, I'm here," she said calmly. "Look at me, Ian. Hear me."

His eyes were crazed, and his roars deafening, but she kept up her soft words. She had no idea how much time had passed. When her legs grew tired from standing, she sat next to the bars, never halting her words.

Slowly, she began to see a change in Ian. His bellows began to lessen. A short time later he stopped hitting and clawing the stones as much. Until finally he sank to his knees, his chin lowered to his chest as it heaved.

"Ian?"

He sat with his back to her, but still made no sign that he heard her.

The fact he had calmed gave her a little peace. Danielle kept trying to reach him with her words. She rose up on her knees when his skin began to flash from the pale blue to his tanned skin.

He gave a jerk, his muscles straining in his neck, and held himself rigidly as if he were in great pain. He threw back his head and roared.

And then collapsed.

"Oh, God," Danielle cried as she rose to her feet. She yanked on the bars. "Ian? Ian, wake up, babe. Wake up and look at me. Ian?"

She pulled on the iron bars, but if Ian couldn't get out of the cell, then she certainly couldn't get in. And she knew Fallon wouldn't give her the key out of fear for her safety.

There had to be another way in. She had to reach Ian. He needed her, and she needed to touch him.

Danielle closed her eyes and called up her magic. She had never tried to use her magic to find something before, but the few times she had searched Saffron's mind had given her the idea that maybe she could.

With her concentration on finding a key into Ian's prison, Danielle moved with the rhythm of the drums she heard in her mind, swayed with the chanting only a Druid could hear.

It would be so easy to become lost in them, but Danielle kept herself from doing so. She thought of Ian, of how she had to get to him, and it helped her to keep her concentration on the key.

She soon found her mind moving all about the castle searching towers and chambers, and even the dungeon. The next thing she knew her mind had taken her outside the castle walls into the village.

After every cottage had been looked at, her mind took her to the ruins of the abbey. But she didn't find a key there either.

Then suddenly, she could feel something cold and metallic through the dirt and the snow. She followed the strange, unusual pull until she found herself outside the kitchen near Cara's garden.

Danielle's eyes snapped open, a smile on her lips. She had found another key.

She got to her feet and looked at Ian. He hadn't moved, and it propelled her out of the dungeon as if Deirdre herself were after her.

Dani only paused when she got to the door leading into the great hall. She quietly opened it, and when no one was looking slipped out and hurried into the kitchen.

She ran out into the snow without any shoes and didn't care. Her only objective was to find the key and get back to Ian. She walked in circles until she found the exact spot. Then, on her hands and knees in the thick snow, she began to dig.

The icy snow cut her hands, and the frozen earth

bent back her nails until they bled. But she felt none of it. Blood oozed between her fingers, helping to coat her hands against the hard soil.

Elation swept through her when she caught sight of something metallic in the soil. A few quick digs, and Danielle held the key in her hand.

With her teeth chattering, she hurried back into the kitchen.

"Dani?" Cara called. "What are you doing outside?"

"Getting some air," Danielle answered and kept walking.

"Is that blood on your hands?"

Danielle didn't want to ignore her, but she couldn't answer her. She stopped in the great hall and looked at Fallon.

"Ian has collapsed. Will you let me in to see him?"

Fallon shook his head, his eyes on the table. "I can no', Dani. We doona know how he will awaken, and I willna put your life in danger. Ian would never forgive me."

Danielle had wanted to give him a chance. She gave a nod and hurried back to Ian. Her hands shook so much she could barely get the key into the lock.

When she heard the latch click open, she threw the door wide and raced to Ian. She wiped her hands on her shirt to get most of the blood off before she touched him.

His skin was on fire and his heart raced, but he didn't move. Not even when she maneuvered him so that his head lay in her lap as she leaned against the bars. She stroked his hair and his chest all the while calling his name, begging him to open his eyes.

Danielle closed her eyes as weariness took hold. Not even Deirdre herself could have made Danielle release

her hold on Ian, not now. Not when she finally had him
in her arms.

And if his god had taken control, Danielle would
somehow find a way to bring Ian back. He'd had control
once, he could get it again.

"You've gone off the deep end," said a male voice.

It brought Danielle out of her thoughts, and she opened
her eyes to find Lucan at the doorway into the cell. "I'm
doing what I need to do."

"And if he awakens with Farmire in control and kills
you?"

Danielle swallowed. "He won't."

"You doona sound so sure. Dani, you need to get out
of there before he wakes."

She shook her head. "No, Lucan. I . . . I love him. I
told him I would help him fight Farmire, and I am. He
isn't bellowing or cutting up the stones anymore."

"How did you get in?" Lucan asked as he fingered
the key in the door. "Fallon refused to give you the key."

"I found another." She was proud of herself. It proved
that her magic was growing. She was becoming the
Druid Aunt Josie had always said she could be.

All because she had wrecked her car, got lost, and
found Ian.

"Shut the door," Danielle said. "Take the key. Whatever happens . . . happens. If Farmire is in control—"

"We've already promised Ian we would end it."

She took a deep breath. "You've been good to him.
You are his family. All of you."

"We are yours as well."

"I know. Please tell the others not to come down
here. I want to be alone with Ian."

Lucan looked at Ian and stepped aside so he could
close the cell door and take the key. "Even if Farmire is

in command, Ian will know what he has done. He'll
never forgive himself."

"Ian is strong. He'll be in control."

"For your sake, I hope you're correct."

Danielle shut her eyes again as Lucan walked away.
She put her hand over Ian's heart and felt the steady
beat of it. Ian had once told her he loved the feel of her
magic.

She called up her magic and let it fill the cell, hoping
he would recognize it and find his way back to her.

Ian felt the strong, steady pulse of magic through the
darkness. He recognized that magic.

*Danielle.*

He fought against that darkness, the cloying, abys-
mal blackness that sucked him deeper and deeper into a
chasm he knew he would never come back from.

The more he struggled against the blackness, the
more Farmire's presence besieged him. Ian was contin-
ually inundated. Ceaselessly beset. Endlessly plagued.

But Danielle's magic was like a beacon in the darkness. He reached for it, for her. It was just out of his
reach, so close he could feel the magic brush against his
face. Yet, Farmire wasn't letting go without a battle.

Farmire's power was absolute. He wanted to prove to
Ian once and for all that he could dominate.

*"Fight him,"* Duncan's voice whispered in Ian's mind
as if it came from a great distance.

Ian struggled against Farmire's hold with all his
might. He thought of Danielle, of what she had given
him. He thought of the man he wanted to be, and the future he desperately yearned for.

Farmire's grasp slipped a fraction.

*"Aye, brother. You can do it,"* Duncan urged.

Ian clung to Duncan's voice and Danielle's magic.

Without them, he knew he would have been lost. The more he pulled against Farmire and gained the upper hand, the more strength he had.

Until, finally, he was the one dominating Farmire.

*"Go to her,"* Duncan said. *"Live your life as I refused to live mine. Forget the past and look to the future. Bring love and laughter into your life, brother."*

Ian didn't want to let Duncan go. He needed his brother.

*"Nay, no longer. You have someone else. Listen . . ."*

Ian heard Danielle's voice in his head like the softest caress. He did as Duncan asked and followed Danielle's magic out of the darkness.

When Ian opened his eyes, he feasted upon Danielle's face. She sat with her head against the bars and her eyes shut, but her hand was over his heart.

There was so much he wanted to say to her, so much he needed to say. But the words lodged in his throat as he drank in her beauty. He covered her hand with his. A moment later, she sucked in a breath and opened her emerald eyes.

"You came back to me," she said with an easy smile.

"I came back for you."

# CHAPTER
# THIRTY-NINE

Malcolm woke to find himself in a field, two sheep staring at him while others grazed unmindful of his presence. One of the sheep baaed and trotted off while the second turned away and began to munch on the grass.

Malcolm sat up and rubbed the back of his neck. He certainly wasn't in Edinburgh anymore, or anywhere even close. It must have been Fallon who jumped him out of the city. But why?

Even as he asked himself the question he knew. Regardless of what he had done or who he was, to Fallon he was family.

For the second time in a matter of weeks, Malcolm had spoken to Larena. How he'd missed her jesting and her easy nature. He could see how the passing of time had changed her, but only for the better. She was stronger than before.

Her words, her urging him to return to the castle with her was difficult for him to hear because it was all he wanted to do. Ever since Deirdre had found him he'd wished he'd never left the castle that fateful day.

But no amount of wanting would change what he had become.

Malcolm rose to his feet and instantly tamped down his god. He turned in a circle, looking around him until he spotted a small two-story house atop a hill in the distance.

He'd stop there first and figure out where he was. Deirdre would be expecting him, and if he didn't return soon, there was no telling what she would do to Larena.

That thought propelled Malcolm forward. He lengthened his stride into a steady run, the ground a blur beneath him.

Ian came up on his knees and pulled Danielle into his arms. He kissed her as if there were no tomorrow, as if she would be taken from him at any moment.

His kiss was full of longing and desire and . . . love.

He ended the kiss and took her face between his hands. Duncan had known what was in Ian's heart even before Ian had been ready to accept it. But now that he had, Ian was overcome with emotion so strong and pure that his chest felt as if it would burst.

"Ian, I was so afraid I had lost you," Danielle said.

"You shouldna have come in here. I could have hurt you. What was Fallon thinking giving you the key?"

Danielle glanced down before she said, "He didn't. I used my magic and found one."

"I told you your magic was powerful."

She laughed and hugged him tight. "I've never been so afraid in my life as when I saw you."

Ian looked at the stones behind Danielle and saw the marks. He could well imagine how he must have looked to her. "I'm sorry I frightened you."

"You didn't," she said. She leaned back, her brows

drawn together. "It was the thought of Farmire taking you that scared me. But you never allowed it."

He couldn't believe how lucky he had gotten in finding such a woman. He took her hands in his and saw her grimace. Ian looked at her hands and saw the cuts and dried blood coating her fingers and hands.

"What happened?"

She shrugged. "The key was buried outside. I had to dig through the snow and frozen, packed earth to get to it."

Ian's heart pounded loudly in his chest. "Do no' hurt yourself so ever again."

"You had fallen unconscious, Ian. I knew Farmire was taking you, and I had to get to you."

He swallowed, unable to believe a beautiful, strong, amazing woman like Danielle would risk her life for him. "I didna think you were so reckless."

"It seems when it comes to you, I am."

Her words, spoken barely above a whisper, sent a thrill running through him. Maybe he did have a chance with her. Maybe her passion for him went deeper.

"Danielle," he said, and slid his fingers into her cool, silky hair. "I . . . love you."

Danielle's heart jumped into her throat when she saw emotion flood into Ian's sherry eyes. Elation filled her, propelling her magic to swirl around her as his words sank into her mind.

The dark, dank dungeon faded away as she lost herself in him. "And I love you, my Warrior."

His devastating smile could melt the stoutest of hearts. He kissed her slowly, seductively. And thoroughly. His hands were on her back, molding her against his rock-hard body.

Instantly, heat flooded her as moisture pooled between her legs. She moaned and tilted her head to the side so he could deepen the kiss.

Deirdre and Declan, Charlie, and all the other evils of the world didn't matter anymore. Nothing mattered but the man in her arms, the man who had fought against a primeval god for control of his body and mind. And won.

A man who made her heart sing and her body melt. A man like no other.

"I didna think finding a woman such as you would be possible," Ian said between kisses.

Danielle wound her arms around his neck, his hair tickling her arm. "I've dreamed of finding you my entire life."

"No more dreams. Now, we make a future."

Danielle winced. "Ah, I think there's some things I need to fill you in on."

Ian sighed and rose to his feet, pulling Danielle up with him. "Then we had better get out of this dungeon and into a shower. I want to hear everything, but first, I want to make love to you."

"Umm," she purred as she rose up on her tiptoes to kiss him. "I'm liking the sound of that."

"How long have you been down here?"

She shrugged. "I have no idea. Lucan came down and locked me in with you, so he has the other key."

"Remind me to kill Lucan when I get out of here."

She laughed and walked to the cell door. "Don't blame him. I wouldn't leave."

"He'd damned sure want me to pull Cara out of this dungeon had she done what you did."

Danielle looked at Ian as he came to stand beside her. "I told you, Ian Kerr, nothing was going to keep me from you."

"I was almost gone. Farmire was so strong, but then I felt your magic. Duncan told me to follow it to you."

"Duncan?" she repeated.

Ian nodded, a half smile upon his lips. "I've thought myself daft for a long time because I heard Duncan in my head. It began after I was brought to this time. He always seemed to be there when I needed him most. He's gone now."

"So, it really was him?"

He nodded. "Aye. It really was him. I doona know how, nor do I care. He helped me keep my head during those long weeks alone in the cave. And between both you and him, I am now in full control of my god."

"You would have done it yourself eventually."

"What?" he asked, his forehead furrowed deeply.

Danielle licked her lips. "While you were unconscious I began to think of what you had told me happened when Farmire took control. When I came down here, your fury was so great everyone else thought you had already been taken by Farmire. You wouldn't listen to anyone, or even appear to hear them."

"Because I didna."

"But I watched you, and kept talking to you. After a long while you began to calm. Eventually, you grew quiet, just sitting there, your back to me."

"I recall Farmire wanting control," Ian said, his voice trailing off, as he looked through the bars.

Danielle rubbed her hand up and down Ian's well-defined arm. "Then the strangest thing happened. You stiffened as if you were fighting something mentally, and then you fell down unconscious. I think all those times you woke thinking Farmire was in control, you got it wrong. I think you were so strong that you lost consciousness when he took control so he couldn't harm anyone."

Ian gripped the iron in his hand until his knuckles

were white. Could Danielle be right? Could he have been in control all along?

"I thought by being in the cave it was too far away from anyone for Farmire to seek them out."

Danielle shook her head of silver hair. "If what you told me is true, Farmire would have walked a thousand miles in order to begin a battle. It was you all along, Ian."

Ian drew in a deep breath and smiled. "It's time we left the dungeon."

Danielle chuckled as he bellowed for Fallon to release them.

A few moments later Fallon, Arran, and Broc were in the dungeon staring at him as if they didn't know him.

"Stop it and release us," Ian demanded.

Fallon cleared his throat and glanced at Danielle. "How do I know it's really you, Ian?"

Ian rolled his eyes. "If Farmire was in control, Danielle wouldna be standing beside me now."

"He's telling the truth," Danielle told them, and wrapped an arm around Ian's waist. "He said my magic felt different to him from other Druids, so I used my magic to reach him."

"And it worked. She pulled me from the depths. Now, I am in desperate need of a shower and at least four meals. Open the door, Fallon."

"Open it," Hayden said. "All you have to do is look in Ian's eyes to see it's him."

Fallon produced the key and unlocked the door. It swung wide, and Ian pushed Danielle through first before he walked out. He was following Danielle up the steps to the great hall when Arran's voice made him pause.

"A lot has happened, Ian. We need you both in the hall."

"I just want a quick shower," Danielle said.

"After you see Sonya," Ian interjected.

When he stepped into the great hall, he found everyone staring at him. Ian looked at them with new eyes. He didn't know what to say to any of them, but then he didn't have to.

They swarmed him, their smiles and words only solidifying his feeling that the castle was his home, and the people inside it his family.

*Godspeed, Duncan.*

And to Ian's regret, there was no response.

# CHAPTER
# FORTY

It was well after midnight by the time Danielle and Ian had finished eating and hearing about Charlie and all that had happened in Edinburgh with Phelan, Malcolm, and the Druid.

"So you didna get her name?" Ian asked.

Broc shook his head. "Nay. She was gone before we could ask, but I can find her easily enough."

"When the time comes," Fallon said. "For now, I just want to be sure she's safe. She's scared and running. She'll hide for a while."

"But for how long?" Isla asked. "Deirdre found her through black magic. She can do it again."

Hayden raised a blond brow. "My wife has a valid point. It would be safest for the Druid to come to the castle."

"Safest, but maybe no' the wisest," Ramsey said as he stared into his glass of wine.

Danielle exchanged a look with Ian. "What's that supposed to mean?"

Ramsey lifted his head. "Nothing."

But Danielle suspected there was a lot more to Ramsey's words.

"I'd like to apologize for no' listening to you more closely about Charlie," Fallon said to Ian.

Ian shrugged away his words. "You've opened this castle up to anyone wanting to fight Deirdre. How can we fight her as a group if there isna trust? You trusted him."

"And made a mistake," Fallon said. "Next time I'm going to listen to all of you."

Ian winked at Danielle and stuffed another piece of Cara's homemade bread into his mouth. "I just wish Charlie were still around so I could kill him myself."

"Trust me, Arran did an admirable job," Quinn said and raised his glass to Arran.

Arran gave a nod. "It felt good to kill the bastard, I admit."

"So, he was working for Deirdre," Danielle said. "Right?"

"That's what we assume," Lucan answered.

Cara shrugged. "We can't really know for sure, can we? I mean, with both Declan and Deirdre out there."

Fallon leaned forward in his seat at the head of the table and placed something small and shining atop the wood. Danielle's stomach fell to her feet when she recognized the key that had brought her to MacLeod Castle.

She looked to Ian to find him watching her.

"I think this is yours," Fallon said as he pointed to the key. "Arran found it after Charlie had been . . . eliminated."

Danielle rose from the table and walked toward Fallon. She stopped beside him and reached for the key. As soon as she touched it, the key hummed.

It was the key's way of telling her it had found its

home. Danielle gathered it in her palm and turned to hand it to Fallon.

"This is what brought me to MacLeod Castle. It wouldn't allow me to give it to you because of Charlie, though at the time I didn't know it was him who was the cause. Regardless, this is the key that will open the Tablet of Orn."

Fallon accepted the key with a slight nod of his head. "You kept it safe."

It wasn't a question, yet Danielle felt she needed to explain. "I wanted to give it to you as soon as I got here. I hated keeping it a secret."

"You did the right thing," Lucan said.

The others all nodded in agreement. Danielle blew out a breath and returned to her seat. Ian reached across the table and held out his hand.

Danielle didn't hesitate to take it. She felt as if a great weight had been lifted off her shoulders now that the MacLeods had the key.

But it wasn't until Gwynn laid something on the table that Danielle looked away from Ian. And gasped when she saw the cylinder shape and the knotwork carved in the gold she had seen in her vision from the key.

"The Tablet of Orn," Gwynn said with a smile.

Fallon shook his head when Gwynn tried to pass the cylinder to him. "You and Logan found the Tablet, Gwynn. It should be the two of you who open it."

Danielle squeezed Ian's hand when she saw Gwynn's hand begin to shake. Logan took the key from Fallon and together he and Gwynn put the key in the lock and turned. There was a loud click and then the cylinder lid flipped open.

"Oh, my," Gwynn said breathlessly as she pulled something out of the cylinder.

Everyone simply stared at the cylinder with its many wooden dials that moved around the tube. Everyone but Ian.

He sat still as stone when he saw the symbols on the cylinder. As if it were yesterday, he recalled his parents carving those same symbols again and again all over their cottage.

"Anyone know the code?" Logan asked with a frown.

Gwynn shook her head. "I've never seen anything like it. I should know it though, right? I'm the Keeper of the Tablet after all."

"No' necessarily," Galen said as he took the cylinder and inspected it. He moved the dials around and around.

"Wonderful," Broc said with a loud sigh. "More waiting. I had hoped this would be the map to Laria's location."

The cylinder was passed around while everyone looked at the symbols. Talk turned to what the sequence could be, and after a bit they began to try different orders of the symbols to no avail.

The more Ian looked at it, the more he realized that somehow, he knew the order.

Ian cleared his throat. "Let me see it."

Everyone looked at him in surprise, but Camdyn passed the cylinder to him without comment.

Ian released Danielle's hand and ran his thumbs over the square pieces of wood carved meticulously with beautiful knotwork.

"I've seen these before," he said, his heart racing with the possibility.

"Where?" Danielle asked.

"My parents' home. These symbols, all eight of them, were carved over and over in our cottage, in our barn, and in every piece of wood we owned." He paused and turned the first row to the first symbol.

"They made me and Duncan learn the order. When we asked why, they said that one day it would be important."

He clicked the second, then third row into place.

"I had forgotten all about it until I saw the cylinder," he murmured, and moved the fourth row into place.

Ian snapped the fifth into place. "How could my parents have known I would need to know this?"

The sixth row clicked into place. "This cannot be possible."

Danielle leaned over the table and touched his arm. "Anything is possible."

He looked into her emerald eyes and at the curtain of silver hair that fell over her shoulder. "Anything," he repeated, and moved the seventh and eighth symbols into place.

The end of the cylinder popped out, revealing a rolled piece of parchment. Ian carefully lowered the cylinder to the table and pulled out the scroll.

"Is it the map?" Arran asked.

Ian cautiously unrolled the parchment and simply stared at the map. "Shite. We're really going to awaken Deirdre's twin."

The hall erupted in cheers as Ian hurriedly passed the scroll to Fallon. Ian and Danielle simply stared at each other, smiling as the realization that it was all about to end sank in.

And for the first time, Ian found himself thinking of a future without Deirdre and her evil.

Danielle linked both of her hands in his, the cylinder between them. "I love you."

"I love you," he said in return. He shoved the cylinder out of the way and pulled Dani across the table into his arms.

He rose and kept a tight hold of her as she linked her

arms around his neck. They didn't need any words. The desire, the hunger was evident in both their eyes.

"Don't y'all want to celebrate?" Gwynn shouted over the noise.

Danielle looked over Ian's shoulder as he climbed the stairs to smile at Gwynn and her Texas accent. "That's exactly what we're going to do."

# EPILOGUE

Two days later...

Danielle rubbed her hands together as she faced Saffron. She blew out a breath and set her hands atop Saffron's.

"You don't have to do this," Saffron said.

Danielle squeezed her hands. "No, I don't, but I know I can now."

"The evil—" Saffron began.

"Is manageable," Danielle interrupted.

Saffron's walnut-colored hair was pulled away from her face in a loose knot, with strands falling about her face. Her soft brown eyes were trained forward, but she wasn't actually seeing anyone.

"I've lived with this blindness for years now. I'd rather stay like this than for any of the evil to harm you, Dani."

"I won't be alone," Danielle said.

Saffron's head cocked to the side a fraction. "What do you mean?"

"I mean that the others are going to lend their magic to mine."

Isla rested her hand on Saffron's shoulders. "What Dani means is that she will be the one searching your mind for the spell, but our magic is going to boost hers."

"So all of you could be harmed," Saffron said.

"No," Reaghan said. "The evil won't touch us."

Saffron took a deep breath and gave a small nod. "All right."

Danielle looked at the other Druids around her with a smile. She saw Kirstin standing with Braden, and gave the Druid a smile. Kirstin had refrained from helping because she didn't have much magic.

With a nod to Isla, Danielle closed her eyes and called up her magic. To her right she could feel Ian's presence as he sat beside her, offering her comfort.

Danielle delved into Saffron's mind, hiding the wince at the slimy feel of the evil that was in every corner of Saffron's mind. Dani didn't know how Saffron was handling such an invasion.

And she also found herself wondering just how much of the evil was bleeding through into Saffron herself.

The evil clung to Danielle, but she ignored it, concentrating on her magic while she searched for the spell to reverse Saffron's blindness.

She was deeper into Saffron's mind than she had ever been before, and the deeper she went, the more the evil was. But just as the evil began to overtake Danielle, her magic caught the spell.

Danielle let her magic follow it until she had it. It was a festering mass of inky darkness that moved about Saffron's mind at will, touching everything.

Dani let the spell fill her before she began to chant the words aloud for the others to hear.

"Don't release her yet," Reaghan whispered into Danielle's ear. "We have to find the spell to reverse this."

Danielle wanted to jerk away from the evil and scrub

it from her skin, but for Saffron, she endured. It felt as if it were moving from Saffron through their linked hands into Danielle's mind.

She tried to turn her head away, her breathing becoming erratic as the evil sensed her fear.

"Nay, love. It willna touch you," Ian said, his deep voice calming her.

Danielle inhaled a steadying breath and faced the evil, daring it to touch her.

Around her she could hear the other Druids begin to chant. Saffron jerked, a cry filling the hall.

"Hold her," someone shouted.

Danielle gripped Saffron tighter as the chant began to work its magic in reversing Declan's spell. Over and over they had to repeat the chant, their magic gaining power each time.

The cloud of blackness began to diminish inside Saffron's mind, but Danielle could see it clinging, trying to dig deep into Saffron.

The longer it refused to leave the more Saffron cried out from the pain.

Danielle joined the chant, pushing her magic strongly against the cloud, until suddenly, after one last effort to remain, it was gone.

Danielle opened her eyes to see Saffron being lifted into Camdyn's arms.

"Did it work?" he asked Danielle.

"Yes," she answered.

Camdyn turned on his heel and walked up the stairs without another word.

"You did it," Ian said as he pulled Danielle into his arms.

She fell against him, needing his strength and his heat. "It was so strong," she said. "I've never felt such evil. It was everywhere inside her mind."

"Everywhere?" Galen asked.

Danielle nodded. "Everywhere. It clung to me as well. It was oppressive and cruel. How could she stand it?"

"We willna know until she wakes," Logan said. "On a more positive note, Broc has recognized the standing stones drawn on the map."

Danielle glanced up at the stairs before she turned to the map as everyone else had. It was exciting and fearful to know they were about to embark on a journey that could get them all killed if they didn't awaken Laria before Deirdre found them.

"Here," Broc said and pointed to the map. "Laria is on the Orkney Isles. The stone circle is called the Ring of Brodgar."

Fallon nodded, his arms crossed over his chest as he stared at the map. "A team of us needs to have a look around first before we bring all of us."

"Aye," Larena said. "Especially since Malcolm told me Deirdre knows we're going to awaken Laria. It could be a trap."

"I'll go," Camdyn said as he made his way back down the stairs.

Lucan nodded. "Good idea. His power to move the earth could prove useful. I'll go as well."

"Include me in this adventure," Arran stated.

Fallon looked around the hall and smiled. "Gentlemen, you leave at first light."

Danielle leaned against Ian as he put his arm around her. "You don't want to go with them?"

"Oh, I'll be there," Ian said. "Eventually."

She turned her head to look at him, her elbow on the table while her hand supported her chin. "What is that supposed to mean?"

"It means I have some other business I'd like to take care of."

"What might that be?"

He took her hands in his and turned her so she faced him. "You are the other half of me, Danielle Buchanan. My heart, my blood. My soul. I want you by my side always. I doona know what will happen with this battle with Deirdre, but I do know I want to call you wife. Will you marry me?"

Danielle blinked back her tears and swallowed. "Ian Kerr, I would like nothing better than to be your wife."

"Even if I remain immortal?"

"Even if you remain immortal."

His smile crinkled the corners of his sherry eyes as he pulled her into his arms for a kiss.

Tara Kincaid grabbed what few clothes she could stuff in her bags from her tiny flat and tossed them in her car. She was used to being on the run, used to moving from place to place. But after four years in Edinburgh, she had thought she'd finally found a place she could put down some roots.

Then the Warriors had come talking about magic. Her grandmother had taught her all about magic, or as much as she could before Tara's drunk of a mother killed her grandmother. And then tried to kill Tara.

She shook her head to clear it of those bad memories and threw the car into first as she pulled onto the snowy road. She had no idea where she was going. All these years she had moved around Scotland, even venturing into England a time or two. Maybe it was time she left Britain altogether.

Because if there were Warriors, more would come for her.

Read on for an excerpt from

# MIDNIGHT'S SEDUCTION

—the next thrilling installment in
Donna Grant's Dark Warrior series—

available in November from St. Martin's Paperbacks:

Camdyn knew the moment Saffron left the castle. He was fishing on the beach with both Hayden and Quinn when the feel of her magic simply vanished.

He went on as if nothing had occurred, because if there had been an accident, someone would have come and gotten them. Still, Camdyn found himself glancing up at the imposing figure of the castle as it rose from the cliffs.

"What's wrong?" Hayden asked him.

Camdyn shrugged. "Nothing."

"You lie poorly," Quinn said with a chuckle before he tossed the net out into the water.

Hayden had already been swimming in the cold depths of the sea and returned with several fish, but Quinn liked to do it the way he and his father had done.

Camdyn adjusted the net in his hands and turned to the side before tossing it out into the water and slowly pulling it back in. "I doona like waiting around is all."

Hayden and Quinn looked at each other and laughed.

Camdyn rolled his eyes. "What now?"

"Have you always been such an awful liar?" Hayden asked.

He knew he would have to give them the truth, or at least part of it. "I felt some magic leave."

"Aye," Hayden said with a nod. "Isla's is gone."

"So is Marcail's," Quinn said.

Camdyn looked at them with confusion. "And neither of you are worried?"

Hayden had opened his mouth to answer when Fallon's voice reached them from behind. "They needn't be worried. Marcail and Isla went with Larena, Gwynn, Dani, and Saffron to London. To shop."

Quinn shook his head. "I figured it was something like that."

"Shouldn't she have told you?" Camdyn asked.

Quinn glanced at him with a half-smile. "I know Marcail would never put herself in danger. She normally tells me when she leaves, and though I'd like to know when my wife is gone, I know through the feel of her magic."

"Saffron didna give them time to tell you or Hayden," Fallon said. "She was bound and determined to leave."

"Why?" Hayden asked. "Surely she knows we need her magic."

"She's returning," Fallon said.

Camdyn didn't want to evaluate how much that pleased him. Saffron was a distraction he didn't need or want. Regardless of how the sight of her caused his balls to tighten or his blood to heat.

"She threatened me with her own jet," Fallon said with a chuckle. "Despite all she's been through, she's kept her backbone."

"Stubbornness, more like it," Camdyn grumbled.

Hayden raised a brow. "I think stubborn can be labeled to every Druid in the castle."

"She should have taken a Warrior with her."

"She did. Larena."

Camdyn shook the net from the water and kept his gaze averted from the others. He shouldn't be so upset that Saffron was gone. Except that he knew how much Declan wanted her ability as a Seer. He could very well get to her again.

"With Larena and the other Druids with Saffron she will be kept safe, Camdyn," Fallon said.

"I know." But it still irked Camdyn that she found it so important to leave the safety of the castle to shop. He might have grasped the difference in the language of this time, but he would never understand women.

"She's been through Hell. Literally," Quinn said after a long moment of silence filled only by the crash of the waves. "Nothing here is hers."

"That's what Larena said," Fallon replied.

Hayden nodded. "Saffron isna so self-absorbed that she would do this if we were awakening Laria tonight."

"She did promise to be back in time to help with that," Fallon said and squatted down to pick up a rock. "You should have seen the excitement in her eyes when I agreed to jump her. It lit up her entire face."

Camdyn growled, hating the way his emotions were rioting inside him. He had seen many of the false smiles Saffron bestowed. They were kind, but they didn't fully reach her eyes. It was a rare thing when anyone saw true happiness on her face.

But then again, who could blame her after all she had been through?

"She'll be back in a few hours," Fallon said.

Camdyn looked at him. "Why are you telling me?"

Fallon shrugged nonchalantly before he jumped back to the castle. Quinn turned his head, but not before Camdyn saw his smile. The only one who would meet his gaze was Hayden.

"She's pretty," he said. "And wounded. A woman like that could find herself leaning on a man who was willing."

"Saffron doesna lean on anyone. She's a strong woman."

"Aye. So is Isla, but she does lean. And it's a fabulous thing, Camdyn."

Quinn nodded. "Oh, aye. A fabulous thing."

"I seem to remember you warning me about love," Hayden told Quinn.

Quinn threw back his head and laughed. "And look where that warning took you!"

"To the love of my life."

Camdyn fiddled with the net, pretending there was a knot in it, when in fact there was a knot in his chest. The love of his life died hundreds of years ago. Not once in all that time had a woman ever snagged his attention.

Until Saffron.

He'd hoped it was simply because he'd been the one to free her from the shackles Declan had used to keep her chained. Camdyn had been the only one who had been able to reach her through the magic of the prison.

He'd been the only one to carry her from that evil place and to MacLeod Castle.

Could it have been the way she clung to him, her body thin and fragile as he held her? Could it have been the way she ducked her head against his shoulder to hide her tears? Could it have been the nights he had been helpless to pass by her chamber as she cried out from the nightmares?

Whatever it was, he'd been powerless to keep his distance.

He'd loved once before and had his heart torn out. Camdyn never wanted to experience that kind of pain again. Ever.

"You're awful quiet," Hayden said as he grinned at Camdyn. "Each Warrior is finding their mate. Do you fear you'll be next?"

Camdyn looked up from the net as he went down on his haunches. "Nay," he answered.

"Nay?" Quinn asked. "What makes you so sure? Love is not something you can run from, my friend."

"Love isn't for everyone. And I've already loved once."

Hayden's brow furrowed. "I didna know."

"It is in the past," Camdyn said with a shrug. "Long ago."

Quinn set aside his net and walked to stand between Hayden and Camdyn. "What happened to her?"

Camdyn briefly closed his eyes and let out a breath. "She died. In my arms. We had years together. She aged while I stayed the same."

"So she knew what you were?" Hayden asked.

"Aye. I showed her."

Quinn shook his head. "How did you stay away from Deirdre and keep your female safe?"

"I got as far from Deirdre as I could. I was in the lowlands near the border with England," Camdyn said, and tossed aside the net. He stood and looked out over the sea.

Hayden clamped him on the shoulder. "You loved her verra much."

"Aye."

Quinn crossed his arms over his chest and rocked back on his heels. "It doesna mean you canna love again."

Camdyn looked at him. "If Marcail died, if you held her in your arms and watched the life drain from her, could you ever imagine loving again? I willna put myself through that kind of pain a second time."

"But Isla's magic prevents the Druids from aging," Hayden quickly pointed out.

Camdyn released his god. Claws extended from his fingers and fangs filled his mouth. A glance down at his skin showed the same dark-brown color as the earth.

He didn't say another word to his friends as he bounded up the cliff, until he landed in the snow. With memories of Allison churning inside him as well as thoughts of Saffron, Camdyn ran into the forest. He ran and ran and ran, never slowing, never looking back.

When he finally stopped, he put his hands on his knees and bent over, his head hanging. He had no idea how long he'd been gone, but he was miles from the castle.

Yet the run had felt good. It was just the thing to calm him.

Camdyn straightened and took off at a jog back to the castle. With his speed, it didn't take him long to reach the outskirts of MacLeod land. He looked to the blue sky and saw the moon. It was too bad the moon wasn't full that night, because he was anxious to end Deirdre.

Anxious and oh, so ready.

He slowed to a walk when he reached Isla's shield hiding the castle. As soon as he walked through it, Saffron's sweet, appealing magic slammed into him so hard Camdyn took a step back.

With a hand over his chest, he paused and let her magic surround him. Enfold him. Embrace him.

And how wonderful it felt. He hated that he yearned to feel her magic more and more each day. The more he felt it the more he wanted it. And the more he was becoming addicted to it.

A very dangerous thing, that.

It wasn't just her magic he longed for. It was her touch, a look, a smile. Anything.

And the more he fought to stay away from her, the more he felt himself being pulled to her. As if Fate were tugging an invisible line between him and Saffron, putting them together.

He shook away such thoughts and continued on to the castle. It was a few hours before the sunset and supper. He wanted a shower and maybe some time playing the Wii Broc had.

When Camdyn entered the castle he stopped dead in his tracks as his gaze locked on Saffron. Her hair, which had been all one length and midway down her back had been cut to just below her shoulders. And wisps of hair now graced her forehead. Her nails had a pale pink color on them, but more than that, she was in clothes that made him all too aware of her curves.

Before, when she was borrowing clothes, everything had fit just a little too loose on her or hid her mesmerizing body. The dark blue jeans she had on fit her perfectly, accentuating her slim thighs and buttocks. But it was the dark purple shirt molded to her breasts and abdomen that made his cock instantly hard. The cream-colored cardigan she wore over the shirt only brought more attention to the shape of her breasts and her small waist.

Arran let out a low, soft whistle as he came to stand beside Camdyn. "Damn. I always thought Saffron was pretty, but whatever she did in London has made her stunning."

Camdyn moved closer to Saffron while she spoke with Cara and Reaghan and showed them the other things she had bought. He didn't care about her clothes; he just wanted to see all the changes she had done.

It was something besides her hair and the color on her fingernails. Camdyn looked at her from head to toe, and it wasn't until his gaze moved back up her body that he realized what it was.

She had pink color on her eyelids and color on her cheeks. Even her eyelashes looked longer and thicker than before. And her lips! God help him, but the way her lips glistened made him want to taste her. A long, slow kiss or a hot, frenzied kiss. He didn't care as long as he could feel her mouth beneath his.

Hayden and Quinn were suddenly on either side of him. Both men with their arms crossed over their chests, staring at Saffron.

"I like the bangs," Quinn said.

"Hm. The make-up is subtle but nice," Hayden added.

Camdyn could take no more. If he didn't leave he was going to do something crazy. Like kiss Saffron.

And kissing was definitely something he couldn't do with her. . . .